D1710305

Liberty
Hou

One Star at a Time!

By

Temperance Johnson

Website: https://temperancejohnsonauthor.weebly.com/

Copyright © 2021 by Temperance Johnson. All rights reserved.

Content editing by: Gernissia Cherfrere

Proofread by: Sherry Chamblee

Cover Design by: Rachel Rossano
https://rossanodesigns.weebly.com

Book Interior Formatting by: Temperance Johnson

Available in print and eBook format on amazon.com and other platforms

Published in the United States of America. Orphans, Faith, Healing, Denver Asylum, Clean Romance, True Love, Orphanages, South

To the caregivers of touched children. You all are heroes and your work is done for the Glory of God.

Well done, thou good and faithful servant.
Matthew 25:21
Also to the children that feel like they have been forsaken. You are survivors! God has great things in store for you. For I know the plans I have for you," declares the Lord, "plans to prosper you and not to harm you, plans to give you hope and a future.
Jeremiah 29:11

Colorado family

Andrew Starry-runs Liberty Ranch and works as a blacksmith

Katrina Starry-married to Andrew, a mother to: Francesca 15, Sara 12 and Carlissa 8

Izzy Donovan-is being courted by Jesse Starry and helps run Liberty Ranch

Jesse Starry-is building a cabin in the mountains and courting Izzy

Dr. Charles and Mabel Alexander- closest neighbors and friends of the Starrys

Timmy Alexander-friends with Francesca

Alabama Family

Julia and Cole now guardians of the young Starry children: Travis 12, Hunter 12, Charity 10, Melody 8, Johnathan 5, and David 5.

Maverick Starry--town deputy of Daphne

Matt Starry -- town Sheriff of Daphne and married to Susan Starry, has an adopted daughter, Mary

Sawyer ---work for the newspaper office and married to Annie

Jerry Emerson—works as a deputy and is married to Gloria

Chapter 1

March 1872

The wind picked up as Katrina Starry made her way to the town of Deer Trail. Despite the cold, she smiled as her friend, Izzy Donavon, walked beside her. Izzy looked like she was used to it, but Katrina would rather be near a warm fire. Luckily, they didn't have far to go. Katrina thought she could see the church bell, or was that her imagination?

As they continued their journey, it started to rain. Lagging behind, Katrina could feel it accumulating on her head and its cold texture falling on her pale face. Pulling her coat tighter she looked up. Katrina soon realized the rain was actually white.

Izzy looked back at her. "What are you doing, Kat?"

Opening up her hands, Katrina let the white rain collect in her palms as soon as she perceived that it was snow. Growing up along the gulf of Alabama, she never saw snow fall. "It's snow," she said in amazement.

"Of course it's snow," Izzy laughed. "You will see a lot of snow while living here. More snow than you want. During some winters, you will even feel like the snow will never end. It will fill your whole house…"

Katrina's eyes widened, "Really?"

Izzy shook her head. "No." She put her arm around Katrina's shoulders. "Honey, if you plan on living in the West, then you will have to grow thicker skin."

Nodding, Katrina giggled, feeling like a child and not her twenty-five years of age. "I will." Katrina walked ahead, putting her hands up towards the sky. "It's just so pretty." Tilting her head back and opening

1

her mouth, she felt the cold flakes on her tongue. She leaned her head back so far that the snow fell on her bad ear. "Can snow make you deaf?"

Izzy shook her head. "Nope, so you are good."

Katrina gave her a dramatic sigh. "Well, you put my worry at ease."

Izzy laughed again. "Let's go meet the boys before they worry." She gently took Katrina by the arm. "And you know how they worry."

Katrina nodded. The snow started coming down heavier. "Have you ever been in a blizzard?"

Izzy blinked. "Yes, but I found a cave to hide in. I wasn't found for a couple of days, and I couldn't get out."

"That must have been scary. I am sorry." Katrina didn't know what else to say. Izzy was so strong all the time, and it appeared as though nothing bothered her, especially at her young age of twenty-one.

Izzy shrugged. "I got out."

Deer Trail was built on a little flat piece of land near the Colorado Mountains. As they entered the town, the first visible building was a doctor's clinic , but Katrina could also smell the bread coming from a diner. It definitely had its beauty; one just had to look deep to find it. Near the middle of the town stood a blacksmith's place where her husband, Andrew, would work part time, and the sheriff's office. Towards the back of town sat the church, like a building for weary people.

Fear ate at Katrina as she thought of what would happen if she and Izzy were back home in the Deep South. The townspeople would have never allowed Katrina and Izzy to walk together holding each other's arm. Izzy had black curly hair and rich brown skin that showed her Mexican heritage. Izzy's black-brown eyes went well with Katrina's curly fiery-red hair, blue eyes, and light skin, which revealed Katrina's Irish heritage.

By the general store, Katrina believed she spotted the brothel or possibly the saloon, but she was unsure because she had never seen either one of those kinds of places before.

Izzy gave her a compassionate look. "You will see them often now that you are out in the West."

Andrew Starry walked up and spoke, "We ain't ever seen one in the South so public. Least not in Daphne." He took Katrina's hand, sensing she was tense. He had a large build with dark hair and even darker eyes. His skin held a deep tan from the hot Alabama spring season.

Katrina squeezed his hand, telling him not to worry with her eyes. They had always spoken to each other with their eyes and hands.

"Well, you are far from Daphne," Izzy commented.

Walking in the store, Katrina spotted Andrew's brother, Jesse Starry, looking at some tack.

Jesse came over to them and took Izzy's hand. "About time you got here, girls. Me and Andrew thought we would have to go through the snow and go find yaw."

Izzy chuckled sarcastically. "Oh, and how horrible it would be for you boys to get wet."

"And cold," Jesse added. "Don't forget the cold."

Izzy just shook her head at the southern brats.

Walking to the front, Katrina took everything in with a glance. She could smell the coffee in the back of the store and hear the fire crackling. She had always imagined what a sweet hometown store would be like, but in Alabama she never got to experience that feeling.

Suddenly the back door opened, and a youthful man walked out. Walking with a limp, his face brightened at the sight of Izzy. Stuttering, and with a boyish grin, he said, "Oh, Bella. You came back to me." He used her nickname from her time at Liberty House.

Katrina had never met a touched person like Billy. From Katrina's recollection, a touched person, or someone who was physically handicapped, blind, mentally ill, or deaf, was often hidden from the public. She wasn't sure how to react. Though her siblings may be touched in some ways, most people couldn't tell. The Starry parents had adopted most of their children. She knew the pain of rejection and what happened to a touched person if he or she was not cared for.

Izzy walked over to Billy and gave him a big hug. Pulling back, she kissed him on the forehead. "It is such a delight to see you, Billy. How is Sissy?"

Billy's smile dimmed. "Not so well. Sissy got taken back home."

Izzy didn't react too much, but now she flinched. "I am so sorry to hear that."

Billy shrugged. "Mama Mabel tried, but no one listens." He smiled again. "Are these your friends?" He looked at Andrew. "You are big."

Everyone laughed, including Andrew.

"He gets that a lot." Izzy's eyes twinkled as she introduced them. "Y'all, this is my friend, Billy. He can play the musician better than anyone else I have ever heard."

Billy smiled. "Billy is the best." He spoke like he always did as he shook Katrina's hand. "You are awful pretty. Cole's girl looks like you?"

Katrina blushed. She had been called nothing but a dull, scared woman before. "Aw, thanks." She was about to pull at her dress collar, but Andrew took her hand. He knew she was trying to hide her ugly scar. What if someone in the store noticed her lisp? "No, we don't look alike, but she is a wonderful woman. Cole is very lucky."

Billy nodded. "Cole is very blessed. We are sure to love her like our Bella. She is the best."

Izzy smiled and looked fondly at him.

Katrina also noticed how, Jesse, was acting now that they had met Billy. His hands were balled in a fist and his jaw popped with anger. If he wasn't careful, he would lose Izzy with all his mood swings. Sometimes he had to learn things the hard way.

"Mama Mabel said to give this to you when I saw you." Billy handed Izzy a letter. He kissed her cheek and then limped to the back.

Katrina leaned over Izzy, just curious about what it could say.

"Why don't you read it, Kat?" Izzy told her.

Katrina backed away. "I didn't mean to."

Izzy shrugged, a twinkle in her eye. "It's fine. The letter is for all of us. The Alexanders want us to come over Wednesday."

"We will be in the mountains starting my place," Jesse snapped too harshly. "I have hired men to come along in a couple days."

Izzy glared at him. "They can still go." She turned to them. "The Alexanders are your closest neighbors."

"It sounds fun. They are the ones who help with Liberty Ranch, right?" Katrina asked. At Liberty Ranch, the Starrys and others would help orphans or touched children and their families get help and healing. They would stay in one cabin we are building. The Ranch will have ten to twenty cabins, each with a full kitchen, living area, and a couple of bedrooms. They would be doing it more in the spring, summer, and fall. The winter might get a lot of snow, but not enough to get snowed in, so the stage coach will still run through once a month, and in the summer once a week, so the people who need help can come and stay. All the families will help by working or paying a small fee. Andrew would help get it started before Izzy's brother, Cole could come in a couple months.

Izzy nodded, "Yup, the Alexanders have worked with Cole and me many times. If you need anything, go to them."

Katrina thought it sounded great. As long as they didn't find out she

4

was partly deaf, she would be all right. No one could know or they would treat her differently.

Keeping her eyes on the road as they walked side by side, Izzy could feel Jesse's anger. Not understanding what made him angry made her even more upset. She was glad Andrew and Katrina were up ahead.

Glancing at Jesse, Izzy stopped walking. She leaned against the fence post on the Liberty Ranch property. "Jesse Starry, what is your problem? Why are you so angry?"

Jesse turned to her. "I don't really know you."

"What?" Izzy had no idea what he was talking about.

"I never saw you act like this." Jesse put his arms up. "In Alabama, you just shut down."

Izzy bit her lip. "Yes, I did. In Alabama, I was not myself." She folded her arms. "If you wanted to get to know me, then you would have come to Liberty House as I have asked. To be a part of my world." She had gone often to visit Liberty House while staying in Alabama. She and her older brother created Liberty House to help people in need and provide a place for families to raise children. They had homes in Alabama, Texas, and Colorado territory. Every Liberty House was like a family.

"What? My family ain't a part of your world."

"No! They are a part of your world not mine. My family is Liberty Home. They are the ones that know me the best." She stood with her feet planted far apart, like she was ready for a fight. "That is why Julia went with Cole to Liberty House. She wanted to get to know his genuine family."

Jesse ran his fingers through his curly black hair. "Well, why did you kiss Billy?" he asked, his brown eyes hard with anger.

Her eyes widened. "What? I only kissed him on the forehead. He is one of my closest friends." She sighed. "When I came here, Billy was the one boy who wouldn't walk away from my rage." At Jesse's surprised look, she continued. "I was an angry teenager, but Billy was always there for me. He taught me how to laugh again, to see the joy in life. He and his sister have suffered beyond belief." Her eyes narrowed. "I love Billy like a brother."

Jesse sighed, stepping closer to her. "Where is the home where Billy's sister resides?

Izzy closed her eyes, pain on her face. "The home is a terrible state-run orphanage. The women who run it leave the orphans in beds all day. Liberty House in Peoria tried to change it, but we haven't gotten far because it's not as bad as an asylum." Izzy opened her eyes, seeing Jesse hide his fear and the pain that showed in his eyes.

"Well, it's not your problem," he said bitterly as he walked away.

Izzy stood there, shocked. She knew the Starrys enough to know they hated asylums and anything to do with them. What was wrong with him then? What was the story behind the anger in his eyes?

Shaking her head, Izzy started towards the Ranch. No one ever said courting a Starry would be easy, but she knew it would be worth it — one day.

The kitchen was cool now that the stove's heat had lessened and a cool breeze had seeped in through a crack in the window. In the deep south of Alabama, cold weather was always a blessing that brought a smile across Julia Donavon's face. Julia sat at the dining room table, which was off from the kitchen, with her sisters reminiscing on their lives.

Susan Starry gently blew on the rim of her teacup, as she reflected on the past few months. "I never thought I could be happier with Matt."

Julia looked to her sister, Gloria Emerson. Taking a sip of her sweet tea, she chuckled. "This time last year, who would have thought all of us would be newlyweds so soon?"

Gloria grinned, "A few years ago, I didn't think any of this would be possible." She pushed back her brown hair. Looking down at her sweet tea, Gloria said, "I wish everyone was here to enjoy it."

The death of her adoptive mother, Ellen, had been hard on all of her siblings. Saddened, Julia nodded as she looked outside to where her younger boys were playing with their dog.

Julia and her husband Cole had taken in her younger siblings when Ellen passed away a month ago. It was a difficult change, but it was going well. "I know. I try not to imagine life in Colorado territory. It's hard to imagine how we'll move on without her." She gave them a soft smile. "Charity and the older kids prefer to talk about the future. It gives them hope for school, a solid church, and real friends."

"I think it is good to talk about the future. Maybe it will help your younger siblings move past some of their grief. Well, I'm not saying to forget grief, but thinkin' about it all the time can't be healthy." Gloria said. She took a sip of her tea and changed the subject of their conversation. "What do you think Katrina is doing right now?"

Susan chuckled, "Maybe she's meeting her neighbors."

Julia almost giggled. "Shoppin'."

"Going to a sewing circle and tea!" Susan added.

"Talking about other women her age." Julia put her hands together. "Maybe she's even going to dances."

Gloria laughed at them. "She is probably scrubbin' her house from top to bottom. Bakin' in the hot kitchen and washing clothes all day long."

They all burst out laughing because it was probably all accurate.

"What is this?" Cole walked in. "A bunch of gossipin' women?" He took off his hat as he sat at the table next to Julia.

Julia shook her head. "Now, what would we gossip about? We don't hear any news or have any friends."

Cole winked at her and drawled, "So when we head to the West, y'all will have something to gossip about."

Julia kissed him as she went into the kitchen. Getting him a tall glass of sweet tea and a plate of cookies, she was glad her ankle didn't give her any more pain when she walked. Finally, it seemed to be healing correctly. "How was work?" He was a deputy in town with her brothers. She gazed at Cole. He was handsome with his dark curly hair, tall build, and brown eyes. One could now tell his Mexican heritage as his skin complexion had darkened from hours of riding the land. In the past, he had hidden his heritage, even from the Starrys.

Cole nodded, taking a sip of sweet tea. His eyes twinkled. "You made this?"

"Actually, Gloria did." She grinned. "I just added more sugar for you."

Looking deeply at her, Cole leaned over and whispered, "I only need you, sugar."

Julia blushed.

The other ladies reacted by playfully groaning.

Cole leaned back, chuckling at them. He always tried to flirt and tease Julia when he could. Being newlyweds with six children could take alone time away from them, but he wouldn't let that happen. Julia said she loved him all the more for it. "I forgot to go to the general store today." He hit his knee. "I'll go in a couple of days unless you need one of the brothers to get something."

Julia walked to the kitchen, grabbed a knife, and started cutting bread for supper. She knew she would have to choose her words carefully. "Well, Susan wanted us to come see her new home, and I thought I would go shoppin'.

Cole turned his attention to her. "Are you sure you want to?" He didn't want her bullied by the very town he protected.

Julia smiled. "I do. I wanted to take the girls to buy some new clothes."

"You know I can pick up clothes for them." When Julia's blue eyes pleaded with him, Cole added, "I just don't want the people in town to hurt you and the children."

Julia frowned. "You can't protect me from everything." Julia had dark blond curly hair and bright blue eyes, but she often wondered what others would think if anyone knew how white his wife was. Though her skin tanned in the sun, it still didn't have the tint Cole or Izzy had. She loved her family. It was just what others might think that made her afraid. She should be used to it by now. She looked down at her hands. "Will they judge me for being married to a Mexican or for being a Starry?" Out of the corner of her eye she saw Gloria and Susan go outside.

Cole got up and pulled her against his chest, using her nickname, "Julia-rose, I am so sorry. You knew marryin' me would bring you more judgment that you don't deserve. I am sorry." He kissed her on the top of her head. "If I could change it, I would."

Julia turned in his arms, facing him. "I wouldn't change a thing about you. No matter what anyone says. I just want to experience goin' shopping." She winked at him. "With the girls."

Cole sighed. " All right, Julia-rose, but stay away from Molly Adams. If you need me, I will be at the office, and your brothers will be around."

Julia kissed him to silence him. "I will be fine." She did a little jump in his arms. "I can't wait to tell the children."

Cole laughed at her childlike joy. He shook his head, not understanding her childhood humor.

Chapter 2

With many rooms and windows, the one-story house was like a huge ranch house. The front side of the house opened up to a wide porch that in the summer held flower pots and chairs where neighbors could sit to visit. Charles and Mabel Alexander owned the ranch house and anticipated helping Andrew and Katrina run Liberty Ranch. Katrina had often dreamed about having kind, friendly neighbors. As Katrina and Andrew walked on the porch, her heart was ready to beat out of her chest, so she tightened her hands into a fist to relieve her nervousness.

Before Andrew and Katrina knocked on the front door, he stopped Katrina and signed, "If you get overwhelmed, tell me."

Katrina nodded, having no choice since Andrew would notice, anyway.

"Good," he said with amusement. He signed, "Have fun tonight."

Katrina cocked her head mockingly. "Yes, sir," she whispered. She felt him playfully poke her side while she fell into his big form.

A woman with brown eyes, bright and clear like she didn't miss much, opened the door. Her graying brown hair was in a tight bun, while her jaw seemed hard and square with thin lips always ready for a smile. Anybody could see in her eyes she looked like a woman who had been through hell and made it out stronger. She was one of the many women that made the West tame. "Hi, it's so nice to meet you. You must be Andrew." She shook his hand. "I am Mabel Alexander." She gave Katrina a genuine smile. "And you must be Katrina. I feel like I know you from Izzy, always telling us about your family." She hugged Katrina.

Katrina stood in surprise. She was unfamiliar with being hugged by anyone beyond her family; however, this lady didn't feel like a stranger. Mabel's hug felt comforting, like the touch of a mother. Katrina hadn't felt that in a long time. Something in her heart softened. "It's nice to meet you too."

9

"Come on in." Mabel took them into the large parlor as a man walked in. He was of a big build with kind eyes. He reminded Katrina of Andrew — big and as gentle as a lamb. "Andrew and Katrina, this is my husband, Dr. Charles." She gestured to them. "Dear, this is Andrew and Katrina Starry."

Charles shook their hands. "It's nice to meet you. I look forward to getting to know you both."

Andrew nodded. "Same here."

After Charles asked Andrew for some work to do in the barn, Katrina asked, "What can I do?"

Katrina and Mabel both got to work. Mabel's youngest daughter, Lucy, helped as well. She set the dining room table as Mabel told her to be careful since they were using the good dishes.

As they worked side by side, Mabel talked to Katrina, and she was glad Mabel was facing her so she could read her lips. The Starrys always remembered to face her when talking. "I am so excited about Liberty Ranch; it gives me hope for the future. See, we adopted five of my children."

"How old is Lucy?" Katrina asked.

"Twelve. She came to us as a baby," Mabel explained. "She has never known the evils of life except for a few scoundrels who live in town. Since we had her for so long, not many people see a difference. See, she is slower."

Katrina had noticed. Again, she had never met a touched or slow person before Dear Trail. "She is so happy with y'all."

Mabel smiled. "Yes, she is our joy, our little miracle. Her tummy ma lived here a few months before returning to her old life."

Katrina's eyes widened. "That is what my mama, Ellen, called our mothers that gave birth to us."

Mabel raised an eyebrow and then shrugged. "It's true. Most of my children have two mamas, one gave them life, and the other gets to love them."

Katrina looked at her carrots as she cut them. "Ellen taught us to care for ourselves and others. She also taught us how to love God. Ben, our pa, taught our boys how to get along and not kill each other. See, my younger siblings and I came to the Starrys as teenagers."

"Was Ben Ellen's husband?" Mabel asked.

Katrina shook her head. A shadow covering her face. "No, Ben was married to Missy. They were both ex slaves and lived on the plantation. Owen was Ellen's husband." Her last words had a bite to them, but she gave a sad smile to cover the truth about him, adding, "Ellen and we were an actual family and in the blink of an eye, Ellen was gone." Katrina rinsed her hands. "It was Ellen's dream to come here." Trying to remain strong, she had not cried since coming to the West, but now she let her tears fall. Soon she felt strong arms go around her; it was Mabel. Leaning her head against Mabel's shoulder, she continued to sob. Eventually, Katrina pulled herself together. She wiped her eyes. "I am sorry."

Mabel shook her head. "There is no reason to be. Sometimes we just need a good cry. How long ago did she pass?"

"A month ago," Katrina told her as she put a cold washcloth to her flushed face.

Mabel gave her a sympathetic look. "I am so sorry. You are still in mourning."

Katrina nodded. "I would wear black but before I left, a few months back, my clothes got burned in a fire."

"Your ma sounds like a wonderful woman."

Katrina brushed away a loose red curl. "She really was. We didn't call her mama often, it was always Ellen. She loved us so much and led us spiritually," she mumbled as they got back to the supper table. Changing the subject, she said, "I can't wait to go to church tomorrow. I dreamed of goin' for years. We've never been to church."

Mabel raised an eyebrow. "I have never met a person who hasn't been to church."

The statement didn't bother Katrina; she just explained, "Well, as children we did, but as we got older, it was too difficult. We weren't welcomed at church or anywhere in town." She sighed a little bit. "See, we didn't look alike, and most of us were rejects from the orphanage. When the war was almost over, my brothers joined the last few battles." She gave her a side grin. "Except they joined the wrong side so we just had church by ourselves on our plantation, Silkwood."

"I'm sorry about that. They were a bunch of hypocrites." Mabel shook her head. "I've also seen it before in God-fearing churches."

"I haven't rejected God because of the hypocrites. I believe a person will go meet God on what he or she has done, not on what others made you think. The ultimate choice to believe is yours and yours alone. My older brother rejects God because of it." Katrina paused, remembering not too long ago. "The words and actions still hurt, but in the long run, you can't tell Jesus that because of His so-called people rejected Him. It has to be your choice to follow Him."

Katrina reached for another carrot when her sleeve came up enough to show her scars. She quickly pulled her hand back to cover it.

Mabel didn't miss a thing but chose not to speak of it. "Those are wise words, my dear."

For Katrina it was just life.

Supper with the Alexander family was similar to how dinner was at Silkwood with Katrina's family. Everyone would talk at once, but no one seemed to be listening to the next person. Oddly enough, they all heard every word spoken. It was fun, and it made Katrina miss her family a little less. She found herself relaxed around Charles and Mabel, which she often didn't feel with others. As Katrina and Andrew's eyes met at different moments of the evening, they quietly shared the same warm thoughts about this family.

Katrina, Andrew, Charles, Mabel and their son Timmy all sat in the parlor while Mabel was telling them a story about one of her sons. "It was the middle of January and my older son wanted to join the club in the treehouse. The only problem was that in order to get into the club you had to lick the metal gate."

Everyone laughed besides Andrew and Katrina, who looked at her to finish the funny part.

Mabel finally asked, "You don't see that as funny?"

"What makes licking a gate funny?" Andrew asked. "I've done it and nothing funny happened."

"Your tongue didn't get stuck on it?" Timmy asked. He was the oldest son that lived at home and he reminded Katrina of her little brothers. He looked like he had Mexican heritage or Italian. There was a dark scar on the right side of his face, but because of his outgoing personality, no one noticed his facial looks.

He spoke slowly due to his stutter, but clear enough to understand.

"No." Andrew shook his head. "Why would it do that?"

"It's in the middle of winter, that's why the metal sticks to your tongue and rips off the first layer of skin." It shocked Timmy. "Oh, no, that sounds painful," Katrina said as everyone laughed.

"So, you have never had your tongue frozen to a gate?" Timmy asked in disbelief.

Andrew laughed. "No, we got snow like twice where we lived, and I would never have thought to do that, but my brothers would."

Everyone laughed this time, including Katrina.

"Sometimes the tongue would get so frozen you would have to wait for it to warm up," Mabel told them.

Katrina and Andrew dropped their mouths open in shock.

Meeting Andrew's eyes, Katrina signed, *Mav would do that in a heartbeat.* For a moment, she forgot that she was sitting around Mabel's family.

Andrew also forgot and chuckled. Trying to hide his hands, he sighed, *Yeah, remember the time he wouldn't let us join his club before we rode his horse.*

Katrina laughed softly and signed back, not hiding it this time. *Yes, we must do that when they get here.*

Andrew laughed, forgetting it all. *Yup. Izzy should have told us about the metal. She spent enough winters here.*

Katrina nodded. *She did. Knowing her, she probably dared her friends to do it.*

Andrew laughed softly. *She probably did.*

Mabel's children ran into the living room, and Katrina looked around, feeling embarrassed. She signed the words sorry out of habit and went to the kitchen without a word.

Katrina found a knife in the drawer to cut out a slice of pie. She felt a hand on her shoulder and knew it wasn't Andrew; Andrew's hand was rough and larger. She turned around to face Mabel and signed *sorry* again, then put her hands down in despair. Katrina began speaking faster, which made her lisp and voice louder. "I'm sorry. I forgot for a moment where I was. I sign all the time with Andrew or one of his siblings. "She frowned. "I've never been to another person's house so I don't know how to act. It was terribly rude of me."

Mabel grasped Katrina's chin and made Katrina look at her. "I am glad you can relax here enough to forget. And honey, I knew the moment you spoke you were hard of hearing. Don't worry about how you behaved. It was nothing." She put her hands down.

"How did you know?" Katrina was calming, though still feeling vulnerable.

"I knew by your voice and how you always look at my lips." She paused. "My sister is deaf and can't read lips as you can, but she can sign."

"So you knew everything we signed?" Katrina blushed, knowing the answer.

She nodded. "I haven't signed in years but it came back to me." She smiled. "Who is Mav?"

Katrina laughed. Having someone know wasn't so bad. "Maverick, he is the oldest brother and the protector of all of us. Andrew and Maverick are known as the brothers, Andrew being the muscles, while Maverick is the brain."

Sandra, Mabel's daughter-in-law, walked in and started dishing the pie out. As Sandra passed Katrina with a piece of pie, she winked. "If you think that was a scene, you should see how my boys behave in one day."

Katrina didn't feel completely relaxed, but she went back out knowing Andrew had told them the truth. The rest of the evening was fun, but she felt like once they found out how she became deaf they would reject her. Katrina remembered what happened back at Silkwood. It was just a matter of time till Deer Trail did the same and rejected her. Her new friends couldn't know her as the burned, deaf, orphan slave girl.

Izzy rode for hours towards the mountains with a silent Jesse. Who said Jesse was worth it? Indeed, it was not her. She encouraged him to speak, but he was still in his mood. She was exhausted and emotionally drained from trying to talk with him.

Katrina had seemed to know a relationship with Jesse would be hard. She'd tried to warn Izzy. Giving her a hug before leaving the ranch, she'd whispered, "Give Jesse some time. I will pray for you both." Izzy was embarrassed that people knew she and Jesse were fighting, but she had lived with much worse.

They stopped for lunch before Izzy headed to Liberty House near Denver. She picked a place alongside a flowing river, the water ran from the side of the mountain and made a spectacular waterfall. Jesse would camp here for the night. Sitting there, Izzy took in the beauty of the Colorado terrain that surrounded her.

Izzy dismounted, then went to the pack horses. She and Jesse had brought six horses, two for pack horses, and four for switching on the mountains. She took the tack off of the gelding. She felt Jesse come up behind her but she ignored him.

He put his hand on hers and gave her a bucket. "Get the water, I'll do this." His voice was light. His eyes narrowed at her in a flirty look.

Izzy obeyed silently, but Jesse became accommodating and talkative. When she came back with the bucket of water, Jesse had her horse almost done. He was trying to win her over by unsaddling Phoenix, but it would not work.

Lighting a fire beneath several pieces of wood, Izzy began cooking dried fish, apples, and beans. Izzy had nearly finished preparing the food when Jesse came over and sat next to her. "I am sorry for the way I acted yesterday."

Izzy wanted answers. "Why did you?"

"I get jealous sometimes. I don't know why, but I do." He took her hand. "Are we friends again?"

Izzy nodded. "But you're not getting' off that easy." She accepted his hand. "I want to know the real you, Jesse!"

"I want to know you, too. I am working on it, I just need time." He drew her close and kissed her.

Izzy put her hand around his neck and kissed him back. She leaned into it and wanted to put her trust in him, but her heart held her back. There were emotional walls Izzy had to cut down just like Jesse, but no one would get in those walls. He pulled her closer to him. She was enjoying his touch but didn't want him like that. Finally pulling back, she leaned her head on his shoulder and looked into his eyes. But did she love him? How could she be sure? Her heart wouldn't let her show it. Would she ever feel love for a man again?

Jesse grinned. "Wow, you never cease to surprise me."

She smiled as she smelled the food. "I think the food is burnin'."

He laughed. "I don't care."

She giggled. "Neither do I." Pulling back, she dished out their plates. "But we need to keep up our strength." It was only a little charred. She doubted Jesse would care about it with the way he was acting.

He hadn't taken his eyes off her as she passed him a plate. "Looks great," he said as he winked.

She smiled. He was funny and sweet but sometimes overly jealous. She took a bite of their food. It wasn't too bad, concerning how much she had wanted to ram it down his throat a few seconds before. She was a girl who knew how to control her emotions and allow people to think what they wanted about her. Her emotions were the one thing she could manage in her life after being raised with an overbearing father and an indifferent mother. She just hoped Jesse wanted her after finding out the truth about her. All she knew was that she had to leave for her friends soon.

Chapter 3

When Katrina got to the Alexander ranch for the sewing circle. This was her very first one and she couldn't wait for it. Though her stomach did a flip. The ladies from church had invited her to sit in the living room where about fifteen women were sewing around a large quilt.

She started threading a needle.

A lady next to Katrina smiled and said, "Hi, I am Diana Tanner. I have three children and another on the way." She held her growing stomach and smiled. "I am Mabel's daughter."

"Nice to meet you. I am Katrina Starry." Katrina tried to hide her lisp by whispering, but it didn't work most times.

They all then started talking, some asking Katrina questions. She answered them and someone noticed how she was sewing without watching what she was doing and a lady asked about it.

Trying to hide her discomfort, she cleared her throat, "When my ma and sisters would sew I got used to looking at them while sewing. My sister, Julia, would end up painting." She looked at Mabel. Mabel gave her a look that said, 'you can trust them.'

The ladies started talking about the orphanage in Peoria. Katrina knew that was Liberty House, the home for unwanted, touched, and child slaves that Izzy and Cole had started. Liberty Ranch would be like it, but for families who cared for those children.

A woman with blond hair was saying, "I have seen asylum children. They are getting many more in, more than they can handle."

"I heard of one child burning down their adoptive parents' home and stealing 'em blind," Maryanne said.

"Talk about stealing them blind, I had two pies gone this week," Gabby said.

"Oh, my. I had some bread stolen," Emily said.

They all looked at Mabel. Mabel put up her hands. "Hey, my boys have been at the ranch lately." She looked at Diana and Sandra, but they both shook their heads, though Sandra looked doubtful.

Maryann spoke up loudly, "What about Lucy?"

Mabel frowned. "Maryann, you know Lucy would never steal."

"What about the incident at the general store?" Maryann glared at her.

"That was a misunderstanding."

"That your boys caused!"

Mabel glared at her but didn't argue with it.

Katrina didn't know what came over her, but spoke up quietly, "Maryanne, I saw your townhouse. The flowers look like they will be beautiful in full bloom."

Maryann turned her angry face from Mabel to smile at Katrina. "Oh, yes. My flower gardens are the most plentiful in the area. I sell them in the spring."

Mabel looked relieved but seemed tired.

All the ladies started talking at once, on different topics. It was all so confusing for Katrina.

Mabel spoke up and asked Katrina if she would like to get the coffee. Katrina couldn't be more grateful for her newfound friend. Reckon they both could help each other out when in need.

Katrina loved the warmth of the sun on her back as she hung the laundry on the line Andrew had just made.

Finishing the laundry, she went to the small shed to see if she could keep goats in there. She loved goat's milk. Back home, she had a job to feed and milk them all on the massive plantation right before she had married Andrew.

Andrew had done a good job at fixing the shed so far, but the roof needed patching. There was a puddle of water in the middle of the floor. She saw a big shelf that held old tools that hadn't been used in some time. Under the shelf was a hole with an old door that had seen better days. Opening the little door, she fell back and let out a cry as she fell in the puddle. She stood and leaned to see in there. There were two girls in the hole. They were curled up in the small area, shoulders touching and legs curled up around each other. "Come on out, girls. I won't hurt you."

The younger girl stepped out first. She was tall and thin, dirty rags hung on her body. Her hair color was hard to see under all the grease. Under bright blue eyes showed the starvation and hunger in deep circles. Her feet were bare, cracked, and dry.

Katrina had seen many children like this, especially during and after the war, the starvation reeked in the south like a spreading disease with no cure.

The dark-haired girl came out. Katrina saw she was around fifteen years old but her body and eyes looked much older. She was small with a big bust which was falling out of her dirty dress. Her hair hung in greasy black ringlets, and her skin was tan under all the dirt. Brown eyes hung in more fear than hunger. She was of Mexican descent. Her dress was worse for wear being much too tight, and shorter than a proper dress. She was also wearing high cut boots, as girls did in a saloon. They were not walking shoes; her feet had to be covered in blisters. This young woman had once been a working girl. Probably a runaway and her saloon owner probably wanted her back.

"What are you two doing in there?" Katrina finally asked, then shrugged. "No matter. Will you come in and eat something? I just finished baking some bread."

They both looked at her with fearful eyes, and then the older girl shrugged. Katrina led the way out, making sure she was standing beside her in case one spoke so she could hear them. It didn't look like that would happen.

When they sat down at the dining room table, Katrina cut some fresh bread for them and buttered it.

The older girl picked it at first, and then ate like she hadn't seen food in a long time.

The younger one looked about to be sick. Suddenly shoving it in her mouth like she was starved. Then abruptly she threw up all over the table and floor. Katrina hurried the girl over to the sink to get some water, ignoring the mess.

The older girl sat there looking unconcerned. Katrina looked at her for some answer and she finally spoke. "She does that all the time. Can't hold down any food, not that we have eaten much. She just throws it up."

Katrina turned back and asked, "Why"

She answered, "How should I know?!"

Katrina was asking more for herself. Standing next to the girl, she could see vermin on her. Having dealt with that many times at the orphanage she knew how to get rid of it. The vermin was a minor problem compared to her health. The younger girl had looked pale before, but now she looked like you could see through her skin. Drinking some water, the girl kept it down. Maybe she should get Doctor Charles.

She turned to see the older girl had cut herself some bread and eaten it, not minding the puke mess. "What do you do to get her to eat without pukin'?"

She shrugged again. "I don't know nothin'. She is a sickly girl. I have seen it before."

Katrina hadn't seen it before. She sighed. "By the way, I am Katrina Starry."

"I am Francesca, and that is Sara." She stood up. "Thanks for the bread, but we should go."

"You're not going anywhere," Katrina told her as she turned back to Sara. "Let's clean up this mess while Sara tries to drink some milk slowly."

Katrina helped Sara sit at the clean end of the table and then handed her a glass of milk. Mabel had been nice enough to lend her an extra milk cow until they could find one. Then she set up to clean the mess. It didn't take much time and Francesca looked at her oddly. Sara sat there drinking the milk. Then it dawned on Katrina. "You're the children that have been stealing food around here?"

Francesca looked at her like she was dumb. "Nothin' gets by you."

Katrina was surprised Francesca would respond sarcastically like that. It made her seem much older, though she couldn't be older than fifteen. "What can I say, I just moved here?"

"When?" Francesca asked.

"I've been here over a week now." Katrina sounded tired thinking about all that happened since she got here.

Francesca looked around. "Cleaned this place up nice."

"Y'alls been here before?" Katrina asked.

Francesca shrugged. "Where's you from?"

Katrina wondered if she meant her lisp or her southern accent. "From the deep South."

"What made you come here?"

Katrina shrugged. "It's pretty and I like it." She looked at both of them. "Now, what do you feel about a bath?"

After both girls bathed and washed their hair, they dressed in Katrina's clothes. These were much too big for them, but their old clothes were not an option. The borrowed items would have to do.

"Francesca, Sara, why don't we head over to a friend's house," Katrina said cheerily. Dr. Charles might be home by now, or she hoped so.

"Is it an orphanage?" Francesca asked, her eyes going wide. "I have seen none in town."

"No, my dears, it's just a friend's house. She has a daughter about your age. Maybe I have some clothes for you."

Francesca frowned but shrugged.

Katrina wondered if Sara was mute? For the child had said nothing.

As they headed to the Alexander ranch, she noticed how pretty the girls were. Francesca was short with a head of beautiful, full, black hair. Her face was round, and her nose was pudgy, her lips full. Her jaw was hard, like she had faced too much in her young life. Her eyes showed it the most; they were angry, fearful, and hard. Behind them showed things she had seen and things she would never forget. She looked like she had built many walls around her heart to protect herself.

Sara was as different from Francesca as girls could be. She was tall for her age, which if Katrina guessed right, it would be around twelve or thirteen. Her hair, now washed, was straight light blond, her face narrow and pale. Her nose was narrow and straight, her cheeks were hollow, her eyes were a beautiful blue with a yellow ring around them. Katrina saw something different in them than Francesca's eyes. It wasn't only fear, but also emptiness, a hollow look like nothing mattered.

Katrina knocked on the Alexander's door, and Mabel came to answer. She smiled at Katrina then took in the girls without missing a beat. "Hi, Katrina and girls, come on in. I just made some lemonade." She led the way into the kitchen, then told the girls to sit while she got them and her children lemonade. As she and Katrina stayed in the kitchen where they could still see the children, Mabel looked at Katrina and asked, "What is the story? I am dying to hear it."

Katrina told her all she knew, especially how Sara couldn't keep anything down. Mabel sadly nodded. "I have seen it before." She sighed. She kept her eyes on the children like a hen mother. "I saw it when I first laid eyes on them. It is in Sara's eyes. Hunger. There's hardness behind Francesca's eyes. Sara can't keep anything down because her stomach is used to being empty and doesn't know how to handle food. My children have had it before. You just have to give them a little food at a time. Also, my Charles can give you something to help."

"I thought he might be able to. Is he home?" Katrina asked.

Mabel nodded, but before they moved, she put a hand on Katrina's arm. "Sara could also be going through withdrawal from alcohol." She added, "I am surprised Francesca is not suffering with it. But she might be moody for a bit due to headaches and body shakes."

Katrina looked confused. "Why would she be addicted to liquor?"

Mabel glanced back at the girls and then back to Katrina. "Because that is what owners give prostitutes."

Katrina flinched, shaking her head. "No, that is wrong. Sara is just a child." Tears filled her eyes.

Mabel didn't argue. "Will that make you not raise the girls?"

Katrina shook her head. "No!" She looked at the girls and then thought about it. "No, my best friend was a child prostitute. Her name was Clara."

Mabel squeezed her arm. "Where is she now?"

Katrina looked away. Not wanting to face her when she said it. "Heaven. She had such faith, even at twelve." She stepped away, wanting space. Wiping at her eyes she added, "I haven't even told Andrew. He wasn't home, so I left him a note telling him to head here."

"How will you talk with him without the girls hearing?" Mabel winked at her.

Katrina signed and smiled. "We know how to talk very well."

Mabel smiled. "How will you deal with this?"

"We have dealt with a man trying to kill my sister for five years."

Mabel looked shocked, "That must have affected how you looked at people."

Katrina had never thought it about that way. And she just shrugged. I will take them home to sleep tonight. After that, I am not sure," she said honestly.

The town of Daphne was hopping, full of people walking, riding horses, and driving in wagons. Julia hadn't been in this town for years and she had never seen so many people. Stopping in front of the general store, she wondered if they would allow her in there with all the children. Because of her newfound wealth, they might overlook it this one time. She could smell fresh food from the diner across the street. Hearing the many boots and shoes on the boardwalk, she worried how she could get past them without being noticed. But the thought didn't bother as much as she just could walk the streets without any fear. For over five years a man was after to kill her. That is how she got to know Cole and he had found the killer. Julia wiped at a tear she would not remember who it was.

Charity jumped happily down and tied Blackie. She had long brown hair, green eyes, and her skin was tan from the hours she spent outdoors with the horses. She was the image of her mother, Ellen.

Julia was glad the horse was fine after it almost went lame a few months before. A shadow passed over her at the memory. She jumped down and helped the excited boys. Taking a look at them all often reminded her of their parents. Travis, Charity, and Johnathan were Ellen's tummy children.

The other three children, Hunter, Melody, and David, had been taken in by Ellen when their own parents has died, leaving them orphaned. Now that Ellen had passed, Julia was raising them as well.

Julia shook her head, trying to shake the memories. She took Johnathan's hand and carried the basket. Charity took David's hand. She knew the boys were excited but also nervous. The first thing the boys spotted was Julia's painting on the wall in the general store. They oohed and awwed over it for a while. Julia just laughed.

"My new mama is famous." Melody stated it to all of them. She and the younger boys had been calling her ma for a while now. Julia didn't mind, it made the children feel safer. Charity and the older boys didn't call her ma, but that didn't bother Julia.

"She will be famous worldwide one day," Charity chimed in.

"I am not sure worldwide, hon," Julia told them.

"Well, at least famous in the South and the West," Charity told her seriously, acting much older than she was.

The girls' faces lit up at all the supplies and material. She led them over to the pre-made dresses. Her girls didn't get pre-made clothes often. She told the boys to stay where they were, and she took the girls aside.

"Now, I am not doing this every outing, but why don't you pick yourself out a dress."

Charity's green eyes got wide. "Will Cole be upset?"

Julia put a hand on her shoulder. "Cole would love new dresses for

23

all of us. I bet he will say you are the prettiest girl ever."

She smiled brightly. "Let's go."

Melody took Julia's hand. "I want the pink one." She led Julia that way, not caring who saw.

Julia loved that about Melody. She was so open and didn't care what others thought. She knew what she wanted and did it. With her black tightly curled hair hanging down her back, her smooth dark skin, and her deep brown eyes that showed so much joy, she was the beauty of the family and everyone knew it.

Charity stood in front of all the dresses. There weren't many to pick from, but it seemed like a lot for the girl who had never been to a grocer.

Julia put a hand on her shoulder. "Any decision you make will be fine. Do you want help, hon?"

Charity kept looking, not used to all the decisions of a store.

Melody just stared, and then she spotted the blue calico one. She whispered, "Cole likes blue."

The comment melted Julia's heart. She wanted to please Cole so much. "He will love it."

Charity excitedly picked out a purple striped one. Julia didn't really care what she picked out for herself, so she had the little boys and the girls help her pick out a purple skirt and a nicely fit white blouse. She picked out two bloomers and two undershirts and hid them in her dress. She whispered to the girls, "Why don't you pick out some undergarments?"

Instantly she regretted asking. She had been so excited she hadn't thought it through. Melody's eyes just got wide and she frowned. Charity shook her head. "Please, no." She shook her head.

"I am sorry girls, I shouldn't have asked. That was wrong of me," she mumbled. "Why don't we try out the sweets? What would the boys like?"

They both nodded, but Julia could tell they were still nervous. She sighed, feeling like she had lost a battle. For over six years their Uncle Frank had sexually abused the girls and older boys. She wished she could give back their innocence, but knew that wasn't possible so she would help them move on. She followed them to the front and bought the items. Thankfully, the lady said nothing but glared at them.

Walking out, Johnathan asked, "Can we go to the blacksmith? Andrew told me all about it."

Julia knew they missed the siblings that were not there, but she didn't feel comfortable going too many places alone with all the children. "Why don't we bring food to the sheriff's office for Matt and Maverick and see how their work is going?"

All the children heartily agreed and they headed out the door as Melody said cheerfully, "Maverick should be getting better."

Maverick had been shot a few months back while protecting Julia. It had almost cost him dearly.

Julia nodded. "He is getting much better, but you know how he is fighting to get back to work."

Before Melody could respond, the boys ran ahead, bumping into a nicely dressed woman on the boardwalk. Julia walked up to them, feeling so embarrassed. She just wanted Gloria or her closest brother, Sawyer, to come. She took the boys' hands. "I am very sorry, miss," she told her and was about to walk away, but the woman spoke.

"You are Julia Donovan?" she asked, looking at her like she was sizing her up.

Julia nodded.

Then Melody spoke up. "She sure is. She is a famous artist. Her name used to be Tommy Starry, but she is now Julia Starry Donovan. She is also our new ma." She smiled like everyone should know that.

The woman's eyes went wide. "I am Molly Smith." She looked over the children like they were on a block for sale. "You are the Washington and Starry children?" She said it like they were nobody's children.

Julia nodded, her gaze narrowing. "Yes, they are Starry children."

"Well, if y'all don't get pushed around." She nodded her head like she figured it all out now. "I knew both of your real mamas. I saw that Starry woman come to town with a baby after that woman died. I know what happened. She had that bastard's kid." She pointed to David. "You are that bastard child, ain't you?"

Julia's mouth dropped open, having no words to say. What was the woman talking about? She had never heard that kind of hatred and been accused in such a way before. She pulled David closer, who looked confused. He would be. He had never heard those words before.

Suddenly Matt walked up like he had been doing rounds. He took David in his arms. He stared at the rich woman with authority. "Why don't you think before you speak? And stop spreadin' such lies! God will judge you for bein' so hateful to others." He took Johnathan's hand and led them to the office.

Julia walked in the back door of the sheriff's office, into Matt's living quarters, still stunned. What was that woman talking about? She had never heard those lies before. Matt told the kids to sit at the table and went back to the office.

Julia poured the children some buttermilk and cut each a piece of cake. She felt guilty as she leaned against the head chair. "I am sorry for what happened. I shouldn't have reacted like that. I am sorry."

Charity touched her hand comfortingly. "It's fine. You were just surprised by what that horrible lady said."

Julia gave her a sad smile and then looked at David. "What that lady said is not true."

David looked calm, "What does bastard mean?"

"Uncle Frank used to call me a bastard," Melody whispered.

Julia gasped. She could tell Melody didn't know what that meant. Charity went pale. She walked over to give Melody a side hug. "I am sorry about that. No one will call you that again." She looked at the boys. "It means a person's parents are not married. Both of your parents loved each other very much and were married. It's not a good word."

"It's a swear word?" Jonathan asked.

Julia wasn't sure how to answer. "Yes, it's a bad word we don't ever use."

Both boys bobbed their heads in agreement.

A little while later, Cole walked in. He greeted all the children and led Julia to another room. He held her. "Oh, honey. I am so sorry this happened. I am sorry I wasn't there."

Julia pushed away. "No, it was my fault. I said nothing. I didn't defend him. I just froze. I didn't do..."

Cole put a finger on her lips. "No, this was not your fault. You just didn't expect it."

"Who would? She was so mean. Why did she say those things?" Tears came to her eyes.

"Because she believes David is Ellen's tummy child." Matt stood by the door.

"No." Her eyes were wide. She had never heard of such a thing. "Why? Why would she think that?"

Matt put his hands in his pockets. "Because Ellen came to town with David, after Ben and Missy passed. While she was here, she nursed him." His jaw popped. "I didn't understand it but they accused her of having Ben's child. They said David and Johnathan were twins."

26

Julia's mouth dropped open. How could they accuse her mother of such a thing? The boys were five months apart, David being the younger. Sitting on the bed, she cried. She wasn't a woman of many tears. She was still learning to let her pain out in tears. As always, Cole was there for a hug and a shoulder to cry on. She cried for a mama she would never see on this side of heaven.

Chapter 4

The sun was high in the sky by the time Katrina woke up. Feeling Andrew's empty pillow beside her was odd. He had liked meeting the girls, Sara and Francesca, and he was ready to jump in with both feet and raise them. Katrina was equally excited. After three days with the girls she had finally slept in.

After dressing in a simple dress, she went to the girl's room across from her room and found it empty. They must be downstairs eating. In the kitchen she didn't see them; she headed outside and found Andrew in the barn milking the cow. "Andrew, have you seen the girls?" she asked, her voice high pitched.

Andrew stood up and faced her. "No, I haven't. I thought after the girls had a rough night, they were still sleepin'."

Katrina nodded. "Let's ask the Alexanders to help look. Their boys can ride the land."

Andrew looked doubtful. "They might be out for a walk."

"Francesca hates walking." Katrina shook her head. "I know somethin' is wrong."

He nodded. "Fine." He handed her the milk pail. "I will go get the Alexanders. I will leave you a saddled horse."

Her hands shook as she strained the milk. Where did the girls go? Were they hiding by the creek? Maybe hiding out in town? They could be anywhere and were used to being on their own. How had the girls come to mean so much to her this soon? Is this how Ellen had felt about the children she'd taken in?

In the barn, she could smell the grain, and the manure pile by the back of the barn. Mounting her small bay horse, she decided to take the south pasture near the road. What if Francesca's boss had found her, and forced her back into that life? What if someone took them? What if they got hurt? God would direct her to the girls. She thought of her future with the girls. What would it hold? She hated that the girls were in danger. She wanted to make sure they were safe all the time. She wanted to have tea parties, late-night talks, to show these children some love. Did she love them? She wasn't sure if she loved them yet. It was too soon to see if she did. Ellen always said love was a choice and not always a feeling. Sometimes feelings came later. She began praying for God to help her find the children. They could be an actual family.

Soon she spotted Mabel and her children on the road. Tears came to her eyes. They began their search.

Having had many siblings that ran away every few months, Katrina was used to looking. But having never searched for her own children, she hadn't been prepared for such fear in her heart. She and the others had searched in valleys, along rivers, in old buildings and barns of neighbors, in meadows, and on more land Katrina hadn't known existed. After getting some coffee, Mabel asked her to take a walk. Her children stayed with Andrew, doing chores.

Mabel spoke first. "When you find the girls, what is your plan? The children will want to know what is happening in their life. Do you want to raise them?"

Katrina shrugged. "I like the girls, Francesca is sweet and scared. Sara is so lost and afraid."

Mabel nodded. "They are sweet, very needy girls. But you might not see them again."

Katrina flinched. "That is what I am afraid of. What if Fran ends up with her old boss? She hasn't spoken of it, but I can see that life. And Sara could get into that life."

Mabel sighed. "Yes, they could. Women and girls alone are in a dangerous situation, especially in the West." They walked into what would be Cole's knew house. It was a bit dusty but pretty clean.

Katrina closed her eyes against the truth. "You could say that again." She softly smiled. "I am glad I met you. You have become a good friend."

Mabel smiled. "I have been praying for whoever moved here. It was God's providential plan. You keep me young." She chuckled. "Now, what do you say we look here again?"

"I did this mornin'," Katrina told her. She could hear the wood creak below her. The house made noises only an older house could make.

"Well, you might have, but my friend owned this ranch; we sat here drinking coffee many times." She took Katrina's hand. "I have an idea." She and Katrina walked down the hallway of Cole's house. The house would be ready for him when they moved to the territory in a few months. The walls and floors were bare. Katrina could imagine Julia's art on all the walls, the furniture, and bright colorful rugs on the floors. It would be a beautiful house one day. One they would share with neighbors. They walked into what looked like the master bedroom. Mabel acted like she knew the place well. She moved the thin dirty rug with her boot and then Katrina saw a trapdoor. Mabel gave her a knowing look, then reached down and pulled it up.

Chaos broke loose. Francesca jumped up and tried to get out the door but Mabel ran and stood in front of it. Nothing could get past her arms of steel. Thankfully, the girls didn't go for the windows.

Sara came out slowly, carefully, as if they would beat her. Katrina knew how that was.

Then another girl came out, much younger, maybe around seven. She looked worse for wear than both of the other girls put together; bug bites covered her legs and arms, her hair hung in greasy knots that would take hours to clean out. Her dress was in rags, really just strips of fabric. Her feet were bleeding. She screamed and ran for the door, running into Mabel. Mabel wrapped her arms around the young child while she continued to scream and fight.

The screaming didn't bother Katrina much, she was used to loud noises, her family was loud. As she looked over the child her stomach tightened to make her sick. She had never seen a child in such a terrible condition. Mabel was talking over the screaming like she knew what she was doing. "Easy child. It's all right. Calm down, my child."

Katrina thought everyone's ears would start bleeding by the time the girl stopped screaming. Her eyes went vacant and her shoulders drooped. She still banged her head on the wall as Mabel held her. She looked ready to kill. Mabel told her, "Stop fighting and I'll let you go so we can chat."

The girl nodded. She started breathing heavily like she couldn't get enough air, though Mabel let her go and she turned to face them.

They all sat on the ground. Mabel asked softly, "What is your name, sweetie?"

The girl swore.

Francesca frowned. "Her name is Carlissa."

"Well, that is a nice name." Katrina smiled at Carlissa, then spoke to

Francesca, "Why did you run away? We've been lookin' everywhere for y'all."

Francesca shrugged. "We ain't staying at your house. We don't want to live in no orphanage or asylum!"

Carlissa moved away, covering her face with shaking hands like she could hide from them. Her breath came out rough like she couldn't catch her breath.

"You are not goin' to an asylum!" Katrina told them. "I would never send you to an asylum."

"Then what do you plan to do with us?" Francesca asked.

Katrina looked at Mabel, then back at the girls. "Andrew and I have been talking about you living with us. We have been prayin' about it." She paused. "My brother-in-law owns the Liberty House, and it is a nice place."

Francesca snorted. "You ever been or lived in one? It couldn't be any worse than a brothel."

Katrina flinched at her response.

Francesca got closer to Katrina's face. Her own face red, jaw set hard, hands in fists. "So you haven't seen this orphanage or an orphanage you plan to send us to. I bet you lived in this perfect little world where nothing bad ever happened with that family of yours." She cursed. "Well, it ain't like that for the lot of us, some don't get as lucky." She turned her face away like she couldn't stand to look at Katrina's shocked face any longer.

Katrina stared at her and saw the hardness, anger, pain, hurt, and the fear of not being wanted. She spoke lightly, "You're right, some don't get as lucky, but luck has nothing to do with it." She spoke with the girls. "Let's go home and get some food. I'm famished."

Francesca just glared.

Carlissa looked ready to run again, but she slowly came along with them as they left the house.

The children ate a supper of fresh bread and salted pork with buttermilk. Katrina was relieved that Mabel stayed after sending her children to her daughter's farm. Katrina knew they needed to look at

Carlissa's cuts and what looked like burns under the layers of dirt. It worried her that the girl had not yet said a thing, only moaned and screamed. She had only eaten a few bits of bread with her dirty hands.

While Andrew stayed home with the two older girls, Katrina grabbed a coat for Carlissa, then grabbed her own jacket and let Mabel take the lead to the doctor's office.

The doctor's clinic was neat and clean. Charles welcomed them in, giving his wife a look he had given her many times in the past. It could only be explained as being between a couple who had been through horrible times and still stood by each other no matter what. Katrina shared that look with Andrew often. Katrina picked Carlissa up and placed her on the table. She was light as a feather, and it made Katrina sick to her stomach. No child should be this thin.

As they looked at the cuts and burns, they got her bath water ready. Mabel went to the cabinet and got some bottles down, and what looked like ointment. *So what are your plans now? With another child, it will get worse,* Mabel signed.

Katrina felt tired but also at peace. Caring for the girls had given her a purpose like she had always wanted. She enjoyed having a purpose, a need to fill. She loved serving and living with Andrew, but she had been missing something for some time. Katrina signed back, *I frankly don't know if I can get through today. Can we talk about it later?*

Of course, it looks like it has been a long three days. She grinned a knowing smile.

It has. Tears came to Katrina's eyes, and she did not understand why.

Mabel put an arm around her and pulled her into a side hug. "I would say it will get better, but it doesn't." She spoke with her lips only.

Katrina looked at her confused, pulled away, and signed, *What do you mean? They won't change? It won't get easier?*

Mabel shrugged. "Not really. Not for a long time."

At that moment, Charles walked up and told them the water was ready.

Chapter 5

Katrina walked over to where Carlissa sat on the table. She looked like she had been through hell and not made it back. Her eyes showed an emptiness Katrina had never seen before, not even in the orphanage, but she hadn't been looking either. Could she have missed it? At the orphanage, she was trying to survive, and it wasn't long until she was at Silkwood. "Carlissa, let's say we take a bath? It's nice and warm," She whispered. "I just love baths. I took one right after I came here to get the horse smell off me. And my horses don't smell like roses, I'll tell you." She smiled brightly and helped her down and led her over to the bath.

Carlissa screamed and cried, though not a genuine cry, but muffled. She started breathing really heavily again.

Mabel walked up to them and told her to stop. She had a rag. She got on Carlissa's level. "Now sweetie, we will not hurt you. I am going to put this over your mouth and nose and you won't feel a thing, okay."

She looked at her hard, much more than any child should. "Wanna bet?"

Mabel put it to her noise as Charles stood behind her. Mabel moved just as Carlissa tried to punch her, then she passed out. Charles put her on the floor. Mabel undressed her from the rags she had on. "Katrina, would you come help me bathe her?" Mabel asked.

Katrina knew she would have to roll up her sleeves to do that. She looked at Mabel, deciding whether to get her sleeves wet or show the ugly scars.

Mabel stood up and walked over to Katrina, then took her hands. Katrina tried to pull away, but Mabel held on. "Katrina, I have seen scars before, it's just you and me. Trust me."

Katrina looked at the scars. "It's easier said than done."

"Yes, it is. Make that step, the choice is yours."

Mabel was right. The choice was hers. It was about trust. Katrina nodded, pulled her sleeves up to show the ugly gray and pink skin.

Mabel acted like she didn't notice.

As Mabel and Katrina bathed her, Katrina saw that Carlissa had whip marks on her back, what looked like burns on her skin, and cuts that looked to be healed over leaving scars. On top of all that, she had bug bites that had left hard spots all over her body.

Katrina spoke softly. "I got burned in a cabin where I lived with the Starrys. The neighbors hated us, for many reasons - Andrew and I were slaves or because a black freed couple lived on our land, or we had two Spanish brothers. You name it, there was a reason. When the cabin caught fire, all the others got out safely. They didn't know I wasn't out yet. I got stuck under a beam, Andrew wouldn't leave without me." She sighed. She had never told anyone. "Besides becomin' burned, I lost most of my hearing. Andrew has as many scars as I do."

Mabel gave her a compassionate look. "I am sorry. They did nothing to those who did this to you," she stated.

Katrina shook her head. "We were slaves. Andrew's brother bought us out of it. Andrew said at least the fire didn't taint our beautiful faces." She smiled lightly.

Mabel laughed. "Good point."

"Ellen and Missy helped me find my brother, Isaiah, after the war."

"So he didn't grow up with you and the Starry's?"

Katrina nodded. "I kept my last name O'Meara till I married Andrew." She looked back to where Charles worked on something in the backroom. "Why ain't Charles helpin'?"

Mabel shrugged. "I have you to help me. We have worked with asylum children for years together. They ain't nothing we haven't seen." She blinked back tears. "We can handle what happened to Carlissa. He has been working a lot lately."

Katrina's mouth went dry. "I am sorry for what you have seen."

Mabel looked up, giving her a sad look, but then turned back to the little girl. "At least we know she can talk, though we might not want her to." She chuckled, though she didn't mean it.

Katrina smiled. "My sister didn't talk for two years and we funned her that when she finally talked, she would never stop."

"She didn't talk for two years?!"

"Yeah, we just learned to talk to her and for her. Ellen was patient and let her talk when she was ready."

Mabel smiled. "Sounds like a family put together by God and who stayed together through a lot."

You don't know the half of it. Katrina thought. "We made it through more than we thought possible." She sadly smiled. "I miss them at times like this. Maverick would know what to do. Gloria and Julia would know how to help them."

"You can learn how to help them."

Katrina said honestly, "I want to learn. I just don't know if I should take them without talking to the family. We should hear from them soon. I just have never made such a big decision without them."

"You know them pretty well; do you know what they will say?"

"Point taken. I'll talk with Andrew and tell the girls soon."

Carlissa's hair was the hardest part; they waited to care for it last. Katrina thought they would have to cut it after washing it twice. The hair color was the same as Katrina's. Carlissa had open cuts on her round face and her pudgy nose. Katrina guessed with some nutritious food and care, she would become a healthy young child.

"We won't have to cut it," Mabel told her.

Katrina's face must have shown her emotions. "What will we do?"

"Run some oil through it and that will get the vermin out," Mabel explained.

"Why did we knock her out instead of working her through it?" Katrina wanted to know. "Why is she so afraid of water?"

"We will work her through it in time, but we had to get her cuts clean and get the vermin out." Mabel paused. "This girl grew up in an asylum, maybe born into it. One of her treatments was cold baths with ice. The scars you see are from whips that marked her body when they thought she was out of control, the burn marks are from a cigarette. The other scars are from..." Mabel paused. Katrina saw she was almost crying. "Those scars are fresh; they are marks of being shocked by electricity. They say they can shock the insanity or the crazy out of them."

"What is electricity?" Katrina asked. It sounded awful.

"It's this shock wave that goes through you so bad it makes your body shake without control. It can cause the shakes, cause strokes, heart problems, and many other issues."

"Do you believe the girls are insane?" Katrina asked.

"No. The abuse they suffered has made them act like this. They need to be in a family that gives them security and safety. They can let the abuse continue to control them or they can control it. They need to choose every day to be free from the past."

Finishing Carlissa's hair, Mabel called out to Charles. They put her on the table and dressed her in a simple pink dress and stockings, leaving most of the cuts open since they had begun to heal.

"The cuts on her legs and arms are from trying to bleed her out, to get rid of the poison, the insanity," Mabel told her.

Katrina didn't know how much she could handle hearing. Bile rose in her throat.

Mabel started brushing Carlissa's hair. It was coming out smooth to Katrina's surprise. To Katrina's dismay, Mabel didn't stop. "She will probably be barren."

"Why? How do you know?" Katrina asked, shocked she would know such a personal thing, but then again her husband was a doctor. She was the midwife of Deer Trail and the surrounding areas.

"At the asylum, any woman or girl child, they make sure they can never bear children from the treatments they do on them," Mabel said. Hardness set in her jaw but she kept her hands gentle. She had almost all the hair done. Mabel leaned close to the scalp.

"Looking for more bugs?" Katrina wondered if she would have to change her clothes and keep them outside until she could wash them. She'd had vermin in the orphanage and hated them with a passion.

"No." Mabel must not have found any. "In the old days at the asylums the butcher would do brain surgery where they would take out part of the brain. If the patient lived through it, the doctor put the piece of the brain in a pouch and put it around their neck for the rest of their lives." She nearly spat, "I have never had a child done that to, but I have seen adults and one child with it. You can only imagine what it did to them. So much was taken from these people."

"Why are you telling me all this stuff, Mabel?" Katrina didn't want to know any more. Her chest was so tight it hurt to breathe.

Mabel looked at her with firmness. "Because if you raise the girls and other children, if you want to help touched families, then you need to know it all. I am not a woman to sugarcoat the ugly, awful truth. So many parents take children in thinking they will be overwhelmed with gratitude or they'll see a perfect child, but that is not the way it is." She softened. "It is hard, Katrina Starry. Every day is a fight with them, every day you choose to love them, every day you do it. Because you know what they can do in life. You believe they can do anything."

Katrina didn't want to hear any more. Raising these children wouldn't be easy. It would be the hardest thing she ever did. But didn't God call His people to do the hard and impossible, and He would give her the strength and power to do this?

"Katrina," Mabel said, "I also want to say God gives you the strength to face it every day, and He gives you a love to treasure, to cherish them every day. He gives you a peace for doing it. Yes, it's hard. But the mothers and fathers who decide to do this are stronger than most. They stay with their children because they have been called to. They love them more than anyone ever could. Why we get called to do this is because we are strong and God knew   that. He made us for this. Sometimes I believe it is to work with us mothers for God to shape, mold us into what He wants us to be. What better way than to parent a troubled child?"

Katrina's face flushed. "Mabel, I don't know if I can do this. I want to adopt, but I am not sure if I can."

Mabel nodded. "No one can. God will lead you."

Katrina loved the old barn. It wasn't anything like the one back home on Silkwood. There was an aisle with four stalls on each side. Then at the end of the aisle was a sizable round area, looking like it could store a couple of wagons and maybe even a sleigh or cutter. There was a loft for hay and other stuff.

After she finished milking Daisy, Katrina let her out in the back pasture. Hearing a scream, she ran towards it to find Carlissa in the loft with a cat. The cat had two newborn kittens and looked like she was having another one. Carlissa glanced at her, "Miss Katrina, mama cat is having kittens."

Katrina sat down next to Carlissa, but not touching her. "Wow, that is fun, sweetie."

Carlissa pointed out all she noticed. Katrina watched her like she was seeing the child inside of her for the first time. The exuberant behavior Carlissa displayed seemed so natural, instead of the fear and terror that usually gripped her. She was just a child that wanted to be loved.

Before she knew it, Carlissa took Katrina's hand as she stood. "Would you like to go see the girls?"

Katrina chuckled. "Let's go." Taking the milk up to the house, she found Francesca drinking coffee and Sara eating cake at the kitchen table. After she strained the milk, she sliced bread for them.

Sara looked up at Katrina. "Can I have a glass of milk?"

Katrina stared at her, then poured her a cup of buttermilk. " So, you can talk, my dear. I am very glad." She kissed her forehead and felt her stiffen.

"You won't be glad after you find out what she says," Carlissa told her.

"That is not true. I will always be glad Sara speaks." Katrina told them. "I always love to hear my girls talk."

Sara didn't respond, she just watched them all.

That evening, Katrina walked out on the porch and watched the sun setting behind the mountains. A chill was in the air. As she pulled her shrug tighter, she watched the bright red, yellow and orange hues in the sky slowly disappear.

"Want to watch the sunset with me, love?" Andrew asked.

Katrina jumped to find him sitting behind her on the swing. "I didn't see you there."

Andrew smiled, looking content. "I noticed."

She settled next to him. "Do you think we are doin' the right thing?" She watched his lips.

"You don't think so?" Andrew asked honestly.

Katrina nodded. "It's just been a rough couple of days. I am afraid that is God telling us that we shouldn't do it."

Andrew looked at the setting sun. "Well, when Ellen took us in, nothing was pleasant or easy at that time." His face was grim. "We were her first kiddos, but she didn't run when most would have."

Katrina couldn't agree more. She tried not to think of that time. It still stung. "She must have really loved us even then. I was always afraid she would send me away because of Clara. Do you want to raise these girls because of what we couldn't do for Clara?" It still hurt to think about Clara, who was Maverick's sister. She had gotten sick, Ellen had come to help. After Clara died, Ellen had taken the children to the orphanage and then home when she could.

His jaw popped. "No, but when I looked at Francesca I thought about it. She is so hard while Clara seemed more weak and fearful. I just wished we could have done somethin' for Clara before it was too late." He looked at Katrina, touching her face. "Maybe I want to do that for Francesca. Give her a chance at a safe life."

"I think I might love the girls. Even this soon."

His mouth turned into a smile. "Me too. Sara is even talkin' now, and Carlissa is actin' more like a child." He chuckled. "Francesca is so

38

sarcastic."

She concurred. "You know Mabel said we can't legally adopt them because of where they came from."

"I know that. Cole explained the chance of adopting Asylum children doesn't happen. He gets approved sometimes but most often the state will just take them back."

Katrina nearly gasps, "That won't happen to our girls." She smiled. "Do you want to tell them tomorrow?"

Andrew nodded. "Sure, after dinner. We can make it special for them."

She smiled, "I have the perfect gift for them." Her mind got busy with ideas. "I am already makin' them dresses. Mabel said she would give me some of Lucy's old ones. They will fit Carlissa nicely."

Andrew's eyes twinkled in the moonlight at her openness to love and care for these children. He loved that about her. He only hoped that she would never change.

Chapter 6

Julia always loved watching her younger siblings play with the ponies. Sitting on the porch swing, she leaned her head back enjoying the cool evening air against her hot body, glad to have some cool nights as it wouldn't last for long.

Out of her siblings, Charity was the best with the ponies. She was very calm and sweet, and could get them into check with one move of her hand. She seemed to know what ponies were thinking. It was wonderful to observe her in action.

One of the ponies followed behind Charity as she walked up to Julia. "Can I go get my pie?"

Julia smiled. "Sure, we'll also have to save a piece for Cole. It is one of his favorites."

Charity chuckled. "Any pie is his favorite."

Julia smiled, knowing it was true. She missed him tonight; he didn't have a choice but to work late at the office. Cole wasn't required to work nights, but Maverick was healing from a bullet wound and Matt needed the night off.

Charity dished out the pie and the children all ate it while sitting on the steps. Though it wasn't dark yet, Julia lit a lamp, because the children didn't like the dark. She leaned against the railing. As Jonathan snuggled up next to her with blueberries on his mouth, she kissed his forehead. She loved him so much.

It was peaceful, even the older children were bubbling with chatter.

"I thought we would start to can the tomatoes. Mama always used to start with them first," Charity told her.

"I remember," Julia told her, wanting to remind Charity that she had been raised by Ellen, too. But she left it alone and discussed what they would do the next week.

A little while later, it was well after dark. The girls took the dishes in, and the older boys went off to put the ponies up. By the time she told the boys to go wash up for bed, Charity had started washing the dishes. "Oh, honey, leave those for the mornin'. It's late," Julie exclaimed.

Charity shook her head. "No, Mama always wanted the dishes done before bed."

Julia's eyes widened. Charity had never told her no before. From the look of it, Charity hadn't noticed how she had said it. "I know Mama always did them, but sometimes she let us go to bed without finishing them. We have worked hard today, let's leave them till mornin'."

Charity looked at her, her jaw firm, but she nodded. "Fine, but one dish will turn into twenty before you know it." She walked to her room without another word.

Julia wasn't sure what to do. She didn't know how much balance there should be between parenting and being a sister to the older ones. They had suffered abuse, which made them behave much older than their actual age. Instead, she decided to leave the situation between Charity and her alone for now. She wasn't one to make a big deal out of nothing.

Approaching the boy's room, she saw her little paint brush tossed around the floor. After picking them up, she went to the boys' room. Lighting their lantern, she put her hands on her hips. "Which one of you got into my pencils? You know that is not allowed without permission."

They both looked surprised at her question.

"What if it was the girls?" David said. "They are children, too."

"The girls were with me," Julia told him. "Now answer me. Who did it?"

Johnathan shrugged. "I was changing into my nightclothes."

David screamed, "It wasn't me! You hate me. I know you just hate and blame me."

Julia's mouth nearly dropped open. Where did this come from? He was totally overreacting. "Davy, I do not hate you. Now just calm down."

Johnathan got in bed and seemed to ignore his brother.

David looked at her with such hate. It shocked her. She wasn't sure what to do. "Calm down now, Davy."

Then suddenly David laughed like something was funny. "I am going to bed now." He got in bed like nothing was wrong.

For the first time, Julia felt so distant from David. She didn't know what to expect from him and she believed he was holding something back. What happened to their close relationship? She was unsure what to do about it. Kissing the boys on the head, she told them, "We will talk about this in the morning."

41

Jonathan looked sad over Julia's comment while David just smiled. However, his smile didn't reach his eyes and seemed very counterfeit.

Taking the lantern, she sat on the sofa to wait for Cole. She knew the dishes called, but she decided to draw. Putting her legs up, she fell asleep, wondering if she should tell Cole about David.

Katrina took the girls on a fun picnic. However, the rain had ruined it, so she ended up having the picnic on the parlor floor. Andrew also took the time to eat with them. After their special big dinner, she and Andrew sat down with the girls. Katrina didn't want to hold back from telling the girls they were raising them. She was just bursting with the news.

Sara and Francesca sat on the sofa, while Andrew sat on the chair.

Katrina set Carlissa on her lap. She looked up at her, eyes wide. "You don't have to say it; we are leaving. Francesca says it's coming."

Katrina was not expecting that. "Carlissa, we will not send you away. That is a promise. We want you to live with us forever and always. How do you feel about that, honey?"

She looked surprised. "Will we get picnics like today?"

Katrina smiled. "Yes, lots of picnics."

"With cake?" Her eyes went wide.

"Only if it is chocolate cake," Katrina teased.

Carlissa giggled. "I ain't never had sugar before. I like it."

Katrina glanced at Sara and Francesca, waiting for them to respond.

"I am too old to be adopted," Francesca stated.

Sara bit her lip, looking scared. "It won't last, nothing ever does."

Katrina knew how she felt. She hadn't believed she was coming to live at Silkwood when Ellen had first told her. What made her believe was that Ellen had learned sign language to communicate with her. "Well, one day you will believe us."

Sara looked at her hands. "I will stay as long as I get my own room."

Katrina nodded. "Well, we planned to build onto the..."

Andrew gently touched Katrina's arm, silencing her. "Sara, look at me."

Sara shook her head. Her face was full of terror.

Andrew continued, "Sara, no one will ever enter your bedroom against your will. I plan to build on a room once some of my brothers come. Do you understand, you are safe here? No one will ever hurt you."

Sara just shook her head again, as she prepared to run.

Katrina felt sick over Sara's questions. She also knew the girls needed rest. "Let's head to bed, girls." Katrina tried to appear cheerful because she wanted Carlissa and the other girls to be happy about it. However, they all looked confused and scared. "I got you all some gifts. They are on your bed. The fastest ones up there will be the winner." They all got up and ran upstairs, even Francesca. Katrina and Andrew laughed as they chased after them.

The girls opened the gifts with surprise on their faces like they didn't know to react.

Francesca put the soft white satin gown against herself. She smiled shyly. "It is so soft. Thank you, Katrina."

"You're welcome, Francesca." She smiled. She wanted to give her a hug, but instead she resisted, not wanting to overwhelm her.

Sara put her peach gown on the bed like the touch of it would burn her. With her back straight and jaw tight, she whispered, "What will I have to do?"

Katrina looked at her. "Nothing. It is a free gift, sweetie."

Carlissa opened her gift, and threw the paper down, then looked at it as though it was the ugliest thing she had ever seen. She exclaimed, "I don't like this color. Pink is ugly."

Feeling hurt, Katrina had always wanted a pink gown when she lived at the orphanage. "You don't have to wear it, but I would like you to wear it, Carlissa."

Throwing herself on the floor like a spoiled little toddler, Clarissa started screaming.

Andrew had never seen one of her fits before. He stared at Katrina like 'what should we do?'

Katrina shrugged, unaware of what to do next.

Francesca told Andrew she was leaving to sleep in Carlissa's bed, and then she took Sara's arm and left.

Andrew nodded. To him, it looked like they would not get much sleep tonight, but he was glad the girls were safe.

Katrina wondered if screaming didn't hurt Clarissa's ears, but the other girls had to live with her and hearing Clarissa holler all night was not a part of the agenda. If Katrina and Andrew allowed her to get away with screaming, then it would happen again. Katrina picked her up while trying to avoid getting a fist in her face. Holding her tighter, Katrina allowed Clarissa to scream, knowing there was no other choice.

Finally, the screaming came to cease and so did the fight. Clarissa went limp in Katrina's arms like she had passed out or fallen asleep. Katrina laid her on the bed but didn't move. She just sat there watching her new daughter while she prayed and thought. What caused this? Would she ever know what made Clarissa tick? At least the other girls remained calm during this one.

Checking on the girls' room, Andrew and Katrina noticed that chaos must be normal for them because they slept peacefully through Clarissa's screams. Francesca slept in her new nightgown with her arm lying over Sara's arm, while Sara slept in her undergarments again. In the heart of the winter; Sara would need to dress warmer. She could catch a cold that could get the rest of the family sick. Katrina remembered when Jesse's twin, Pedro, came back sick and no one but Ellen was allowed in the room. Katrina never wanted to face anything like that again.

Andrew took Katrina's hand and they walked away from the girls' room. In the kitchen, they felt like they could talk. Andrew spoke first, "You're right." He shook his head. "That was strange."

"You thought I was lyin'?" Katrina snapped.

"Of course not," Andrew told her. "But I never thought a child could scream and act like that. How did you know what to do?"

Katrina shrugged. "I don't, I just did what I could." She unloaded the groceries Andrew had bought in town.

Still in shock, Andrew didn't know how to take this all in. Was he willing to put Katrina through this? Was it worth it when she had been through so much already?

Katrina slammed a bag of sugar on the counter. "Don't even go there, Andrew. I can handle this and I plan to do it, so don't change your mind because of me."

"But what if they physically hurt you?"

Katrina shrugged. "I love them and I will fight for them."

44

Andrew nodded. "This will be rough."

"God sends us challenges," Katrina told him. "He did it in the image of three little children."

Andrew took her hands. "God sent us these children."

"I agree, love." She looked at him with a flirty look. "Are you going to let my hands go so I can put away the food?"

He did and winked at her. "We can do things like this."

"You need to go to bed. You have work."

"What, do you think I am an old man?" he teased her.

Katrina pulled away and went to the other end of the kitchen. He enjoyed watching the way she moved her hips. "Well, Andrew Starry, you ain't any younger. And let's just say you ain't as strong as you used to be."

Andrew caught onto it and chased her around the kitchen until he caught her. "Let me show you who's weak, woman." The food didn't get put away for some minutes.

"Francesca, I want you to do this right now," Katrina told her, keeping her voice even.

"No." Francesca crossed her arms firmly.

"Then you will have to be disciplined." Katrina shook her head, her mind running on how to do this. "What chore do you like to do, because work is a part of life."

"What am I good at?" Francesca threw her arms in the air. "Come on, you don't know? I am good at entertaining men. That is what I learned since I was a young girl. It's all I know! It's all I will ever know."

Shocked, Katrina's mouth dropped open. She didn't know what to say to Francesca. She couldn't believe how Francesca viewed herself and felt like crying for Francesca, for what this child had suffered at a young age. She was glad the two other girls were outside.

Francesca shook her head at Katrina's shock. "Oh, you are so ignorant to the world around you." She swore. "I wish I were that lucky in life."

Though Francesca's words hurt, in some ways Katrina agreed. She was naïve to what Francesca had suffered. She knew Clara, her first friend, suffered, but as a child Katrina couldn't help her. Nightmares of the way Clara died still haunted Katrina. For a moment, she recalled seeing Clara lay in her own blood from what men caused, but she quickly blinked against the memory. Besides Clara, Katrina was still innocent to the life Francesca and Sara lived. Could she be a good mother to them? The mother they needed. She opened up her mouth, then shut it when she didn't know what to say. She saw Francesca's gaze go behind her. Expecting to see Carlissa, Katrina turned around, but instead she was surprised to see Izzy standing in the door. "Hi, Izzy, this is Francesca." She looked back at Francesca. "Fran, this is my friend, Izzy Donavon."

Izzy nodded to her. Then laid her eyes on Francesca, her face expressed love and open honesty. "You just need to learn a different trade."

Francesca's eyes turned from Katrina to Izzy.

Izzy walked in like she knew her way around the place. She nodded to Francesca and looked at Katrina, "You don't mind if I take Francesca with me, do you?"

Katrina shook her head. "Francesca, we will talk about this later."

Francesca glared at her.

As they walked out, Carlissa strolled in carrying the milk pail. Katrina assumed that Andrew would bring in the rest of it.

Carlissa set it on the counter, her face angry. Unable to assist Carlissa in time, Katrina watched Carlissa dump the milk all over herself and the clean floor.

"Carlissa, why did you just do that?" Katrina asked.

Carlissa ignored her question. "Who is that Spanish lady? I don't like her. She was signing with Andrew."

Katrina wouldn't let her change the subject, "Carlissa, answer my question. Why did you spill it?"

She looked up with an innocent expression. "I didn't! You bumped me."

"Carlissa, you know that is a lie." Katrina sighed. "Well, I'll get you a bucket and you can clean up the mess."

Carlissa screamed at Katrina, but with Katrina's help she cleaned up the spilled milk.

Chapter 7

Izzy walked to the paddock where they kept the horses. Francesca walked beside her with her arms crossed. In those beautiful brown eyes was anger and fear.

They came to the fence and looked out at the most beautiful animal God had ever made. "Francesca, pick one of them. You can keep it forever."

Francesca didn't believe her. "I don't like horses."

"A person without a horse is like a person with one leg," she exclaimed. "This is a workin' ranch. Everyone needs a horse, so go out and pick one."

Francesca looked out at the horses, trying to act bored and indifferent. But Izzy saw the light in her eyes and the softness that came to her face. Izzy was seeing a glimpse of the child in her. She just stood there silently, waiting. Finally, Francesca opened up the gate and walked in.

Entering the paddock, Francesca's back went straight, and her hands balled into fists. Izzy wasn't surprised that she was afraid of horses. "Come on, Francesca." Walking closer to them, Francesca followed. "Any one horse can be yours, to care for, ride, or train. These horses are green."

Still gazing at the horses, Francesca asked, "What is green?"

"They are still in training," Izzy explains. "But none of them should buck you off, though. Donovans know how to raise good stock." She was proud of her horses and her hard work to get the Donovan name back after her dad had destroyed it.

Francesca pointed. "What about the black and white one?"

Izzy smiled. The little gelding was a feisty little spitfire. "Well, he doesn't like to listen to anyone. I have far to go with him."

Francesca frowned; her shoulders sagged. "You said I could have any horse out of this pen."

Izzy nodded as she took a rope off the fence. "All right, just don't expect a miracle." She heard Francesca's gasps, as she pulled the rope to find that the feisty horse wasn't having it. She walked up to the horse and placed a halter on him. She stood watching him run around the pen, near his pasture mates. "He is a paint; When we got him as a yearlin,' he was pure wild and ran the range up in Texas. He's about four years old now and as grumpy as a turd, but he'll show you what to do."

"Is he a mustang?" Francesca inquired in awe. She seemed a little nervous at first, but the fear left as she continued watching him. "So you're from Texas?"

"Yup."

"What made you come here from that barren, hopeless state?" Francesca asked bitterly.

Izzy didn't have to look at Francesca to see the evidence of the broken girl. She could hear it. Her brokenness came out at the oddest times. Izzy figured that many of Francesca's abusers were from Texas. Francesca probably missed the loveliness of Texas. She shrugged and was honest. "To get away from my pa, who beat me." Keeping her eyes on the paint, her voice still light, she said, "I found out I liked it here, near the mountains, rivers, valleys, and even the winters." She paused. "So where're you from?"

"You wouldn't believe me if I tell ya," Francesca said in a hard voice.

"You won't know until you tell me," Izzy spoke in Spanish.

"Yeah, right!"

Izzy handed the rope to Francesca as she gave her directions to repeat the same actions she had seen Izzy performing. Francesca obeyed, but the horse sensed her fear and tested her control. He started bucking a little.

"He didn't do that for you!" Francesca cried.

"He is only testing you. Now show him who's the boss. He needs to know you will protect him by making him have rules. You're doing fine. Keep at it."

Francesca did and Izzy walked to the paddock boards next to Sara, telling her what to do. "Now get him going faster."

As Francesca did, Izzy talked to her. "With a horse, you can do anything. It feels as if you are truly flying. It will take your breath away every time. When you have a relationship with a horse there has to be a leader. Work through your problems together. Sometimes you will fail, but ultimately you are gaining trust. Once a horse's trust is gained, it is hard to lose it. If you lose their trust, you can always gain it back. It is never hopeless when you have the love of a horse."

Izzy noticed Katrina and Sara had walked up and were standing by the fence. Sharing a smile with them, she turned back to face Francesca. "Now stop in the middle, Fran. Turn your back to him." Francesca's back was straight with fear again. Izzy encouraged her, "Just relax. He won't hurt, he is learning to trust you."

"Really?" Francesca asked. She seemed to relax her body a little as the horse walked behind her. Francesca touched his nose with her hand. The smile on her face showed it all.

"Yup, he is bonding with you. Now walk away."

Francesca obeyed and the horse followed her. The horse moved with her as if they were one.

"With a mustang it is easier because they normally have never been abused by a person. While a horse that has been abused may be angry and very fearful." Izzy paused. "I have worked with both. Based on the ones I worked with, I realized that it has to be the horse's choice. They can choose to obey and live a healthy life by doing a job they love. On the other hand, they can choose to fight me every time, and live an unhappy life. It's all about choice and change. They always have an option to change their ways with help from a loving owner."

Izzy spoke up, "So Franny, what do you want to name him?"

She looked up at her. "You mean I get to choose?"

Izzy nodded.

Francesca turned and looked up into the horse's eyes, and then said, "Your name will be Poder. It means power."

Izzy smiled at the pair. Hopefully, Francesca would see the healing power in this horse. And so much more to come.

I hated mucking stalls. Francesca thought as she shoved another pitch fork of horse poop into the wheelbarrow. *All they want me to do is work. When they know I am so bad at working, then they won't want me to do more. I could just stop working and they would kick my butt in this place. They really don't like me. Katrina wants me for work and Andrew doesn't know how to treat a girl. My daddies never treated me like Andrew. What is wrong with him? My daddies never made me...*

Suddenly she saw a boy walk into the barn. His face had a scar or birthmark right down his face, it was hard to miss. His broad boyish smile made her heart feel light.

"Howdy, Francesca. I am your closest neighbor, Timmy, next door," he stuttered.

"I ain't livin' here." She frowned. "I am just passing through."

"Well then, I will be next door as long as you stay," he told her. "You are about a thirty-minute ride or hundred steps from my house."

"Why in the world would you count your steps?" She looked at him like he was crazy.

"My brothers are blind and our friends used to live here."

She leaned on the pitchfork. "Why do you talk so funny?"

"Some people say it's because my brain didn't develop right. My mom says cuz I'm special." He grinned. "But most moms are supposed to say that, right?"

Francesca blinked.

"What are you doing?"

"Picking up horse poop with a knitting needle," Francesca said, then swore.

Timmy laughed. "My favorite chore in the barn is mucking stalls. It gives me time to think. I talk to my horse and God."

"Who answers?"

"My horse does when he's not mad at me, and God always responds."

Francesca smiled. "You're different. Most people would freak when I swear."

"I just figured it was between the good Lord and your parents." He held up his hands. "Okay, the people you live with."

Again Francesca smiled at him. She couldn't help it because he was so boyish.

"My brothers will probably tell you to stop, though."

"Why? They want me to change, too."

"No, they've just been where you are."

Glaring at him, Francesca said, "You are a..."

"Good looking, kind gentlemen." He grinned. "You don't have to say it."

Francesca rolled her eyes. "If you say so."

"Want some help, Fran?" He said her name like a song almost, smooth.

Francesca didn't like how he was treating her like a child. Or maybe it was something else. "I would never turn down help even if

50

it's from a stuttering, ugly boy."

Timmy just smiled and got another pitchfork off the wall. "If you plan to offend me, Fran, you will have to come up with something better. I have heard it all." He shrugged. "You'll like it here Francesca, and one day you will feel like this is home."

The kitchen was toasty and warm as Katrina baked a cake. Too bad her mind wasn't entirely on the cake. The girls still didn't know she was half deaf and it was bothering her. They would talk and turn their head away or mutter, but it was difficult for Katrina to read their lips or overhear them. She was tired of hiding it from them but didn't know how to tell them. In the past, people had just known she was deaf.

When Katrina asked Francesca to bring her the flour, Francesca dropped the full bowl of flour on the floor. Unsure if it was an accident, Katrina asked, "Francesca, why did you do that?" Glass and flour covered the floor. "That is wasteful."

Francesca glared at her. "You don't care a wit what I say. Why do you ignore what I have to say?" She looked hurt before she covered it with anger. "Why?"

Katrina realized her mistake. She should have told them sooner. "It's not that I ignore you, dear. It's..." She stopped. How did she tell them she was deaf?

Just then Sara walked in, giving Francesca a smug look. "She's deaf as a post."

Katrina saw Francesca look shocked and hurt.

Carlissa walked in, looking confused.

Katrina sighed. "No, I am not. I am half deaf." She bit her lip. "I was born not hearing in most of my right ear and then lost some of it in my left ear. I can still hear." She sighed. "That's why I miss what you say sometimes, Fran. I can't read your lips when you look away or mutter." She paused. "I should have told you sooner, I'm sorry about that, my sweeties."

Francesca just gave her a shrug. "I just didn't know. I thought you didn't like me or something."

Katrina took her in her arms. "No, it's not that at all. I like you a lot, my dear." She looked at both of them. "I like all of you." This was the first time she had held Francesca.

Francesca pulled away to look up at her. "That is why you sign, right?"

She nodded and looked at Sara. "How did you know I was deaf?"

Sara muttered, "I heard you and Izzy talking."

"Back home, the deaf people didn't know how to get out of the way of the matrons and men. They would get hit more often because of it." Carlissa stated like it was the truth. "They were dummies, so they got beat more."

Katrina bent down to her level and took a chance to take the small child in her arms. "No one will hit you here, ever. Deaf people are not dumb, they are just different. No one deserves to get hit. Ever. Will you forgive me for not telling you, Carly?"

She nodded. She didn't relax in her arms, but she stayed there. Katrina picked her up, settling her on the counter. She was still too thin. "Well, at least there is no real secret between us."

Francesca nodded. "Will you teach us sign language?"

Katrina wasn't sure she wanted to. She signed with Andrew alone. "Sure. Can you read and write, Fran?"

Francesca nodded. "Not well, but I had a friend in the daytime learn me."

Katrina flinched. She knew what that meant. She covered it, or she hoped she did. "Good, then it shouldn't be too hard to pick up," she told her. She looked to Sara, "Can you read?"

Sara shook her head.

"Well, we can work on both together, how about that?" she said cheerfully.

Carlissa tugged on Katrina's sleeve. "I can read."

Katrina didn't believe her for a second but smiled, "Oh, can you now? We can work on it then."

Carlissa nodded.

As they were cleaning up the mess, Katrina told the girls how they could get her attention when she didn't hear them. They all came up with their own ideas. She didn't mind that her daughters were aware now. It was a relief, but would they tell the entire town?

Chapter 8

Katrina was up before anyone, wanting to get the baking and cleaning done for the day, since she hadn't gotten to it the night before. She liked the quietness of the early morning. A lot of times she and Andrew would share breakfast together before he left for work.

When he didn't work in town, they would eat with the girls. It helped them start the day on a good note, though it might not end that way. They seemed to enjoy being together for breakfast. The part they didn't like was when Andrew read the Bible every morning. They sat there solemnly and sometimes would interrupt him, but Andrew, with a gentle, firm hand, put a stop to that.

Izzy walked into the kitchen, wearing a fashionable dress. It was a light pink blouse with a long straight blue skirt. Putting her hair up, Izzy said, "Mornin', Kat."

"Morning, Izzy."

Izzy got the bacon out of the cooler. She looked refreshed after sleeping in the bedroom down the hall. The bedroom was supposed to be Isaiah but he gave it up for her.

As they were getting breakfast started and talking lightly, Francesca walked in, her hair a mess. She was wearing one dress that Katrina had altered to fit her. It made her look like a young child. "Mornin'," she muttered.

"Morning Francesca. Did you sleep well?" Katrina asked.

Francesca was normally honest. She shook her head. "No, not really." She looked at Katrina with those dark, pretty eyes. "Do you still want to adopt us even though we don't really listen? We lie and don't treat you nice. Do you want us?"

Katrina wasn't surprised Francesca asked her. She had asked Ellen the same thing about the bad boys. "Yes, I do."

"Why? Do you like us making your life miserable?" Francesca asked as she shuffled her feet.

Katrina chuckled dryly. "No, I don't like it, but I pray, and I will help you girls work over the years to get over the bad memories and obey. I want so much for ya'll to become anyone you want to be. Francesca, what do you want to do when you grow up?"

Francesca looked at her like she was crazy. "I am grown up. I am too old to be adopted."

"No, you're not. You are never too old to be adopted. Adoption is like being adopted into God's family. You are never too old and in this family, you can do nothing too bad to be kicked out." Katrina gave her a serious look. "Believe me, you can do nothing that some Starry ain't done before. Once a Starry, always one."

"So I could do nothing that would make you want to kick me out?" Francesca swore. "You know my daddy could come back and kill you all."

Katrina flinched, "Starrys are used to it being hard. We've never given up yet. We mean this forever and always."

Francesca gave her a look. "The Starrys reminds me of odd folk."

Izzy and Katrina laughed.

Izzy teased, "Now you're getting it. Starrys and Donovans are not normal folk, but we make it through pretty much anything."

Carlissa and Sara walked in the kitchen looking hungry as usual. Katrina tried to keep some kind of food upstairs so they wouldn't feel afraid of going hungry, but it didn't work. They still acted out in the morning. Carlissa looked at them, grumpy. "What is so funny?"

Katrina came over to give her a hug and smiled. "Well, we were laughing about our families. I can't wait until you can meet them. I told them about y'all." She gave Sara a side hug.

Sara looked at her as she pulled away. "We probably ain't staying, so we won't have to meet them."

That hurt Katrina more than she thought. Had they never known unconditional love? Love forever? Probably not. "No, they know you are staying here forever. They will love getting to know y'all." Neither girl reacted. So she changed the subject, picking up the bowl, "You have a nice soft voice, Sara. Did you know…" She stopped as she saw Carlissa take a hot greased biscuit off the stove. She didn't seem to notice the heat.

Katrina put the mix down and pulled the hot biscuit out of Clarissa's hand using her apron. "That was hot." She looked at Carlissa's small red hand. She knew about burns and how they hurt. She took Carlissa's hand, then ran water over it. "What were you thinkin', Carlissa?"

Carlissa started screaming, loud and in terror. She fell on the ground and screamed, crying out. "You starve me. You don't care about me. I hate you. I hate you all."

Katrina regretted how she handled it, though it was an honest question. She put her arms around the young girl and just sat on the floor. Katrina hadn't checked on the table for a note from Andrew. At any moment, he would be in from milking.

Katrina thought she would try something new. She began singing "Amazing Grace" as Carlissa continued to scream and fight. Francesca set the table for breakfast while Sara started beating the bread, like Katrina had been teaching her. Izzy sang with Katrina while putting breakfast on the table.

If only her family could see her now. What would they say? As she held her baby girl, keeping her safe from herself, she felt God's peace.

This is My Beloved child. Love and Raise her to serve Me, good and faithful servant.

Yes. I will, my Lord. Katrina thought. She felt such love for this child. It was powerful and magnificent. She felt like she could do anything with this kind of love. She could do anything if God was with her.

As they sat at the table for breakfast, Carlissa began shoving food into her mouth. She acted like she hadn't eaten in days. However, Katrina acquiesced to her behavior as long as she remained calm.

Isaiah, Katrina's brother, ate with them this morning. He had been avoiding them like the plague.

"Katrina, how did you know Sara had a nice voice?" Francesca asked. "If you are deaf?"

Katrina smiled softly and looked at Sara. "Well, I can read her lips. Everyone's lips are different. Sara has a soft, quiet voice from what I noticed."

Francesca grinned. "Her voice sounds like that, so what is my voice like?"

Katrina chuckled at her youthfulness. "Your voice is sometimes teasing and sarcastic. It is hard, but still feminine. It holds a little

Spanish accent and when you're mad or passionate, it comes out more."

Francesca dipped her head. "You're right. No one ever noticed anything but what came out of my mouth." She swore, then asked like nothing was wrong, "Do you want me to call you ma now?"

Katrina didn't notice her brother's face and just replied to Francesca's question. "If you want to, that's fine with me, my dear. Do you want to?"

Francesca shrugged. "I still feel too old to call you that, but I'll think about it."

"I hardly ever called Ellen ma because I was her oldest girl," Katrina told her. "But I don't think it's what you call the person as much as what they mean to you."

Sara spoke up. "Did you ever call your real mother, ma?"

Katrina glanced at Isaiah, who had known their parents longer. But he was much younger when they lived together, so they didn't have any shared memories. Katrina only had a few personal memories of her parents, and they weren't pleasant ones. She looked back at Sara, took a sip of coffee, and explained, "Aww, no. I didn't know how to talk until I left home."

Francesca's eyes shone. "But you got a second ma." Her smile seemed real. Glancing at red-faced Isaiah, she frowned, sensing his anger. She ran a hand over her hair; a sign that she was uncomfortable.

Katrina saw Isaiah pull at his collar and his face redden. The tension in the room grew thick. "You can't be real to raise them!" He yelled.

Andrew narrowed his eyes at him. "Yes, we are." Then added, "Isaiah, we need to head out early to get to the auction today."

Isaiah got up and stormed out.

Andrew stood ready to follow him. He smiled at the girls. "Why don't we make a day out of it. Would you girls like to come along?"

Katrina took his cue and acted like all was well. "Yeah, I was going to look for goats and maybe some chickens."

Francesca smiled. "I've never been to an auction before. Sounds like fun."

Carlissa spoke up, "Could we get a puppy?"

Katrina looked at Andrew, and he nodded. "We can get one soon."

Carlissa screamed, "I want one now!"

Katrina stood and looked at her. "Well, you will have to wait until later because they don't sell puppies at the auction."

Andrew also stood next to Katrina. "You will wait because we told you to."

She screamed again, "I told you I don't want to wait!"

Katrina looked at Izzy and signed to her, *Watch the girls for me.*

Izzy nodded.

Katrina looked at the girls and said, "I'm going to the barn with Andrew for a minute. If you wouldn't mind, please help Izzy clean up so we can go to town early."

Andrew took her hand, and they headed out to talk to the younger, furious brother. "I can't believe he is reacting like this."

Katrina frowned. "He doesn't like change and he came to the plantation late in life. And he wanted to live here before he found his own   place."

"It doesn't matter. He should know better." He slammed the barn door.

Katrina hadn't seen him this mad in a long time, but she understood his feelings towards Isaiah. He had no right to do that to her children. This was their decision. Not his. He called for Isaiah.

Isaiah walked out of the stalls looking equally upset with his face red and hot. "How could you want those girls to stay forever? You hardly know them. It has only been a couple weeks."

"It is our choice. What does it matter to you?" Andrew told him.

"What does it matter?" He yelled. "I live here too, last I remember! I gave up my bedroom for Izzy because of them. Now I have to give up my home for them. You should have told me before tellin' the girls."

"You're right, we should have told you. I am sorry for that." Andrew looked at him. "It doesn't matter now. We are raising the girls."

Isaiah's mouth dropped open. "Why? You don't know what they will do to you or your life. That little redhead hates both of you."

Katrina stood next to Andrew and took his hand. "I know they don't like us right now, but we love them. I want to give them a home and to show them a little bit of love. We talked about this before."

Andrew spoke, his voice steady. "Katrina is right, we want to show our daughters what love is."

"They are so messed up. How can you love them? They got problems as big as the gulf." Isaiah ran a hand through his dark red hair, his green eyes glaring at them. "This is so messed up. It's nothing like we planned when we came here. What will the rest of the family say about this?"

"Some things have to change, and this is one of them," Andrew told him.

Katrina spoke up. "It's not like you want to fit in. You don't come to anything besides church. What do you want?"

"When the rest of the Starrys come and life will get back to normal," he told her angrily. "I don't want to trust the Alexanders or any other neighbor just to lose them."

Katrina saw the hurt in his face. It scared him to let someone get close again and just lose them like they lost Ellen and loved ones. "I'm sorry you feel that way, Isaiah, but you can trust these people. They are good."

"It doesn't matter." He paused. "What will the family say about this?"

Andrew stated the facts. "I telegraphed them and they like the girls."

Isaiah looked at them with such hurt and anger. "You told our family that lives five hundred miles away before you told me."

"You don't visit us in the evenings anymore. You only come by for meals. How are we supposed to tell you?" Katrina told him honestly.

"It doesn't matter." He looked at her with disgust. "I don't want them here. That Spanish girl is a whore, for Pete's sake."

Katrina didn't see what occurred, but the aftermath was visible. She saw Isaiah on the ground holding his jaw and Andrew standing over him holding his fist. Katrina took Andrew's arm, trying to calm him.

"You ever say something like that about my daughter again, you won't be talking for a long time," Andrew spat at him.

Isaiah stood up, still holding his jaw. "Fine, pick a bunch of girls over your own kin. Have it your way," Isaiah yelled as he stormed out.

His words stung Katrina more than she wanted to admit. He was her only blood brother, and he had turned his back on her again.

Andrew put his arms around her. She closed her eyes, trying to shut out the world. He held her while she wiped her tears on his shirt like so many times before. She felt Andrew pray for her as he held her. And she did the same as she cried for her brother and her broken daughters.

Chapter 9

Walking into the kitchen, Izzy heard yelling coming from the parlor.

"I don't feel like it," Francesca yelled.

Katrina yelled back, though not angrily. "I don't care what you feel. It needs to be done."

Izzy walked in at the right moment, as Katrina looked at her in relief. The girls needed to know Katrina was strong enough to handle their anger. Izzy looked at Francesca and spoke in Spanish. "Do it now! For your ma. She needs your help to show the other girls how to work."

Francesca glared at her and started doing her chores.

Katrina stared at Izzy wondering how she did that.

Izzy shrugged and signed, *You can do it. Just hide more of what you are feeling and don't show them that you are bothered by what they do. If you reveal all of your emotions, then it shows them that they won the battle. You can do this.*

Katrina nodded and signed, *I needed to hear that.* She paused. *You don't sugarcoat things, do you?*

Izzy signed while Katrina watched her, *Nope, it does no good.*

Thanks a lot. Katrina chuckled, then signed, *I just don't know how to get them to do anything.*

Izzy signed back, *Have you ever worked with cattle?*

"Of course, I have. Well, a few times," Katrina spoke.

"The girls aren't used to hard work, so let them get used to it by working cattle with them. Andrew can show them the tricks. We need to do that before fall anyhow. Just do it sooner," Izzy explained.

Katrina thought about it for a moment. "I'll talk with Andrew about it. They have to get better at riding."

Izzy nodded. "I'll take Fran out today. Why don't you take the little girls out on a ride? I have a good saddle for Carlissa, and Sara will be fine in the saddle. She has a good body shape for it."

Katrina nodded.

Izzy added shyly, "You're not offended by me telling you what to do?"

Katrina thought about it. "Not really. I lived with Gloria and Julia for a long time. They can both be bossy. And then Susan moved in and you know how she is, so I am a person who just goes with the flow."

Izzy laughed. "Oh, you might change after living a life with these three little angels." Izzy knew Katrina's life would get much worse before it got better.

Before stepping outside, Izzy grabbed her jacket, knowing she might need it where she planned to go. Heading to the barn, her eyes adjusted to the bright sun.

"What are we doing out here?" Francesca asked, still upset for having to finish her chores.

"Why don't you figure it out, girl? You look smart enough to me," Izzy answered back. She pointed to the saddle. "Get me that tack and I'll show you how to saddle the paint." Poder and Phoenix stood tied to the hitching post.

Francesca grumbled as she obeyed. Izzy patiently showed her how to saddle. She was becoming more comfortable around horses.

Izzy grabbed Phoenix's white mane as she mounted. The horse was a palomino and was thick as well as tall. He was white up to his knees with a white blaze down his face.

Francesca sat on the horse like a statue as her horse picked up speed as they rode out of the barn.

"Do you want to try something?" Izzy said. Remembering how she felt the first time she ran on a horse.

Francesca nodded slowly. "Sure, why not?"

"Hold onto the saddle's horn and tighten your legs." Multiple times Izzy showed Francesca how to hold her legs, but she still held them like she had no control over anything. "Lean a little forward like this," Izzy explained, as she dug her fingers into Phoenix's white mane. As the wind blew, Izzy got a whiff of him. She loved his smell because it brought a comfort. Waiting for Francesca to follow, she smiled at her, saying, "Now hang on and say yeehaw."

Francesca smiled, knowing what was coming, and nodded.

Izzy's horse took up a ground-eating gait. Glancing behind her, she was pleased to see Francesca laughing. Phoenix knew this land better than she did. Izzy could remember riding from the time she was two years old, sitting on the horse behind her brother or cousin. She thought that what she experienced was typical of how every child grew up. At a young age, she found out why she rode the range with the cowboys. Her pa had hit her when her brother or cousin weren't there to protect her. She decided it was better on the range. By the age of six, she was riding her own pony and cooking for her cousins. Horses were safe. They didn't tell secrets and never left an owner when they were needed. Phoenix was there at the worst times. Glancing again behind her, at the edge of the open field, Francesca was still smiling. She pulled Phoenix up at the river.

Izzy smiled back and dismounted. "You rode very well."

Francesca tried to dismount the same way and fell to the ground. She just stood up and brushed herself off, not caring. "I suck at riding. This mare is just dull."

Izzy ignored how she dismounted and liked how Francesca got right back up like nothing happened. "No Donavon horse is dull, honey. They are just well trained," she told her. "Actually, your pa trained that mare."

"When can I ride Poder?"

Izzy knew Francesca hated asking, but she didn't have much of a choice. If she didn't let her ride Poder soon, she might ride him by herself and that would be a big mistake. "I'll ask Andrew what he thinks. But with how you rode today, you can ride him soon."

Izzy took off her stockings and boots, then waded through the water, letting her divided skirt get wet.

"What are you doing?" Francesca asked as she sat on the ground.

"Cleaning out the dam, I noticed it the other day when I was finding more stray cattle," Izzy told her as she moved the branches from the dam.

Francesca pulled the branches away from the river.

As she worked, Izzy asked, "How do you enjoy living with the Starrys?"

Francesca swore. "Kat is so bossy; she tries to make me something I ain't."

Izzy shook her head. "All good mamas nag their kids like that. She wants to help you make the best out of this life and wants to help you know that. She loves you, you know."

"She's never told me," Francesca muttered.

Izzy knew it was probably because Starrys didn't say "I love you" lightly. She should know that. Maybe Katrina didn't want to overwhelm Francesca by being too overbearing. She might say something, but Katrina needed to learn things on her own because Izzy wouldn't always be here for her. "But she does, she gets everything you need, she takes on the fights with you because she loves you enough to make you do it. If she didn't care she wouldn't take the time to fight, she would just do it herself."

Francesca pouted. "She doesn't understand me. She has lived such an easier life."

Izzy came up and sat on the ground by the river, letting the water run over her feet. She motioned for Francesca to do the same, so they might have a wet ride home. The sun warmed her against her back. Staying silent for a while, they just watched the river run. "Maybe God gave Katrina to the Starrys so she could raise you. I don't think I could do it."

Francesca looked at her in surprise. "Why not?"

Izzy looked away. "My past wouldn't let me. Growing up was rough. After my pa beat me most of my childhood, I didn't think much could be worse. But it got much worse."

Izzy could hear the shock in Francesca's voice. "How did you live through it and get past it?"

Izzy scoffed. "I didn't get past it. You don't get past something like that, but you live through it and live with it."

Francesca asked again, "How do you live with it? I feel like the only thing I am good at is sex."

Izzy thought she might throw up. She hated thinking about it, let alone talking about it. Francesca needed to know someone else had been there and gotten through. And she knew girls like Francesca were used to talking about sex, just like the weather. "Horses - they saved me. I found my Phoenix." She tipped her head to where Phoenix was grazing. "He was a wild abused mustang. He was so broken and so was I. You can say we saved each other. I felt again while riding him, for I had to hold on with my knees and legs. I had to feel my body and emotions again." From the look on Francesca's face, she knew what Izzy was talking about. She should be a young woman, worried about school and cute boys, not worried about what men had done to her. "I also had a cousin help me. She put her life on hold for me, literally. She stayed with me till I could make it on my own." She smoothed out her skirt. "And definitely I had God."

Francesca moved away a little more but stayed sitting. "If God was so strong for you, then why would He let it happen in the first place?"

"I asked my God that so often. I thought I would cry my tears out." She took Francesca's hand. "Men who wanted to get back at my white family took me. I can say God didn't want it to happen but evil men made that choice. I believe God helped me get through so I could say there is hope at the end of the tunnel. I told so many ladies before that they could get through, but I didn't know what that meant till I walked in a month in their lives." She paused again and made herself say the words, "When I was in slavery I got two other women out of the prostitute life, I couldn't have done that if I hadn't been there."

Francesca looked at her in disgust and despair. "You lived in prostitution for a month." Her face was angry, and she tried to pull away from Izzy.

Izzy didn't let go, she was much stronger. "Talk, yell, tell me what you think."

"You lived a month in that life?" Francesca cried. "I bet they found you because of your wealth, right?"

Izzy didn't answer. It was a miracle they found her by her cousin that day in Reno. She didn't know why some got out of it sooner than others. It wasn't so easy to answer. Including why her sisters were never hurt by their father, while he beat her, her brother, and their ma.

Francesca cried out. "The same kind of men took my baby stage since my ma was working for them." She didn't let the tears fall, just glared in such rage. "I was seven when I first knew a man, they took my childhood. They took my teen years and then they took my entire life. They changed how I look at life. They didn't care what they did to me, only what it did for them."

She tried to pull away again, but Izzy now took her hands in hers and didn't let go. She had met her match, Izzy was hard core.

Izzy knew from the other girls that Francesca was younger than seven when the abuse started. The children were tied under their mamma's bed or locked in a closet while men raped her ma.

Francesca cried in despair. "They took my past, my thoughts, my future, my will, they took my body." She finally stopped fighting and sagged her shoulders. "They took everything. Men and sex took my childhood and my teens. It's all I think about! Sex is all I know. I hate it, but I am addicted to it."

Izzy nodded. "You just admitted it. Admitting is the first thing to beat it." She looked at her with such love and understanding. "Let God help you take it away."

Francesca looked despaired. "I will never be the same again. I can never get it back."

"But God can restore you as a person." She bit her lip. "Francesca, there is something to remember. Those men that did that to you, it was their filth, their sin, not yours. God will judge those men one day for what they did to His precious children."

Francesca shrugged with anguish.

Izzy looked away for a moment. "It was so important for parents to protect their children better, even adult children. They went on working saying that will make it end, never speak of it, do nothing about it, bury it and it will always go away." Izzy had needed to talk about it and she had to her cousin, but sometimes she still felt broken and everyone saw that. She felt it even more when she was with Jesse. He didn't seem like he was a man who would understand her past. "You can always talk to Katrina or even Andrew about this."

Francesca made a face. "Normal people don't talk about unspeakable things.."

Izzy smiled. "Well, then it's a good thing the Starry ain't normal folk. Just ask any of their old neighbors." She added, her voice hardened, "Francesca, I was kidnapped because of my wealth. I was a Cooper. Cole and I changed our name to Donavon."

Francesca stared at her. "I'm sorry, I didn't know."

"Every woman's abuse is hard. It's how you handle it. They also took my future." She looked away. "I can't bear children because of that month of abuse."

"No!" Francesca cried.

"I told no one that, not even my brother."

"Why not?"

Izzy sighed, thinking of the man who raised her. "Cole was so hurt and angry over what happened. I couldn't burden him with more."

"Why not tell Annie?"

Izzy laughed harshly. "Annie wouldn't understand and we ain't close."

"You haven't told Jesse?"

Izzy stayed still. "No."

"Why?" Francesca looked at her. "I thought you were healed?"

Izzy looked at her. "I am by the grace of God, but it doesn't mean I don't struggle every day." She whispered, "Find a man who will understand."

Francesca nodded sadly.

Izzy tried to lighten the mood. "Talk to Katrina about it, one of my struggles was I didn't talk about it."

Francesca shrugged. "I'll try."

Izzy stared at her feet with the water running over them.

She looked into Francesca's hurting eyes. "You know when you step on the ground, it is where a dozen other people have stepped, dirty and ugly. But a river, when you step in a river, it is always a fresh step, never the same, always clean and made new. When you bathe in the river, the dirt goes away down the river and you are clean again." She paused. "This life takes you through the dirt and the filth that men caused, but God takes you through the river. You might make mistakes, but He is always at the river making you clean. Making you pure and whole again. Because He paid the price when He died for you. He took your dirt and filth on Himself to make you whole again because you are His beautiful child."

Francesca looked at the river, not fully understanding this kind of love. Maybe the Starry family would make her see the truth.

Not for the first time, Katrina realized how sheltered her children were. "You mean you have never been in a store at all?" She wanted to make sure but not put them on the spot as the girls and Izzy walked into town for the first time. They had just finished breakfast and planned to have lunch with Mabel, who was meeting them in town.

Sara shook her head.

"Nope, never been to one," Carlissa said.

"I stole food from the store," Francesca whispered. "A store owner gave me a doll once." She added bitterly, "Ma's men broke it."

"I am sorry about that." Katrina put her arm around her shoulders and gave her a brief hug. "Well, have to make a day out of it, my dear." She kept her voice light.

Izzy nodded like she did the right thing. "Kat, I am running by the bank. I'll check up with you later."

Katrina walked down the sidewalk and towards the general store. She noticed Carlissa's back went straight as a board, her eyes wide, her hands into fists. Katrina laid a hand on her shoulder and got no response, which was a surprise. Carlissa continued to look around. She hadn't acted that way in church, but she still seemed a little dazed.

In front of the store, Carlissa started screaming. The scream was fake and loud. It embarrassed Katrina since people were watching in the street, but she was more worried about why she was doing this.

Carlissa fell on her back, still screaming with not a tear on her face and her eyes glaring as if she could kill.

Katrina tried talking to her over the screaming. "Carlissa, what is wrong? Calm down, dear. It's okay. Nothing bad will happen. I am here, Carlissa."

Nothing Katrina said helped at all. She prayed God would help the child. Then she saw Mabel come onto the walk. She nearly cried in relief.

Mabel grabbed Carlissa's shoulders gently. "It's okay, love," she said over the screaming. "It will not hurt you; nothing will hurt you. It is just a store that you buy food in." Carlissa's screaming quieted just a little. "You don't even have to go in. Easy, baby."

Carlissa quieted down a little more, but her little body was still shaking. She screamed in Mabel's face, "I hate you. I don't like you."

Mabel didn't even flinch. "I understand more than you know." She paused. "You are afraid, and that is why you're screaming. You need to control these emotions. No one will hurt you here. That is a promise."

Carlissa stopped screaming but still shook. "I hate you."

Mabel stood but still held her. "Katrina, why don't you go shopping with the other girls. I'll stay here with Carlissa and my youngins'."

Katrina looked at her like she was crazy. *Are you sure?* She signed. Mabel just nodded.

In the store Katrina found some flowered fabric and she asked, "Do you like this fabric, Francesca?"

Francesca shrugged like she didn't care, but Katrina could see the fear behind those pretty eyes.

After getting some candy, and looking over some toys for Carlissa, Francesca began to relax and the day wasn't a waste. Francesca enjoyed looking over the material.

"What color would you like to wear?" Katrina asked her.

Francesca showed her age, wringing her hands. "I am not sure. What do you think?"

"This purple would look good on you," Katrina told her.

She nodded. "Sure."

As Gabby cut out three yards, Katrina turned to look at the undergarments, stockings, and other items they would need. The girls walked to another part of the store.

She felt someone tap her shoulder; she expected to see Francesca or Sara. Instead, she was faced with a lady who had not been at the sewing circle, someone she hadn't met. Katrina had learned to know faces since she only missed some of what they said. She spoke, hoping she didn't miss something. "Can I help you?"

"I told you already. I am Nancy Graham," she said through gritted teeth. "I heard you are the new one in town with your young husband. I thought you would be normal, but you are just like Mabel Alexandria. You know she is half crazy with those children she has. You must be just as crazy. They are trouble."

Katrina gasped, taking a step back. Her thoughts went back to the past after Andrew and Katrina had been burned in the fire, a former Matron had seen them in the street and yelled, "You's just a pretty face with no brain, dummy. And now your body is scarred and ugly, just like your brain." The lady seemed to look under Katrina's scarf she had around her neck. She was the only child who wore a scarf in the heat of summer. "Least you's have you's hair. Maybe a man would want you. Maybe your face will get a man. Cause your body won't." Katrina had such a hard time after that, and it didn't help that she had been struggling with the hearing she had lost and the amount of pain she had suffered. Now she patted her hair as if she were trying to hide the scars that were still there.

Coming back to the present, this lady sounded like the same ignorant person who did not understand what those girls had faced in their young lives. She felt like yelling, "You try living a day in their life and find out how you deal with it." She told her instead, "What does it matter what I do with my life now that I have moved here? I don't plan to go near you." She paused. "And I never want to hear you ever talk about my daughters that way because it is very untrue and they will prove that to you one day."

Mrs. Graham went silent.

Gabby nodded. "Bout time someone put Mrs. Graham in her place."

Katrina stepped out of the aisle, then saw Francesca and Sara behind her. She took Sara in her arms. Katrina just hoped the lady stayed silent. Too late. She did not get her wish.

"Well, since you're as crazy as Mabel Alexander, guess nothing can be done," Mrs. Graham said. "You know there are children like that at Liberty House, and that place is a mess. These children are from asylum. You want children to control your home?"

Katrina wasn't sure how she knew the girls were from the asylum but it didn't take long to figure that out. She felt Sara tense even more and Francesca stepped away from her. "It is my home, my life, and I love these girls. So we don't mind if they are in my home controlling it, as you say." Both girls were looking at her to see her response.

"Well, I just hope you know what you're getting into." Her face was still hard and set.

Katrina felt someone behind her. She looked to see Izzy, looking in control. "Hi, Mrs. Graham, I am Izzy Donavon. We have met in the past." She paused. "I was there when you adopted your children from Liberty House. I was sorry to hear it didn't work with your children." She paused, choosing her words carefully. "Only a mother's heart can understand that love and pain you suffered. Just don't let the bitterness of your children hurt others like Katrina. And you turned your back on the only friend you had at that time. Who was there for you when you sent the children back to us? It was Mabel Alexander and you know it. She never once judged you when it wasn't the right home for them."

Mrs. Graham's face didn't change, more angry and hurt than Katrina thought possible. "I just didn't love my children."

Izzy walked up to her and put a hand on her arm. "You and I both know that is not true, because if you hadn't loved them you would have sent them back to the asylum and not to my home. You knew they needed a loving home and not a government mental place. I know you loved them and gave them all you could. Don't let it destroy who you are. Let God help you through this pain."

At the mention of God, she pulled away. "God didn't heal my children when I begged Him to. God didn't give me children who could be loved." She walked away on that note.

Katrina gave Izzy a soft smile. "Thank you."

Izzy shrugged. "She is in a lot of pain."

After collecting their items and heading outside, Katrina handed Carlissa a piece of candy. She looked at it funny but didn't take it. "What is it?"

"Candy, Carlissa," Katrina told her.

Carlissa still looked at it like she'd never seen such a thing before.

Katrina bent down to Carlissa's level. She seemed calm after the screaming fit. "It's something you suck on, sweetie. Here, put it in your mouth."

Carlissa looked shocked. "I am not a baby. Only baby's suck."

Katrina smiled and told herself not to laugh at Carlissa. "No, you lick it."

Carlissa licked it. "It's sweet! I've never had candy."

Katrina's mouth dropped open. "You have never had sugar?"
She shook her head and moved her eyes all around.
Katrina noticed her distress and wasn't sure why. "We must get you lots of sugar cause you are so sweet." She tickled her and kissed her cheek.

Chapter 10

As Katrina, Izzy, Mabel, and the girls headed to the Alexander ranch, Francesca asked what happened to Mrs. Graham's children. The younger children ran up ahead, but Sara had stayed back. Katrina took Sara in her arms again. Katrina noticed she didn't mind being touched in public. "Well, Mrs. Graham doesn't understand some things. She has the view many people have of orphans."

Izzy spoke honestly, "When we first started the Home, we let anyone adopt. That was wrong. So many children were being sent back to us. It was hard on the parents and especially the children. Well, Mrs. Graham was one of our first to adopt two siblings, a boy and a younger girl. I won't bore you with the details but improper things happened between the children and they needed to be away from each other. They sent the boy back to the home. We found him a family. She had also sent the girl away to the Home where she also went with another family. They lived with Mrs. Graham for over five years. She did her best for them, they were just too much."

"How are they now?" Francesca asked bitterly.

"The boy ran away soon after they brought him there; he left to join the military. That was the last anyone heard from him. The girl did remarkably well in the new home."

Mabel spoke up. "I helped her out through that time. It was very hard on her. She had been unprepared for the events that went on. It has made her hard; we just need to pray God will heal her heart."

"Why do some mothers act like that? I have seen it before." Francesca crossed her arms.

"Hardness. They put walls up around their heart like their children so that nothing gets through," Mabel answered. "The mother and child have a hard time healing when they harden their hearts to God."

Izzy added, "You have to love like there is no such thing as a broken heart. And lay down your heart for your child just like Jesus did."

It surprised Katrina they were talking about this in front of the girls, but Francesca seemed to take in every word while Sara didn't react.

Francesca looked at Katrina with her eyes guarded. "Are you willing to do that for us?"

Katrina looked into those beautiful hard eyes. Sara was looking up at her. This was her choice. Was she willing to give everything to her child? Love, time, energy, and patience. "Yes, I am. Forever and always." She took the young woman in her arms and into her life.

"I've never had sweet tea." Francesca sipped the southern drink.

Katrina's mouth dropped open. She had found Francesca in the stall with the scared horse and given her sweet tea. "They have sweet tea in Texas, right?"

Francesca shrugged. "Yeah, but I never drank it. How do you make it?"

Because she was so busy, she hadn't made it often. "I will show you next time I make it."

Francesca drank it and smiled. "This is so good, Katrina. It is sweet." She acted like she didn't expect that.

Katrina smiled. "Of course it is."

Francesca reluctantly put it down and started to groom the horse.

Katrina did the same. "You know Maverick's horse drinks sweet tea just like water, more than water."

She saw Francesca's smile. Katrina was tall, and the horse was smaller than the drafts they normally bred, so she could see Francesca's full profile. "The big stallion also loves orange juice and apple juice, cider is his favorite."

"What is orange juice?" Francesca asked curiously.

"They make it from oranges from a tree that grows in the south. I brought some with me; they handle the ride pretty well."

"They are the color orange?" Francesca asked in wonderment.

Katrina chuckled. "Yes, they are."

"There was some in the cellar and it wasn't any too good. No wonder a horse ate it," Francesca said honestly.

That was something she liked about Francesca. She never tried to cover the truth, she just said what she thought. "The horse can't peel it, but a person has to peel to taste the juice."

Francesca looked shocked and even met Katrina's eyes for a moment.

Katrina let the silence reign. It didn't happen often that the girl was silent or surprised. "What do you think your owner should name you, horse? You can't be called horse your whole life."

Francesca shrugged.

"I know, we can name her Bella. It means beautiful in Italian."

Francesca kept brushing quicker, like someone was holding a gun to her. "I wonder how a deaf person knows Italian."

"I knew some from when I lived with rich folks," Katrina explained. She leaned over the horse to look at her daughter. "Do you think Bella suits her?"

Francesca shook her head. "No. Horse works, it's better to not get used to names, no one cares to remember them anyhow." She swore. "Horse is ugly."

"On the inside, she is beautiful. She likes people, and she loves you."

Francesca touched the whip scars across the mare's back. Her face went hard. "This will never heal, it will never go away. How can she be so nice when men did this to her?"

Katrina walked around the horse to face Francesca, leaning against the horse's butt. "She is beautiful because beauty comes from the inside of the body. This horse can heal on the inside because she had love. She has you caring for her. She can tell you are a nice, kind, and hurting child." Katrina did something she hadn't done often. She didn't want to, but she looked in those pretty, hurting, dark brown eyes. She had to. She pulled the neckline of her dress back to reveal the scars. "Fran, I never told you why I lost most of my hearing; it was a fire I got burned badly in. These are scars that will never heal."

Francesca looked at her for what seemed like the first time. She looked into Katrina's eyes, and then reached out to touch the ugly white pink scars on Katrina's chest right about her breasts. Her face was so broken, so exposed.

Katrina could see in her face she was wondering how Katrina moved past this. It surprised her she didn't feel as valuable. She felt love for her daughter, a God-given love that was so strong, it shocked her. "Men who never got a thing for causing these burns. The scars on the inside were so much worse. I was so bitter, so angry that they would do this to me. I realized something when I found God. He

72

could help me take away that anger and He would make my enemies one day pay for what they did. They would pay for their evil-doing; God would take care of me. Because He says he will take care of His fatherless children and I was one of them, though my parents probably ain't dead. I healed because of Christ and what He did for me on the cross and what He did by giving me such a wonderful family who love me as their own." Katrina took her hands. "He wants to do that with you, my dear. He wants to let you know he loves you before you were even born. He chose our family, the Starrys, to be your family forever and always. I love you, Francesca Starry." Katrina felt her heart swell at the words.

She wasn't sure what she expected. Francesca to tell her the same thing and to call her Ma the rest of their days. To hug and be more open and not so afraid. Though she now knew it was never that easy for Ellen. She wasn't sure what she expected, but this was not it.

Francesca backed up like something had stung her. She shook in fear or anger. "No one can heal from what men do. You're wrong. You're ugly. Men make things ugly. I hate you," she screamed with such anger on her face. "I hate you."

The words cut Katrina like a knife, taking her breath away. Why did Fran hate her? What had she done besides try to show her love and comfort? Why was she so horrid? Katrina knew she wasn't ready to face the girls, so she just stood in the stall, with the horse munching on hay, and let the pain wipe away in tears again. How did one child have the power to hurt her so badly? Was it selfish to not want a daughter to scream?

She felt the ground move a little under her feet. She knew it wasn't Andrew's horse; his horse was too big for that little movement. Ignoring who had ridden up, she just cried.

She felt a hand on her shoulder and turned to see Izzy. She hugged the smaller lady and cried all the harder while telling her what had happened between the tears.

After Katrina finished the story, Izzy gave her a hankie. "Know not is all lost. In your childhood, did you ever feel like telling someone you hated them?"

Katrina thought about it and nodded. "I never did, but I thought about telling Maverick. I hated him and even Andrew sometimes."

"Now why is that?" She smiled. "I can see why you would hate Maverick, but Andrew, he's pretty much perfect. Why did you?"

Katrina smirked. "They were teaching me sign language and how to talk properly. I didn't understand it, and I was just tired of trying to learn it. Everything to them was a lesson, never did they ever think of just having fun, and if it was fun, it had reading in it or speaking. I didn't understand it all."

Izzy nodded. "You didn't understand it."

Katrina wanted to cry more when it hit her.

Izzy shook her head, telling her no more tears. Katrina figured for this tough cowgirl they were a waste of time. "Now you understand a little more about what makes your daughters tick."

Katrina nodded and explained, "It helped me come out to understand. They don't know what love is, don't understand and don't know how it can make them have a future, just like I wouldn't have much of a future without Maverick and Andrew trying so hard. The girls need to understand in their hearts, and not just their minds, that God loves them." She smiled. "So my daughter doesn't hate me, just what I am trying to make her understand and feel."

Izzy didn't need to respond. They both knew it was true.

Katrina put an arm around her. "Let's head in before the girls destroy the house."

Izzy touched the buttons on Katrina's dress, though she tried not to look as Katrina buttoned them up. "It was brave of you to show them."

As they walked up to the house, Katrina asked, "How are you so smart?"

Izzy chuckled. "Well, I ain't that smart." She paused. "I've just been where your girls are at."

Katrina noticed a shadow pass over Izzy's face. "Well, I am forever grateful." She looked up to see smoke coming out of the kitchen window. No more time for talking.

"Izzy! Izzy-baby! Come back," Cole squealed with agony.

Expecting the cry to be one of the children, Julia abruptly sat up, her covers falling to her lap. Instead, she found Cole screaming. Trying to wake him, she began shaking him, but he continued screaming. She shook harder. "Honey, Honey, wake up. You will wake the children." And the children hadn't been sleeping well.

He finally opened his eyes and looked at her, his throat hoarse as he spoke. "What happened?"

Julia took his hand, looking down at him. "You were screamin' about Izzy again."

"Again?" He looked confused.

Julia nodded, "It happened a couple of nights ago, but you didn't wake up."

Cole's face flushed with sweat.

Julia couldn't handle the look that came into his eyes. She leaned down and kissed him. Putting his hands in her hair she felt his passion. She pulled back; she put her head on his. "Tell me, Texan." She knew he needed to tell her what he had never told her before their wedding. When Izzy was still there.

Taking her hand, Cole sighed and sat up. "Let's get some air."

Julia let him lead her to the porch, the bare boards were cool against her bare feet. They sat on the hard dew-damp swing. It was muggy, and hot like most Alabama summers. The dew clung to their skin. Julia's long, curly blond hair felt wet and hot against her back. Listening to the crickets, Julia waited for him to speak first.

He looked out into the darkness, his face tense and pained. He spoke so softly, Julia could hardly hear him.

"We wanted to get away from our pa, so we started rescuing children and people from slavery. We traveled everywhere and went into any situation, no matter the danger. Then we hit a big powerful man. He wanted us gone, so he took Izzy." He had to stop. "I almost died in that month. If she hadn't come home, I would have never stopped looking and rescuing. I would have gotten myself killed, I know it now. I gave up the rescues when she was found. I came here while Izzy went to Colorado."

Julia remained silent through it all. Nothing would help the pain he still felt. She knew from Maverick that pain never went away. She just took Cole in her arms as he usually did to her. He was so big compared to her slight form. "I am so sorry. I love you so much, Cole Donovan."

Julia could feel his tears soaking her nightgown as Cole put his head on her chest. She held him as he cried his pain away. As Julia closed her eyes and squeezed Cole gently, she finally envisioned her experience as what an actual marriage looks like.

The next morning, Julia walked in the barn to find Cole trimming one of the pony's hooves. Melody was holding the pony's lead calmly, look as steady as if she probably wouldn't move if a gun went off. The little boys stood around him. "Looks like all of you have been having fun without me."

Johnathan and David came up to her and hugged her legs. "Come look, mama. Pa's trimmin' Snowflake's hooves," David told her.

David spoke up as they walked a little closer. "Why are we naming it Snowflake?"

Melody answered like they all should have known. "Because she is white and snow is white."

"How do you know? You ain't ever seen snow." David told her.

Melody put her nose up at him. "Well, it is still white."

Cole had missed none of this and smiled. He put the hoof down, patted the pony, and looked at them. "We will see plenty of snow this winter."

Just then Julia turned to see her brother, Sawyer walk up, on his arm was Cole's sister, Annie. Sawyer smiled. "I figured I would find you here with the pony. What is that song, when you wake up you will have all the little ponies?" Sawyer came over to hug Julia. "And now you have them all." He chuckled.

Julia laughed and hugged him back. "That is every child's dream. How was your trip, Sawyer?"

He laughed, taking Annie's hand while she giggled.

Cole stood up and looked at them. "What is up, sis?"

She giggled again. "We got married!" she said excitedly.

Julia's mouth dropped open.

Cole walked closer to them, unbelief on his face.

Even the children stared at them in shock.

"Well, I can't imagine what the other family will say or do when we tell them," Sawyer said, amused.

Julia opened her mouth to say something and then shut it with no words coming out. She felt so betrayed.

Cole saw it on Julia's face, hurt and shock over Sawyer not telling them first. He also knew because he was feeling it. He had always hoped he would get to walk his little sister down the aisle. "Well, that was fast." He forced a smile. "I'm happy for you both." He hugged Annie and shook Sawyer's hand. He took Julia's hand back and grasped it, telling her to be honest.

She smiled, though it looked strained. "Wow, this is such a surprise and such a joy." She hugged Sawyer again, and then Annie.

Cole asked, "So what are your plans? Where do you want to live?"

"Well, we have been thinking about heading to Colorado early. I have been looking into a newspaper job in Deer Trail, so I might take it when we get down there, and we will find a place." Sawyer smiled. "We're thinking of movin' soon, maybe a few weeks."

"Well, if you want to, you can bring some stock to Liberty Ranch. Andrew will run them for me till I can get there."

"Yeah, I'll help you round them up."

"That would be great." He paused. "You know we heard from Andrew."

"What's up? What did you hear?" Sawyer wanted to know.

Julia spoke up, "They have settled pretty well. They like the people there, and they found three girls in their shed."

Sawyer looked surprised. "What are they goin' to do?"

"They wanted to know what we thought," Julia said carefully. "But they plan to raise them."

"Wow, that is not what I expected to hear."

"Well, we both got a shock today," Julia whispered, a small bite to her words. She was glad none of the children picked up on it, just the adults. Annie looked more hurt than Sawyer, but he was better at hiding it.

Cole clasped her hand, and then spoke to Annie, keeping his voice light, "Now I want to talk to my baby sister at the house so she can give me every detail of this eloping. Come on, kiddos." He put an arm around Annie's shoulder and they walked out.

They walked over to a bench. Both sat on the same bench they did when Sawyer told her he was a believer. Julia hadn't been one and found it shocking and even felt hurt. Like today, but for two different reasons. She was now a mother, but still was a beloved sister. She forced herself to be honest. She looked up at him. "I am surprised about you two eloping. How could you not tell us?"

He sighed. He took her hand. "It was a quick decision, Julia. And since the whole family couldn't be there, we didn't want to wait."

She nodded. "I understand. But what about Izzy? She is not close to Annie and wants to be. This will hurt her."

Sawyer looked at her like he knew that. "But like you said, they ain't close. I know they have struggles, but nothing they can't get over."

Snowflake ambled up to see if Julia had any treats. She patted her head. "Being married is hard sometimes, Sawyer. We married siblings. I have found out things about the Donovan's no one knows because I am one." She looked at her brother - the one who had been there since she was born - though they shared no blood. She let a tear run down her cheek. "You are now married to a Donovan."

"What is it?" Sawyer asked, concerned.

"I can't say, but when you can, help your wife. Help her love Izzy, Cole, and even Amy. It takes work, but keep at it." She paused. "You know, over the last few months, we have really become a family and started healing. Well, it's our turn to do that for the Donovan's." She squeezed his hand. "Now that we are both married to them."

Sawyer sighed. "I have tried to help her with it but she is distant with anyone but her ma. She just doesn't seem to care to fight for it."

"She doesn't know what she is missing. We both should know that with our past. The Donovans have a secret like ours in their family and I believe soon enough it's going to come out."

Sawyer nodded, knowing she couldn't say more about it. "Let's pray, sis, for our spouses and our new siblin'."

"I think that is a wonderful idea, and then I can tell Annie how happy I am to have another sister in my family," Julia told him.

Sawyer's smiled said it all, although he couldn't stop the worry in his eyes. The Starrys knew what this kind of pain was like. God would see them through this.

Chapter 11

"Katrina, come sit with me?" Mabel asked as she sat at one of the many tables in the churchyard. The men had built the tables for times like this gathering; weddings, funerals, and fellowship. There was talking, eating, and laughing going around. Children ran about and adults visited. Everyone seemed to be having a great time. Some of the women had welcomed her to the church. Many ladies gave her a homecoming gift like bread, cheese, and small items to help her in the home.

Katrina nodded and headed that way. She had already gotten the younger girls' food. All the children were eating with other girls their age. Katrina was excited to see them have fun. The rain they got yesterday had held off today, though there was a dampness in the air, and the cloud looked ready to drop more rain. Katrina was glad it held off for the time being. It was just so nice having fellowship. She noticed Izzy laughing with someone. Many of them had met Izzy since she worked with Liberty House.

Katrina greeted Mabel and Dinah as she sat down.

"How are things going?" Mabel wanted to know.

Katrina chuckled. "You don't waste any time, do ya?"

"Nope, not when you need to get things figured out." Mabel smiled.

Katrina made a face. "That is so like a Starry thin' to say."

"You miss them?" Dinah asked.

Katrina nodded. "More than I ever thought possible. With the busyness of the children, it has gotten better. I miss their advice. They were always there." She looked away. "I reckon I never expected to lose another parent."

They both looked at her tenderly. Katrina didn't want their pity. She changed the subject and asked something that had been on her mind. Talking so much, she almost forgot to eat. These ladies told her about motherhood, funny things they and their children did. They advised her how to teach the girls, discipline, and love them without having them freak out. She took it in like a bee to honey.

Suddenly Katrina heard a scream and turned around to see Carlissa on the ground near a group of other girls her age. By the time Katrina got over there to her side, the whole church was watching. Her cheeks burned.

Andrew and Mabel came up beside her. Andrew picked Carlissa up as she was stiff as a board, and carried her inside the church, with the young girl screaming the whole while.

Charles met them in there, but he stood back.

Katrina looked at him for an answer. "What can you do?"

Charles shook his head. "Nothing, she will stop when she is ready."

"Why does she do this?"

"If we knew we would write a book on it," Mabel told her dryly. "Prayer, love, and time do help sometimes."

"Are there any treatments?" Andrew asked.

Mabel gave him a sarcastic look. "Yeah, they made her into this mess."

Charles cleared his throat.

"That is why you are running Liberty Ranch to help families," Mabel told him. "So they can treat and care for their children."

Andrew had never been so embarrassed. His new friends had seen Carlissa screaming like she was mad. What must they be thinking? He wished some of his siblings could be here. Julia or Maverick would know what to do. What was wrong with her? And to make it worse, Mabel and Charles acted like this was no big deal. Well, it was a big deal to him. He wanted it to stop.

"I am not sure what to do when this happens," Katrina admitted, and she moved to pull Carlissa into her arms as she screamed.

Mabel signed quickly, "Even if you are unsure, never admit that when the girls are around. It shows them you can't handle them, and they don't feel safe." She smiled. "Just think you got this, even if it's the furthest thing from your mind. God gives me the strength to do all things, all things, even this."

Katrina nodded.

Is there anything else we can do? Mabel signed.

Andrew finally spoke up, "No, we are fine. We have this under control."

He saw Katrina stare at him, thinking, we have nothing under control, don't send away my help. But he ignored her look. He didn't

80

need anyone's help. They had always done things by themselves and they did just fine.

Charles took Mabel's hand and nodded to Andrew.

"We will pray for you all," Mabel said as she left the church.

Katrina glared at him. He knew they would fight about this later. Ellen had taught them not to fight in front of the children.

He prayed Clarissa's screams would end soon - for all their sakes.

Izzy watched Francesca's face turn red and her lips get tight.

Alice, Mabel's granddaughter, who sat next to Francesca with other girls their age, was trying to talk to her about something. Maybe it would help to have Mabel's granddaughter as a friend. The sun bore down on them, showing them that summer was coming.

As Izzy cleared the plates since it didn't look like they were coming back for it, she could smell some of the leftovers and what smelled like apple pie. A boy ran up to her, "Miss Donovan?"

"Yes."

"This telegram came for you and the Starrys." He handed her the note.

"Thank you," Izzy told him and dug in her purse for a dime.

His face lit up as he took it from her. "Thank you, Miss."

Izzy nodded. She noticed his clothes and voice; he was a poor immigrant.

She opened the telegram:

To Mr. Mrs. Andrew Starry, Mr. Jesse Starry, and Miss Izzy Donovan of Deer Trail.

Hope this finds you all well. Sawyer and Annie along with Jerry and Gloria will leave on Wednesday. They have a surprise. With all my protection. Maverick Starry

After putting the letter away, she looked to see Katrina and Andrew getting ready to leave with the now calm, perfect child.

She spotted Francesca talking to a young man by the tree a little away from everyone. Izzy knew Timmy and knew he was a good young man.

Francesca was smiling like an innocent young schoolgirl. Izzy knew that feeling. She laughed about something he said. He laughed along.

Izzy walked up to get Francesca. "Hi, it's nice to see you again, Timmy."

Timmy stepped back from Francesca a little. "You too. I was so excited to hear your family is moving here."

"Yes, Deer Trail is a great town." Izzy smiled. "Well, we have to run, but we will see y'all soon."

Timmy laughed.

Francesca smiled.

"What?" Izzy asked the youth.

Francesca chuckled and winked at Timmy. "Timmy thinks we talk funny since we are from the south."

Izzy grinned at them; she took Francesca's arm in a teasing way. "We are one of a kind."

Timmy grinned. "That is for sure."

Izzy didn't let her go, but they headed over to Andrew's wagon. She rubbed the mare as she passed. "Do you want to walk home, Fran? It's such a lovely day."

Francesca shrugged and started for home while Izzy told the others.

Katrina looked surprised, but nodded.

Izzy caught up with Francesca. They walked in silence till they were out of town. Trees lined the side of the roads.

"So what, you will tell me it's terrible to talk with a boy? Or to have a beau?" Francesca asked Izzy in haste.

Izzy grinned. "No, you probably wouldn't listen."

"Nope," Francesca said firmly.

Izzy kept her voice light. "But I will tell you anyhow."

Francesca looked at her like she didn't care, but behind her eyes, Izzy saw confusion. She understood that. "It's not wrong to talk to boys or have beaus; just watch how you act with them. Since men scare me, I have to be careful how close I get to one."

"Why?" Francesca sounded like she cared now.

"Because when you have been intimate with a man, even if you don't want to or wanted it, it opens you up to those feelings. Sometimes people think the only way to know love is through sex. However, there is much more to love. That kind of love belongs in a marriage, not outside of it. And real love is carin', kind, and bein' patient. My father beat me growin' up, so I had a hard time feeling what real love means." She paused. "Would you have let Timmy kiss

82

you?"

Francesca shrugged like it didn't matter. "Men have kissed me lots of times. I am used to kissin'. I don't think whether I like it."

"You should. You shouldn't do something if you don't like it."

"It happened for so long, I don't see why not," Francesca told her flatly.

"That's what needs to change in your heart. Just be careful with him."

Francesca defended herself. "Many girls have had their first or second child by my age."

Izzy corrected. "Being married, they have." She rolled her eyes as she spotted the ranch come into sight.

"That is a given."

Izzy nodded. "Yes, many girls are courting by your age but just be careful just the same." She wondered if only Timmy could handle Francesca's past. Few men could handle having an ex-child prostitute as a wife. Maybe that is why Izzy thought so much of Jesse, because he wanted her. But then he didn't know about her past. She knew it was time to tell him, but she was afraid of it. Afraid of how he might handle it.

"What's wrong?"

Izzy looked out over to the beautiful Rocky Mountains on the edge of Liberty Ranch. "Just thinkin'."

"Of how unfair it is that we have to look at life differently? It's not fair," Francesca said in despair.

"You're right, it's not fair. I've wondered in the past if God disliked me."

"He hated me. My ma said He hated me for letting me be born."

Izzy stopped by the paddock at the gate of the ranch, watching Francesca as her eyes followed the grazing horses. "He loves you more than Katrina or Andrew ever could. At times you will feel the love and at other times it feels so lonely that depression sinks in." She paused. "God didn't let it happen, it happened because of a sin of this world. Sin of men. Because everything they did to us was a sin, but not our sin. God made this world perfect and because of people there is now sin, and because of that, free will."

"I don't see the point," Francesca said as she pulled away.

Izzy let her, feeling her pain, knowing how much she understood. "Just keep talking about it, at least you can. Sara can't. And Carlissa can't talk about much without screaming."

Francesca frowned at her. "You think she will one day?"

"That will be up to her. You always have a choice." Izzy kissed her forehead like a child.

Chapter 12

"Watch this, Julia!" Travis yelled as he took a sturdy branch and swung into the pond.

Julia smiled, waving at the boy. She didn't mind that the older children didn't call her ma. She was too much like an older sister.

Jonathan came up and needed her to cut a piece of rope. Julia knew Cole had a knife, but she just reached in her boot, pulled out her own knife, and cut it for him. Putting the knife back and leaning against the tree, she went back to thinking of the children. Talking to Melody about Ellen passing, and even Missy passing, had helped Melody. It was bringing up those memories and the memories of the abuse from Frank. Melody could talk about it easier than Charity. Julia still didn't know what to say over it. She just felt so guilty that she hadn't known the truth for so long. She blocked those thoughts out. Today was fun with the children and Cole had taken the afternoon off.

He leaned over and kissed her. He held her hand all afternoon. She felt like a young bride. But then again, she was. It was tough with the children, always demanding attention. "I am glad you took a break."

"I need to do it more," Cole told her. "We need more alone time."

Julia teased. "Being a deputy, helping find a new matron for Liberty House, and working the ranch keeps a body busy."

Cole rolled his eyes. "You could say that again. You make me tired thinkin' about it. I like workin' the ranch with the boys."

Julia agreed the boys were good. They acted like perfect gentlemen, which sometimes had her worried. She didn't want them shoving their feelings away as she had done as a child. Or now. She knew she could be honest with Cole, and she was mostly. Sometimes it scared her to be fully honest. What if he rejected her? Couldn't handle the truth? She wanted to tell him how she was struggling with David. But Cole was so good with them he might not believe her.

Cole eyed her. "What's going on in that pretty head?"

Julia shrugged. "Nothin' worth much."

David ran up to her and wanted to get something from the house.

She needed to go get the drinks, so she took his hand, and they went. David ran off ahead, not listening when she said to stop. She just shook her head, though she was surprised he didn't listen. He was always so obedient.

In the cabin, she got a pitcher of orange juice from the cellar and a cup. She would miss these hot summer days. They held such fond memories with the family.

Katrina had written to her about the pond they had there and the hot springs. She would learn to love Colorado just as much as she'd loved it here in Alabama. She couldn't wait to try the warm water. How nice would that be while washing her hair?

David ran all over the house, acting wild, touching things he wasn't supposed to touch, and moving stuff around.

Julia told him to stop, but he didn't listen. She put down the pitcher and took his hand. "What is wrong? I told you not to do that." She tried to be clear, but she was confused by what he was doing.

David screamed. "No, I won't stop!"

It shocked Julia. Where was this coming from?

David hit her with his fist and screamed again. He tried to get away from Julia, but she held unto his hand. She knew she had to deal with this or she would lose his respect. She honestly wanted to cry. She didn't know how to handle this. What had happened to her sweet boy? She got down to his level. He wouldn't look her in the eyes. What was happening? "David, what is wrong? Why would you hit me?"

He shrugged his little shoulders. "I felt like it."

Julia didn't know what to say. "Well, you can't do that. You have to be disciplined."

Suddenly his face was repentant, but his eyes held an edge to them. "I'm sorry, mama. I love you." His voice cracked. Then he hugged her like she was his best friend.

Julia hugged him back. Maybe it was a one-time thing. Her little boy was back. She kissed him on the head and told him she would deal with him later on his punishment. He even helped her carry the cup to the pond.

The kitchen was stuffy and hot as Julia boiled the green beans for canning. Her sister, Gloria, pulled up her sleeves as she finished the dishes.

Charity and Melody were helping and always teasing each other or making jokes about the new crazy thing the pony had done. They could laugh for hours about the ponies.

Julia was sending Charity and Melody out to swim in the pond with the good watch dog, Bunny.

"Oh, thank goodness," Charity laughed. "We will be back to help."

Julia shook her head. "I will call you in for supper. Take the rest of the afternoon off, honey," she told her. The girl acted too much like an adult. "The little boys are playin' with Matt, so you don't have to worry about them." She hit them playfully with a towel. "Now go, girlies."

Charity squealed in delight. "No boys and no chores. Let's go." Then she added nervously, "Will you make sure the boys stay away?"

Julia smiled lightly, trying to cover her discomfort so Gloria wouldn't notice. "I will make sure."

The girls ran out chasing each other.

Gloria put the pan on for the canning and sat at the table with a piece of plum cake.

Julia took the break they needed and poured them a tall glass of sweet tea.

Gloria took a sip and winced. "All we need with this heat is a sugar rush," she said dryly.

Julia rolled her eyes. "Not too hot to be sarcastic." She felt at peace with Gloria, like she didn't have to be a parent or protector. She could just relax and be a friend like she was. She had thought about it for a while but didn't know how to bring up her issues with David. He was so good with Gloria and Cole. It seemed like he was only angry at her. Maybe it was just her. Maybe she wasn't bonding with him enough. She felt like it was something she was doing wrong. She put the rest of the green beans on the stove and then sat back down. She pulled back her hair and tied it with a ribbon. "I can't wait for this heat to end and for us to be in Colorado territory."

Gloria nodded. "I miss Katrina so much. Her letters or notes just ain't enough."

Julia nodded. "I wish so much I could talk to her in person. That I could talk to a parent."

Gloria looked surprised. "What is wrong? You can talk to me."

Julia knew she could, but she wanted some help with some of her struggles as a mother and she didn't want to burden Gloria with it. She knew Gloria was her only option for talking. Sometimes she longed for fellowship. "I just feel like I need to be a better ma."

"You are a wonderful mother," Gloria reassured her. "You love them and that is most important."

Julia drank some tea. Maybe it was a little sugar high. If only loving them was enough, but Julia wasn't so sure. It was painful to have her son hurt her with his words and rage. "It's David. He is so hard to deal with. When I try to discipline him, he just laughs or fights me. Nothin' I do fazes him. He does nothing I ask him without putting up a fight. He yells and screams as I have never seen him do with anyone else." She sighed and didn't know if she should tell all the stuff he did. If she told Gloria everything, would she believe it? Julia struggled to believe it, and she saw it every day. "David is so mean to the other kids, especially Johnathan. He hits, yells, and fights with Johnathan all the time. I couldn't find out who was breaking all the children's toys, along with the girl's dolls. I found David broke them. He destroys everything. He looks at me with such anger in his eyes. It's like he hates me. We have always been so close before. I don't understand it." *I didn't expect this when adopting him. It wasn't in the plan.* Suddenly she felt guilty for thinking that.

Gloria's eyes were wide. Before speaking, she took another sip of tea. "That doesn't sound like David at all. He is such a sweet boy."

Julia nodded. "I know, but he is so angry with me."

Gloria shrugged. "Maybe you are reading into it wrong. I am sure if you show him extra love, he will come around. Remember what their father Owen did, betraying us like that. Shooting Maverick. It was such a big shock and so hurtful especially to ones so young." She leaned closer. "Maybe you are just seeing it differently than it is."

The words cut at Julia's heart. Oh, how she wished it were different. Though maybe Gloria was right, maybe she just needed to love him more, care for him more. Now she was just confused. Just then David and Jonathan ran in.

Johnathan ran to Julia, and she pulled him into a hug and kiss while David ran to Gloria. In his happy bliss, David talked all about the day he'd had with Matt.

Gloria gave her another look like maybe Julia could be wrong and David was just fine.

All Julia knew was she was starting to wear thin from not knowing what she was doing wrong.

The sun was high in the sky by the time Izzy got back to the house; Katrina was still out with the girls. It was a beautiful day for a ride; she loved it here. So much beauty in one place. How had she gotten so lucky, or blessed, to be here with all of this?

Only one thing was missing, Jesse. She missed him so much. Since he has been away setting up his homestead. She knew that land was his pride and joy. If she married him they would have a good life together. More than she'd thought she would.

As she walked to the house to get some lunch, Katrina and the girls were eating bread and smoked turkey on the trail like the old days. Francesca had told them they were eating like cowboys did.

It surprised Izzy how well the girls were learning to ride, but out here what else was there to do. Though if they tried to run away, they could get farther and get there much faster.

Izzy shrugged. Better to let them deal with that if and when it happened. Walking into the kitchen, she remembered she was making supper; she had agreed to do it since Katrina was gone and wouldn't get back till later. She wasn't a cook, her brother and sister were the cooks of the family.

She got some bread out and ate, trying to think of what to make for supper. She heard someone behind her; Andrew was at work and Isaiah was working on another farm. As she turned, she pulled her gun, to find Jesse putting his hands up.

He grinned. "I didn't expect this kind of welcome."

Putting her gun away, she ran to him. Wrapping her arms around him, he looked so good. His black hair still wet from washing in the creek. "Oh, I've missed you," she whispered.

He pulled her away to look in her eyes. "Not as much as I missed you." When they kissed it was like they became one. She felt something open inside her heart and some fear left. She felt such a love for him.

When she finally pulled away, they were both breathless.

Izzy smiled. "Do you want to eat?"

Jesse pulled her close again, kissing her. "I just need your lips."

Izzy giggled. "Well, you will have to just live with my cookin', cause I am doing supper tonight." She turned to cut the bread and then put some bacon in the pan to fry. "Katrina is out ridin' with the girls, so I got supper tonight."

"What girls? Gloria and Julia are here already?" Jesse asked as he sat down at the table.

Izzy turned halfway to meet his gaze. "Oh, we can't get a hold of you easily, so you don't know about Andrew and Katrina's girls." She continued to tell him as she toasted the bread. As she finished, they sat down with their lunch.

Jesse poured two glasses of buttermilk. "So these girls came from an asylum. How do Andrew and Katrina not know these girls will steal them blind?"

Izzy shrugged. "I don't think they would." She winked at him. "Couldn't have been any worse than you boys?"

Jesse frowned.

"Let's pray." She took his hands.

"Lord, thank you for the food you provide and my beautiful girl made. Bless and watch over the family in Alabama. Amen." He squeezed her hands before letting go.

"Oh, I forgot to tell you," she told him. "Gloria and Dave, Sawyer, and Annie are on their way. They are leaving tomorrow."

"That will be nice," Jesse said as he ate. "So Julia, Matt, Cole, and Maverick are the only ones left there."

She nodded. She knew it was hard for him to be away from them all, but especially Julia. "They should be here by fall. They said they are bringin' a surprise."

"Wonder what it is?" Jesse took a bite.

Izzy frowned. "I don't know, but I wish I did. Surprises from my family normally ain't great."

"Mine neither, and with them comin' together, I can't even imagine what it is." He winked at her. "It could be good."

Izzy shrugged. "That is true. So how is the farm comin'?"

"Good. I finished the cabin. It ain't big, but it can be added onto later." His eyes lightened. "And the barn is near finished."

"You should stay here for Founder's Day. It's next Monday." She gave him a soft smile. "We could go as a couple."

"I'll see," he muttered as he finished his lunch.

90

"What horses did you bring with you? I didn't see them in the barn."

He grinned. "What, and ruin my surprise? They are in the back paddock, the one you can't see from the barn or house. I brought four with me to bring stuff back on. Want to go shoppin' with me later?"

"Sure." Izzy stood to take the plates to the sink. "But it will have to be tomorrow. I have to make supper." She made a face.

He laughed. "You don't sound so excited." He got up and kissed her cheek. "I am sure you are a great cook."

"Yeah, over a fire or smoking and caring for meat, but not on a stove."

He kissed her. "I have faith in you."

She made another face.

He took her hand. "Take a break and come to the barn. I want your help with somethin'."

She looked at the kitchen and it was clean. She had planned on making a venison steak, along with potatoes and carrots.

In the barn, they sat on hay that Andrew had brought in from of one of the biggest fields.

"Now, what do you need help with?" She asked when she saw nothing.

Jesse pulled her closer and kissed her. She let him and kissed him back as they lay there in the hay.

She pulled back and sat up, looking down at him. "What else did you want help with besides this?"

Jesse teased. "Well, I can't do this alone. I need you."

"Seriously, Jesse," Izzy pleaded.

He sat up, sighing. "Fine, I want you to write out what you want for my cabin, everythin' from kitchen stuff, livin' room stuff, to fluffy girl stuff, whatever you want," Jesse told her.

"Why?" Izzy asked.

"Why?" He mimicked her. "I love you, Izzy, and I want to marry you!"

"You do?" she asked, surprised.

He took her hand. "Of course I do. And I want to get married when the whole family gets here. What do you say?"

She stared at him in shock. He hadn't really asked her to marry him, but who needed fancy words when you got this man. She loved him. She wanted a life with him, that is what she needed. She nodded. "Yes, I will marry you, Jesse. I love you and I want to be with you."

91

She kissed him. This was the first time she had chosen to kiss him, made that first move. Like she told Francesca, she needed to make that choice to be free from her past, and that is what she was doing by marrying him. She was choosing to let go of her past and forget it happened. It wouldn't matter now; she would be a new person with Jesse.

He pulled away this time and said, "Thank you, Izzy. Besides my family, you are the only one that has chosen me."

She touched his cheek with her hand. "You're wrong. God chose you, and I will always choose you." She grinned. "We have to send a telegram to Cole and my cousins. I have to get a dress." She got up and went to the office, bringing back a paper and pencil, then she sat down and started talking a mile a minute.

Jesse smiled as he watched her. She was so much fun, her eyes were alive, her cheeks were warm from excitement, her hair shone despite it being a mess from her ride, her lips were full and red; how he loved kissing them.

She is not yours.

He heard a voice. He frowned as he didn't want to listen. He loved Izzy, and why not treat her like he loved her?

Love is kind, patient, and selfless.

He frowned. He wasn't any of those things, but he ignored the voice. He knew how to live his life; to have fun with his bride-to-be.

You are my beloved son and she is my beloved...

No, he wasn't listening. It was his life. He turned back to listening to Izzy as she continued to talk. He talked with her and decided he liked this time with her; it was almost as good as kissing her. He was finding out new stuff about her.

Time seemed to stand still as they talked of the wedding, the girls, the younger siblings and how Julia had written to them telling how they were changing, the family farming and Jesse's ranch. Izzy thought she knew all she needed to know about Jesse, but now she knew so much more than before. They were really talking and not just kissing; it felt good.

"I love you, Izzy. You are like an ocean breeze, fresh and good," Jesse told her as he lay on the hay.

Izzy sat up on her elbow. She smiled at him, though she felt less than confident. What if he knew she was not fresh or good? What was she thinking? What would Jesse do if he found out? She didn't trust herself to talk, so she just leaned close and let him kiss her, let herself get lost in those kisses. Maybe he wouldn't care that others had kissed her lips before. She shut her eyes and made herself forget, but her love for Jesse...

"Izzy! Jesse!" Katrina yelled.

Izzy pulled away as fast as if she had been burned. She looked to see Francesca standing next to her and to see Carlissa and Sara tying their horses to the post. She stood up, as did Jesse.

Katrina frowned at her, and then turned to Jesse. She let go of her horse's reins and went to hug him. "Hey, Jesse, it's so good to see you." She stepped back and introduced her daughters to him.

Jesse nodded. "Glad to meet you girls."

Francesca held out her hand to him. "So you're Jesse, Izzy's young man. Nice to finally meet you." She didn't seem happy at all to meet him.

Jesse shook her hand. "Same here."

As they put up the horses, Izzy declared excitedly, "I have news."

Katrina looked over her horse, her eyes curious.

"We are getting married." Izzy laughed.

Katrina came over and hugged her. "I am so glad." She hugged Jesse again. "I am so glad, Jesse-boy." She touched his cheek. "Pedro would be happy."

Jesse pulled away from her touch as he gave her a sad smile.

Francesca walked up. "What? Where will you live?"

Izzy hadn't thought about that, but the move would be hard on Francesca.

Jesse answered, "At my place. It is about a six-hour ride from here. I hope to make it easier to travel, but it will have to do."

Katrina might not have lived here long, but she knew once they left for winter, they wouldn't see them till spring. "Do you want to get married before winter then?"

Izzy nodded, still watching Francesca, who went to Poder and took off the saddle like someone was holding a gun to her.

They finished the horses in silence. Francesca walked off. Izzy went after her.

"Francesca, wait."

Francesca turned and glared at her. "I ain't hungry! Just leave me alone."

Izzy covered her face with her hands. "I forgot to make supper." She looked at Katrina.

They both burst out laughing. Francesca looked at them like they were nuts, but even she saw the humor in it and laughed along. Sometimes you just had to laugh at yourself.

They all headed to the kitchen where they put supper together. When Andrew got home, they were still making it but laughing all along and none of the girls were upset. For one of the first times, they were a family with no moods ruining it.

Chapter 13

Riding into town with Jesse two days later, Izzy gazed at the trees that lined the road as rain softly fell. At least they would get soaked through their coats. Izzy thought it fit her mood as she couldn't ignore Jesse any longer. She stayed silent; she had turned numb again. She had in the past. It was better than feeling pain all the time. She hadn't known how hard relationships could be. She wished Ellen was here to talk to. She might know how to help her son in all his moods. She was, of course, not showing any of this to Jesse because she was good at hiding what she felt. By the time they ordered their supplies at the general store, Izzy was feeling much better. Somehow getting out and doing normal things had put her in a better mood, lightened her heart to see some of the people that she came to care about.

"What restaurant should we go to?" Jesse asked.

"Hattie's Place is the best place in town." She grinned., "And the only one."

"Then Hattie's Place it is." Jesse took her hand, walking towards the restaurant.

Izzy greeted many people as they passed. Sometimes she even introduced Jesse as her fiancé. Once they arrived at Hattie's Place, they found a table towards the back of the room. Jesse hadn't eaten in a restaurant since the trip West because Starrys weren't allowed in Alabama's restaurants.

Millie came to the table. "Hi, Izzy, so is this your fiancé?"

Izzy nodded. "Milly, meet my fiancé Jesse. Jesse meet Millie." She smiled. "You don't miss much, do you?"

Milly laughed. "I sure don't. Now what would you have to drink?" She winked at Izzy. "I have tried that sweet tea. Want some?"

"Sure." Izzy winked back. "Bring a cup of sugar."

Millie hit her shoulder playfully. "Well, I might put some pepper in it."

Izzy laughed. "You wouldn't dare."

As Millie walked away, Jesse commented, "You have made yourself a name here."

"I love it here, more than I thought I would," she admitted honestly. "We will have to visit often in the summers."

He took her hand from across the table. "Sure, you don't mind moving then?"

"I want to be with you. Let's just not forget about our families."

"Our family is hard to forget."

After Millie dropped off their drinks, Izzy put a couple spoonfuls of sugar in her tea. She was at two spoons when Mabel walked in. She spotted them and headed their way. Izzy didn't miss it and told her of their engagement.

Mabel laughed and pulled Izzy into a hug. "I am so happy for you, honey." Still holding Izzy, she looked down at Jesse. "You are getting a wonderful woman."

Jesse smiled. "Yes, I am."

Mabel turned back to Izzy. "How are things at the ranch?"

Izzy looked at her and knew she wanted an actual answer. "It will take time for them to get used to the fact that I am moving." She added, "We have been using the hot springs. Carlissa almost got in yesterday."

"That is wonderful and such a big step." Mabel hugged her again. "Well, I have to run. Enjoy your life with Jesse." She smiled at Jesse. "Nice to meet you too, Jesse."

"Same here." His face remained guarded.

Katrina smiled as the ladies started to sew. She was more relaxed this time around than the last time, though she wasn't sure why, maybe because these ladies had becomes her friends. Francesca, Sara, and Carlissa were outside with the children having an enjoyable time, but Katrina was still monitoring them. Mabel told her they all watched the children like a hawk. Katrina relaxed then. She sewed a flowered dress for Francesca as she watched the faces of the ladies. They all sat around   a   circle.

Her heart felt joyful as she thought about the next sewing circle when Gloria and Annie would be sitting by her. They had just received the telegram that they had left Alabama. She could hardly wait.

"So you're actually raising the girls?" Mrs. Bly asked.

Katrina nodded. "Yes, I am."

"Why?" another woman asked. "You know that older girl is Mexican."

Katrina looked at Izzy, who didn't look bothered, or hid it well. "Yes, I know that. She is a lovely girl."

"Well, no matter. The other two girls behave so well and are sweet. I am sure you all will be happy together," Mrs. Bly responded like she had figured everything out.

Katrina smiled anyway. "I hope to be."

"How can you sew and not look at what you're doing?" A new lady asked. She hadn't been at the last sewing circle.

Katrina looked down at her hands and then at the ladies. Before she could speak, Izzy spoke up. "She is one of the best seamstresses in the family and they would do it in the dark. Julia, who is married to my brother, is the best painter you have probably ever seen. She can paint while looking at other things. She is raising her six siblings, so I wonder if she still finds time." Izzy smiled. In the past, she had met most of these ladies.

"The children are mixed, colored, then?" Mrs. Maryanne asked. "I heard rumors."

Katrina saw Izzy didn't even flinch. How did she handle this so well?

"Well, two couples lived on the same plantation. Almost six years ago the Washington, who were colored, passed away. So Ellen took the children in. In March their ma, Ellen Starry, ended up passing away."

Katrina picked up from there. "See, the Starrys took us in as teenagers."

"Will you keep the children at your ranch?" a lady asked. "Or do you want to wait to have then move in untill they get here?"

"No, we want them to have a stable home."

"That is what they need." Dinah smiled. "You're being a great ma."

Katrina smiled back at her. "I never planned to adopt so soon, but I guess God had different thoughts about it."

"Doesn't He? He knows our needs and shapes us with our needs and wants." Mabel chuckled. "Tell God your plans and watch Him laugh."

Later, Katrina got food for the girls as the ladies' snacks were light.

Mabel stopped next to Katrina. "Here, take some of ours. We always bring enough to feed an army."

"You bring food everywhere you go?" Katrina asked.

Mabel nodded. "Almost everywhere, for meals at least. It's important for children that have starved."

Katrina nodded, making a mental note of it.

Mrs. Bly and Gabby were talking to Carlissa as they ate. She sat and read their lips.

"What is your favorite animal?" Gabby asked.

"My new lamb and the kid goats are sweet, too. We got a calf too," Carlissa answered. "We are getting a puppy soon. Maverick Starry is coming with a bunch of dogs."

"I bet you love having tons of uncles and aunts."

Carlissa looked confused at those two words. She looked at Katrina like it was normal. "What does aunt and uncle mean?"

Katrina was glad she had been watching. "It means our sisters will be your aunts and our brothers will be your uncles. Izzy will be your aunt. When she is married to Jesse, you can call her Aunt Izzy. My brother Isaiah is your uncle."

Carlissa nodded and made a face at Gabby. "Uncle Isaiah doesn't like us none. Pa hit him!"

Katrina gasped. "Carlissa, Isaiah likes y'all just fine. He says you're as pretty as a peach."

Carlissa looked back at her. "So we are pretty as fruit, that's really nice."

Izzy chuckled. "No, saying pretty as a peach is a real compliment in the south, darlin'. It's like saying you are pretty as the queen of England."

Francesca spoke up then. "I always wondered why people said you are as pretty as the queen of England. She is born the queen. She ain't picked for her beauty. So she could be as ugly as Whisper, and still everyone would say she looked like the queen of England."

The ladies who were listening chuckled.

"You got a point, lovely," Katrina told her with a chuckle.

Katrina turned to look at Carlissa as she spoke again. "I's like the ranch a lot, though I'm sad sometimes."

"Oh, why honey?" Gabby asked.

Katrina noticed Mabel try to speak up, and then watched as Carlissa pulled her world down a bit. "Well, my new ma is deaf, and she just ignores me sometimes when I talk. I don't know why. I am a good girl."

Gabby and every other head turned to look at Katrina, their faces questioning.

Katrina, who didn't handle attention well, blushed to her roots. "I am almost all deaf, but I can hear pretty well out of my right ear. I read lips and sign." She cleared her throat. "It's hard for me to tell people."

Mabel smiled. "She is one of the best speaking hard-of-hearing persons I have ever met. She is like Allie and I told her you all accepted Allie well."

"You knew about this?" Mrs. Bly asked, sounding offended.

Mabel shrugged. "I didn't think it was your business if Katrina wanted to tell you or not."

"How do you expect to raise hearing children having this problem?" Mrs. Bly asked.

"You lied to us?" Maryanne said.

"They can't bond with you. You are so different from them," a woman told her.

"She's not their real ma any how, so what does it matter," Maryanne said.

This was like salt to Katrina's wounds. The worst yet, her daughters were sitting with her, listening to it and maybe agreeing. She looked to see Sara had gone cold. Carlissa looked smug. Francesca's face was hot with anger.

Katrina stood, ready to get the girls and leave.

Izzy spoke up. "How dare you talk about Katrina that way. You say you are Christian ladies, but have you ever taken in an orphan or helped one of their families out? Or maybe talked to the saloon girls in town to see why they are in that life and to help them get out?" Izzy moved her hair back, calm as she could be. "I have seen people like you all my life and I don't care what you think about me. Y'all have heard lots of rumors." She winked at Mabel. "Only about half are true. What if you looked beyond the outside and into the person. God didn't reject Zaccheus for being short. He let a former prostitute, Rahab, be in the lineage of Jesus. He let a liar be one of His men. He washed Judas' feet, knowin' he had betrayed Him. What if God's people rejected Mary in her time of need? Ask yourself what God would want you to do. And not believe the world's lie."

By this end of her speech, the ladies just stared. Katrina wasn't sure what to say, but she sure was thankful.

Maryanne snorted. "I always heard Donovans had a big mouth, with their uppity living and all."

Mrs. Bly came up to Katrina. "I apologize for what I said."

Katrina nodded. A couple of other ladies apologized too.

Maryanne and several other ladies stormed out.

Katrina realized that being honest and open with people didn't hurt as much as she thought it would.

Chapter 14

On the way to the Founder's Day picnic, Carlissa asked Izzy, "Why are you and Andrew riding your own horses?" She sat next to Katrina on the wagon.

"Well, there will be a horse race that I will win," Izzy told her smugly. She lifted her head up to the sun. It felt like the sun was coming down and giving her a hug. She loved when it would warm her cheeks against the winter chill. She always imagined the sun was the way God watched His people during the day. She also believed He protected them with the stars as they slept. It warmed her in her darkest days.

Andrew challenged her. "Oh, you think so, huh?"

"This horse is from this country, unlike that beach baby you have," she told him.

He looked shocked. "This stallion is one of the fastest Starry horses."

"He's faster than Maverick's horse?" Izzy smiled, knowing he wasn't.

Andrew held up a hand and said, "Let me repeat myself, he is the fastest horse in Colorado."

Izzy laughed. She was going to enjoy today even if Jesse hadn't stayed. She understood his need to get back to build their home. They had both lived in poverty and neither wanted that life ever again. Though Izzy had cousins who had cared for her and never let her go hungry, Jesse wasn't that blessed. Izzy still missed him and felt his absences.

In town, Katrina saw it was busier than they thought it would be. It had been a week since she had been there. She was trying to put a normal house together for the girls. Some things were going better and more workable. However, she continued to worry about Carlissa and

Sara, who still became scared of unfamiliar events.

After tying the horses to the hitching post, Andrew helped her down, and then helped the girls get down from the wagon in their new dresses. Katrina had taken a lot of time with each of their hair. They had wanted to look good. Though she wasn't sure what the girls would say to Carlissa after what she did. Carlissa didn't seem worried at all.

Katrina put their food on one of the tables. She saw Mabel and waved to her, making her way over there while holding Carlissa's hand.

Mabel greeted her and then spoke to Carlissa. "That is such a pretty dress. Did your mama make it?"

Carlissa nodded.

"What do you say to Mrs. Alexanders, Carlissa?" Katrina asked her.

Carlissa looked up like she forgot what to say.

"Say thank you," Katrina told her.

Carlissa looked up at her, but not in the eyes. "Say thank you."

Mabel smiled. "You're welcome. You have the prettiest eyes."

Carlissa looked in her eyes and shook her head. "I have been told I am a terror child. I ain't pretty."

This statement shocked Katrina and she didn't know how to respond.

Mabel got to her level. "Well, those people were not telling you the truth. God created you and you know what, Carlissa?"

Carlissa shook her head, not looking in her eyes.

"Jesus made you in God's image and He knew you before you were born. He brought you to your ma and pa's home to live." She paused. "God loves you and He made you a delightful girl."

Carlissa shrugged, and then pulled on Katrina's hand. "Mamma, can I play with my friends?"

Katrina looked at her gently. "After dinner, honey, we can do all the games."

Mabel looked at Clarissa, noticing her frown, and said, "Can you ask your mamma if you can eat with my table, and then after you eat you can play with Lucy?"

Carlissa laughed and looked at Katrina. "Could we, mamma?"

Katrina chuckled at them. "Sure, Andrew won't mind."

Supper was over and some games had started, but at the moment, Katrina and Mabel sat back and were talking. "How did you get Carlissa to laugh like that?"

"Oh that, it was easy for me. I am not her mamma who she

struggles with and I try to do that with my children. With touched or asylum children, remember to use small words, like when she says bad things about herself. Build her up little by little with short words. Not a lot or she will stop listening." Mabel smiled like she knew they did that. "With Francesca, and even Sara in a little while, use more words for them; but remember, Sara doesn't have the knowledge of words we do."

Before Katrina could say anything, Sara ran up and took Katrina's hand. "Mamma, the first game is about to start."

Katrina laughed. "Sure, let's go. What do you want to do first?" She ran with her to the first event.

Katrina couldn't remember when she had laughed this hard or played this much. She ignored the looks she got from a few people about her children. At least she was used to this in Alabama. Long ago she had learned to ignore it. Most were kind and welcoming.

The mayor spoke, then it was time to call Katrina's husband Andrew to speak about Liberty Ranch and their mission work there. Months ago, Cole and Izzy had written a report explaining everything.

Katrina walked up to him as the girls sat at the table eating a snack. "You ready?" She knew he was nervous.

Andrew looked at her like she was crazy. "Yes. I hate giving speeches. Mav is better at it."

Katrina smiled, "Just do what he does."

Andrew shook his head and laughed. Maverick said imagine where a sniper would sit to hit them, then how he could kill the sniper before he got any of them. It was just how his mind worked. "You're horrible." He kissed her nose.

When they called his name, she whispered, "Just look for my eyes."

Katrina walked closer to the stage, caught his gaze, and he smiled. She knew that smile was meant for her even though many thought he was just being polite.

All of Katrina's dreams were coming true. Overwhelmed by it all, she wiped at joyful tears. Andrew had been open and honest in his speech. He and Izzy had worked on it for hours.

She looked around to see where the girls were when her eyes were covered by hard, callused hands. "Well, I know it is not one of my girls or Andrew since he couldn't get over here soon enough. Isaiah?" She smelled his cologne, but knew it couldn't be him.

"Well, you weren't none too good at guessing." The voice came to her ears she hadn't heard in months, how she missed it.

She turned around and burst into laughter as she hugged Sawyer. She moved to hug each of them. It was getting crowded around them and they were getting looks, so Katrina led them a little away from the crowd. "Oh, when did y'all get here?" She hugged Gloria again.

"Three days ago," Sawyer said sarcastically.

Annie smiled. "We just got here, just in time to hear the end of the speech."

"He did a great job," Sawyer added.

"Well, thank you," Andrew said as he walked up, and then gave the same greetings.

The crowd had grown since the speeches ended. Izzy had enjoyed writing that speech with Cole. It spoke of their dreams and future. On how they had gotten close after many years. Though her future had changed a little, it was still wonderful to see it come true. Izzy spotted a woman who looked like Annie through the crowd.. Her sister was back already. She jumped up and started over there, bringing the girls with her.

Carlissa whined, "Where are we going?"

"My sister and the Starrys are here," Izzy told them.

Francesca looked at her. "Where?" She looked around and spotted them. It wasn't too hard. The town wasn't large, and Francesca now knew many of the people. She whispered, "Is the dark-haired one your twin?"

Izzy shook her head. "No, the blond one."

Francesca responded like she wondered how Izzy was even related to the blond woman, let alone came from the same womb. Drawing near, Izzy heard Katrina ask what the surprise was.

Annie looked at Sawyer, beaming with joy. "We got married!"

Izzy stopped walking. It felt like a bullet had hit her. How could her sister get married without telling her anything about it? What did Cole say?

Katrina spotted them first and introduced the girls as Izzy hugged the girls.

Francesca looked to Izzy. "You came from the same woman and man as your sister?"

Izzy nodded, trying to make it light. "Yup, it keeps people guessing."

Francesca chuckled. "You keep everyone guessing."

Izzy picked Carlissa up, knowing she was probably overwhelmed at meeting all of them.

"Did you hear the news?" Annie asked.

Izzy smiled, though it didn't meet her eyes. "Yeah, congratulations." She was glad Carlissa was on her hip, so she wouldn't have to hug her again.

Francesca whispered to her, "You can't be in her weddin'?"

Izzy shrugged.

Sara whispered to Izzy, "She has your nose."

Izzy met her eyes, surprised she would say that in her quiet wisdom. No one had ever said they looked alike. She whispered back, "Thank you, dear."

Suddenly the last event of the day was to start - the horse race.

Andrew smiled at his brothers. "Did you bring the horses to town?"

"No, we left them all back at the ranch and walked to town," Sawyer said sarcastically.

Andrew laughed. "Want to race like old times? Now that Mav ain't here, I can win."

Both of them argued but agreed.

"You don't have to argue, because I will win," Izzy told them smugly.

The guys groaned and Andrew eyed her. "The challenge is on then."

Francesca stood next to Izzy. "Izzy will win for sure."

Annie glanced to Gloria and then Sawyer. "Are you funning? We have done nothing but travel for the last fourteen days."

Sawyer shrugged. He kissed her and then laughed. "It'll be fun, hon."

Izzy put Carlissa down and kissed her on the head. "Stay by the front, sweetie, and you will see me win." She wanted to get out of the sun and go swimming instead of racing. But maybe winning a race would help.

Katrina looked at her curiously, but said nothing.

Izzy walked over to Phoenix, and leaving him bareback, she

mounted, then followed the boys to the starting line.

Hank, who was in charge, came over to her. "Are you sure you want to ride? This is a hard race."

Izzy nodded confidently. "This horse knows this land better than I do, and I've lived here most of my adult life."

Andrew spoke up, "Let her ride, boss. She is a fine rider."

Hank seemed to take in Andrew's words, then nodded. "Okay, may the best man or woman win."

Andrew smiled at her. "Be careful. If you get hurt, Annie and Katrina will kill me."

Izzy smiled. "Kat would kill you." She knew Annie wouldn't care that much. "I won't get hurt, I will just win."

"We'll see," Andrew said.

When they fired the gun, Phoenix had been in enough races to know what to do. He stayed a little behind Andrew's and Jerry's horses. She knew more about her horse than she did her own twin. God had given her such a gift when He gave her Phoenix. He was her friend, her protector, her stability, throughout life; she loved him to the earth and back. She wished just once she could feel that for Annie.

She felt it for Cole. They had gotten very close in the last few months, but it had taken work. Annie always said they were fine, but Izzy knew they weren't. She wondered if God had made a mistake by making her Annie's twin. She felt the tears burn her eyes, but she wouldn't let them come. By the end of the race, she knew what she had to do. Tomorrow she would leave for her mountain, to her future home. She felt God tell her not to go, but she needed to.

She heard everyone say congratulations, and she saw them put roses around Phoenix and hem them in. This means she must have won the race. She didn't really care, but smiled, anyway.

Francesca gave her a big hug and laughed, telling her she would win her own race one day.

Katrina eyed her again with concern. This time Andrew did the same. They knew her well enough to know something was wrong.

Hank gave her some money for winning and a silver cup. "I didn't think you could do it. Congratulations."

Izzy just wanted the day to end, so she could sleep in the hay until she could leave in the morning. It couldn't come fast enough.

Chapter 15

Julia laid the baby, Mary, in the basket when she finally fell asleep. Mary didn't seem to mind the soft voices of Susan, Jerry, Gloria, Matt, and Cole.

The girls had gushed over her, especially Susan. "So what do you plan to do, Jules?" Susan asked. They had all had supper and then had coffee and cherry pie in the parlor.

Julia shrugged. She was feeling tired after a full day of traveling to get this little one from the asylum. Cole was called the night before about her. Julia knew this might be the way things were being married to Cole, though he normally had help in places where asylums were at. "I would rather find a loving home for her. I don't know if it would be good to bring another child into the family."

Cole nodded, taking her hand on the safa. "We would love her, but the children have been through so much already." The baby stayed sleeping while they softly talked.

As Susan smiled big, she looked at Matt, he was the second oldest brother, who sat next to her on the other sofa, and then back at Julia. "Why don't Matt and I adopt the baby?"

Matt nodded. "We would love to bring this little one home. She has been through so much in her little life."

Julia glanced at Cole and then back at Susan. Cole spoke first. "Susan, Matt, taking on a child like this, even a baby, can be very difficult. When she is older, it might not get easier, just harder. It will be a lifetime of working with her." He chose his words carefully. "I don't want to discourage you, but it is a hard life even for an infant that didn't get any love or a touch of kindness."

Julia spoke up, "Cole's right. This week I have spent a lot of time with Melissa. She knows about this kind of thing. It's hard. I just don't want the two of you deciding in haste and regretting it later. Many parents can't handle them, even a baby Mary's age. Melissa thinks she is around half a year old."

Susan's eyes narrowed. "We still want her, and we won't give her back when she gets older," she defended herself.

"Susan, I didn't mean it like that," Julia told her honestly.

Matt was a quiet man, but he spoke up when the time called for it. He was the spiritual leader of the family. He had been the first to believe. "I know what you meant, Julia." He took Susan's hand. "Two families adopted me and gave me back when I was too much trouble." Pain still showed on his face from what those families did. "Which I probably was, but sometimes parents take the child in haste and don't consider the child." He looked at Julia and Cole. "We have been praying about it for a while and have wanted to help you with this. We want to help a child who needs safety and love."

"Normally, I don't allow a couple who hasn't been married for at least two years to adopt a child," Cole stated. Since he got the baby out of the asylum he had the choice to where the baby went. "That is what some of the leaders I have worked with have agreed to."

"Why on earth not?" Susan asked.

Gloria spoke up for this one. She was curled in a chair, her knees pulled up, comfortable in the house she spent many years living in. "When you have your own child, we don't want the adopted child to get put aside because some parents can't afford both. I was in a home where my stepfather didn't want me after my mamma died. He wanted his real child."

Susan looked at her sadly. Out of all the adults in the room, Susan was the only one to grow up in a normal two-parent home. Susan started out gently. "We would still want to adopt her."

Cole nodded. "Since you are family, I will bend my rules." He smiled. "I don't mean to be imperious, but when you have so many children under your care, you learn not to bend rules often. If you do, then other people will try to swindle their way in. Give it a couple weeks, then we can sign the adoption papers. It doesn't matter to the asylum but it does matter to the child. We always put the adoption in the family Bible." His jaw went hard. "If the asylum wants the children back, papers don't matter, but like I said, it doesn't happen often. The owners shouldn't come after Mary."

"Thank you, Cole." Matt stood up, breaking up the party, for the hour was late. He hugged Julia. "Thank you for findin' us our daughter, Julia." He kissed her cheek.

Susan went to hug Julia. "I am sorry if I am rushed about this. I am just trying to understand it all."

Julia smiled. "We can learn together. Being married to Cole helps me. He knows the system like the back of his hand." She leaned close. "You have Matt too. He is wise and has been there."

"Thank you, Jules." Susan then took the baby girl to her new home and to their future together. Julia sent a prayer to the new family and for her new added family member.

Susan had thought having a baby wouldn't be so hard, but Mary was proving her wrong. She took a bottle and only that, but would cry and scream until Susan put her on the couch or her bed. Every time she would hold the baby, her back would be straight as a board and she would try to pull away from any kind of touch. Feeding her baby food would end with more food on Susan than in the child's mouth. She liked baths but still never played or smiled. She just screamed or acted like a statue. It was heartbreaking. When Mary threw food at her again,. Susan fed Mary a bottle and put her down for a nap, then sat crying in the parlor.

Matt found her that way. He sat beside her and took her in his arms. "Susan, honey, what is wrong?"

"I am a terrible mother," she cried. "I can't get her to eat and I'm afraid she is losing weight. She hates me and it's only been a couple of days."

He picked her up and placed her in his lap. "Susan, it's only been a couple of days, give it time." He wiped her tears with his handkerchief. "Have a good cry, and if you are that worried, go to Julia's."

She stiffened. "Just run to your sister if something goes bad. She can fix everything, but I don't see it that way. She and Cole don't think I can parent."

"That is not true, Sue, and you know it, too. They wanted us to know what we are getting into with adopting." He paused. "Go to Julia, she will help you."

She looked away. "I don't know. She might judge me for being a terrible mom."

He pulled her face to his. "Julia would never do that. You can trust her."

Susan wasn't so sure about that.

Susan finally agreed and headed to Julia's house three days later. Matt had planned to come for supper. The family always did that, dropped in for lunch or supper, there was always enough to go around. She was holding Mary to her chest as she lay there not moving or relaxing. Just unhappy empty eyes showed through.

She knocked on Julia's door, though most of the family just walked in and out. Susan had lived in this cabin for two months before she married Matt, but she still got nervous.

Charity came to the door holding the rope of her pony. "Why are you knocking, Susan?"

She just smiled and walked in, heading to the kitchen where she knew Julia would be. There she was, her arms, hair, and face covered in flour, as was the floor, the counter, and David, who was sitting at the table pouting. "I was going to ask why there is a horse in your house, but I'll ask why there is flour everywhere?"

Julia looked discouraged. "Someone had a poor attitude this morning, and he is paying for it now."

Susan nodded. "Would you like some help, Julia?"

Julia gave her a look like she thought she'd never ask. "That would be great. You can put Mary in that basket. Is she ready for a nap?"

"Yeah, she just ate a little." She held up a bottle. "I brought this too."

Julia said lightly, "She is demanding when it comes to eating."

Susan laid her in the basket. It was lined in blankets. "No, she doesn't cry when she is hungry, just when I am holding her or trying to comfort her." She turned to get some water to boil.

Julia looked concerned. "It has been that rough."

Susan nodded. "I never realized. It has been one battle after another." Susan told her all she had been dealing with.

Julia nodded. "Give it time. It has hardly been a couple of weeks." She gave her a knowing look. "I keep telling myself that."

"Why would a child act like this?" Susan sighed.

Julia tried to save as much flour as she could without it being dirty.

110

From the look of it they would have to throw out most of it. "Well, she is scared for one and has never had a kind touch. She doesn't know how to deal with it so she just lets it out in anger, and even hatred it seems like, but it is fear behind those emotions." Julia started washing the floor. "Just love her and it will be enough, but it might go on for years."

Susan's mouth dropped open. "If I love my child for years, it might not help. She might act this like forever."

Julia looked at the children who were helping clean. "Can y'all run outside for a moment? I'll call David in to clean up the floor, but for now, go do your chores?" She looked at the older boys. "Can you boys help David clean up his clothes, and don't use a lot of water or it will clump."

They both nodded and headed out.

Charity called to Firefly, the pony obeyed, and they walked off together. She muttered about something like a sunflower liked the flour.

Julia smiled at the two, then turned back to Susan. " Since the day we heard about our children or met them, we have loved them and wanted the best for them. We want our children to reach the sky. And they can do it, but it won't be easy. It has to be their choice when they are older on how to handle life."

"Why don't they heal? Why doesn't God heal them?" Susan cried.

Julia looked at the floor full of flour. "My son has spilled almost four cups of flour all over the floor, himself, and me. I can and will clean this up with his help, but it will probably be in the cracks, the seams. With work and more work we can get it clean, but it will still be there just like our children's scars. Mary might be a baby, but she still has never had a mother's love or care. It leaves a big hole in their heart that only God can fill, but it may still have cracks."

Susan nodded. Point covered. "Thank you, Jules."

Julia looked at her. "For what?"

"Not judging me for not knowing all this," Susan admitted.

Julia hugged her. "Well, how could I judge you when you are a great and loving parent? If you weren't, you wouldn't come to me about this."

Susan smiled. "I do love her. She is so beautiful. I like to think she looks for me when I walk into a room and to think I see her smile." Susan wiped her eyes. "Good thing I have a big imagination."

Julia hugged her again. "I know how it is. You want to see them

111

happy and not so afraid." She wiped at her own tears. "It's harder than you ever thought."

They were still hugging and wiping at tears when Charity walked back in with Firefly. "Julia, Firefly loves the flour. She wanted to come back to eat some more. At least she is cleaning it." She walked Firefly over to the flour and the pony began to eat.

Julia and Susan looked at each other and burst into laughter. They had more tears coming down their cheeks as they laughed. Charity laughed with them, not being offended at all. "Well, it is true; I am not bluffing, Susan, Julia."

They laughed all the harder. Some days you just have to laugh or you will end up in tears. Life with these children was never boring, that was for sure.

Izzy hadn't slept well and now she was waking up in the barn loft. She hadn't wanted to sleep inside because she would wake up screaming in terror. She was dreaming of going into the night with Cole doing a rescue. She hated when the nightmares got that bad and she wanted to just forget it all. After getting ready for the day, Izzy walked to the house, and entered the kitchen. The soft voices brought peace to her.

The kitchen smelled of sweet rolls, which reminded Izzy of when she went home to her aunt's cooking. However, it wasn't just the food, Izzy also felt safe with her aunt. She never got hit there.

They sat down for breakfast and the boys came in from chores outside. Watching them all mess around the kitchen laughing and talking all at once felt like being home. Annie and Gloria fit in like they had always been there. Izzy enjoyed it, though she still wanted to go away. As they sipped their coffee at the end of the meal, Izzy said, "I'm heading out today to Jesse's cabin. We need to cover details like the cattle he wants to buy and getting the land ready for them."

Francesca looked at her. "Do you have to leave?"

Izzy sighed. "It might be easier for me not to be here all the time because I will be married soon." When she saw Francesca worry, she added, "I will visit. If I leave early in the morning, I will be here for supper, so I will be back in the spring through the fall till it gets too cold to move." She made a face and Francesca smiled, her head still lowered.

Andrew looked at her. "You think you will be alright making that long trip?"

Izzy rolled her eyes. "I have been farther by myself."

Andrew just nodded. "Be careful."

"I always am." Izzy said.

As they cleaned up, the men left to look over the land and make plans.

In the kitchen, Annie tried to not look miffed about this change. She finally said, "Why do you have to leave now? We just got here."

Francesca said under her breath, "Why do ya think she is leavin'."

Izzy looked at her hard like she'd have her hide if she said another word. She shrugged. "I need to get stuff down before winter starts, and we need to talk about those things."

"It's burning hot out right now and you are talking about winter."

Izzy turned her back to her while she got food together, trying to remember what Jesse had brought. "Winter comes early here especially in the mountains. You got married without me knowing. Why should you care if I leave or not?"

Annie gasped. "I thought you were happy I got married."

Izzy shrugged. "I am." Her eyes darkened. "How did Cole and Julia react to not being at the wedding?"

Annie smiled. "They were happy for us like I thought you would be."

Izzy looked to Gloria and signed, *Answer me honestly, did Julia handle it well?*

Gloria looked uncomfortable but looked Izzy in the eyes. *It hurt Julia,* she signed and gave her a sad smile that said she'd known Izzy would be hurt too.

Annie looked at Gloria. "Don't talk when I can't understand you. It's rude, Gloria."

Izzy just shrugged and put her stuff in the bag. "You should have learned it."

"Why? You and Cole were never around long enough to teach it. You were off saving the world," Annie snapped.

Izzy looked at Francesca, then hard at Annie. "We stayed home when we could, but we had to help others and not sit back in that wayward town."

"Even if it cost you..." Annie didn't finish.

Izzy glared while keeping her voice even. "Yes, I would do it again and again." She glanced at the girls who just stared at them, showing no emotion.

Looking at Francesca, Izzy's heart stung. She couldn't handle this anymore — it was too much. Walking out, she shut the screen door behind her.

She stopped when she heard Francesca shout at Annie, "You have no right to say that to your sister. She is the most wonderful woman I have ever met. She would do anything for anyone and you know what? She even loves you, though I do not understand why."

Katrina stepped in, "Francesca, stop. This is between Annie and Izzy. If you would like to say something to Annie, do it respectfully."

Francesca must have been livid. "Ma, you don't understand. I know what Izzy has to live with every day! But at least I don't get family rejecting me yet." She swore at Annie. "I am sure glad Cole is a better siblin' than you. She talks about him and all he has done, but she has mentioned you like twice. I know why now."

Izzy started walking when she heard Francesca slam the door behind her. She shouldn't have gotten angry. It was bad for the girls. But at least they knew the family wasn't perfect, which she was sure they had thought before.

She saddled Phoenix, deciding it would be faster on just one horse.

Francesca walked up behind her, then started helping without saying anything.

Exhausted although it was still morning, Izzy spoke softly, "I started going into brothels, villages, cat houses, and anywhere there might be a slave. Then Cole and I would buy them or steal them from their abuser. We did it all over Texas and the West. I felt good doing it, like I was making something good out of the mess my grandparents caused, but we got cocky and sloppy. We bought women from a man known as Cutty. We planned to go into hiding after this, but Cole wanted to do another rescue first. My cousin agreed and of course I never said no. However, I had a bad feeling about it…" Izzy put her hand on the saddle horn and her eyes burned into it like it held a message. "We stayed in a hotel, when my mom and sister came into town to try to convince us to stop before we got hurt or worse." She made a sarcastic sound. "You know us, we were never going to get hurt. We were too powerful." Her face went pale and she said right above a whisper, "After my mom wouldn't stop nagging me, I walked into the hall to Cole's room. He was coming out to meet me when the men showed up out of nowhere. Before I could get away, they put a bag over my head and the world went black." She moaned. "I woke up and you could only imagine what I faced for a month." She refused to let a tear fall. "We looked for him for years after I escaped, but we found nothing. I told Cole to stop so we could get on with his life. Cutty was never caught."

Francesca just stood in shock, not moving, her face pale, eyes moist. Her jaw was hard. "When I was little, I wanted you to rescue me. I heard of you. They said an Angel and a Knight would come rescue us and give us all families. When you stopped rescuing, I became more hopeless. I thought you gave up, moved on, or got killed."

Izzy took her hand. "I wish I could have rescued you, Fran." She wiped her moist eyes. She knew how to hold off the tears. "I might not have been able to rescue you, but you came to be my family anyway."

Francesca's face showed all her emotion, bitterness, anger, and longing. So much longing at what was lost. "If you never got a thank you before, thank you, Izzy, for doing it. For loving people you don't even know. For saving lives." She waited so long that Izzy didn't think she would say it. "I love you."

Izzy hugged her for a long time. "I love you, Franny." She mounted and waved as she rode away. Still holding off her tears until she got to the mountain.

Chapter 16

"How are you doing, Ma?" Susan asked her mother as she visited with Mary. Susan was sitting in the parlor of the plantation house her parents owned. Susan had never thought her parent's parlor was big, but it was twice the size of her kitchen and dining room. Even though they were from the north, they now fit in the South very well.

"I am doing well, Susan." Her mother, Hannah, was still a young woman with jet black hair and piercing blue eyes. However, she was a hard woman in that everything had to go well and look good. She had wanted her only daughter to marry well and wealthy. Instead, she had married a deputy who no one liked. It was not what she wanted for her only daughter, and Susan knew that. She looked down at the baby in the basket. "Who is this?"

Susan picked up Mary out of the basket and expected her to arch her back and try to pull away from any touch, but this time she stayed relaxed in her arms. "This is Mary, she's around nine months to a year old."

"She's pretty." Hannah said like she didn't mean it. "What do you plan to do with her?"

"Well, Matt and I are going to adopt and raise her." Susan told her cautiously. She sat on the couch.

"Raise her for how long?" Hannah asked like they were going to send her back in a couple of days. She also sat across from Susan.

Susan retorted, "Until she is of age or out of the house."

Hannah looked at her like she was crazy. "It's all right. I know your husband put you up to this. He is a bastard orphan and needs to save others."

"Mother, don't call Matt that. He is my husband," Susan told her. "And this is my daughter. It is my idea. When Julia and Cole came back, Matt and I chose to take her in. It was my choice just as much as it was his." She paused. "We should have told you sooner. I know this came as a shock. I wanted you to love her and treat her like your grandchild."

"Well, I would, my dear, if she was my grandchild, but she is not. Where did she come from, anyway? Who are her parents? You know nothing of this child?"

Susan knew this was going badly and she did not see it going any better. "I know she is my daughter, Mary Starry. She will be raised by Matt and Susan Starry. She will have many loving uncles, aunts, and cousins, and have grandparents."

Hannah almost glared at her daughter. "Why are you doing this? Out of pity for your man?"

"No, mamma." Her mother shocked her. Was her mother this way before she married Matt? She had changed so much, she hadn't seen how close-minded her own mother was. The Starrys dealt with this every day. It was exhausting. "I love my daughter and I want to raise her. It might be hard, but I feel God calling me to do it. I have been talking to Matt about when we move to Colorado territory to live on Liberty Ranch with the Donovans and some of the Starrys."

"Move to Colorado? You are still thinking of moving there? Why in heavens would you want to move even more into the west, with no civilians at all out there?" Her voice became high pitched.

Susan tried to explain. "At Liberty Ranch we will help orphans or touched children and their families get help and healing."

Hannah looked at her daughter like she had grown two heads. "How could you do this? What if the people don't have enough money to travel?"

Susan hadn't thought of that. "I must talk to Matt about that. He wants to be the pastor there. Juan Jose, Cole's cousin, is going to train him and he is doing ministry part-time while being a deputy. Matt is a Godly man who wants to preach his word."

"So you are serious about this? You want to move to God knows where to help kept children."

"Ma, don't call them that. They are God's children, just had a harder life is all."

"Like that clan you married into."

"Yes, just like the Starry Yankees," Susan told her. "Some of the family is already there. Sawyer and his wife, Annie, Gloria with her husband Jerry, are leaving next week. It means more work for deputy Job, but it will be fine. We hope to move there by late summer or early fall, before the heavy snow falls. I have missed having snow for Christmas."

"You're moving for snow! It is so hard to live in the West. Why would you want that? You won't be able to have servants or as many hired hands as we have here." Hannah spread out her hands as if showing her all she was missing.

"I would never use servants here, anyway. It might be hard, mamma, but my husband wants to go and so do I. I want to have a church family again." Susan had missed her church family since leaving the north.

"If you hadn't married into that family, you would have friends and be a part of the social crowd," Hannah told her like she had a dozen times before.

"Mamma, I don't want those kinds of friends and I would choose my family over that any day. Sometimes it's difficult, but I have come to love them so much." Susan thought of a way to make peace and make her mother happy. "Why don't you come over to my house on Monday night?"

"You mean to the sheriff's office?"

"Yes, were we live," Susan told her, suddenly tired of all the years of being her perfect daughter until now. She knew then what she wanted. She wanted Matt and his way of life. And she would never regret marrying him, choosing his family. "We can eat on the back porch. It is so nice out there and you can try my sweet tea. I almost make it as well Julia."

"Matt says your tea isn't good?"

Susan covered a sigh. "Of course not. He just knows his sister's tea is better."

"Fine, your father and I will come, but don't expect me to call or treat this grandchild as my own." She added, "Now when you start a proper family, I will love my real grandchildren."

Susan stood up, knowing she couldn't take much more of this. She needed to leave. She went to the door. "Thank you, mother, for coming to my humble house." She left too fast for her mother to say anything in return, which was her plan. She would have a good cry at home, trusting their old mare to get her home. This hadn't gone well at all.

Susan was so excited about her mother coming, yet nervous.

However, she was also disappointed, but not surprised, that her father wasn't coming. He had missed most of her childhood due to work. Her small house was spotless and neat; she had done supper perfectly and it was ready when her mother got there. However, Susan was still all nerves. She had finished feeding Mary when Matt walked in from the front door. He was off duty, while Cole and Maverick still worked. She was so glad to see him because she didn't want to be home alone when her mother came.

She put Mary in the crib, then let Matt pull her into a hug. "How is my wife?"

She smiled. "Feeling better now that you are here. I just don't want my mother to say those things again."

"I won't let her," Matt said firmly but gently. "I think she will try to keep peace for now." He looked down at her. "She came to our wedding, which surprised me."

"So was I." She paused. "Most of her friends didn't come."

"What about your friends? Did they come?" He grinned.

"Yup, all twenty-one of them." She kissed him. "I loved having them all."

Matt laughed and kissed her. "I love you, Sue."

Before she could respond, they heard a knock on the back door. Most of the Starrys came through the front door to see them all and then walked through the office to the back.

Matt opened the door and greeted Hannah, then they sat in the parlor as Susan checked on supper. Matt picked up Mary. He didn't ask his mother-in-law if she would like to hold her. Instead, he decided to make small talk and he wasn't good at it. He almost sighed when Susan said supper was ready.

As they settled in, Hannah asked why they didn't put that child in the highchair.

"I was just going to feed her a bottle, but she just ate so she should be good for a bit," Susan explained. "We like to hold her as much as possible, and she doesn't like the chair."

"Well, make her like it; you can't hold her forever," Hannah responded.

Susan said nothing, thinking this was going to be a long evening. She warmed milk for Mary and fed her when they all sat in the parlor after supper.

"What kind of milk is that?" Hannah asked as she looked at the child like she would give her the fever.

"Goat's milk. We buy it from a farm next to Silkwood."

Hannah grunted. "You should use cow's milk."

Susan looked at Matt with long eyes, and he gave her a compassionate look. How could her mother be this hard? Had she always been this way and Susan just hadn't noticed? Just then, Mary pushed the bottle out and screamed.

Hannah looked at the child, disgusted.

Susan just got up and excused herself, knowing it would take a while for this one to end, and went to the bedroom.

She prayed Matt could handle her mother until she got back. She then began to sing to her baby; she loved lullabies. Her nannies had sung to her, but her baby would not get nannies. She would be her mother forever and never pass her on to nannies while she was busy in society.

Matt heard his wife singing over their child's cry. He loved when she sang to their daughter. He had never heard a lullaby as a child. He loved that he was giving his child a chance to hear a lullaby. It was the little things that made him love being a father. He hoped he was a good one, he prayed. If he was just a little like Ben, then he would be great.

"She really loves that child," Hannah mumbled, more than she had said anything that night.

He nodded. "We both do."

"Why?" she hissed, like they loved someone horrible.

"She is our baby daughter. We are raising her. Do we need another reason?" He added in a soft voice, "I love her so I can sing her lullabies." He knew his mother-in-law hadn't sung lullabies, nannies had. "It's never too late to learn."

"Yes, it is too late." She frowned at him. "I don't want you taking my daughter to Colorado or anywhere. You never told me you were going to leave before you married her. Or was that your plan?"

Matt sat up. "No, Ma'am. I did not do that, but Susan and I have been talkin' and we want to raise our daughter, our future children. We reckon we need a new start. And the family agreed on Colorado." He noticed the baby had stopped crying as Susan continued to sing to her.

"Well, I don't care why you are doing it." She told him angrily, "You have no right to take my daughter away from me."

"I am not takin' her away from you. You can visit any time you want, and I am sure we will make it back here." Matt wasn't sure when.

Neither of them wanted to come back to visit, but if Susan wanted to, they would.

Just as Hannah was about to say something, Susan walked out carrying a sleeping baby. She sat down next to Matt, trying to relax.

Hannah glared at them. "This child is going to be the end of both of you. I won't ever see her as my grandchild, and now you are leaving." She stood up, her chest rising and falling in anger. "Susan, I told you this family you married into would destroy you and now look at you. You could have anything." She looked around the small house. "And you have this." She nodded to Susan. "If you want to leave this place, you can always come home. But if you leave for that land full of outlaws, never come home, you will not be welcomed," she shouted. "And neither will your real children. They probably will be touched, like your man and that child."

Susan had tears running down her face as she held her sleeping baby closer.

Matt stood up, holding his temper. "Don't you ever talk to my wife like that again. Her home is with me. Our home is anywhere we are together." He moved closer to her. "And don't you ever call your grandchildren touched ever again. Me, on the other hand, that might be true." He paused, holding his anger. "If you ever speak like this again, you will never come around here again. I am your daughter's husband and that will not change, ever! Do you understand?"

Hannah looked shocked and stared at her daughter with disgust and disbelief.

Susan stood up, standing next to her husband in more than just support. "Mother, I love you. I want you to love me and what I have chosen to do in life. My life is with Matt and Mary."

Hannah looked at her daughter. "Then I guess I got my answer. I will never come back here, or that forsaken land you move too." With that, she stormed out and slammed the door.

Susan sat down as the tears came. Matt took her in his arms with Mary between them. "What will your pa say?"

"He always goes along with mother. He has never cared for me. He wanted me to marry wealthy." She cried to him, trying to not wake Mary.

Matt held her and his daughter; he loved them so much. He would give anything to take away her pain, but only God could heal her. He just prayed, held them, and kissed her head and Mary's head.

Chapter 17

The sun was setting and beginning to disappear behind the trees on the mountains. In Colorado, it was so beautiful, with clear creeks and land as far as an eye can see. It was like Izzy and Jesse were on top of the earth.

Izzy laid against Jesse's chest as he rested against the cabin; she sat between his legs. He smelled of smoke from the fire and wood. His rough hand ran through her curly hair. She enjoyed the feeling. She could even smell the leftover blueberry pie she had made in the dutch oven. That was her way of cooking. The ranch hands had eaten and left to bunk in the barn.

Izzy laced her fingers with Jesse's, then asked ever so gently, "Jesse, can you tell me how you came to live in the asylum?"

Jesse's back went hard, he kept still.

He stayed quiet so long, Izzy wasn't sure he would answer, but he talked in a monotone voice, "I was having a hard time with Ellen. I was always angry, and I honestly hated her sometimes. It was hard because Pedro was better than I was. The war was about to start, and Ellen kept being told her Mexican boys needed a Mexican home. When I kept hearing that I just got worse. I broke Gloria's nose and Maverick nearly killed me, which I deserved. I am ashamed of how I acted now. One night, Ellen fought with Ben, Missy, and Owen. After crying, she told me I was going to a Mexican couple." He cleared his throat. "I was so afraid. Ellen cried many times after that, though she tried to hide the tears. The couple came to pick us up. I don't remember much about the couple, just that they hated the Starrys, which made me angrier. Pedro got sick and he wasn't getting better," he muttered. "The couple hated me, so I arrived at a huge building. It was so cold and full of sick and evil people. They told me I would only stay there for a little while." He made a humorless laugh. "It was hell on earth. After a few months, I ran away. I don't know how I got out, but I did. Ben always said if you got lost, follow the smell of the ocean. I got on a wagon which was headed for Daphne and then I walked home." Letting his hand fall on her shoulder, he continued, "I was filthy, and they didn't care. Ellen just held me. She had prayed for me every day I since I left; she knew I would come home. She had more faith in me than any other woman. I told her about the asylum, though later she knew more through the nightmares." He kissed the back of her head. "I tried to kill myself while living there, but Maverick and Ellen saved my life. I was in a dark place. Julia finally came to me and cried. She didn't cry often, if you remember. She cried for me, 'Killin' yourself is only hurting the ones you leave alive to mourn you. Do you know what we would do without you? We are already missing a family member; we can't lose another. If you want out of this life, go fight in the war where hundreds of men are dying or stay here and live.' Julia really helped like she did to each of us."

"I didn't become a believer until I was sixteen, after moving out of the Starry's house and raising my own crops at my own cabin. That is really when the change started. I let go of a lot of things I held in my heart. God is still workin' on me." He paused. "I am glad I believe because I will see Ellen, Ben, and Missy one day again."

"You will. It gives me hope to see Lucida and Sophia in heaven one day," Izzy told him. They were her friends that were killed months ago. She still missed them and their help with Liberty House. "Thank you for trusting me. I know some things aren't easy to talk about."

"That's the truth, but what could you be hiding?" Jesse teased lightly.

Izzy half laughed. "I am a Cooper. Remember we have things in the closet to fill half of Colorado."

Jesse grunted. "That is probably true, but you're a Donovan now."

"Jesse," she said roughly. All the humor left her voice.

"Yes, my love." He knew she needed him to be serious, and he was, though he did not understand what she would say.

Her back went hard and straight like she was distancing herself from him. "I can't bear children." She could hear the variability in her voice, and it made her feel like shooting something. Tears stung her eyes as she waited for Jesse to respond. it was like her heart stopped and she held her breath. And then he squeezed her hand. It was like an anchor she waited for.

"I am okay with that," he said softly.

Izzy's heart wasn't as ready to believe him. "I know you want children; I can see how you are with children and your younger siblings."

"I do," Jesse admitted. "But I love you and we could always adopt a baby in the spring."

Izzy smiled brightly. Her heart was starting to soften, to trust him. Love was happening for the first time for her. She just hoped it lasted. "I love that idea. It will give us a good start for a little one."

"But I want a baby," he said,. Then he added, softer, "I need time to bond with a baby and understand how to raise one."

Izzy nodded. "I agree."

Jesse ran a hand through her hair. Izzy knew she should tell him about her past, but she couldn't let the words get out. She didn't want to see the shock, disgust, and then pity that would come into his eyes. She knew he might be all right with it. But then he might reject her. What if he didn't love her anymore?

She closed her eyes against the nightmares she had to live with. Jesse wasn't the only one with nightmares. She needed to call it a night. She was so tired that she couldn't think straight, and things went badly when two people weren't thinking. "We should go to sleep. I want to mud the cabin tomorrow with you," she told him sleepily.

"I was thinkin' the same thing." Jesse's voice sounded too light.

Izzy knew what he was getting at. "You are sleepin' in the barn, mister." She said it strong enough for him to get the point.

Jesse grunted. "Did Andrew tell you that?"

"No," she said as she stood up. "We are adults. He wouldn't treat us like children, but I don't want to fall off that cliff."

Jesse stood up and said angrily, "We will be fine. I would never do that." He came up behind her and whispered in her ear, "But doesn't mean we can't dance around it." He kissed her cheek.

She turned around in his arms and frowned. "It means we don't, Jesse."

He just kissed her frown away. "I love you, Izzy," he whispered.

Izzy kissed him back. His arms went around her, holding her so close. She knew she had to stop. He got more passionate.

Izzy finally had enough and pulled away. "I am going to bed. See you in the mornin'."

"One more kiss?" He begged, giving her a flirty wink.

She shook her head but smiled. "Go to bed, Jesse."

Katrina woke up to screaming. She ran to Francesca's new room. They had split Sara's room in half to make one for Francesca. Katrina tried to wake Francesca up while she shook all over. "It's okay, baby girl. It's all right." Taking the girl in her arms, she moved her head before Francesca could hit her. "It's all right, baby. No one can hurt you again. It's okay." She whispered comforting words. It didn't hurt her ears as much as it would others. Maybe the reason she was deaf was to help her screaming children.

As Katrina rocked Francesca back and forth, she thought of how most of her life others had considered her weird for being so tall and built so big. Now she was almost happy because of it. She was strong and could hold her girls where they couldn't hurt themselves or each other. She had never before thought maybe that was why God made her so tall, but He must have planned it. He knew of all she would do in her life.

Finally, Francesca stopped the screaming and then opened her eyes. Her eyes were bloodshot and dilated. When she looked up at Katrina, the only light coming in was the sun beginning to lighten the sky. She closed her eyes again and her face paled.

Katrina did not loosen her hold, Francesca might need to feel this safe.

Francesca sighed and opened her eyes. Her voice was rough, just above a whisper. "I never had nightmares before. Had never had the time to have them. I knew women who had them after leaving that life. I don't know which is worse, living that life in body or living it in my mind."

Katrina kissed her forehead. "We will move on from the nightmares. They will end someday."

Francesca moved from her arms. "How do you know?"

"All of my sisters had them, and I did after the fire for a long time. Giving your fears to God and receiving His everlasting peace is what worked for Julia. And Gloria just had to trust God with all she felt. For me it was forgiveness. Sometimes the nightmares come back to us after, our mind plays games on us, but we heal if we trust and depend on God with our hearts."

"Why doesn't God take it away?" Francesca was waking up.

125

Katrina felt like this was the first time Francesca was open — no sarcasm or anger hiding her true emotions. Katrina said softly, "God heals, but Satan plays with the doubts and replays the nightmares when God has healed our hearts. We have to let go and sometimes the nightmares will stay. I have been getting them bad lately."

"Are your nightmares from takin' us in?" Francesca said sarcastically.

Katrina shook her head. "They've come since we lost Ellen. I wake up crying for her." She felt vulnerable saying that. "Just so you know you're not the only one with nightmares, we all had them."

"Even the boys?" Francesca asked in disgust.

"Yes, the boys were hurt just as us girls."

Francesca looked at her like she couldn't be serious.

"Francesca, some boys hurt just as much as girls. One of the brothers still wears the scars that his drunken father gave him. Another one of them carries around scars on the inside, they cut deep. A big brother still cries for his twin brother. A boy wears scars from a kidnapping that happened to him and his younger sister. Believe me when I tell you that the men in this world wear their own scars. But it also means they are still being healed by the grace of God."

Francesca nodded.

Katrina kissed her forehead. "Go back to sleep. I'll make sure the girls don't wake you up. Get some rest." She got up and shut the door as she left. She decided to just go downstairs and start her day. It was early, but she probably couldn't get back to sleep anyhow, so she might as well get some bread started. She liked when the girls did it with her; they liked to pound and kneed it. She also found it funny when they had flour all over their faces and hands.

Chapter 18

"We want to make sure we don't tax our land with too many cattle. Next year when we get some hay up, we can get more, but we got too late of a start this summer," Izzy told Jesse as they sat around the fire eating supper. It had been fun working with him and it gave her a glimpse of what their future would look like. Izzy was becoming open and honest with herself. He could see it as well. He just remembered to keep her trust so that light would always stay in her eyes.

Jesse nodded in agreement. "You know this land more than I do, so I guess I better listen to you."

Izzy laughed. "I can get used to hearing that."

Jesse made a face. "Don't get too used to it, I won't say that too often." He put another biscuit in his mouth. "Izzy, you got to be the best cook ever."

Izzy raised a brow. "You have Julia who knows how to cook as well. I can't match her."

Jesse shook his head. "I can taste your food. Julia's food is so hot. After my mouth stops burning, there is no more taste. You cook like Gloria, though she has a sweet tooth."

"I know the way to a man's heart is through his stomach." Izzy laughed, feeling a sense of playfulness she hadn't felt in a long time.

Jesse said playfully, "Let me show you the way to my heart."

Izzy made a shocked face, but got up and ran into the cabin, laughing all the while. The cabin wasn't that big, so she stopped at the sink as Jesse's arms came around her. He took out the hair clips and her hair fell in a mass around her shoulders.

She moved out of his arms, needing room to breathe. She looked around what would be her home for the rest of life. "When we add another room for our future children and maybe even a guest room, it should be on this wall." The cabin held a large bed on the left side of the door and a big fireplace. The kitchen held a stove he had brought from town on his last trip. There was also a sink, but no pump yet. Talking about the house helped him refrain from kissing her.

127

Jesse watched as Izzy talked about the house. She was his life. The reason he had made the cabin was for her and their future children. He didn't mind if they had to adopt a Mexican baby. He had hoped to have his own, but he couldn't give up a woman like Izzy. No one had ever wanted him, but she really accepted him.

He felt a voice tell him he should leave. It was getting dark, and he hadn't slept well. He never slept well after talking or thinking about his past. From the look on Izzy's face, she hadn't slept much either. She drank nearly two entire pots of coffee by herself.

Leave now. I provide a way from temptation. Take it and leave.

He frowned. He could handle himself. He wouldn't fall off the edge, and he was strong enough. Anyway, now that Izzy couldn't bear children, if they did something, she wouldn't be with his child. He shoved that thought away. He would never do that to his Izzy. She was the one good thing in his life. And if he did, he couldn't bear the look that would come from Julia's eyes or the anger from Maverick. Cole would probably kill him. There were things you just couldn't cross in the Starry family and he had crossed almost all of them. However, doing this with Izzy would be the end of his family being there for him. He couldn't lose them, so he just wouldn't.

She is My Beloved Daughter and you are My beloved Son; remember to honor My ways. Love is patient.

He ignored the voice. He didn't care what anyone had to say. He would give her one last kiss. Then head out to the cold barn.

He started walking towards her with such an intense look in his eyes, Izzy knew she should send him to the barn for the night. It wasn't right being alone this late. It was like falling off that cliff Andrew talked about. To make it worse, she hadn't gotten much sleep last night. She couldn't keep living off of a few hours of sleep. "Jesse, we should go to bed," she told him.

"Just one last kiss then." He smiled and took her in his arms.

She kissed him back, feeling his passion more than last night. She got lost in his kiss. She knew this wasn't right. She told herself to stop. She didn't really have a desire to be with him, just like she had told Francesca, but she wanted to feel loved for once in her life. She wanted to know what it felt like to be treasured by a man.

His kisses got deeper, as his hands tangled her hair. She finally snapped and pushed him away, but he didn't move.

"Izzy, I love you more than I ever loved anyone," he said breathy, and kissed her again.

She kissed him back and let herself get lost in his arms, forgetting everything she knew to be right, keeping the thought that she wanted to be loved and feel love in her heart. She gave him her body, but she kept her heart far from him.

In the barn, Izzy felt every part of a fool. How could she have done that? Defiled herself. Forsaken all she believed in. After brushing Phoenix, she saddled him. Hearing Jesse come in, she ignored him.

He started, "Izzy, I am so sorry. I never should have..." He cleared his throat. "I'm sorry. I should have never done that to you."

She put the bridle on and said nothing.

"I am sorry," he pleaded. "What else do you want me to say?"

She turned to him and glared. "Did you do it because you know I can't bear your children? That no consequence could come from this?"

The look of guilt on his face showed too much and then shock. "No, Izzy that was not it. I was a fool. I thought I was strong enough. But I ain't strong. I should have treated you like the maiden you are."

She looked at him in disgust. If he only knew. His words meant nothing. She had also been a fool. It wasn't only Jesse, it was her too. She shouldn't let herself be in that position. Andrew was right. They had walked and danced around the cliff until they fell off. The fall left her feeling ashamed and cheap. She mounted the horse, ready to take off.

He walked up to her and took Phoenix's reins. "Izzy, please let's talk about this."

She let the tears run down her face. "I can't." She wiped her eyes. "Let go, Jesse."

"But we need to talk." He tried again.

She wiped at the tears so she could see him. "No." Phoenix took a bite at Jesse's arm. He let go. Taking off at a full-speed run, she didn't look back. Digging her fingers in Phoenix's white mane, she let his mane dry her tears. Remember how Phoenix came to have his name — rising above ashes. She was in ashes when Phoenix found her and now she was in ashes again. This time by her own making.

Jesse watched Izzy ride away as her hair blew in the wind and her skirt flared from the ground-eating gait. She ran like he had burned her. She ran away from him, and that hurt more than he could explain.

How could he have been so stupid, thinking he could do anything? He had been such a fool, Ellen would have told him that. He would have gotten on a train to Alabama to talk to her. She was one woman who would have listened and tried to fix his problems. He hadn't mourned her death, and now he ached to talk to her one more time. He just wanted to feel her motherly touch on his face. He longed to see the look in her eyes that she really loved him. Ellen cared for him even after knowing all that he had done. She was the one woman who loved him unconditionally and could make his heart soft again.

Jesse didn't want to grieve losing her, but it had caught up with him. It was one reason he had left Alabama — to get away from the memories. He needed time because every time he saw her children he thought of her. Every time he looked in Charity's eyes, he saw Ellen.

Now Jesse had made the biggest mistake in his life and she wasn't there to help him through it. He knew the family might assist him, but he wanted an adult to help him out. Suddenly, the image of Mabel came to mind. She had a way about her that looked right through him like Ellen had. He ignored it. Mabel could never take Ellen's place.

Jesse fell to his knees and wept for making Izzy feel used and for not treasuring her. He also cried for his mother that he would never see again.

Chapter 19

Katrina could tell this would be a long day the minute she didn't find Francesca and Sara in their rooms. However, she found Carlissa still sleeping.

When she didn't find Francesca and Sara in the barn, she went straight to Andrew. This was a runaway. However, it didn't come as a surprise to her; the girls were pushing their limits with Katrina and Andrew to see whether the Starrys would go after them. After the last few nights of Francesca's nightmares, she was bound to run away.

Andrew was in the kitchen. "Andrew, Sara and Francesca have run away!"

Andrew looked up in surprise. "Are you sure?"

She nodded. "My guess is that they couldn't get Carlissa past our bedroom."

"I should have heard them." He ran a hand through his hair.

Izzy walked in from her room, dressed in her ranch clothes — a big shirt and divided skirt. She had been back for a couple of days and was very quiet. "This is bad if Sara gets caught by the asylum. Liberty House got her out of it, but there would be no way to get her out again. Francesca probably wouldn't go back to Denver, but it doesn't take a bright person to find out what she was from."

Andrew nodded. "I'll find them." They knew he had gone to find his brothers because that is what the Starrys did.

Katrina sat on a chair by the table. "What if the Starrys can't find them?"

Izzy went over to her. "Pull yourself together. Andrew and the Starry brothers will bring them home. I will go look for them as well, but it would be good if you stayed with Carlissa. She doesn't know Annie or Gloria enough to stay with them, but she might stay with Mabel." Izzy began operating like she had done this before. "Just make everythin' stay normal. I'll run by and tell Mabel, but don't let another soul know that the girls are gone."

Katrina nodded. One of her worst fears came true. What if the saloon owner came for the girls? Sara would be trapped in that saloon life. What if a bad, vile cowboy found them? The way Francesca acted had her worried. *Oh, God, keep my babies safe. What if...*

Izzy made her look at her. "Katrina, snap out of it. We will find your girls."

Katrina nodded. Her mind cleared. "I can do this. Find my babies."

Izzy headed out the door, ready for a lengthy ride. These girls knew how to hide, and they didn't want to be found.

Andrew had searched for children and women for years, but never thought he would have to do it for his own daughter. Andrew tried to imagine the lies Francesca and Sara believed in order for them to go back to the saloon. Walking in, he looked at the men of all ages and races looking to fulfill a need that only God could touch. He saw all the saloon girls that got caught in this saloon life because of lies, deceit, or just for the money. He saw the emptiness in their eyes. Again, only an emptiness God could fill.

He walked up to the bar, looking like a normal cowpoke, only with a full beard. He kept his eyes from searching for her too much. He didn't want to raise suspicion. He never planned to do it this close to Deer Trail; it was dangerous. Dangerous for his reputation and if the saloon owner came back for her.

"Whaddaya want, mister?" The bartender asked.

"Straight whiskey." His voice had no accent. "And some company if I can." He cleared his throat. "A young Mexican girl."

The bartender poured his whiskey and smiled, his brown teeth showing over his full beard. "I got a couple of those. They came from Texas, didn't you know? A young one came in last night, but she won't let a man touch her yet. She just wants to serve. Like that will happen for long." He gave a humorless laugh. "She ain't fresh, I can tell you that. But she ain't too used up." He whistled and called out, "Franny, got a man interested."

Andrew was careful to hide his face, but he saw her walking up and looking as mad as a wet hen. "Whata yaw want? I told you I ain't ready for that!" Francesca spat. They did her hair up in curls, which made her look like a child who got into her mother's powder and curlers. However, her dress fit like a second skin. She had gained weight while living at the ranch.

The bartender raised his arm, but Francesca put her arms up to protect herself. Andrew was faster than Francesca and pulled her back so the man hit Andrew in the arm instead. It didn't even make Andrew flinch, but would have hurt Francesca's tender skin. He glared at the bartender.

Francesca looked up at him. Her eyes widened even as she stepped closer to him.

"I like treating my own women my way." Andrew spat at him. He looked at Francesca, and hated doing this. "You will do. Come with me."

Francesca's eyes got wider. She bit her lip, and Andrew could feel her shaking under his arm. He prayed like never before. *God help her.* He felt weak in the knees. He hated doing this to his little girl, but God gave him a peace like he had never felt before. He could do this to save her — even from herself.

He put more than enough money on the counter and pulled her roughly into the back room. He hoped there was a back door or window. He didn't want to take her out the front door. He knew she might be too afraid to go. She was used to men's control. In her mind she thought they were saving her. He knew what the room would be like before he entered it. It would have a small horsehair bed, a nightstand with a wash bucket, and maybe a rug on the ground. As they entered, he was right, only this room smelled of cheap whiskey and who knows what else. Right away, Francesca ran from him and leaned against the wall. Her whole body was shaking. Andrew had to ignore her and went to the only window in the room; it was locked and boarded up well. "If you wanted me, Andrew, why didn't you just do it at the ranch? Were you afraid Katrina would find out?!" Francesca spat at him. "Why pay to have me now?"

He glanced over his shoulder to find her glaring at him, blood running from her lip to her chin. "I will not touch you, sweetie." He touched her arm. "Do you want to go home?"

She looked up at him. Her eyes wide. He could hardly see a nod. But that was enough for him to get to work. "I need you to start crying and make it loud."

She looked confused. "I don't cry."

He didn't argue with her. When he had passed her bedroom on

other nights, however, he would often hear her sobbing in her sleep. He wasn't about to tell her. "Well, then act. You are pretty good at acting."

She gave him a small smile. "You got that right." She winked at him. "I learn from the best." She leaned against the door and started to cry.

Andrew turned to face the window. He looked towards her and nodded for her to get louder. When she let out a scream, he ripped off two boards. He set them down softly and kept on working while Francesca cried. He had to shut down his feelings as he listened to her cry because he knew this wasn't the first time they had hurt her. The pain she felt was so great, not even tears could wash it away. Taking his knife, he broke the window seal and slowly opened the window only to find more boards. He felt like swearing. If girls wanted to work at the saloon, why lock them up?

He moved fast and got the boards down. Francesca ran to him. He helped her out, and then got out himself, which wasn't easy for his big size. He felt his back rip open. Ignoring it, he took Francesca's hand and ran to the back alley where his horses stood. He picked her up and set her on a horse. Mounting his own horse, he took the lead and ran at a ground-eating gait.

Andrew looked behind and knew they had to stop. Francesca's hair was a mess, her makeup ran down her tired face, and her head was bobbing like she was about to fall asleep. He had found Sara early and left her deep in the woods. Dismounting he walked over to Francesca, he reached up to help her. She pulled on his full beard. "Where did you get this thing?"

"It grew quickly." He shrugged. He took off the full beard and mustache. He would wash the grease paint off later. "It works for what I need."

"I almost didn't recognize you, but it was your eyes that revealed your identity."

Andrew nodded and helped her down. "I walked past Katrina dressed like this once, and she didn't know a thing. In the South I dress fancy."

She looked confused. "Kat doesn't know what you do?"

Andrew shrugged again. Taking his jacket off, he put it around her shoulders. It went to her knees. Then he took off the horse's tack. "Yes, she knows," he drawled. "Will you start a fire, Fran?"

Putting her arms in the warm coat, she frowned as she spotted something on his back. She decided to gather some sticks instead of mentioning it.

When Andrew finished, Sara came out from behind the trees. Her eyes widened at the sight of him.

Andrew just let them wonder and got the food started. "We will stay the night here. It's too late to start back now." It wasn't really but the girls needed a break.

"How long have you been doin' this?" Francesca asked as she sat by the fire.

"Long enough," he answered.

"Your voice, how do you change it?" Francesca seemed interested in this.

"Decades of training," Andrew muttered. "You can't tell a soul what you saw today, you know that right."

Sara gasps and nodded.

Francesca shrugged. "I won't. No one would believe me anyhow."

Andrew agreed with that. To the world, he was easygoing and fun. It was a good cover. In work he was confident and could outsmart nearly anyone.

Francesca moved closer to him and muttered, "Your back. You got a cut."

Andrew looked around and couldn't see it, so he pulled up his shirt to see blood over it.

Sara gasped and turned away, hiding her face.

Andrew knew it was the scars and not the blood that made her ill. He handed Francesca the canteen and a clean rag that he had brought in case the girls got hurt. "Would you mind putting this on it? Katrina will fix it up when I get back."

Francesca hesitantly took the bottle and started to clean the wound. Her hands shook as she gently pressed the rag to it. "The scars are everywhere."

Andrew nodded. "They hurt for years. I was blessed that they didn't go deep." Not like Katrina's who still had pain.

Francesca swore. "How did you get over what they did to you?"

Francesca was gentle, but it still stung. He bit his cheek. "I had to let go of the bitterness. It only hurt me. Bitterness is like givin' yourself poison and expectin' the other person to die."

Francesca dried the wound. "You're lucky it didn't go that deep. I have seen worse." Taking a strip of cloth, she wrapped it around him a couple times. "If I had Katrina's dress on, I could rip some cloth off and wrap it more." She moved her leg out to where she got more

135

comfortable. "If I did it in this dress, I wouldn't be wearing anything."

Andrew didn't answer. She didn't need one. She was trying to flirt with him, but he wouldn't have it. When she finished, he dished out the food. As he prayed for the meal aloud he silently prayed that his girls would be free of the lies men held them in.

Chapter 20

Andrew walked into the barn because he couldn't handle the emotions in the house a second longer. Katrina kept checking on the girls to see if they would run away, while looking like she would burst into tears. Sara was angry and moody and Carlissa just kept sobbing. Izzy, while the normally calm one, was also having as bad a day as the rest of the ladies. He wondered if they had adopted a boy instead, would life be calmer? Nah, probably not.

Yesterday, when he came home, Katrina had hugged the girls for way too long, while Izzy looked at his face and she knew where he found Francesca. He was sure it made her sick.

He remembered how Katrina sat at the table sipping coffee, glancing up at him, expecting him to tell her everything, but he couldn't. No words could describe the pain he felt. He shook his head and turned, feeling bruised all over. He hadn't felt this beaten in a long time.

Katrina stopped him. "You're bleeding."

He glanced at her concerned face, and then looked at Izzy, who also looked scared. Izzy's eyes showed a deep sadness that only they could understand. She knew what he saw in the saloon and her awareness made him angrier. He didn't want her to know what he had seen. No woman should have to experience a brothel or saloon. He frowned. "I'll go change. It's just a scratch." He walked to his room, hoping Katrina wouldn't follow. He didn't feel safe with anyone.

In his room, he dropped by the bed and washed away his pain. He shed tears for a daughter who couldn't be a child ever again. He cried out to God in his heart, to take away the hate for those men who hurt his little girl. He asked God to keep letting him love Francesca despite her mistakes and to heal him over losing Clara. He would make sure Francesca would get the chance that Clara never received.

Leaving his memories he opened his eyes, he spotted Francesca mucking out her stall.

"Saddle up. I want to show you something," he told her.

She looked at him questioningly.

He nodded. "Just do it."

Francesca nodded. Her curiosity got the best of her.

In ten minutes, they were riding out of the ranch yard. When they reached the woods going up the hill, Francesca couldn't handle it anymore. "So where are we going?"

"It's a surprise," he stated.

She made a face. "I don't like surprises. They end badly for me."

He shook his head, not bothered by her. "This ain't a bad one, just trust me."

For the next three hours Francesca rode on Poder. She enjoyed moving with his gait and feeling his power. He made her feel safe though he was grumpy. She listened to the woods speak to her. She had learned a lot about the land and she came to love the beauty of it. No loud, aggressive, vile men. No smell of beer and smoke, and no sad-looking women.

Finally, they came to such a wide clearing of green grass and trees that she couldn't see to the other side. Andrew dismounted and tied Blade to a tree.

Francesca did the same, as her shaky legs followed Andrew. He walked through the trees. She caught her breath. The mountains were so high that she could see the snow that always hung on them, as well as the rolling hills spread out below. From her view, she could also see Deer Trail and Liberty Ranch in the far distance. Not taking her eyes off of the view, she leaned against a tree.

Andrew said nothing for some time. "I thought the same thing when Katrina and I saw this, the first day we got to the ranch. Julia would say it's God's most beautiful canvas."

Francesca looked down as she moved her booted foot along the rock and sighed. "So much beauty and evil in the same place."

Andrew nodded. "We humans make a mess of this life, that is for sure." He chose his words carefully. "Francesca, look at me."

She obeyed, feeling uncomfortable.

"Why did you run away?" he asked gently.

She flinched and shrugged. "I don't know."

"Yes, you do." He urged again, "Why?"

She looked out at the mountains. She didn't want to talk about it with him.

"Answer me, Francesca."

She glared at the mountains and her mouth set in a firm line, saying nothing.

"You know why I think you ran away? Because you are afraid that we won't love you when we find out what you have done. Or is it that you are afraid that a man from the past will come and make our life hard?"

Francesca's eyes flew to him. How did he know that?

"I am right?" Andrew knew he was. "Darlin,' why would we hold it against you when Jesus doesn't? We love you. What can we do to prove we love you and always will?"

Francesca glared at him. "You think my past wouldn't matter in your eyes." She swore. "You gotta be lying to yourself."

"No, child, I am not. I am trustin' in Jesus to show me how to love you properly. To show you real love." Andrew walked a little closer and leaned against a tree. He acted like he didn't have a care in the world.

Francesca glared at him. "You think you love me. You don't know me. I have been hiding like I always do."

"You might hide your true self, but I want to know who you are." He cleared his throat. "You can't keep running away. I will come after you forever, but there will come a day where I can't bring you home. It has to be your choice."

Francesca frowned. "I heard that your parents always went after you."

He nodded. "They came after us. However, when I ran they didn't come after me because it was too dangerous and I knew it."

She looked out at the view. She couldn't take much more of this.

"I kept goin' back to my old life because it was what I was used to. The feeling of family and havin' a mother scared me more than danger. Ellen prayed for me every day. Ben visited when he could. But it was my choice, and I was makin' stupid decisions. I had never been so unhappy." His eyes were moist. "Finally, a little blond mute girl gave me something."

"Katrina?" Francesca was sure of it as she watched him.

Andrew shook his head. He went back to the horses and came back with saddlebags. He took what looked like a picture. "Julia is the sweetest little mute girl I have ever met. She never said much, but she handed me this picture and told me two words — come home."

Francesca took the picture. It was beautiful drawing of all the Starry children. She could see they looked like the ones she had met. The edge of the paper looked like something had burned it. The frame and glass looked new. "Who drew this?"

"My eleven-year-old sister, Julia."

Francesca looked up at him in shock.

"Yup." He smiled. "She was good even then. She is the one who got me to come home with those two small words. It took me a while to become a Christian."

She gave him an amused hard look. "Why? Were you just being stubborn like every other Starry?"

He chuckled. "Probably. But I think it was because we needed time to understand what God did for us. We had to come at our own time and not be pressured into it. It needed to be us wanting it and not our parents doing it for us."

She raised an eyebrow. "You don't think you are pressuring us girls to believe?"

He shook his head. "We are trying not to. What Kat and I want to show you is that God loves you. He died for you and wants to heal you." He frowned. "We might have been too stubborn to believe God at first too, but it hurt us by not trustin' Him."

Francesca handed the picture back. "God would shut me out if I went to Him with my sins."

Andrew shook his head in disagreement. "No, my child. He knows about your sins already. He loves you despite knowing them. I know what it's like to be afraid of not being enough in front of good people and a perfect, loving God. All it takes is trusting Him. He will make you a new person on the inside."

"It can't be that easy, nothing is that easy." Francesca shook her head and looked away into the woods.

Andrew shook his head. "But it is that easy. God did the hard stuff for us, He paid that price."

Francesca shook a little. "No, if He knew what I have done. How used up I am."

Andrew stood in front of her, not touching her. "Honey, Jesus knows all those inappropriate situations men put you in. He also gives you the grace to handle the memories of that time. He loved you before you were in your mother's womb. He will always love you, child."

Francesca fell to her knees and cried out, "Where was He when I went through hell? Where was He when a man took me at seven?

140

Where was He when I was sold at eleven? Where was He when the matron took my babies from my body!" She held her stomach where her babies were ripped from her. Her heart split open.

Andrew kneeled by her, being careful how he touched her. She might shrink back more. His heart cried out to her, "He was right there and His heart was breakin' with you, child. He was there through it all. He never stopped lovin' you and being there. He sent you to me. He gave me a daughter I always prayed for." Tears ran down his face. "I love you so much, Francesca."

Francesca glared at him. "How can you feel anything for me when you know what I am?"

Andrew took a chance and took her small hands in his large ones. "I know who you are. You are my daughter. And you are the daughter of the Kings of kings and Lord of lords. You love to cook, you have learned to ride like an angel, you are funny, honest, and you say whatever pops into that pretty head of yours. I love all those things about you. That is who Francesca Starry is to me."

Francesca stared at him in shock. He was crying for her. She had never had someone cry for her, not anyone. She had never felt so valuable and open. It was an unfamiliar feeling and she hated it. Her voice was hard. "You will see one day you are wrong."

Andrew showed he loved her with his eyes. "No, daughter. You will see I am right."

Chapter 21

Katrina woke up listening to Andrew softly snore beside her. Dressing in a light, navy blue dress with frills at the bottom, she tied her hair into a tight bun as she made her way to the kitchen. Starting the first pot of coffee for the day, she thought, Today might go as bad as yesterday.

Carlissa had a "terror," which is what Katrina called it. It had happened right before supper and lasted till long after bedtime. Katrina still wore the bruise on her cheek from Carlissa's elbow. Andrew had not been happy about it, but Katrina did not know what to do next. She just wanted help for them. Maybe she could go to Mabel's and see if she could get advice, though Andrew had not wanted to get help from them. Wasn't that why they built the ranch, to get help from others and to help others? She knew his reluctance to ask for help had to do with their pasts. She didn't know how to help him get over what Frank did to them. Normally she would talk to Ellen about it. Consequently, Katrina still ached to talk to her just one more time.

She saw her old leather Bible on the kitchen table. The beloved book had her name on the cover in gold. She treasured this book given to her by Ellen for her twelfth birthday. She felt guilty she hadn't had time to read it like she should. Ellen had always found the time. Sitting down to read, she knew only God could heal her girls. She certainly couldn't do it. After reading five chapters of Proverbs it made her feel like she could be a parent.

Then she started up donuts and sourdough biscuits. She always enjoyed sweet food. She glanced behind her to see Carlissa walk in the kitchen with her hair ruffled, eyes puffy, and telling Katrina she was about to take on the world.

Katrina sighed on the inside. She should have read the whole Bible, and then maybe she could do this parenting thing right.

Carlissa was worse in the mornings and before almost every meal. Katrina did not know why. She had been trying to watch her girls, to see what made them tick or react. She had come up with nothing, but she wasn't one to give up without a fight. This was a fight she would win. She prayed she would. "Good morning, sweetie," she said cheerfully.

Carlissa grunted to indicate she didn't agree with it being a good morning.

Katrina made sure Carlissa could not touch anything on the stove. In the morning, Carlissa would just grab whatever food was in sight and it was normally hot. This was another behavior she did not understand about Carlissa.

Turning back to put the donuts in the pan, she cracked eggs into a bowl. "If you set the table, girls, then breakfast will be ready in a few minutes. I made some special things this morning." She knew neither girl had tasted donuts before. Another thing she would explain at breakfast. Almost everything they ate was a new experience. She had eaten horrible food in the orphanages. Asylum food had to be so much worse.

Sara obeyed silently.

Carlissa folded her arms and pulled her legs apart from each other like she couldn't move. "I don't want to, Ma. I want to eat now!"

Katrina turned to see Sara had stopped working and planted her feet like she was ready for a fight. Often Sara would play off what the other girls felt. That is why she tried to keep Francesca away from them. She looked at Sara. "Set the table now, Carlissa, you will help," she tried again.

Sara obeyed and got out the silverware, slamming them down on the table, but she did it.

Carlissa stood there.

Katrina didn't know how to get her youngest daughter to obey. "Carlissa, I need you to help or you will have to wait to eat breakfast."

Carlissa's eyes rolled back in her head, which Mabel had told her was a brain issue, and Katrina knew what was coming. Carlissa threw herself on the ground and pretended to scream. Katrina ignored her like she had in the past, but then Carlissa took her nails and dug them into her own skin. Katrina took the girl into her arms. Sitting on the ground, Katrina put her legs around her daughter's legs to keep from being kicked.

An hour later, as Carlissa continued screaming, Katrina thought she would lose her mind. She ached from hunger and her ears felt like they were on fire. Katrina's arms were wearing out, her back was killing her as she rested against a cabinet, and her legs had gone numb. Carlissa

143

hadn't worn down one bit. She sounded like she could go on forever and never wear out her body or voice.

Sara, Izzy, and Francesca had eaten breakfast while Katrina dealt with Carlissa. Sara, after eating a few donuts, raved about them. She was calm. Like this altercation with Carlissa was normal. Katrina prayed this would not continue to be normal.

Katrina looked at Andrew. He looked like he wanted to do something. He was a man of action. He was used to fixing problems. This problem was not easily corrected, and he felt helpless. Katrina muttered low, "Go get Doc. Maybe there is a medical issue."

He nodded. He looked to Izzy and said, "Why don't you take Fran and Sara to check the cattle today. I can clean up here. Take lunch with you." Izzy got the picture of what he was asking.

Francesca gave him a smug look, raising an eyebrow like he couldn't clean the kitchen by himself.

Andrew squinted his eyes with a twinkle of mischief. "Yes, darlin', I can clean a kitchen."

Izzy snorted in amused disbelief and nodded. "Sounds good. I wanted to work with the girls anyhow." She nodded to Katrina, telling her she would be praying. Her eyes held such compassion and understanding.

Katrina softly sang while she waited for Andrew to get Dr. Charles. Katrina wanted to tell Andrew to get Mabel, but she knew that he wouldn't have liked that. She needed to talk to him about the girls and their problems. She needed more help. She was about to lose it and she knew it. When she would be able to talk to him she didn't know. Maybe she could wake up in the middle of the night and talk. That thought made her more tired. She prayed out loud for her daughter.

Andrew and Charles walked in. Charles looked around to see a pretty clean and organized kitchen. He didn't react to seeing Katrina holding her daughter. Even the screaming didn't seem to bother him. He got down on Katrina's level, watching Carlissa closely. He didn't touch her. He stood and took the mug of coffee Andrew handed him. He put both hands around it, feeling the warmth.

He spoke so Andrew could hear him over the screaming, looking at Katrina so she could read his lips well. "Medically, I can do nothing. I could give her something to sleep so she will stop the screaming, but that will not help the next time. I only use it when they haven't slept in days. It doesn't correct the problem—just ignores it."

"Why is she doing this?" Andrew asked.

Charles shrugged. "Hard to say. I believe it occurs when she can't let out what happened in her past. See, her body knows what she went through, but her mind can't remember. Either she was too young or her mind won't let her remember. Mabel believes she is in a flashback or just can't handle what is around her at the time." He sounded so relaxed.

"When will it stop?" Katrina asked, begging him to tell her it would end soon.

He shook his head. "I can't answer that. One of my sons screamed for over twelve hours, though he stayed on his bed. However, he didn't try to hurt himself." He saw the shock on their faces and added, "That was an awful time for my son. He has gotten much better. Actually, my asylum boys are doing better than the boys I got off the street in Denver. Why? I don't know."

"What heals them? What makes it stop?" Andrew wanted a fix. He wanted to help them.

"Time. Being there and supporting them." He paused. "I can't do much more, but I can see if Mabel can come over or one of my daughters. As a family, we also work out a system if parents need each other. We are always there when a family member or friend needs help."

"Yes!" Katrina said desperately.

"No!" Andrew said sharply.

Katrina had never felt such a wave of anger at him. She could even call it hate. How could he deny her a lifeline like Mabel?

Charles nodded. "I try my best as a father, but it is my wife that softens them first."

"I'll walk you out," Andrew said lightly.

Katrina met his eyes. They had always talked with each other through their eyes. She let her anger show. His face showed guilt and then hardened. He gave her a look that said, I am doing what is best for all of us. It also showed something more before he walked out the door. Katrina wasn't sure what it was. Sorrow? Grief?

All Katrina knew was when Izzy got back, Andrew and she would pack supper and go on an overnight trip and talk. She wanted to find out what was wrong with the man she married. This had to stop.

She rested her chin on her screaming daughter's head. Katrina was glad that Carlissa stopped shaking her head. She let Carlissa's soft red hair dry her tears.

Stepping outside, Andrew could breathe, though he could still hear the screaming. He was embarrassed that Dr. Charles had seen his daughter like this. It helped that Dr. Charles' children did it, but not by much. "I don't understand why she is doin' this."

Charles nodded. "I ask myself that all the time. We may never know." He acted like Ben in his wise confident ways. "Have you seen a child do this before?" he asked.

Andrew froze in time. His mind went back to the first time Jesse tried to hurt himself with a knife right after he came to Silkwood for the first time. He could still smell Jesse's blood as he held him down, could see the rage in Jesse's eyes. Jesse hadn't been hard to hold but he had been so angry. It hadn't been long after that Andrew had to deal with him. Ellen and Ben didn't want the others to know, so only Maverick and Matt knew. After Jesse became a believer the screaming fits had stopped. Even when Ben died, the terrors didn't come back.

Andrew didn't want to answer Charles. He just wanted Charles to back off, mind his own business, and leave them alone.

He knew it might be childish fear, but the man he called father had shot him. He didn't want to let himself get close enough to get hurt. Worse, he didn't want Katrina or the girls to be hurt again. He could hear Ellen's words, "Don't hold onto your bitterness. Love others and let them love you, my son. One day will come when people will want to help for real. Let them in your heart."

He ignored her voice.

Charles put a hand on his shoulder. "Are you all right, son?"

Andrew nodded. They both knew he wasn't. "Everythin' will be fine. Thank you for the help today."

Charles got the message. "Just so you know, I am around whenever you need it." He patted Andrew on the shoulder like his pa, Ben, used to. "I'll see you around."

Andrew nodded and watched him leave, knowing he should probably give the man a chance, but Andrew's heart was so broken and angry at what Owen did to them. He couldn't make himself do it. He could talk to Sawyer about it. Sawyer would probably understand, but he decided against it. Sawyer was newly married and busy with his new newspaper job.

Suddenly he wished Maverick or Matt were there with him. The kidnapper and murderer, who had sought them for years, had almost killed Maverick with Owen not caring a wit. Maverick would understand. And Matt would set him straight spiritually, like he always had in the past. Matt wouldn't say much, he would sit and listen.

Heading back into the house, the sound of his daughter screaming returned. He didn't mind facing her, but he didn't want to face his angry wife.

He should have told Katrina what he was thinking. He had always been open in the past, but now it seemed hard. Maybe he was afraid she wouldn't understand. Katrina had forgiven Owen and moved on, but he wasn't there yet. Ellen had prayed that he would forgive Owen and let God use Andrew to the fullest.

His face went hot. He didn't know if he could do that. The man was dead and Maverick couldn't believe Owen had betrayed them. He walked back into the kitchen. He sang old hymns over the screaming, as he showed Francesca he could clean a kitchen, thanks to Ellen who taught him. He did this for the next two hours until she finally stopped.

Then Carlissa sat down at the table and ate like nothing was wrong. She ate with her fingers like she did when she was stressed. It shocked Katrina at the difference in the child.

Two days later, Katrina stirred the fire one more time. Taking much needed time with Andrew away from the noise and business of life, Andre took her off the mountain. She could the beans and smoked beef as it warmed up in the kettle. She put the biscuits on the rocks to warm them up.

While swimming in one of the hot springs, Katrina had kept it light and didn't talk about what was between them. The heat felt wonderful against her back. She looked at him over the fire as he sat against his saddle, his hair still wet, sending a long dark curl down his forehead. She had married such a handsome man.

He had a grim look. "Just get it over with and spit it out, Kat."

"I want to know what is goin' on with you." She shook her head. "Why won't you let anyone in?"

"I let you in and family," he muttered.

"That's not what I mean and you know it. Do you not like the Alexanders?"

"They are fine, I just don't think we should dump this all on them."

She folded her arms and put her legs out, watching him. "Then why did we say we want to start Liberty Ranch with Cole? It was so we could help families and help people understand what is going on behind closed doors. Is that not what you wanted?"

"No, it is, but that is it. We help others, but we don't have to accept help from others."

She looked at him like he had lost his mind. "Then what is the point? We won't be a help to anyone if we are too tired and worn out! If you haven't noticed, I am at my wit's end and I don't know where else to turn." She stood up, pacing. "I need help. I have to can and dry the vegetables, make more candles and knit winter clothes. I will also begin teaching school since none of the girls can go. If I could just teach the girls one thing, that would be nice. They listen to nothing. I need help!"

He stood up. "You have Izzy."

She glared at him. "Izzy ain't a parent. She has helped me out in so many ways, but this is not what she wants to do. She and Cole left the children to their parents for a reason." She knew what he would say. "And I can't go to Gloria. She might understand it, but it is too much in her new marriage. I won't do that to her." She turned around. She didn't know how to deal with him.

"I'll help you," he pleaded with her.

She turned back to him, glaring. That is not what she wanted to hear. "I know that. But Sara won't let you near her. Carlissa just doesn't care, and Francesca wants you too much. I am worried about Fran the most. I need to bond with her more. When Izzy gets married, Francesca will have a hard time with it. I can't bond with her well when the girls come between everything we do." She explained, "Mabel and her daughters get together and teach the children school since most ain't allowed in the school. They take one or two children and teach them to do basic things. Mabel or one of them could watch the girls so I could get alone time with Fran. Mabel said it works since it is one-on-one time with each of them. I think she wanted to do it more often with the others when Julia gets here." She threw her hands up. "I am done. I don't remember how Ellen and Missy got us to obey. How did they make enough food to last the winter? Make enough clothes."

Andrew shrugged. "We lived in Alabama. Everything in the winter was easier," he muttered. "We can always buy from town, if we run out."

She frowned. She had never bought from a town to survive—ever. They had always grown what they ate. She shook her head. "We are not dependin' on the store for food. I will can it all myself before we do that." Depending on a store for food was way too close to how it had been during the war. The stores had nothing. Which meant many went hungry. The Starrys didn't because they grew and canned enough.

"Now who won't depend on others?" he asked sarcastically.

She walked up to him. "That's it, ain't it? You don't want another person to get close enough to hurt you like Owen and leave you like Ellen." She could tell by his face, she was right. "So you won't trust Juan Jose when he gets here with Mav?"

He got closer, raising his voice. "I don't want another person to have that much control over me again. Juan Jose is family."

"Owen was family." He had never yelled at her. How had they come this far? "He raised us. So what, you ain't going to let anyone close because of one man?"

"You don't know what it's like," he yelled as he turned away.

She got in his face. "You think I don't know what it is like. I had that man walk me down the aisle when it should have been Ben doing it. I trusted that man with my life. I still cry myself to sleep for a father who hurt us. I know what it is like trustin' someone who has that kind of control over you. I feel it all the time when I look at pictures of Owen. We can't erase him from them. It was difficult to forgive him. I wanted to hate him. I hated him. But it was only hurting me. Ellen said all those years of bitterness hurts the person who is bitter."

Andrew's face went hard as he looked at nothing. "I can't let it go."

Katrina let a tear fall for the man she loved, but she just didn't know how to help him. Ellen was right. Owen's betrayal would be harder to deal with than anything any of them had faced before. It would have to be up to each of them. She touched his clean-shaven cheek. "Ellen was right, that bitterness will destroy you, love."

Chapter 22

The door hung open, letting a breeze enter the parlor as Julia sat on the sofa. She hadn't drawn in some time. With all the busyness of life, she was tired in the evening. She drew the outline of the horse. Feeling the emotion in the horse as it ran, she brought it to life on paper. Horses were her favorite animal to draw. She loved the movements and emotions behind the drawing.

Cole came to sit by her. His arms circled her waist. He snuggled against her neck. She knew he was in the mood to cuddle, but she wanted to draw some more and maybe talk. "How is my rose?" he muttered.

She put the drawing aside. Cole took that as a sign and moved her to his lap. She leaned against his shoulder to where she could see his face. "Love, we need to talk."

Cole turned serious. "Yes."

Julia brought up what the children needed and wanted. Cole had ideas and solutions to the issues. Julia began to feel hopeful, but she failed to mention David's anger and disrespect. He seemed fine with Cole, but what if Cole didn't believe her, or worse, didn't support her?

Cole seemed to know her look and touched her face. "Hey, Rose, what is that worried face for?"

"I am afraid," Julia finally admitted. "I am afraid that I am failing the kids. They need more than I can give." She didn't want to admit that there were days she just wanted to stay in her room and paint. She loved them, but some days it was so hard. She wanted to just paint and forget about life. She felt guilty about feeling this way. Ellen never felt this way.

Cole shook his head. He made her sit up, with his hand on her cheek. "Rose, you don't see how wonderful and carin' you really are. You doubt yourself." He kissed her nose. "Why don't you see yourself the way I see you? You are a wonderful mother. The little boys seem to be the best. I think some of that is because they weren't abused."

Julia almost flinched. He thought she was doing a wonderful job mothering the boys. David hated her. She felt the walls coming up around her heart. She couldn't speak. It was too hard fighting David every day.

Cole's voice became soft. "Your value is far above rubies." He kissed her eye. "You are kind." He kissed her cheek. "Loving." At every word, he kissed her. "Patient. My love. My help meet. My beloved. Your children will call you blessed. You love far more than others."

Julia closed her eyes, feeling his lips on her. She knew he was supposed to be comforting and supporting her. But at every word she felt the pressure to perform. He expected so much from her. She couldn't measure up. David hated her and Johnathan still asked for mama often. The girls still hurt in so many ways. She couldn't measure up to his expectations. As he kissed her, he spoke softly. She kept silent, feeling trapped in another secret she had to keep. She put her arms around his neck and felt his curly hair in her fingers. How she loved him. She would just forget her many problems and let Cole's hand run through her hair. "I love you, Cole." Meeting his lips, she kissed him back with all the passion that filled her. She was crazy in love with this man. No matter the problems they may face in the future, he would always be by her side.

Katrina loved peaceful sunny afternoons like this, where family and friends would gather and talk after church services, before the drive home. This time there was no Sunday picnic, but still some ate in the churchyard before heading home.

Diana walked up to her. "Would you like to eat with us? We always eat before heading home."

Katrina looked around and saw Izzy talking with Mabel. Andrew was out of town for a job and would be back the day after. "That sounds fine. I am sure Annie and Gloria will want to stay for lunch as well."

"How are they settling in?"

"Very well."

After settling in for lunch, Katrina looked around, seeing some other church families also staying for lunch. She saw Annie and Gloria laughing with some ladies. She smiled peacefully, knowing they had never felt accepted by people either. She hoped they could keep friends with these people. She thought it would all go away and they would just be a family again, with nobody else. She felt alone and still, like she didn't fit in. She was half deaf and would always be.

Watching where the girls were, she saw Carlissa smiling. She didn't see the girls smile often, but Carlissa was with some other girls her age. Sara looked out of place, so she stayed by Izzy. The girls all loved Izzy so much and would miss her when she moved away.

Francesca was talking with Alice. Her eyes were light, even if she still looked hard often. Alice was probably used to the mood swings. God had really blessed them with people who understood. It had helped more than if she still had Ellen in her life.

"How is it going at home?" Mabel asked.

"Well enough, I reckon," Katrina answered. She wasn't being honest with Mabel about her marriage and how the girls were bringing her down. She held back. Had Ellen talked about her marriage with anyone or was it too private? She was afraid to be a bad wife, and she knew she was a terrible mother. At least she could try being a good wife.

Andrew had left with the brothers to see Jesse's place. He had given her a long passionate kiss before he left and told her he loved her. She knew it was true. She never doubted his love, but she felt her needs were being misunderstood.

Mabel put a hand over hers. "It's all right, I understand." Her eyes said she did.

Katrina's eyes went moist. She looked away. She didn't know how to handle all this and she was so tired. Tired of Andrew ignoring her. Tired of fighting with the girls, and so tired of crying every morning because she was a failure as a mother and wife. She looked to see Francesca standing by a tree talking with a boy from town. He didn't go to church. She was smiling and moving her body in a flirtatious way. Katrina frowned, ready to go over there and set her straight. She did not want to fight with her all the way home.

She knew she would have to walk back over there and get her. She didn't know how Andrew always handled her when she acted like this. It drove Katrina nuts. She looked back at Mabel who had watched her gaze.

Mabel looked at her in a way that indicated she understood. "It's hard understanding them. You are not always sure what to do," Mabel told her.

Katrina nodded. "Izzy seems so much better than me. She is so patient and kind. I feel so lost in my own home."

"Like the children have taken it over." Mabel smiled a little. "You just have to set what your home will be and make sure nothing comes between you and your man. It will not help the girls if they know you two are at odds."

Katrina's face crumbled. How could Mabel guess that she was not on the best of terms with Andrew? She must not be hiding it well. She didn't want others knowing she was having a hard time in her marriage. She had never had a hard time before. Spending time with Mabel made her want Ellen here more than ever before. Why wasn't she here to show her what she should do with Andrew? Ellen would know what to do, how to get Andrew to open up. She would know how to handle the girls better. She would be more like Izzy, patient and strong.

Not knowing what to say, she looked back at Francesca to find Francesca's back against the tree with the boy's body pressed against her, kissing her. His hands held her tightly against him. Her arms were around his neck as she kissed him back.

Katrina stood up and started over there, and Mabel followed. She passed Izzy, who noticed and kept Sara at her side. Before she got over there, Timmy walked up to them and pulled the boy away from her. He stepped between them, his hands in a fist, ready to throw one. "How dare you touch her like that, Joe Taylor? Francesca is a precious, priceless ruby who needs to be treated with respect."

Joe swore. "You are talking about that who..."

Joe didn't get the word out when Timmy punched him right in the mouth, knocking him to the ground.

Katrina came over to take Francesca's hand and lead her away, but Francesca just stared at Timmy and stayed there. "How could you?!" she asked in a quiet, angry voice.

Joe stood back up, wiping his lip.

Mabel walked between them and stared at Joe. "That is enough, Joe Taylor. Go home and I better never see you doing this again with any girl. Do you understand me, young man?" She said it with such an authoritative voice that few people would mess with her. "Cause if you ever do this again, you'll be fighting her father, not my son."

Joe stepped back and bobbed his head. "Yes, ma'am." Then he left without looking at anyone.

Katrina yelled, "What were you thinking, Fran? What you did was so wrong."

Francesca ignored Katrina and stared at Timmy in shock. She tried to step closer to him, but Katrina held her back. She stood there and yelled, "How could you do that, Timmy Alexander? What Joe says is true." She stated it like she didn't care.

Katrina looked to see the church members and some town people gathered and watching. Sara's face was hot with anger and shame. Her face was hard. Katrina had to look farther to see Carlissa was still playing with her friends on the other side of the church.

Timmy walked up to Francesca. "No, he is a liar! A bad boy. He is wrong about you. You are a valuable treasure. You are a beloved child of God."

Francesca stared at him in shock. Her mouth dropped open. For once she had no words. No smart comeback.

Katrina looked in shock. She wanted to take this boy home because he had gotten Francesca to be quiet. "Timmy is right," she mumbled, then kept hold of her hand and led her to the wagon.

Izzy had an arm around Sara, who still looked scared, but now she was red in the face, her hands in a fist.

Katrina looked to Gloria and asked her if she could go get Carlissa, who had thankfully missed all this for once. Her eyes looked hard at Francesca, she couldn't help it. She could have ruined their name by admitting to being a whore. She could lose it all. What would they think of Andrew? She knew what could become of their reputation. She had lived in that reputation for decades in Alabama. It scared her to live that way here.

Katrina put an arm around Sara's waist and led her away. This day couldn't get any worse. "Sara, you are a good girl. You are my daughter. The church will think the same thing I do, that you are a beautiful sweet child."

Sara glared at her with scared eyes. "You can't really believe that, Ma." She moved her arms to show the biggest gossipers of town. Both of them knew this would be around town by tomorrow morning.

Katrina kissed her forehead. "Let's go home, baby. We can talk later." She kept her in a side hug like she normally did when they walked.

Izzy took Francesca's arm. "We will walk home, Kat."

Katrina looked at Francesca and then Izzy and nodded. "All right." Katrina looked back at Francesca. "We will talk at home, young lady." She watched Izzy and Francesca walk away.

Katrina's eyes met Mabel's, whose expression said she would be by this week to talk. She almost cried. Katrina knew she had messed up today more than once.

She knew what Francesca had just done would get to the ears of Pastor Peter. He would no doubt be by, telling them how to parent properly. Andrew had told her he was surprised he hadn't come yet. She hoped Andrew was home by the time he came over. She wasn't in the mood to deal with a self-centered, self-righteous pastor, as Ellen often called them.

Chapter 23

Izzy walked home, ignoring Francesca who followed. She could not believe Francesca had done that. Francesca caught up with her and folded her arms, acting like a spoiled child who got caught in the cookie jar. "So why don't you just get on with it and tell me how I am a bad girl for kissin' Joe!" Francesca told her.

Izzy could say that was more than kissing. Both were way too close. She knew how that could go bad fast. "I ain't going to scold you. Kat and Andrew will when he gets back."

Francesca unfolded her arms. "You ain't. Then why did you ask to walk home with me?"

Izzy shrugged. "I needed to get you away from Sara. You might be all right with boys, but you really freaked her out."

"Everything scares Sara. I can't help it." She didn't seem to care.

Izzy stopped in the road. She turned to face Francesca, her eyes narrowed. "What do you think? What we do affects others. Do you want Sara to be kissin' boys like that, or maybe going farther?"

Francesca frowned. "No, but I wouldn't do anything with him. Joe is a good boy."

Izzy shook her head and started walking. "Kisses like that can lead to more, quickly!"

"So what? To do things like your brother did. I hear he didn't even kiss his wife till their weddin' day!" Francesca said, as if Cole was crazy.

Izzy cocked her head. "Somethin' like that wouldn't be bad. I wish Jesse and I did it more like them. They are a sweet couple, and I think some of it was because they got emotionally close first and not physically."

Francesca stopped walking and swore, glaring at Izzy. "That might be great for them. But I have nothing to give a man. Everything I had got taken by hundreds of men. Not a couple, but hundreds. I have nuthin' to give my husband. They took everythin', my kiss, my touch, everythin' I have done. I have nothin' left. I am nothing to a man. So I don't have your brother's power to not touch. What does it matter? I can get none of that back."

Izzy froze. What Francesca had just said was why she had let Jesse's kiss go farther with her. What did it matter? She had nothing to give Jesse that hadn't been taken. She took Francesca by the shoulders. "That is not true. You have a lot to give. You have your personality and talents. What they took from you was not your choice and a good man will know that. It was their filth that took from you, not yours. God will take that pain away and make you a new person." She let her go. "A good man will love you for who you are."

Francesca didn't soften. "Jesse doesn't know about you! What if he did? What would it matter if I gave Joe what every man wants?" She added like Izzy didn't know what she was talking about. "Sex."

Izzy got in her face. "I know the world says sex outside of marriage is fine. They just say give in and have fun, don't think about what will happen after. God forbids two people to burn in sin. God did not just forbid it because He wanted to make rules. He had our best interests, and He knew how we give into temptation." Izzy faced her until Francesca's back was against a tree, having her full attention. "Giving in to sex before marriage is not the answer. You will wonder if the man wanted you for you or your body. You will also wonder, can I ever trust him after being married? He broke his commitment to you before marriage, why not after? Sex and children belong in a union called marriage for good reasons."

Izzy leaned her hand above Francesca's head, breathing hard. "You will always wonder if he married you because of your body or guilt." She softened her voice. "Marriage can be a wonderful thing. I have seen it with people around me. But it takes work and patience and not giving into everything you want. Wait for the best, Fran. If you give yourself to God's hand, He will bring a man you can't imagine. He has so many plans for you, you've just gotta let him." Izzy gave her an amused look. "Remember, no scolding." Moving away, exhausted from more than just the heat of the day. "Let's get home. I need some iced tea."

Francesca caught up. "You mean iced sweet tea."

Izzy grinned and put an arm around Francesca's shoulders. "Is there another kind?"

Francesca shook her head. "Nope." They walked for a bit in silence, then Francesca spoke like she didn't want to say it but like it didn't matter. "I have thought of going back to the saloon."

This didn't surprise Izzy. It was the only way Francesca knew love.

"When you feel like leavin', talk to Katrina or Andrew right away."

"Katrina would freak out if I told her my feelings!" Francesca stepped away. "Andrew doesn't love me. Not really. He doesn't show it like others have."

Izzy stopped Francesca by taking Francesca's arms. She tried to meet her eyes, but she kept looking away. "Andrew loves you. He is showing you love by not doing what anyone else has done. He is showing you what a father's love is. It is not what you experienced before." She paused. Bad-mouthing her abusers would not help, even if she felt like it. She had yelled and ranted about them. Her favorite thing to say about them was God had a special place in Hell for those monsters. "Andrew is kind, patient, and shows you what healthy love is. Those bad men were not showing you love the right way." She added, "Katrina will be just fine if you talk to her."

Francesca met her eyes, glaring. "I can talk to you about it because we are made from the same cloth. It will be no time till they realize who I am and then tire of me."

Izzy shook her head. "That will not happen! Ever!" She lowered her voice. "But you have to believe that in time. It has to be your choice to believe them." She knew it was hard to believe that because if the town ever found out what she had been, they would treat her and anyone around her like an outcast. She had scolded several pastors for not welcoming former prostitutes or child slaves in their church. She told them if they knew how these victims had lived, they would have a little more compassion. It normally didn't help. Juan Jose had opened many of the pastor's eyes. She put her arm back around Francesca's shoulder and started walking home. "You have to let it go, retrain how you think about love, especially a father's love."

"Did you feel loved by your pa after you came home?" Francesca asked.

Izzy gave her a rough laugh. "No, he hit me six months after coming home. It shocked me, I thought he had changed. He hadn't hit us in years. He beat Cole up and we left soon after. I came here and Cole went to work with the Starrys in Alabama. I got a father figure through my cousin. And Cole was always there. Cole is a lot like Andrew. They are made from the same cloth." Growing tired from the heat and emotions, choosing a lighter subject. "We could have a tea party with lots of sugar with the girls. The men will be gone for a bit still."

Francesca shrugged. "Kat is still mad. She probably won't want to."

"You could try givin' in and obeyin'." Izzy winked at her.

Francesca moved back and gave her an amused look. "Now what fun is in that." She gave her a sassy look. "So this tea party, let's invite all the boys in town."

Izzy tried to playfully smack her, but she took off. Good thing Izzy was a good runner.

"Ma, can I take Whisper up on the north pasture to look for the new foal?" Sara asked from the kitchen door.

Izzy had let her go up there before, so Katrina didn't see why not. She nodded. "Let me pack you a snack to take with you." She got out some salted pork and cheese, then a slice of bread and wrapped it in a towel. "Put this in your saddlebag, hon." She kissed her forehead, then handed her the bag and the canteen.

Sara nodded silently.

A few moments later, Carlissa walked into the kitchen looking very mad. Her hair was all full of hay, and she had water running down her face. "What happened to you, sweetie?" Katrina asked.

Carlissa put her hands out like she had done nothing to deserve this. "Fran dumped me with water when she was watering Poppy, Mama."

Katrina nodded, trying not to laugh at her pouty lips. She was just so cute when she did that, so much younger than she was. She was good at getting sympathy. "Did Francesca water Poppy and Poder?"

Carlissa looked shocked and held out her arms. "Yes, but I am all wet!" she explained, like Katrina hadn't noticed.

Katrina nodded. "All right, I will deal with Fran in a minute. Why don't you take this towel and dry your hair? After I am done cooking supper, I will brush it." Francesca wasn't normally mean to the girls. Carlissa was probably bugging her. Getting her wet was the only way to get her away. It worked. Though she would have talked to Francesca about that.

Carlissa stuck her tongue out. "I hate when you brush my hair."

Katrina ignored the attitude for the moment. When they were alone, she let some stuff slide trying to not fight with her at every moment. She knew it would be a big fight for her hair.

Carlissa tried to dry her hair and was just making it messier. "My hair is ugly," she declared.

Katrina looked at her lovingly. "No, I love your red hair with curls. It's getting so long and lovely."

Carlissa made a disgusted face. Her anger grew as it did.

"Right now, you look madder than a wet hen," Katrina told her softly as she finished cutting the tomatoes.

Carlissa was about to answer back with a comeback, but then she shut her mouth and stared at her with a confused look. Then her eyes got wide. "I look like a chicken?"

Katrina burst out laughing, shaking her head as her girls took everything so literally. "With the hay on your head, you kinda look like a hen, sweetie." She laughed till Carlissa joined her.

Carlissa smiled up at her. "When the hens get wet, they look awful mad for sure. Well, I saw the boy bird get just as mad."

Katrina just laughed away her seriousness. "I was funning with you, Carlissa."

Francesca walked in. "What, are you trying to explain yet another saying to her?" She smiled a little, knowing how the two younger girls just didn't get most of them.

Katrina nodded, still smiling. "Yup."

"When will Izzy be back?" Francesca whined. She didn't like it when Izzy did anything with anyone else. At the moment she was with Annie in town, shopping. Francesca got insanely jealous of her. Katrina couldn't imagine how she'd react when Izzy moved and wouldn't be back for over six months or more. She was trying to bond with Francesca herself.

"I am not sure. Did you finish your chores?"

Francesca nodded.

Before anyone could say anything, there was a knock on the kitchen door. Turning, she knew who it had to be. Almost everyone else went to the front door. "Come on in, Mabel."

Mabel came in and smiled at the girls. "I brought my granddaughters and Lucy if you girls want to go play." She looked to Katrina to answer.

"Sure, you girls can go on out," Katrina told them.

Carlissa looked up and smiled brightly at Mabel. "I like your grandbabies. They are nice." Then she ran out the door, slamming the screen, with Francesca following.

Katrina put the stew on to simmer. "Want some coffee?" she asked as she buttered two slices of cinnamon bread.

"Sure." She took a seat at the table after looking outside.

Katrina set the plate down and poured coffee for both of them. She took a long sip of coffee. Looking at her older friend, she asked, "How do you do it? Timmy is such a good boy."

"You're not missing a beat." Mabel grinned. "Timmy came to me as a baby, he didn't have the amount of neglect my other boys had. Though he still has a hard time with losing his tummy ma. He is a Godly young man. Your girls can be the same one day." She took a sip of coffee.

Katrina looked at her in surprise. "You really think so?"

Mabel nodded. "Remember, you have only had them with you for a couple of months now. It will take time to heal their wounds. Maybe decades."

Katrina nodded. "The nightmares are terrible for both of the older girls right now. Before they wake up from their nightmares, it is almost like I can feel what they went through. They never remember what they say, but they cry out for the men to stop." Katrina wiped at a tear. "I hate what they did to them."

Mabel laid a hand over hers. "I know that feeling well. My boys were hurt by so many. Sometimes they don't remember, but their bodies do."

"Do you think the town knows what Francesca and Sara were in the past?" She hated to ask, but needed to know. She hadn't been to town since the incident outside the church, and she worried. Andrew said some were talking, but not as bad as Alabama would be. "I thought I heard Maryanne say somethin' about it."

Mabel shrugged and took a bit of the bread. "Maryanne is the biggest gossip in town and is always nasty. But really the neighbors talk. They have nothing else to do. Nobody is saying the actual words. It will die down soon enough. I don't think there is much harm since both girls are so young."

Katrina sighed. "I worry. In Alabama we were the brunt of the gossip and had no one to stand up for us." She took a bite of the bread, enjoying the yeasty lightness, but more enjoying fellowship. "This is what Ellen had missed for decades. It is what all the Starrys missed."

"I am glad you came here, though I am sorry you felt like an outcast. I think this town needs Liberty Ranch. It needs healing for our families, our children." Mabel meant it.

Katrina bit her lip. "I think you have too much hope. Hopefully, with Juan Jose and Cole coming, they can get it too, cause I don't see us doin' it at the moment."

Mabel looked at her. "You are putting yourself down. You are doing a splendid job with the girls. Remember, we will help as much as we can."

Katrina nodded, "You don't know what that means to us." She didn't have that kind of confidence. Mabel had too much faith in them. She felt pressured. Maybe that was what was wrong with Andrew, too much pressure.

Chapter 24

The dark clouds forming overhead looked like they were about to downpour soon, probably making it much cooler. The rain had lightly started to come down on the roof, sounding like soft pings. Then suddenly, thunder went off, and it made the barn echo. The thunder made Andrew think of how Julia hated storms and how they made her cower in the corner of a room. While she had gotten better, it was still a strong fear. He could feel the rain was about to come down.

Francesca ran in with a rush. "Where is Sara?"

Andrew frowned. "I don't know."

Francesca swore as she passed Whisper's stall. "She ain't in the house and Whisper is gone. I will go find her." She sounded too old, like this wasn't the first time rescuing her.

Andrew grabbed his reins. "We will find her together." After they tacked the horses, they mounted and headed to the north pasture. It didn't take long, but Andrew found her tracks.

Francesca chuckled. "Izzy said she is a hard woman to track. She can almost always cover them."

Andrew narrowed his eyes with humor. "It depends on how good the tracker is. And my brother, Maverick, can track the best of men."

Francesca's eyebrow rose. "I bet she would put you to the test."

Now Andrew chuckled. "I reckon that is true."

Just as they reached the top of the hill, the trail stopped in the rocks. "Sara! Sara, are you up here?"

As the brush got thicker, their horses were too big to get through. A pony like Whisper wouldn't be. Dismounting, Andrew tied their horses. He loved the mountains. It was nothing like Alabama.

Suddenly he heard a whimper. Moving towards the sound, he called Sara's name again. This time Francesca called as well. He saw Whisper standing a few feet away.

Then he heard Sara scream from beyond the edge of the rocky open cliff. Getting on his stomach, he felt the rocks dig into him as he leaned over the edge, careful not to drop the rocks on her. He saw Sara holding onto a tree root. From the look of it, the root wouldn't hold up much longer. His hand could touch the top of her fingers. "Sara, honey, you are going to have to grab my hand. I can't go any farther."

Francesca screamed above him. Terror filled her voice.

"Please, love, take my hand. It's the only way." He tried to show he loved her through his eyes. He knew telling her he loved her right now would not help. Many men had said those words so expertly while not caring about her heart. "Please, Sara, take my hand."

Finally, her small, blood-stained hand went out to him and he grabbed it with both of his and gently lifted her up. Getting her to the top, Francesca screamed again and grabbed Sara so fast that it nearly knocked them over.

"Don't touch her!" She said with an authority that didn't match her youth.

Andrew didn't know what she meant, but he nodded, knowing she was upset. Everything was fine. Then he noticed Sara's arm looked twisted. He reached out to her, only to have both girls start screaming. He pulled his hand back and took a deep breath, thinking of what to do. "Girls, I think Sara broke her arm. See, her arm doesn't look good."

Neither girl even looked at the arm. They just stared with wide scared eyes. Francesca swore and her lip shook.

Andrew bit the inside of his cheek. Not knowing what to do, he went to Whisper. Bringing the pony to the girls, Francesca helped Sara up as she held her arms close to her body. He wished he could make a sling to make it better to ride in, but he knew that would be a mistake. Both girls were having a bad day.

As they walked to the horses, he remained silent, and after riding back to the ranch, not a word was said.

Katrina ran out to greet them. Andrew could see the worry in her eyes, and he saw her eyes go wide as she saw Sara's arm.

As Andrew dismounted, he signed, Don't get her down. "Let's just take her to Doc. Francesca and Sara have had a bad day."

Katrina just nodded like she knew what Andrew meant. "Girls, why don't we go to town. I will ride with Andrew and…"

Izzy rode up with Carlissa in her lap. "Carly is riding with me." As always, she was one step ahead as she looked at Sara's arm.

When they got to the edge of the ranch, Izzy signed, You need to tell Sara we are going to doc's.

Katrina nodded from the back of Andrew's horse. She signed, It's

164

late, let's go to the ranch and see if he is there first.

Izzy looked uncertain but didn't argue.

The ranch was right outside of town. As they rode up, Francesca swore. "Why are we here?"

Izzy dismounted, turning to her. She didn't miss a beat. "So you can play with Alice." Carlissa dismounted.

"I don't play!" Francesca dismounted and tied Poder next to Phoenix.

After Andrew helped Katrina down, Katrina went over to Sara who still sat on Whisper, looking very pale. Her wet hair hung in ringlets. The pain must have been great, but she had yet to complain. "Now honey, I'm pretty sure you broke your arm. I need you to be strong and Charles is going to set your arm."

With a movement Katrina didn't think she could make, she moved the reins to run, but Izzy grabbed the pony's halter. "No. Sara, you need your arm fixed." She was gentle but firm.

Francesca screamed and then yelled. "Charles ain't touchin' her!"

Andrew decided to just knock on the door and see who was home. Charles greeted them at the door. "Well, hi, Andrew, how are you doing? Why don't you come in out of the rain?"

Andrew nodded to the girls just as Sara dismounted, wincing with the pain. Katrina went right to her. She moved some wet hair from her face. "Now, honey, it will be fine. Let's go inside out of this rain."

Sara went along almost like a shadow. While Francesca tried to stop her, Izzy took her hand and let them go in first.

Andrew waited until they were all inside and then he heard Katrina softly tell Sara, "Honey, Charles is just going to look at your arm. It looks broken."

Sara shook her head. "No!" she yelled.

Just then, Mabel walked in with Alice behind her. She took in the girl's broken arm but waited for Katrina to respond.

"Honey, your arm is broken. He needs to look at it." Katrina tried again.

Before Sara could respond, Francesca took Sara by her good arm and pulled her close. "And what will Charles get for fixin' the arm?"

Katrina blinked. "We can pay him money. I don't know how much, but you don't need to worry about it. We have it covered."

"I bet you do!" Francesca swore again.

"What is the matter, Francesca?" Katrina asked, more confused than hurt at the moment.

Mabel told Alice to take Carlissa in the back. They walked out without being noticed. Then Mabel walked closer to them but still didn't speak.

"Fran, we need to get Sara's arm looked at. She is in pain. You can see that." Katrina touched Sara's shoulder. "Now, please let her go so we can give her medicine and fix her arm."

Francesca held on tighter. "No. I knew it was just a matter of time until you and your people did what you wanted with us. Well, that ain't happening."

Izzy stood in front of Francesca. "Fran, that is not happening here. That will never happen. I have the money for Doc right now. No one will use you. Ever." When Francesca didn't respond. Izzy looked at Mabel and then continued, "You know, I heard Mabel is pretty good at fixing arms. Why don't we let Mrs. Alexander do it."

Francesca swore. "No! Her husband will use her and I can't be there. I told you, Sara ain't ever being a workin' girl again. She ain't made for it."

Katrina gasped.

Andrew's jaw hardened. But he knew if he said anything right now, it would just put her off. He could see by her eyes she was in shock, or near to it. She wasn't hearing anything, but Sara needed to lie down. She looked ready to be sick. Her normally pale face was even more pale.

Izzy nodded to Mabel, who then stepped behind Francesca. Francesca didn't seem to notice, her eyes just locked with Izzy. "You should know men are bad. All men," Francesca yelled.

Izzy put her hands on Sara's shoulders. "Honey, you need help. Mabel will help you and no one will hurt you. Mabel is a good Christian lady."

As Francesca screamed and looked like she would attack Izzy, Izzy wished she could take those last words back, but it gave Francesca a rough surprise that Izzy grabbed Sara and picked her up. Careful of her arm, she held her behind her as Francesca fought and screamed from Mabel's hold.

As Izzy took Sara into the other room with Katrina by her side, Andrew wished again he could help do something, but touching Francesca would freak her out even more. He had seen it with saloon girls he had helped. But this pain hit his chest deep. He ran a hand through his wet hair just as Izzy walked back in.

Izzy took Francesca's arm as she spoke softly to Mabel. "Sara threw up."

Mabel nodded and spoke to Francesca as she continued to scream. "Are you going to calm down so I can help your sister?"

"No!" Francesca said in a rage.

Izzy's eyes got light. "At least she is honest." Then she nodded. "Go to the room."

Mabel let go as Izzy kept a hold of Francesca's arm so she couldn't get away, screaming, "I will let you go if you promise to not go after Sara."

Francesca just shook her head and continued to scream.

"Fine," Izzy responded. "I might be small, but I can be just as tough. I have taken down a twelve hundred pound steer."

Andrew almost smiled at the image of that. For a petite little lady, Francesca could fight with the best of them.

Charles stood next to Andrew. "Why don't we pray?"

Andrew looked at him with weariness. He wasn't sure if he wanted to pray openly with this man. He came for medical help, not spiritual. But Izzy said sometimes people need more spiritual help than medical help. When their spirit gets worked out, then the medical is fine. He nodded. He was too tired to think of what to say.

"Lord, we all need Your presence here. Give your children comfort right now. We need you in this room to help us. Give us guidance and strength to know what to do right now. Be with us, Lord. As always You are the King of kings. Be with your children. In Jesus' name, Amen."

It seemed forever until finally, Francisca stopped fighting and screaming. Andrew saw Izzy loosen her grip but not let go. He could tell Izzy was getting tired by the look in her eyes. It was more emotional than physical.

Then Francesca moved from Izzy and ran back outside. Andrew went after her and she stopped by the horses. Her hand rested against Phoenix's butt as she looked off to the woods. Her face was hard as a rock. "I hate you," she muttered.

Andrew just stood there in the rain watching her.

"You know Sara came from an asylum. The owners raised her in a brick room until they deemed to let her out." Francesca's voice was soft with a bitterness to it. "They kept Carlissa in a cage and never let her out. Sara taught her to talk and fed her what we could find. Then Carly was let out. She became the terror child running through the halls of the asylum. No one knew what to do with her. Then a man came to

Sara's new room. He said she was old enough now." Francesca's face went hard, her lip quivered in fear like remembering her own nightmares. "She wasn't old enough for that! No girl is old enough to know the evils of a man. Then she stopped bleeding. That man made her bleed so badly she almost died. I found her then. She and Carly had run, and since she was near dead, they didn't care. I took her to the brothel. There was nothing else I could do. I couldn't stay on the streets with her. It was too cold, and she was so sick!"

Francesca defended herself. "She wasn't supposed to work. Ever. Really, I tried to stop her from working. But after getting better and knowing she would never bleed again, the matron put her to work. Sara cried so much the first week, the matron hit her until her ear started bleeding. The bouncer was worse; he took what he wanted whenever. He said since he took us in, we owed him." She touched her face as she could still feel the sting of his fist. "We owed him."

Andrew couldn't watch her face anymore. It hurt. He glanced at the porch to find Izzy standing there. She had tears silently pouring down her face. The pain in her eyes cut at his heart.

Francesca continued, "Carlissa would do laundry when she wasn't screaming. The matron didn't feed her, so Sara and I gave her our food. Sara didn't eat often anyhow. By the spring, Carlissa went to the streets during the day. A church lady would give her food to bring back to us, so for once we weren't always hungry. She never made sweet tea or peach pie. We were so tired of working, but then the matron threatened to put Carlissa to work if we didn't see more men. So we did. Then it got worse, until the matron told us Carlissa was working." She closed her eyes in pain.

Andrew prayed someone hadn't hurt Carlissa. Somehow he didn't think she had been. She was the healthiest with him. She didn't cling to him, and she didn't cower from him.

"So we ran. I stole Sara a proper Christian dress. It was old and dirty, but it was proper. Sara and Carlissa went to that good Christian lady's house. Her husband took one look at Sara and saw how Carlissa screamed, and he sent them packing." She crossed her arms across her chest and looked at the ground, leaning against Phoenix. It was like she was trying to hide the dirtiness that man made her feel.

What Andrew wouldn't give to punch that man out for rejecting his girls once more. Another slice to their hardened young hearts.

"We had to get away from the matron, so we traveled to Deer Trail. We found out they didn't have street children like Denver did.

We couldn't beg. So we ended up stealing food and living at the ranch till you got there. Carlissa was in the woods that day Kat found us." Her eyes went to Andrew. "Don't let Charles take Sara because we owe him. You saved Sara's life just like that bouncer did, and we owed him."

Andrew, who had years of training, flinched. His breath caught at the pain. He found his voice. "Francesca Starry, you or Sara owe me nothing. I saved Sara's life because I love her. I would do it again and I would expect nothing in return. Do you understand me?"

Francesca's eyes went to Izzy, who came closer. Izzy's wet hair hung on the side of her face. Her face was still wet with tears. Then Fran glared at Andrew, swearing. "Men are all alike. It doesn't matter, I guess men will always use us since that is what we are born to do." She looked ready to be sick at her own words.

Izzy touched her shoulder. "That is not true, Fran. Men are different. You were not born for that work. No one was. God created you for much more."

Francesca's eyes got so dark, Andrew thought Izzy would back down, but she didn't. She was one tough woman. "If you believe that, why haven't you told Jesse the truth? Because you know he is a man and one day all men want one thing."

Izzy took a step back like the words had slapped her. She said breathlessly, "You are wrong." She didn't meet Andrew's gaze, she just backed away and half ran away, but then she stopped and whistled. Phoenix untied his own rope and ran after her. She mounted and ran away.

Andrew didn't know if he should rebuke Francesca for doing that to Izzy or leave it, because Francesca had turned a big circle today by talking about her past. But he could still see the shame on Izzy's face, and he was pretty sure it wasn't because she and Jesse kissed. It was deeper. Like it was about her past. He had come to care for Izzy deeply. She had become a sister to him. "Francesca, one day you will see how wrong you are about life. Izzy loves you and wants the world for you." He took her hand like he would a child. He wanted to hug her but knew that would be a mistake. "Francesca, no matter what happens and how much you push us away, I will always love you."

Her eyes showed so much disbelief. Then her eyes went empty. "We will see about that," she muttered with hopelessness.

Watching the sunrise, Izzy walked until she hit the back of the barn. Thinking about how bright the sun was after yesterday's storm, she wished the outward storm was the only one going on, but she knew it wasn't. The morning sky contained hues of vibrant pink, yellow, and orange. However, she didn't feel the beauty of it. She heard something behind her and thought it was Phoenix coming for a snack or to comfort her. He always seemed to know when she needed him. Feeling a touch on her shoulder, it was a rough big hand. She reacted, pulled her gun, and held it against Andrew's chest.

Andrew held up his hands. "I am sorry. It's just me, Izzy."

She put her gun away and wiped her eyes, making sure there were no tears. Feeling Francesca's words between them, she knew she had to say something about it. "So how long have you known?"

Andrew's body relaxed, but Izzy knew better. "Since we found out who Cole was. We looked for you for months and then found out you were safe." He ran a hand through his hair. "I am sorry that happened."

For some reason, Izzy didn't feel the old shame she once experienced as she talked to him about her past. She felt like he understood somehow, but how could he? Clara may be the reason. Maverick and Jesse talked of their sister Clara. She just nodded. "I got through it and so will the girls."

He put both hands through his hair. "I can handle them thinking I will beat them. I have had sisters look at me and think that. But not my daughters. They think I will hurt them in different ways." A tear ran down his face. "It hurts more than words can say. I wish I could change how they think of me."

Izzy crossed her arms, feeling for him. "It will come in time and they will learn."

Andrew glanced at her. "Can I ask you a question?"

Izzy knew she didn't want him to ask her, but she nodded.

"Are you afraid of me because of my size?" He was so gentle with the question — so open and not judging.

She told herself to be honest. Shaking her head, she said, "No, I have forty-six male cousins. I just have a hard time with men in general. Francesca is afraid of you because you are a man, not your size. For Sara, it could be both."

Andrew seemed to respect her answer. "I don't think Jesse will reject you. Being a Starry, you learn to understand people's pasts, and we all do that pretty well. Or we try to. I believe God brought you into Jesse's life for a reason."

Her eyes watered. "Thank you."

"You might want to tell him before my loud-mouth daughter tells him when he comes back," he said dryly.

Her eyes lightened. "You're probably right." She needed to do so much to repair their relationship. It hurt deep inside because she still loved Jesse. She decided to be honest with him about his own past. "Who else knows you are the raider?"

He had told her he was the Striker when they first met. He didn't need to say much, Izzy understood. Striker was his cover name for rescuing people and children. "Just Kat and Ellen. It brought them closer. When I would be gone for days, Katrina would stay with Ellen. And I know their prayers brought me back. I have thought of giving it up though..."

Her eyes went wide. "No, don't," she whispered. Then she added softly, "I understand. It takes innocence from you every time you do it to rescue a child." She looked down at her muddy boots. "To know you are rescuing a child who is being sold for her or his body. To know that the seller could be the father, mother, brother, and even son. It takes something from you every time you step into those doors. It takes something from you no one will ever understand. Not a wife, a husband. No one but that person."

Hand in fists, he nodded. "I am sorry," he said again.

She could almost feel him look at her neck. "No, Cutty didn't tattoo me yet." She snorted harshly. Cutty tattooed his women on the back of their neck. "I wasn't branded by him yet."

He wanted to say sorry again but that was getting old. "I had never seen a Cutty...mmmh... survivor get out. I looked for you, but I knew my chances." His face softened. "I heard you got two girls out when you were there. Still rescuing."

She made a humorless laugh. "Yeah, that is me. I was so arrogant. They weren't the Cutty's girls." Her face crumbled. "One of them was murdered. They said it was payback for me." Before Andrew could say it wasn't her fault, she added, "I think she knew too much. Cutty didn't leave survivors."

"You know Maverick is still looking for him. For him it is something personal."

"Well, everyone knows Lucas worked with him. We just aren't sure how close."

Andrew's face lightened. "Is there anything you don't know?"

Izzy smirked. "Not much."

He sighed, "Do you know Ellen used to pray for you every day after they rescued you? Even before we met Cole. She called you a guardian angel. She said, 'Angel will do great things for God.'"

She closed her eyes, feeling tears come. Angel was the nickname Jesse gave her. Ellen had talked to Jesse about her without giving away her secret. No one had done that for her. All those talks she had with Ellen alone and then with Jesse, Ellen had never treated her differently. Like she wasn't ashamed of her being a daughter. Instead, she had unconditionally loved her. Something her own mother had never done. She cleared her throat. No words came, and they needed no words for this moment.

"Well, I am headin' in." He passed by her without touching her. "The Starrys were blessed the day you entered our life, Izzy." He handed her his handkerchief and walked away.

Izzy felt her knees give out as she slid down the barn wall. Letting the tears come, she sobbed this time. She let the tears come deep from her soul. Tears she had built up from when she sinned with Jesse, she now let out. She repented for what she had done. And then felt Jesus take her in His arms as she had felt in the past. She felt Him say she was a gift to Jesse. That He could still make them work for His glory. She wiped her eyes with Andrew's hankie. Whispering to the dying sun, she prayed, "Father, if You want us to work out, it will have to be You doin' it."

Chapter 25

"Hey, yellow rose, how's my spice?" Cole leaned in and kissed her soft cheek.

Julia was stirring the pot on the stove, putting hot spice into the stew. Cole almost sneezed. She turned in his arms and kissed him. She noticed all the children were watching their every move. Cole was very careful about how he acted with Julia in front of them. He wanted to treat her properly while still treating her like a young bride. They made it work.

Cole pulled away, draining the rest of his coffee. "I need to go check the south pasture. Mav wants to move the horses into that pasture before the sale," he told her. "We might not be back for lunch."

Julia nodded. "You go saddle up and I will pack you some lunch."

Cole saddled up his best stud, and Travis and Hunter got the new green geldings. They were good at training horses. They were firm and gentle. It was from the older boys and their father, Owen, that they had learned so much. Starry horses were known all around as the best stock.

Mounting, he waved at them. The boys rode on ahead.

After a long ride fixing parts of the fence, Cole spotted a mare stuck in a pit on the hill. He dismounted and handed his reins to Hunter. Hunter tied the reins and moved to stand next to Cole.

"This is Angel." Travis stood next to the pregnant mare. "She likes to hide when she delivers, but she is a great broodmare and delivers on time."

Cole nodded, respecting his opinion on the mare. "It looks like she is in labor. This was a small pit to deliver a foal in." He looked to see a small hill that the mare could get out of. He could see the mare start to push. "We have to get her out before she delivers. Hunter, get my rope. We are going to need to help her get out."

Using the rope as a halter on Angel, and then looping the other rope around her rump, he gave Hunter the halter rope and told the boys to pull. They all pulled, but Angel fell back in the middle of the pit and slid down.

"Maybe we should wait till she has the foal," Hunter told him. We don't want her to lose the baby."

Cole nodded. "I reckon we have to, son." He put a hand on his shoulder. "Why don't we build up this hill so she won't slide?"

They all got to work, and after a bit, they got a wooded path under her that might give the mare enough support not to slide down farther again. As they did this work the mare started to push more. Her stomach contracted.

Travis grinned and pointed. "Look! Look, the hooves are coming out."

Cole sat where they could watch. "Travis, why don't you get lunch? We can eat while watching her."

Travis nodded and jumped to get the food. He was never one to wait when he could eat.

After blessing the food, they dug into freshly made bread with ham and cheese, nut cookies Charity had baked, and cool water to wash it down.

None of them spoke as they ate. By the time most of the foal's front legs were out, Cole thought he should talk about his own past. He wanted them to know the truth about what could happen, even in a Christian family. "You might not have known, but I grew up with a father that talked with his fist more than words. He would beat me from the first day I could remember. I hated him." Both boys were watching him. "I often wondered why he even had me if he was going to beat me. I couldn't defend myself — I was too young and small. When I grew up, I made sure no one took something from me again. I hated that man." He looked back at the horse, feeling vulnerable. He knew he had to be honest. "If anything ever happened to you like that, it will be all right to talk about it."

Travis looked away like he wanted to hide.

Hunter's face went red, his lips set in a firm line. Angry, he was thinking about what Cole said. "What did you do about it?"

Cole wanted to reach out and touch him, but he didn't want to cause a flashback or bad memory. "It filled me with rage and hate for him. My pa made me feel worthless. When he hurt me, I felt so alone and angry."

Hunter frowned. "Why do men hurt others?"

"Sin. I know that sounds simple, but wickedness and sin have been

174

around since the garden of Eden. I also felt guilty, like it was my fault he hit me. If I had done somethin' better, then he wouldn't have hurt me. I had to realize my pa was in the wrong because he was the one who hurt me. I also had to let go of what he did to my sister and mom because I felt guilty over what he did to the ones I loved."

Travis put his hands to his sides, ready to run. "I need to relieve myself." He got up and nearly ran away.

Hunter watched him leave. "Uncle Frank... hurt me." He stammered and twisted his hands. "I felt some of those things. I didn't know he was hurting the girls. I should have told someone."

Cole touched his shoulder. "You did nothing wrong. Frank was wrong." He paused. "Thank you for telling me."

Hunter nodded. "I can't tell the brothers. They loved Frank." He looked away. "I loved him, too."

Cole could hear the tears in his voice. "I loved my pa, too." He wanted to hug him. "Can I hug you, Hunter?"

Hunter nodded.

Cole pulled him into a hug. "You can talk to me about it at any time."

Hunter wiped his eyes and nodded at Cole. He looked at him. "I might do that."

Travis came back and looked at them like he didn't want to come back. Travis sat and looked at the mare. "Look at the head."

Cole smiled. "The head is the biggest part to get out. When that is out the rest comes easily."

Travis now looked relaxed, as did Hunter.

The mare pushed and the foal nearly came all the way out. After another push the foal came out, and slid onto the ground. The mare licked the baby. The colt looked like he was mad about being woken up from his nap.

The boys chuckled at the colt's response.

Travis smiled. "Today's been a good day."

Hunter looked at Cole and nodded. "Today has been good."

Cole knew most of the days since the passing of their parents had been hard. He was glad the days were getting easier for them. He prayed as they got the colt up and got the mare out of the pit, that the boys could also get out of the pit Frank had made for them. His young boys were as innocent as the newborn foal at one time, but one evil man had taken that innocence from them.

Katrina watched Francesca storm away. The wind blew her blue dress, and blew her hair in her face. Her boots had mud on them from the night's rain. Choosing to wait to deal with Francesca, she met Sara's eyes.

"I think Fran hates you sometimes," Sara stated.

The words stung Katrina. "Do you hate me?" She knew she risked hearing Sara say yes.

Sara stared out in the pasture, putting her good arm on the fence. Staying silent so long, Katrina was sure she would say yes. "Not all the time," she whispered. "I think deep down you might even love us."

Katrina stood next to her, waiting for her to continue.

"I never had a ma before," she said with no emotion. "Fran's ma would stay in the room while daddies hurt Francesca." Sara closed her eyes like she almost remembered it for Francesca. Or her own memories. "Only men hurt me. Francesca told me if her mama hadn't sold her, she would have killed her. I believe it, too."

Sadly, Katrina also believed her. Sometimes it kept her up at night to know how much rage was in Francesca. Would she take her rage out on her new parents? Putting her arm around Sara's shoulders, she said, "No one will ever hurt you or your sisters here."

"I wonder if my ma sold me to the Asylum. I often wonder why," Sara told her.

Katrina took a chance. "I asked myself that often after my parents sold me."

Sitting up, Sara stared at her. "How? Did they know you would get a safe home?" she muttered. "Away from men?"

"Actually, the man I was sold to. He sold his own daughter as a sex slave, who was my best friend." This shocked Sara. "I was protected, so I didn't know the evils of men. But I was still so afraid."

"Isaiah says you had great parents," Sara commented.

Katrina shrugged. "I remember parents yelling and getting mad at me for being deaf. I left when Isaiah was a baby, so Isaiah remembers when my parents sang, pa played his guitar, and other moments of happiness. We don't talk about our family often anymore."

"Does Fran know?" Sara wondered.

Katrina shook her head, "No, in time I will tell her. You are the first to know."

Sara looked proud of this. "Why?"

"Because no matter what you go through, you can always overcome it. Unspeakable things happened to the Starrys. We overcame it, knowing we are God's Stars." She kissed her head. "One Star at a time."

Francesca laughed loudly. "You are too funny, Carlissa."

Katrina chuckled with her. It was so good to see the joy on her daughter's face. Since Jesse had come, it had disrupted their life again. "You're such a sweetie."

Katrina laughed until she had tears in her eyes. She put her arm around Francesca's shoulders, touching the back of her head. She chuckled. "I don't know how you handle your hair down on such a hot day."

Francesca jumped away like a frightened animal, her arm hitting Katrina in the eye. She turned, glaring at Katrina. "Don't touch me."

Katrina wasn't sure what she did wrong. She touched the younger girls on the head. Her eye was stinging. The girl could really throw a punch. "I didn't mean to. I meant nothing by it, honey."

Francesca's eyes darkened. "You think my hair is ugly, don't you?"

"What?" Katrina looked at her confused. "What are you talking about?"

"You said my hair was down, so it looked ugly!" Francesca accused.

"No, I said, I don't know how you can have it down when it is so hot," Katrina corrected her.

"Well, then why do you put up with my ugly hair?" she whined.

Katrina was quickly growing tired of this conservation. She bit off sarcastically, "You don't like me doing your hair, remember?"

Francesca stuck her tongue out like a child and walked out.

Katrina looked at the tired girls. "Let me go talk to her, girls." In the barn she saw Francesca standing by Poder.

Katrina stood next to her and stayed silent. Normally she would talk. This time she felt like staying silent to listen to her daughter though she might not say a word. "Why did Izzy save Poder and all the ponies? When there are so many other horses that are better. Poder is like a grumpy old man all the time. They didn't deserve it."

"No animal deserves to be treated badly. Everyone deserves to be rescued. Izzy saw the good in the horses. There might be dozens more that need help, but for the ones Izzy rescued, it mattered to them." Katrina petted Poder on the head. "For this one, it will make a difference. He will live a happy life here." She touched her face. "One horse at a time. One Star at a time."

Francesca put her chin on her chest. Katrina took a chance to put her arms around her. She pulled her away and sat down with Francesca in her lap like she was a baby. Francesca put her head on her chest, her hand on Katrina's shoulder.

Silently Katrina held her. Francesca spoke softly but loud enough for Katrina to hear. "My friend Anna had a mom that held her like this. I watched from the window." Gently Francesca pulled Katrina's hair clips, weaving Katrina's hair between her fingers. "My ma never let me touch her hair. She said it was meant for men. When she was in bed with a man, I would touch her hair." Katrina felt something different in Francesca. "It stunk and was stringy. Your hair is soft and smells nice. I never saw such a bright red." Francesca swore. "I found men like hair. They pulled mine when I wasn't good."

Katrina stayed silent, so still while she opened up. Her heart beat a mile a minute.

"My friend Anna got a home away from the brothel. She was still good enough to get a home. Her mama baked and smelled good. She had it good till she had to come back to the brothel. She told me every day her mama would be back. At her mama's home, a man would come into her room at night. It was her pa."

The man might not have been her adopted pa, but any man in her life. When the child came from that life, it made her very easy prey. Katrina never had to worry about the Starry men.

"When the madam sold Anna, she never said her mama would be back again. She knew dirty girls don't get homes."

Katrina felt Francesca's tears on her shoulder. Her hair-covered fist was in her mouth like a baby, making a sound like a small broken animal. Katrina stayed silent as her own tears covered her daughter's hair. No words would cut the hurt her daughter felt. Her daughter wept like the little girl she never got to be. Katrina felt like she was getting a glimpse of her little girl for the first time.

Chapter 26

Andrew walked into the kitchen, spotting Katrina at the stove. He just watched her. She was so beautiful with her curly red hair pulled up. Some little ringlets hung down on her cheeks. Wearing her old apron did nothing to hide her figure. He needed to make more time for her and show her, in small ways, that he still cared. It just wasn't as easy now with their busy lives. He wondered what would improve his marriage. Ben would tell him it was because he wasn't right with God. It would be his fault if the marriage wasn't right. Andrew didn't disagree. It probably was him.

Walking forward, he slid his arms around her. She leaned back. As he kissed her neck, she smiled. "What was that for?"

He growled into her neck and kissed her lips. "Do I need a reason to kiss my woman?" he drawled.

"Someone will see us," she told him playfully.

He heard some laughter in the living room from the sewing circle. He knew she was nervous about it. "Well, you'd better go see your guests." He gave her a pat on her backside. She eyed him like there was something wrong with him.

He was about to go back outside to finish some chores when he heard Mrs. Walker ask Carlissa, "Where is your mama?"

"Outside," Carlissa answered.

"No, I mean your real mama," she said.

Andrew waited to hear what Carlissa said.

"What do you mean? She is my real mama."

"No, someone gave birth to you." Mrs. Walker was getting impatient.

Andrew could see Carlissa's face full of confusion. "I didn't know that," she stuttered.

He couldn't take it anymore and he walked in. Carlissa spotted him and she ran to him. He picked her up. "Pa, who is my real mama?"

He wanted to swear. Not at his daughter, but at this woman who had caused this confusion. "Well, your real mama is Katrina just like

Ellen was my real mama. But we are special. God gave you two mamas. One gave birth to you and the other one gets to love you bunches." He tickled her a little, she was still a child. Unlike the older girls, he could keep her young and still very much innocent. "Why don't Mama and I take you to Hattie's or a picnic, your choice! We can talk more about it later."

She kissed him on the cheek. "Just us and no sisters."

He chuckled. "No sisters."

She jumped down. "Let me go tell Mama." She laughed. "I want peach pie and sweet tea." She waved a finger in his face to make her plan clear.

He nodded, chuckling. "Yes, ma'am." He had turned his western kids into southern brats. As Carlissa ran away, he faced Mrs. Walker. "I would appreciate it if you didn't bring up my daughter's family that she came from."

"But you should look for them." Mrs. Walker pushed her lips out. "She deserves to know her real kin."

"I would agree. Everyone should know their family that gave them life, but that doesn't happen often." Andrew tried to get her to see the truth. "Looking for her parents would be like looking for a needle in the hay. It won't happen."

"Why ever not? Every child should be with their real mama."

Andrew sighed. "She is being raised by her real mom. Living the life my young child led, it would be a surprise if they are still alive." Then he thought, If you tell my daughter her real parents are in heaven, it will be my first time hitting a woman. "I would like it if you didn't mention it to any of my children again. We will talk to them about it. If you and others do, it just confuses them."

Putting her nose in the air. "And if I don't stop?"

Andrew's eyes widened. "I will have to ask you to leave my girls alone and not talk to them again."

Her mouth dropped open. "You need to respect your elders, young man."

"Ma'am, I believe I am," he drawled. "But protecting my children is more important."

She grunted and walked away.

Stepping into the barn, Cole's eyes adjusted to the light. He knew he would find the boys in their favorite spots with the ponies. The ponies were like dogs to them. David ran up to him. Cole picked him up. David always seemed in a good mood lately and he started talking his ear off like he always did. Sometimes the non-stop chatter gave Cole a headache, though he would never admit it. He carried David as he walked into the back paddock.

He saw Travis out there looking furious. He was yelling at an untrained filly. Putting David down, Cole ran to see what was wrong. Before he could reach Travis, Hunter came out and yelled at Travis.

"Get it together!" Hunter shouted.

Travis raged, shaking his fists at his brother. "The filly won't do what I want," he yelled. "I don't need you to tell me what to do!"

Hunter shook his head like he was dealing with a child who just wouldn't listen.

Cole stepped between them as Hunter looked like he was about to throw a punch. "Boys, calm down." He looked at Hunter. "What is wrong, son?"

"First, I ain't your son!" Travis shouted angrily. "My real pa was killed for what he did to his family! My real pa is killed! You will never be my pa." His eyes got wide as he realized what he had said. He turned and walked away in anger.

Cole had never been so hurt. The words cut deep. He knew it was emotions talking. He looked at Hunter. "Let me talk to him. Take the boys to the house."

At Hunter's nod, he followed his son.

Travis stopped at the fence. He put his head against the board like he carried the weight of the world on his thin shoulders. Cole knew that feeling. It took so much to make the feeling go away. He just stood next to him, waiting for Travis to speak first. It was hard to wait. He prayed God would give him the right words. He hoped the words would be nothing like his father's words. Both older men in his life had spoke like christians but aced very different. It left a foul taste in his mouth.

Travis finally sighed. "I am sorry for yelling." He said it like that was what Cole expected to hear, his voice void of emotion.

Cole wanted to punch someone for making this lively boy a robot with no voice and no feelings. He knew acting was easier than a feeling. "I accept your apologies. I don't like how you handle that, but I want to know what you feel. You can tell me what is going on inside."

Travis shrugged like he didn't care.

"I know when Owen betrayed everyone it hurt as nothin' else could." He looked at the younger boy. "I have felt betrayed as well."

Travis shot his dark, angry eyes at Cole. "Your pa kidnapped your sister and planned to kill her? Did he break your mama's heart?" His voice was even. He was a hurting boy who wanted answers. "Did he call you and your siblings liars when you were finally honest about what his brother was doing?"

Cole didn't flinch. His eyes met Travis' hurting eyes. He kept his eyes light. "In the way, my pa beat my ma, my sisters, and beat me often. He never once defended me on anything. It was always a fight with him. In many ways, my pa betrayed me. He had been dead for many years, but I had to forgive him even after he was dead. I had to let go of the bitterness I had harbored for years." Cole told him.

Travis's eyes clouded with tears, confusion, and pain. "I fear others."

Cole nodded. "You can always come to me with your fear and your anger. Taking your anger out on your siblings and the animals will not help."

Travis looked guilty at what he had done. "I am just full of hate. I can't think straight."

Cole understood that. "You come to me when you feel those feelings coming on. Or you can go to Matt or any of the brothers. You can always go to God in prayer."

Travis shook his head but shrugged like he wanted to end this topic.

Cole didn't want to push, asking, "Can I pray with you, Travis?"

Travis nodded again, his emotions shut off, his face guarded.

Cole prayed for God to heal Travis and help him open up. In his heart, he was asking God to take away his own anger at a man who had hurt so many of his loved ones. Again, he gave his pa over to God, holding no anger or bitterness, knowing it wasn't easy.

Walking outside, Izzy's hair blew into her face, feeling like a tornado was nearby. The sun was so bright it nearly blinded her. The wind was probably bringing in colder weather, but nothing like the deep freeze of winter. She didn't want to think about winter because it would mean that she was married and in the mountains. She hadn't really thought about the wedding, let alone planned it. She wasn't sure what would happen.

She pulled her hair back with a thong and put her hat back on. After getting Phoenix saddled, leading him out she nearly ran into a figure standing in her way. Looking up, her eyes met the man she loved more than anything. And the man she had tried so hard to forget.

Jesse smiled. "Hi, Iz."

Izzy closed her eyes. The sound of his voice was making her long for him, and also feel like hitting him. She felt his hand on her cheek. She pulled away and turned into Phoenix. She hadn't been touched by a man since she had seen him last.

"Izzy, can we talk?" Jesse said lightly, though his voice held some defeat.

Izzy looked at him and saw he was trying so she should at least do the same. "Sure." She mounted before he could help her. "Let's go for a ride."

He sighed and then mounted his own stud.

Izzy took the lead without being asked. She rode for some time and knew she had to stop at some point. Finding a peaceful place by the river, she stopped and stared at the running water, not thinking about the beautiful view at all.

Jesse walked up to her and held out a hand. Looking down at him, she frowned. This was so hard for her. She finally took his hand and dismounted. He tied Phoenix for her, then sat next to her on a huge rock overlooking the river. Izzy kept her hands in her lap.

Jesse put his hands behind him, leaning. "How have you been, Iz?" he finally asked.

She didn't want to talk, but knew they had to. So why not talk about stuff no one cared about? "Fine, the girls have been doing pretty well. We even held a sewing circle with the ladies at the ranch. The stock is buildin' up for Andrew and for when Cole gets here. It will be good. I bought some more stock." She finished with that.

"That is good. We needed more for the land than we have," Jesse told her.

Glaring at him, she asked harshly, "So everything is fine and back to normal?"

Jesse flinched and shook his head. "No, I messed that all up. I came back so maybe we can start over — start new. A second chance at love. Let's do it right. Will you give me another chance?"

Izzy looked back over the river. She didn't know what she wanted. She loved Jesse, but knew she couldn't get married the way she was at this point. Moving a strand of hair from her face, she thought Jesse was right, they had to do something. Finally nodding, she met his gaze. "Fine, but we start new with not being alone, and we don't touch as much."

Jesse looked at her, full of pure love, not that passionate love he had that night. "Let's agree to touch on your terms. If you want me to, I will."

Izzy nodded. They gazed at the beautiful view. After a bit, Izzy leaned over and laid her head on his shoulder. He never moved or took her hand. Cole would say that her heart was as far as Texas. It would take a miracle to get it back to Jesse.

Chapter 27

Gazing out the window, Katrina felt like a mother waiting for her children to return home from school. Is this how Ellen and Missy felt when their children ran away? Katrina couldn't believe Francesca had run away again. How long would it be till she felt a part of the family? Watching the rainfall, she held back the tears that threatened.

It didn't help that since Sara had opened up about her past, she had been much worse, from throwing things to swearing about everything. It was like she was asking Katrina to kick her out.

Turning, she saw Izzy walk in with two steaming mugs. She sat on the other side of the sofa and handed over the steaming mug. "Andrew will find her." Izzy took a sip.

Taking a sip of the hot chocolate, she savored the sweetness. "I don't understand why she keeps going back to that life. Are we not good enough? Am I such a bad mother?!"

Izzy shook her head. "No!" She bit her lip. "It's all she knew. She doesn't see herself as a victim or a survivor yet. She was just going to live in that life for the rest of her life. She didn't think of anything else. She was born to it. Some even said it was in her blood."

Katrina flinched. She was not used to that world. It scared her. Maybe that was why she wasn't a good mom. "How do you know so much? Like I know you work with Liberty House, but none of this fazes you. You seem to know the girls' feelings."

Izzy put the mug on the table and pulled the blanket next to her around her shoulders, putting her feet under her. Katrina wondered if she shouldn't have asked. Izzy spoke softly, facing her so she could read her lips, but not meeting her gaze. "I once lived the life Francesca was born into."

Katrina gasped, hoping she had heard wrong but knowing by Izzy's face she hadn't. "I am so sorry, Izzy. I would have never known. You are so strong."

Izzy dipped her head and gave a hard laugh. "So you think."

Katrina set her mug down and placed a hand on her shoulder. "But you are so strong. None of this shocks you."

Izzy narrowed her eyes and cried, "I want to be shocked. I want to say I know none of what the girls are feeling. I want to have the liberty to know nothing of what they are going through. I want that. But they have taken it from me!"

"I am so sorry, I didn't mean it like that." She chose her words more carefully. "What I mean is you're a good person for them to depend on. You understand though, that is hard to do." She sighed. "I don't know what I mean..."

Izzy whispered, "I understand." She took another sip.

Katrina stayed silent for a long time. "Can I ask you something?"

Izzy shrugged. "I might not like it, but I will answer."

Katrina bit her lip. "How did you get through it?"

Closing her eyes, she spoke, "God, my family, and knowing what I did, knowing how it affected them. Family got me through it, but you never really get over something like that." She met Katrina's eyes, though it was hard. "Francesca will believe that one day. You and Andrew are doing a good job with her."

Katrina shook her head. "I don't think so. I think she hates me."

"She probably does," Izzy stated dryly. "It comes from the same place, hate and love. It will be up to her to choose."

Katrina's mouth dropped open. "How are you always so calm about it?"

Izzy chuckled softly. "Believe me, I am not. Cole says the Donovans have an outrageous sense of humor. It comes from people hating us. Really the truth is, I am just good at acting." She shrugged again. "And I will be leavin' with my man in the fall. You have them forever and always have to plan for the future."

Katrina nodded. "Does Jesse know?"

Izzy shook her head. "I am afraid of what he will say."

Katrina agreed. Jesse had a way of not handling things well. "Don't be worried. God gave you a good man. He might act out of emotions first, but then he will think with his heart." She smiled softly. "I would tell him before my loud-mouth daughter tells him."

Izzy chuckled. "Yeah, I better."

Katrina took Izzy's hand, turning serious. "Missy had two children with her master before she met Ben. They were both sold. They were to never see them again."

Stunned, her eyes wide, Izzy said, "I didn't know that. Jess doesn't talk often of Missy and Ben. We have talked often of Ellen and are working on talking about Owen."

Katrina gave her a sad look. "Losing them was hard, no matter how long it has been. We don't speak about that time often. Though Missy had Hunter pretty soon after marrying Ben, their marriage was hard at first. She had a hard time with the angry boys. That was one reason us girls moved in with them."

"She couldn't handle the angry boys physically or mentally. The boys triggered flashbacks from her abuser." Izzy spoke from experience. "I could never do it."

"Why can't I believe that? You are so good with the girls."

"They ain't that hard, you just have to live day by day." Izzy took a sip. "Thanks for telling me about Missy." Setting her empty mug down, she felt exhausted.

"Anytime." Katrina could see the fatigue in her eyes. She put a pillow on her lap. "Why don't you try to catch some sleep?"

Izzy shook her head. "I... might..."

"Wake up from a nightmare," Katrina finished for her. "Well, I have seen worse, I am sure."

Izzy doubted it but lay her head down in slumber, which was peaceful for once in a long time.

Francesca had gotten used to getting up early and going to bed early. Exhausted from the night before, she hated how she felt. Not that it was an unfamiliar feeling. It made her feel old.

She already missed her morning cup of coffee while talking with Katrina. Sometimes Katrina got out a treat just for them before the other girls woke up. Looking around the smoky saloon, she knew she wouldn't have sweet tea again. Andrew had told her love and sweet tea made a home. She rolled her eyes now. Only a good old southern boy would say things like that.

A hand touched her shoulder. She wanted to ignore it and tell them to get away, but she turned, putting on a fake smile. Expecting to see another cowpoke who didn't know how to bathe, she looked up and met the eyes of the man she had never expected to see again. Not after seriously working again.

Closing her eyes, she almost leaned into him. Andrew had come for her. She hadn't expected him to come for her. Not like that other time. But this time was different. This time she had worked. Looking up at him, she saw his anger as he looked at her. From his face, he knew what she had done. She could tell by the anger, but what did she expect from a saint? He still came for her.

"Do you have a contract?" Andrew asked.

Francesca shook her head. She hadn't gotten one. She had been too afraid of being locked in, being owned again. But deep down she was afraid of Andrew not coming for her. She was afraid he wouldn't pay for her.

He took her hand like she was a child. After the work she had just done, she was anything but a child. "Let's go," he said more gently, leading her to the door. He added, "Let's go home."

Francesca looked up at him like his words meant nothing to her. She shrugged. She was going home for sweet tea and Poder.

After two days of Francesca being missing, Katrina was a complete mess. Both girls had been terrible that day, which was to be expected. Katrina walked back into the kitchen, taking the cookies out of the oven. She prayed again that Andrew would find Francesca safe. She glanced at the tub, not feeling like getting in, but since it was nearly ready, she might as well.

She felt the ground move before she heard the horses ride up. Running outside, she saw Andrew pull in with a rough-looking group. Francesca was riding in the middle of the group. By the light of the setting sun, Katrina saw a bruise forming on Francesca's cheek and her hair was in knots all over her shoulders. She looked like she had been to hell and not gotten out.

After getting Francesca inside, Katrina just hugged her. She felt such relief even if Francesca remained stiff in her arms. Katrina stepped back, taking her into the warm kitchen, taking off Francesca's soaking wet coat. Then she saw a peek of her daughter's only way of life. Her dress sleeves were on her shoulders, leaving her bruised chest bare. The skirt was cut short to show off her boots and stockings.

Like normal, Izzy looked at her with one glance and shrugged it off.

She started filling the tub.

"I am so glad you are home, baby," Katrina said as she sat in the kitchen chair.

"I ain't anybody's baby and this ain't my home." Francesca glared at her.

Katrina flinched at the harsh words.

Francesca gave her a smug look.

"Stop it, Fran!" Izzy snapped as she poured boiling water in the tub. "Now undress and get in," she ordered in a no-nonsense voice.

Francesca looked at Izzy, then Katrina, and back again. She looked down and took her dress off, and then her undergarments.

Katrina saw Izzy's face crumble and for the first time, she saw terror on the young woman's face. Signing sorry, Izzy left like someone had lit her on fire. Katrina had seen her act nothing but strong. Praying for her, Katrina turned back to Francesca.

Katrina's eyes watered at the bruises on her daughter's legs, and her young full breasts. There was blood on her upper thighs. She wanted to weep at what they did to her baby. But like Izzy said, crying was useless.

"You don't have to look so sad. It's not like this ain't my life or a hundred other girls live every day. This is the west, not your good old south," Francesca slurred as she ran water over her face.

Staying silent, Katrina handed her a mug.

Francesca drank from the cup. Her face was emotionless. She handed the mug back, Katrina put it on the floor next to her. "Honey..." she started. "I don't have all the answers of what to do. Honestly, I don't know what to do right now. I am trying to keep Sara from fallin' apart. I am trying to keep Carlissa from destroyin' the house." She put her arms on her knees and leaned forward. "What you do affects others. You don't live in a bubble where you affect no one. What you do affects the other girls that live here. You have to face that, and that this life will get you nowhere." She bit her lip. "These men don't know what love is. They can't. It's not in them. The Bible says men that hurt His children will burn in hell. They will pay one day for all they took from you." She took Fran's cheeks in her hands and looked in her empty eyes. "I love you, child. Andrew loves you. We will always love you. Nothing will change that. Nothing. We just want you to be safe. To feel the right kind of love. I love you, baby."

Francesca pulled away, glaring at her. She yelled with such fury, "You really love me? Would you love me after I sleep with every man in the west? Would you love me after I slept with every man in your family? Would you love me even if I destroyed what you had with your brother? Would you love me if I destroy your home like the terror does? Would you love me even if I destroy everything I touch?"

Katrina saw it was a child asking how far her love would go. Her eyes begged Katrina just to reject her, but beneath the anger and the hate, there was a longing. A child's longing to be loved. "Yes, I would still love you if you destroyed everything. I would still always love you. Nothing will change that."

Francesca still glared, shaking her head in disbelief. "I reckon you're up to the test."

Katrina was afraid of what Francesca meant.

Izzy stood back and watched the builders swarm around Juan Jose and Maverick. After a bit, Juan Jose made his way over to her. She knew he wouldn't try to hug her. She hadn't touched him in nearly six years. He stood in front of her, his eyes looking down lovingly at her. She smiled, leaned over, and wrapped her arms around his waist. She knew she took him by surprise. It took him a minute to hug her back. He put his face in her hair. "Oh, I love you, Iz," he whispered so lovingly.

Stepping back, she saw his eyes were moist. He looked over at Jesse, giving him a glance that said they needed to talk. Juan Jose knew she hadn't told Jesse the truth yet.

Jesse stepped over to her, softly taking her hand, and held out a hand to Jose Juan. "Good to see you again, Juan Jose."

"You too," Juan Jose greeted him.

Izzy leaned into Jesse. She was enjoying how he touched her softly, as if something more would break her. It wouldn't break her, but this soft, slow touch and love was healing her, even if he still didn't know the truth. "You ready to work, or too tired from your trip?"

Grinning, he winked at her. "I have waited a long time for this." He turned to Jesse and challenged, "Let's see who can put up the first wall."

Jesse chuckled. "You're on, man."

Katrina giggled, knowing her dream was coming true. She smiled as she watched the men putting up the last wall. The chapel would be beautiful. A little piece of heaven. Leaning against a large oak tree, she imagined her future here. This would be where God really moved and worked in His children's lives, even the touched and soiled. This is where they would all be accepted. Just like all men and their families who came today to show their love and support of Liberty Ranch and what it would do. It made it even better that Juan Jose and Maverick had arrived to help just in time. She loved seeing Andrew and Maverick work with each other again. It felt just like at home.

Mabel came over and handed her a glass of punch. "You know I have prayed for a building like this for some time."

"So have I. I thought I would fit in at the town church, but it has not happened yet. This will be a real blessing to this town."

Mabel nodded. "We needed it for some time." She watched the men work.

"Do you think Pastor Peter will be all right with this?" She took a sip of her punch. Her sweet tea was better. She knew Pastor Peter didn't let Mabel's touched children do the same thing other children did.

Mabel sighed. "Oh, I am pretty sure he will not be all right with it."

Katrina looked at her friend with surprise. "Do you think he will come to the opening sermon Juan Jose has planned?"

"Oh, he will come just to see what it is about, but I am sure he will be uncomfortable with it." She sighed. "He doesn't like change or touched people."

"Jaun Jose is different." Katrina looked over at him working. He wasn't a big man, but he was fit and strong. His faith was unshakable. "I don't know him that well, but he is a good man. So much like Ben," she whispered.

Mabel squeezed her hand again. "You miss him."

"More now that Ellen is gone. I always thought Owen tried to take his place, but he never did. No one can take the place of Ben. He was the first father I loved." She let a tear fall. She was tired of hiding her grief from her girls and Andrew. Losing Ellen was bringing all those feelings back of losing Ben and Missy all over again. She leaned her head against Mabel's shoulder, even if Mabel was much shorter.

"It's hard always being strong for others," Mabel mumbled, like she understood.

Chapter 28

After supper, the church walls were up and standing tall. They would get the chapel done today so they could have church Saturday afternoon. Most of the men had the day off. Andrew was looking forward to it. Walking over to get a drink, he drank the cool water, thankful the weather wasn't as hot here as it was in Alabama. Nothing was that hot.

Charles came over and took a cup to get a drink. For a doctor, he was a fit man. He could work like a horse. He took a long drink then looked at Andrew. "How are you doing? Are plans coming along well?"

Andrew nodded. He looked at Charles, who gave him such a compassionate, caring look. The emotion of the man surprised him. For that he opened up. He shrugged. "I am trying to do the plans. Some things are going as well as I wanted. I never thought it could be so hard."

"Have you prayed about it?" Charles asked.

Andrew almost nodded, but then thought about it. Had he taken time to pray or had he just done things his way? Had he asked God how to love his girls? He blinked. When was the last time he had prayed with Katrina? Like deep intimate prayers. He shrugged. "I could probably pray more often."

"Just don't try to do it all on your own. You need God and friends." He patted Andrew on the shoulder. "Trust takes time, just don't let it take too long. The damage will already be there."

Andrew stepped back. He looked over at Katrina, who was chatting with Mabel. She looked so trusting and at peace with her — eating up everything Mabel said. He looked back at Charles. "Not everyone is trustworthy." He took one last sip and got back to work.

David was in full force this evening. He was throwing things at Johnathan and Julia again. It was after supper and the boys were out doing chores with Cole. The girls were locking up the ponies because of the summer storm coming in.

Julia shook her head and told him to stop it. The storm was already making her edgy. She didn't need this.

David picked up one of Julia's paintings and held it over his head, ready to throw it. The painting was one of Cole when Julia was starting to fall in love with him. She loved that painting. It showed his strength and gentleness.

"Do not throw that, young man!" Julia told him firmly.

David gave her a critical face, claiming she couldn't stop him.

Before Julia could move, he threw the picture. Her only reaction was to shove Johnathan out of the way as the wooden frame hit her in the face, then it fell in a pile of glass. She moved to take David in her arms, but what she planned to do with the boy was beyond her. She told Johnathan to go outside. The boy just shrugged like he was used to David's rage.

David kicked and tried to hit her. Julia could feel her cheek swell and hurt. She needed to put ice on it. She moved over away from the broken glass and brought him into the parlor. She sat on the sofa and just held him.

Making David face her, she didn't know how to get him to calm down. She just held him and prayed for him as he screamed.

Later, Cole walked in on David kicking and screaming in Julia's arms.

As soon as David saw Cole he stopped and smiled at him and became peaceful in Julia's arms.

Julia looked at Cole's shocked face and couldn't understand what overcame David to change like that. It had happened in the past, but never like this. She let him get down as she moved into the kitchen, tears building in her eyes.

Cole told David to go outside and then followed Julia as she swept up the glass, crying.

Julia felt so bad Cole had come in to see her being a bad mother. Cole came in and took the broom from her. He took some ice from his glass of water, wrapping it in a towel. "Come here, love." He gently took her in his arms and then carried her to their bedroom.

Julia leaned into his neck as she cried. "Oh, Cole, I am a bad mama. I did everything wrong and now you saw that."

Cole kissed her on the head and laid her into bed. "No, love. I am the one who should have seen it. Just lay down and sleep or draw." He gently put the ice on her cheek. "I will put the children to bed."

Julia shook her head. "No, I should do that and…"

Cole gave her a kiss to silence her.

Julia closed her eyes and drank in his touch, his kiss. It could always affect her. She loved to feel his passion as he touched her. Pulling away, she felt exhausted, but they had too much to talk of.

Cole just shook his head. "Tomorrow Matt and Susan are watching the children and we are having a day to ourselves, love."

Julia sighed. "That sounds wonderful, but what about the children?"

"They will have fun with Susan and the baby," Cole assured her. He knew he couldn't leave the children alone for much longer.

He kissed her again. "I will be back later to tuck you in, love."

Julia felt so tired, but her mind needed time to unravel, so she did what she did best when she needed to rest. While holding the ice on her face, she drew from her heart. When her paper filled and her pencil was dull, she fell into a fitful sleep.

"Julia, I am sorry for not seein' what David was doing, what he was like," Cole was saying, as he leaned against the palm tree for shade. The waves beat softly against the sand. The sun was high in the sky beating down on them like a soft blanket on a cool day.

Julia shrugged. She leaned against him, loving the feeling of the sand on her bare feet. "I should have been honest with you about how he had been acting," she said. It felt so good to talk to him like this. "I just didn't want you to think I was bad at taking care of them."

Cole took her hand in his and intertwined their fingers. "Oh, hon. I could never believe such a thing because it could never be true. You are a wonderful mother. David is just struggling with you being a parent."

"He is fine with you!" She nearly shouted.

"He is for now, but that may change. He doesn't see me as a threat." Cole chose his words carefully. "He is strugglin' with you because you are trying to be his ma and that scares him. See, he never bonded with his ma."

"Do you mean Ellen?" Julia listened to every word. She pulled her skirt up, enjoying the air on her legs.

"Right. I am sure he treated Ellen much like he does you. He bonded with Missy and when that bond was broken, it crushed him. He didn't understand what was happening. He didn't have the emotions to deal with the loss, so he just reacted and didn't bond with Ellen. And now he is struggling with you." He paused, choosing his words carefully. "He might be this way because he has been living in fear for so long. Getting shot at, knowing his older siblings and even Mama weren't safe. I don't want you to feel responsible for it, but it is also somethin' we need to deal with."

Julia closed her eyes. "I was so wrong for not tellin' the family for so long. It is probably one of the reasons I didn't tell you about David. I fell back into that trap."

Cole kissed her on the top of her head. "We will just pray that you will overcome this. And when you feel yourself unable to talk or be open, come to me and we will pray, and I will just hold you. Showing you I will never leave."

"Hold me now," Julia whispered.

"I always will." Cole ran his free hand over her hair, which she had pulled back in a bun. She loved the feel of his fingers. He let his hand slide to her neck. "I also need to apologize for not getting someone to help you, especially after Gloria left. It was the one thing I promised Ellen I would do."

"Who could I go to around here? Is there someone who doesn't believe the lies about Ellen? I can't deal with that."

"Of course not. Not everyone believed the lies. I was thinking maybe you could confide and talk with Melissa."

Julia liked what she knew of Melissa but didn't know if she could trust her enough. What did it matter? She would be in Colorado territory by the end of the month. But she did need someone to ask how to be a good mother. Maybe she could even ask her about more things. "I will think of it." She sighed. "I just miss Ellen so much."

Cole nodded against her. "As do I. I think of her often, especially when I see you with the children. You reminded me so much of her."

Julia looked over the waves lapping on the beach. "How? I look nothing like her."

"But she raised you. You act like her. It makes me fall in love with you all over again."

Julia felt tears sting her eyes as she turned to look at him. "Do you really love me?"

Cole ran a finger over her cheek. She shuddered under his touch. "Do I make you doubt my love?" He needed to remember her faith was young and needed more time to keep the doubts out.

Julia shook her head. "No, but sometimes I feel like I don't deserve it."

Cole shook his head like he didn't know what to do with her. "Aww, love. You deserve so much more. Don't you know you are a child of the King? You are worthy of so much."

"Sometimes I need the reminder." She softly sighed, this time from contentment.

"Don't we all." He pecked her on the lips. "I will make sure you never, ever, forget it." Then he pulled her closer and kissed her more thoroughly, reminding her how much he loved her.

Chapter 29

Katrina sat back on the hardwood chair as she enjoyed a cherry pie with tons of fresh cream while sitting across from Andrew. The room smelled of leftover coffee and the biscuits Francesca had burnt. Katrina enjoyed these talks with Andrew about the ranch, the talk in town, and of course the girls. It made her feel like they could do this.

"How are the girls doing?" Andrew took a sip of coffee.

"Fran was worse than normal." Katrina shook her head. "Sara did a great job on the pie."

Andrew smiled. "She sure did. It was a little crispy." He winked.

Her eyes lightened and she added, "Carlissa didn't have a rage today. Which is good, I don't know if I could have handled it." She kept thinking about the other rages and how bad they got. Her body was getting used to it. With the last one, Carlissa calmed before she let her go and Carlissa even looked at her gently as she got up, not with the hate she normally had in her eyes. That was the first time in a while Carlissa allowed her to hold her.

"What do you mean Carlissa didn't go into a rage?" He looked confused. "When was her last rage?"

She looked at him, placing her head on her hand. Why did it matter? She glanced in her journal. "She only had one in the morning. Which she almost always does in the mornin'."

"Except this mornin'? What did you do differently?"

She took a sip of coffee, trying to clear her mind, to remember. "We didn't do school. We did chores, cleaned, and then cooked." She made a wry face. "Okay, we made way too much food, but both girls enjoyed it."

"So the only thing you did differently was cooking and eat all day." He looked like a man that was trying to figure out a mystery.

"The girls ate." She corrected him. "I just snacked."

"So could it be the food?" he asked. He looked puzzled and then a light came into his eyes. "She goes into a rage almost every mornin', and almost always around supper. What about lunch?" He was working most afternoons.

She nodded, feeling his emotion. This was it. It could be the answer. "Sometimes, but not as often. I give her snacks when I am cookin' lunch." Her eyes got wide. Feeling like this could be a breakthrough for the very first time with the youngest child. She stood up and threw her arms around Andrew. "So she goes into a rage when she is hungry. She doesn't know how to handle the hunger feeling. We have the answer."

He hugged and pulled her onto his lap, smiling. "Yes, I think we do."

She looked into his dark eyes. He kissed her and whispered, "Hey, darlin', this is a big step. We can keep her safe now."

She giggled. "Let's go tell Izzy!" She jumped up and ran out to the parlor where Jesse and Izzy were talking. She felt lighter than she had in days.

"The preacher is here," Katrina groaned, more like her children than herself.

Andrew's jaw set. "It will be fine." He snapped. He saw the man ride up on his wagon.

Izzy spoke up. "Why don't we take the girls fishin'?"

Jesse nodded and winked at Carlissa. "You girls can help by looking for worms."

Carlissa laughed. "I've been worm searchin' with pa."

Francesca eyed Andrew as she walked into the room, hearing Peter was there. She seemed to challenge him. "I slept with many preachers. One time this priest didn't want to pay me." She walked, hips swaying. Andrew watched where his eyes landed. She started unbuttoning her dress. "He said he would forgive all my sins if I gave it to him free." She made a hard humorless laugh. "He really thought I got paid for anything. I told him I didn't want to pray to his God. Not for my sins." She was now right in front of Andrew. Her eyes challenged him. Her dress was unbuttoned to right above her breast.

Andrew took a deep breath. His face showed no emotions. His eyes never left hers. "How old were you?"

Francesca gave him a smirk and put her arms around Andrew's neck like a young woman would in love. "Young enough to be fresh. Old enough to give him what he wanted." She swore. "You think that is bad, I had a doctor who liked me. He came often, and he liked his women hurt so he could heal them. So, the bouncers would beat us before he got there." She touched her cheek like she could feel his fist on her face. "He beat me so bad once my teeth became loose."

Only decades of training could keep him from flinching at her words.

Katrina swayed slightly like in a daze.

Jesse held Izzy's hand. His other hand was in a fist. Izzy showed no emotions at all.

Sara crossed her arms over her chest while Carlissa was getting her doll ready for fishing.

Andrew buttoned up her dress. "Oh, honey. Sex is not love. Love is standing by someone when you don't feel like it. Love is real. What happened to you was wrong. Those men didn't love you. They abused you." He finished buttoning her dress and took her face in his hands, being extremely gentle, knowing the pastor might be at the door by now. "You are beautiful. Your beauty is far above rubies. I see your worth every day."

Her eyes got darker. He could tell he had lost her again, but he had to try. He wouldn't give up on her. "I see you as a priceless beauty. You are so much in your mind and brain. You are my sarcastic, funny, caring daughter and no man will ever hurt you again."

Francesca backed up, shooting daggers at him. "You might be the man that believes that. That pastor out there will tell you, I will be nothing but a whore because my ma was a whore. She became one at four when her mama died." She stepped to the back door, never taking her eyes from him. "I will never be wanted for anything other than my body. You will come to see it one day."

Andrew gave her a fatherly snapping look. "I will never see you that way. Ever. You are a child. My child."

Francesca hit the wall with her fist. "I was sold at seven years old! My mama told me I was older than her, so I was old enough to do it. Daddies would take care of me. Before that, they had hurt me in ways that would make even a man like you blush. I will be nothin' more than a whore."

Sara spoke up, looking sick. "If you believe that, death would be better."

Francesca's gaze never left Andrew's eyes. Her eyes almost went out, but it was more pain than Andrew had ever seen. His heart cried for her. "I have been dead since the day I was born." And with that, she slammed the door.

Andrew turned to where the pastor was now knocking.

Katrina kept it light. "Just ignore your sister, she doesn't know what she is saying."

Carlissa shrugged like this was normal. Nothing would affect her fishing today.

Izzy ushered them out the door.

Katrina walked up to Andrew and looked into his face seeing tears run down his face, something she was not expecting. But he had to let go of his emotions. She did at night when she was alone with him or Izzy. He had to let go of his anger. They heard another knock. "I can't do it. I can't face that self-righteous man out there."

"Ellen handled it when they did it to her."

Andrew took Katrina by the shoulder and got close to her face, but kept his voice low. His face was full of rage. "Those preachers said it about us boys. Not you girls. Had we boys left we would have ended up dead from the war, in prison, or barely surviving somewhere. If our girls ever leave, they have one choice. One way or another, they will be abused. And that man out there doesn't care who has hurt my little girl. Almost everything Francesca said about him was true. And it makes me sick."

Katrina cried as she nodded. "It is true. What if Francesca was his daughter? Would he reject her then?"

Andrew took her deep into her arms. "I love you!" He felt so much emotion.

He heard the pastor call to them. They had to go. He wiped his eyes and handed Katrina a hanky. Then he walked out to meet the man. The man, they were not ready to face.

He greeted Pastor Peter, and then invited him to sit on the porch. Pastor Peter sat on the chair and Andrew took the swing. They talked lightly till Katrina came out and set the tray of coffee and cookies down on the coffee table. Pouring the coffee, Andrew could see the tension in her. Her back was straight; her lips in a straight line, and her hands were shaking just a little. Through all the Starrys, pastors had hurt her worst. He prayed it wouldn't happen again today. He took his teacup, and took Katrina's hand as she sat down. Katrina's free hand held her skirt.

There was some silence as Peter drank his coffee. Finally, he set it down and looked over at them, not seeming to read them well. Andrew had been trained to read people extremely well. He saw right through this man. Peter cleared his throat. "So you might guess why I am here. I am wondering how you are raising your girls, especially those two older ones. The Mexican child is way out of hand. What are you doing about that?"

Andrew shook his head. "Well, the Mexican girl has a name. Her name is Francesca. We have gone to your church for about five months now and you still can't remember her name. It's Francesca."

Peter looked at them like he didn't care. "Well, she's foreign and could even be a half-breed!"

Katrina moved in her seat. Andrew squeezed her hand and she bit her lip, probably all the way through. Peter was probably right, Francesca was half or full Mexican, but she was not Indian by any means. "What does that matter? Whether she is half Mexican or even Indian. Charles's grandson is Indian."

"Adopted grandson, and you have become just like them. I have never liked Liberty House and all those younguns'. Now you are becoming just like them."

Katrina spoke up. "I am glad to be compared with Mabel and her family. They get stuff done and they care for others."

"And what are you going to do with your daughter that is out of control? All of them but your oldest. She is wild."

Andrew made a hard, humorless laugh. "And I am sure no one in your church has done nothin' wrong. They are perfect, or maybe they just hide it from you because of what would happen. What gossip you would spread?" He looked at him hard. "My daughter is a child. Yes, she gets disciplined when she does wrong, but you have never tried to teach a child how to do right when they have never been shown kindness or love. They believe what's right is wrong and what's wrong is right."

"Every person knows right from wrong." Peter held his head up high like he taught that, so it had to be true.

"That is true." Katrina squeezed his hand.

Katrina spoke up. "Think of it like this. When a person is getting ready for a bath, they are so cold and have been so cold for so long, that when they get in the warm water it feels hot. And they can't handle it on their skin because they have never felt any warmth in the first place." She added, "When a child has never felt love, it feels like pain."

"Now you sound like Charles and Mabel, all they do is give those sayings." Peter put up a hand. "I just say you need to get your daughters under control. Especially that oldest one! Discipline better. Spare the rod, spoil the child."

Andrew squeezed Katrina's hand. She was shaking with anger, his jaw set hard. "My daughters have never lived a spoiled day in their young life. They have never known love, care, or kindness in any way. They have only ever known filth." He took a deep breath. He wanted to put his hand around the pastor's throat. No, he wanted to let the man live a day his girls had lived. Few men could. His girls were strong in so many ways. "Is that how God treated the woman at the well who had five husbands? He forgave her and told her to sin no more. My girls didn't have a choice of what people, especially men, did to them. God had mercy on that woman, and it was her choice to have that many men while my girls don't get a say much in life."

"Don't you dare preach to me, boy." Peter glared at him. "This preaching is coming from building that chapel and taking my members."

Andrew would have smiled if he wasn't so angry. So the man had gotten to the point of his visit. "We are not taking any members. We just meet on Saturday night and Sunday night." They also met when church family member needed it, but that was normal at the house, not the chapel.

"But when the rest of that family gets here, and those touched families come, you will meet on Sunday morning and take my people."

"They are not your people, they are God's. They can go wherever they like."

Katrina calmed down a little now. "One reason they want to come to the chapel is to be treated like an equal. Lucy can sing in the chapel. Timmy will do things in the chapel-like the boys his age do in the church. They won't be treated differently in the chapel."

"You have listened to the Alexanders all too much. They told you those lies." Peter almost raised his voice.

Andrew blew out a breath. "We have seen it for ourselves. Juan Jose is very good at teaching God's unconditional love and mercy." His anger almost got hold of him, but he thought if he could sit with a man who had sold his own mother into slavery, he could sit here with one self-righteous pastor.

"What? And I fail at my teaching?" Peter's jaw was hard and set. "I can't have Lucy or Timmy do things in my church. What if someone new or even my members saw that? What would they think if I would accept touched people?"

"Maybe they would see that you accept God's children? God's people. Oh, how could we accept that?" Andrew responded sarcastically. "We might even be following God's ways by not just accepting but loving the touched."

"That is another thing. I have questions on why you took the girls in the first place." Peter accused him.

Andrew couldn't believe his ears. He had never been accused like this to his own face. Behind his back, he wasn't sure how much everyone said. Still, no one had ever accused him of being immoral or abusive, as this pastor's eyes said. He put his arm around Katrina which to some might be possessive, but he was trying to get her to stop freaking out.

"How dare you accuse Andrew of somethin' like that! He loves our children and he would never hurt them or me," Katrina yelled. Her eyes filled with fire.

"Then why do you come to church with bruises?" Peter acted like he was back in control.

Katrina's eyes filled, her hand went to her neck. "Somethin' fell on my face," she muttered.

Andrew knew she couldn't answer with the truth. Sara had gone into a rage and hit her with a metal plate. It was better than glass. Ellen always said to look on the bright side of things. Peter would never understand a child that angry. "I have never ever hit a woman. I never have, even at the worst part of my life." He glared at Peter. "I wish I could teach my girls. Men are not always mean with a fist. But havin' men like you around, they will just have to learn it from others, that men are good. Because there are always more men like you to say different."

Peter stood up and looked over them, unrelenting. "How can you say that?! Your daughter has done immoral things with men in the past. Who knows she ain't doin' it now with men in my church or your family. It's in their blood."

Andrew moved faster than he thought possible taking Peter by the shirt collar and holding him up to get his attention. Katrina stood next to him holding his arm but not holding him back. "If you ever talk about my girls like that again, I will forget I am a gentleman." He let him go with a jerk.

Peter stood back. "You are an angry young man who needs to learn to respect your elders. I won't be coming back here till you learn some respect', young man!" He went down the stairs.

Katrina still held onto Andrew's arm. "We do respect men who deserve it. I never thought I could respect such a Godly man again after my pa passed away. But Juan Jose came into our life. You're right, we do need help, but you are so limited in believing what God can do." She stepped closer. "But better you go, Peter, before my husband does get abusive."

Peter got in his buggy, looking back at them.

Andrew took Katrina's hand. "You will never know what God can really do believing the world's lie. The world believes we would be better off without the touched. But look in the Bible and see what God has done to move His kingdom with touched people. Then look in the Bible and tell me where God believes we'd be better off without them. Or in man's lie." He gave him a sad look. "You are missin' out on so much life."

Peter shrugged. "It's my life to live and you are living in a world blindly." He slapped the reins and was out of the yard in no time.

Katrina put her head on his head and cried. He wrapped her in his arms and let her cry. In some ways, he wished he could just cry all his pain out, but he couldn't. It wouldn't fix a thing.

She finally wiped her eyes with her handkerchief and just leaned against him. "I don't know how Ellen handled self-righteous people like that."

"She was a saint."

"Nah, I think she was just like us. Trying to do what is right."

Izzy laid back on the sofa as she listened to Jesse read as the rain came down. It was a cool, rainy afternoon. After chores, Jesse read to the girls as Francesca and Sara sat on chairs and Carlissa played with her doll on the floor.

By the end of the story, Izzy and the girls were all laughing.

Izzy sat up from laughing so hard. Catching her breath, she took a sip of Katrina's sweet tea. Hers was better, Jesse always said. She enjoyed these times with him, even if the girls were with them. He had gotten used to them being around, he even enjoyed it some. Other times he just ignored them, though he wasn't good at it. So Izzy would tell him to stop arguing with an eight-year-old child who could argue over how to argue.

Jesse's gaze met hers. He had gotten so much softer in the looks he gave her. She was getting to know him so much more now. Something more than physical touch. He didn't touch her cheek, but Izzy knew he wanted to. It helped to have three sets of eyes on him, watching his every move. "I love you so, Angel. You're so perfect..."

Izzy knew he meant that she was perfect for him. She smiled, never thinking she would feel like this for a man. She wanted him to herself. She wanted to reach out and touch him. She never thought she would get that physical touch back. It had been hard for her cousins and loved ones to see how she had changed after it happened. She had seen it too, with Cole and how he had changed. She was getting back some of what she was before, but it didn't mean she didn't have fears. Just that maybe God was healing her heart. Giving back some of what she had lost. Like she had prayed for since it happened. Like they were patches on her heart and it was finally healing in the places that hurt the most.

She heard Francesca clear her throat like what Jesse had just said was anything but true. "Jesse, you are just so naive." Francesca had been on the warpath recently, ever since Jesse had begun to stay there. Izzy was sure it was because she would move away soon. In Fran's mind, she blamed Jesse, so whenever Jesse was around, she almost always lashed out in anger at him. Unfortunately, when Francesca was this bad, it made the other two girls worse.

Izzy ignored Francesca. She would have to get over the fact that Izzy was leaving. Maybe it hadn't been good that they got so close. Izzy wasn't sure anymore.

Francesca got louder. "How can you call Izzy perfect for you? She is about as perfect as any other soiled dove. She is about as used up as I am in that life."

Izzy didn't look at Francesca but kept her eyes on Jesse, in disbelief. She stood up, needing space between them, though there was enough already.

Jesse stood up in shock, shaking his head, his eyes trying to meet hers, but she couldn't look at him. She would tell him, but not this way. This wasn't how Jesse was supposed to find out.

Francesca kept talking in a light naïve voice like she didn't mean any harm. Izzy rolled her eyes and stopped listening to what she was saying, just looking at the ground, then she finally looked at Jesse. She was unsure if Jesse was mad or still in shock.

Jesse shot imaginary darts at Francesca. "Shut up, Francesca Starry," he yelled in a no-nonsense voice. His gaze met Izzy's eyes, but his eyes were now guarding what he was feeling. His hands were shaking, his voice rough with emotions. "Is it true?"

Izzy nodded softly, looking down. "I was rescuing until I just got caught when I was almost seventeen. Then got the raw end of the deal for a month." To say the least. "I was going to tell you." She had been telling him about the girls being rescued. He liked how much rescuers did, but to know the woman he was marrying rescued girls until she got caught herself. This information was hard to deal with for anyone. Izzy looked at the girls.

Sara looked up between Izzy and Jesse. Her face showed shock, anger, hurt, and some hope. Like how Izzy could marry a man after being a soiled dove, like there might be hope in the end.

Izzy's eyes finally came to Francesca, who looked furious and in a rage. She turned her dark eyes on Izzy, angry for leaving. It was all too clear.

Izzy shook her head. She couldn't do this. One reason she couldn't raise girls like this was because her relationship with Jesse would end. She couldn't handle the emotional strain of it. She couldn't even meet Jesse's eyes again. She didn't want to know how he felt. She felt so worthless. All that love she had been learning was stripped from her, which left her feeling raw and vulnerable. She started for the door, hearing Katrina and Andrew come in.

Running out into the rain, she headed to the barn. She was feeling such despair, she threw up.

Chapter 30

The wind blew hard as the rain came pounding down, but nothing was louder than the pounding and the breaking of Jesse's heart. *I just got caught when I was almost seventeen. Then got the raw end of the deal. For a whole month.* Izzy's words ran through his mind. He dug his heels into the mare's sides and lunged forward. Feeling the rain sting his face, he would never forget the image of Izzy's face, she looked of hopelessness and worthlessness. Oh, how he wanted to kill the men who touched a hair on her head. He pulled his horse to a stop. The mare was breathing hard as he dismounted. Dropping the reins, he walked over to the wooded area. So thick were the trees, he could hardly feel the rain. The wind got softer as he entered a valley with a hill on each side.

This area reminded him of Izzy. She loved the mountains so much. They were a part of her. He leaned his head against the tree, feeling the bark, hard like his heart. He wished he could stop feeling. He cried as he punched the tree with his fist. It did no good. Anger helped nothing, Ellen always said.

So much of how Izzy reacted to things made sense now. How she froze at his touch. The lack of emotion she showed. The times she flinched and backed away like she didn't want him to notice. All of it made sense now knowing she'd been used by men. Men who didn't care about what it did to her soul.

Jesse thought of all the times he had taken from her. She did not belong to him. She was the Daughter of the King. Not his bride or wife. Then it hit him like a rock. When he had slept with Izzy, he imagined what that must have felt like to her. He had used her body for his own selfish desires. He had not looked at her heart. He had only been going with his emotions that night. He had so much ground to make up with her. He knew where to start. It was time he really repented and talked to God like he should have months ago. It was time he made amends for what he did. He had been a foolish, rebellious prodigal son.

He looked up at the sky now that the rain had stopped. But it was time he poured his heart out to God. Even if he was mad or angry, Ellen always said he could be honest. He wasn't always good at honesty. *God, why didn't You protect your daughter? Why did you let it happen? She deserved so much more. She deserved the best, and she got abused and beaten. She got rejected by everyone. Why didn't you fight for her?*

He almost cried. He almost let the tears fall, but he knew he couldn't. He wouldn't be a man. Suddenly he felt a hand on his shoulder. Standing, he turned and swung first. Juan Jose caught his fist like he'd expected it. "Calm down, Jesse," he ordered.

Jesse glared at him. "You want me to calm down! Why didn't you protect her? All the good she did, and she is the one who got hurt! Why?"

Juan Jose shook his head, full of guilt. "We were prideful and so she got hurt. The men we had taken a lot from wanted to get back at us. They did more than we can say." He paused. "I am so sorry you had to find out that way, man."

"You knew she didn't tell me when you got here?" Jesse asked, feeling like he should have been told by Izzy. He had told her about his past.

"I figured." He sighed. "So what are you going to do about it now that you know? Going to break it off with her?"

Jesse caught his breath. Calling off the wedding was never in his mind. Not even close. He loved her more than life itself. He knew no matter what happened, cutting it off with her was not an option. "No. I never even thought that." He shrugged. "Missy had two children before by a master, and she had a good marriage with Ben."

"You think it was all perfect, and they didn't have struggles?" Juan Jose asked.

"No. Ben was the only reason we had our sanity. He was the first to win most of our hearts. It wasn't Ellen's man for sure." He thought about it. Was Juan Jose right? Did Ben struggle with Missy's past? Did Missy struggle? How did Ben handle the fact that he wasn't the first one Missy had been with? Even if it wasn't her choice, like Izzy. Could he handle not being the first? Could he handle knowing men had abused and used her for their own selfish desires? Could he handle her struggles? He wanted to scream. "How bad was Izzy when she came back? What did it do to her?"

Juan Jose shook his head and looked down. "No, you don't want to know."

"Tell me!" Jesse demanded. By the look on Juan Jose's face, he regretted asking.

"Do you really want to know?" Juan Jose met his hard gaze. "Well, we had never found a Cutty victim alive before. The Cutty didn't leave survivors. He branded and broke bones on his girls the first few months." He grunted. "They hadn't done that to Izzy yet. It took a month to find her. We had no idea where they took her. We found her in undergarments, but they hardly fit her thin body. She had lost nearly forty pounds, and she was never a big person." Juan Jose's face twisted in pain. "Nothing was as bad as how they took her mind, her broken heart. She would scream and cry out if a man touched her. Her eyes were empty. No life in those bright eyes. For so long she stayed like this. It took years for her to be like she is right now. But she made it through when so many don't."

Jesse backed up and leaned against a tree. He couldn't breathe. He wasn't ready to hear what she went through. He wanted to throw up.

After Jesse caught his breath, Juan Jose crossed his arms. "I am only tellin' you this because you will have a long winter in that mountain and you won't see many people." He spoke calmly. "Izzy might have a hard time desiring you as a wife should. It may take time for her to look and act as a wife should without fear or even some shame."

Jesse wasn't ready for any of this. It hit his pride. He wanted his wife to want to be with him. He desired her more than he had ever thought possible. But he never thought she would struggle with desiring to be with him. He wanted her to feel safe with him, not be with him out of duty or fear or apathy. Did Missy desire Ben? They had three tummy children. If not, how did Ben handle it? Oh, how he wanted to talk to the man one more time. "I would never make her feel shame," he muttered. He felt the burden of so much to make up for between them.

"No, you would not, but because they forced her to do unspeakable things, the bed can bring shame to her heart. It may take time for her to feel love truly in her heart. And it may take years to desire you as a wife should."

Jesse shook his head, feeling so angry. So broken over his bride. They would have to move past so many problems due to this. He looked at his boots. "How can I help her?"

Juan Jose put his hands in his pockets. "You really want to hear it? There will be a long road ahead of you. But I can tell you it will be gratifying in the best way. First off, get to know Izzy emotionally. You don't know what is in her heart."

Jesse glared at him.

Juan Jose held up a hand. "No, hear me out. You see the woman she is now. She is beautiful, Godly, a woman that gives her whole heart. What you don't know is what she hides from men. You don't know how she can grow in your love. From God's love. As a husband and even now as her man you can show her how to come out of that shell to you." He crossed his arms. "You used to farm in Alabama. I bet it took time and care to get that ground ready to plant. It took getting the rocks and weeds out of the ground. It took putting good dirt back where the filthy had been. You never gave up and before you left, you had the most superb, most abundant gardens I had ever seen. It took time. You see, having Izzy come out to be your loving wife and the woman she is meant to be will take time and care. Get to know her by caring and being there even during her struggles. Some struggles she may never be free from, and others she could be free from through time. There is always hope through love. Giving that love to her will be like a salve to her wounds. You will reap what you sow. You will see the woman I know. You will find a woman who is set free from the past and is continuing to be set free. You will know the woman I know is in there."

Jesse looked away. "I know how hard that is sometimes. I have seen Ellen do it and get hurt. I see Andrew and Kat do it with their daughters. It's hard."

"Yes, it is. And you might fail her and she might fail you." Juan Jose nodded. "Love her as Christ loved you. If you do this, you will be blessed in ways you can't even imagine." He patted his shoulder and walked to his stallion. Mounting, he looked back. "Love her like this, Jesse Starry, and Isabella will be like an angel flying into your arms."

Jesse watched him ride away in the drizzly mist of the mountains. When Juan Jose was out of sight, Jesse fell on his knees and cried out to God, this time humbly and repenting. 'Oh, Father God, help me. Forgive me for hurting Your beloved Daughter. She wasn't mine. I abused and used her. Forgive me, Father. Oh, make amends for the mess I have made by my sin. He wept. He wept to a God who knew pain. Who felt his pain when he had been abandoned like Izzy. He wept for the only one who could know his pain. He felt a peace he hadn't felt in so long. He was going to be the man God called him to be.

The evening was warm with a soft breeze after yesterday's storm. Sitting with Jesse on Annie's front porch, Izzy gazed over the quiet little town. Izzy loved Deer Trail, it was a quiet little town most of the time. Annie's front porch chairs had come from Denver, a wedding present from Gloria and Jerry. A table sat between them, holding a pitcher and two glasses of sweet tea. Annie's sweet tea was not as good as hers.

She put her knees up to her chest. Her breathing came out rough. *Calm down*, she told herself. Jesse had said little. Giving her time or he didn't know how to end their engagement. "I did not plan for you to find out about my past the way you did. I wanted to tell you myself, but every time I tried to, I stopped myself." She froze. "You know my pa wasn't a kind man. My pa would hit me and Cole often. Ma would get it as well. Annie was always too sick to hit. Amy stayed out of the way most of the time, so he didn't go after her. The hittin' stopped mostly when Cole got the grandparent's money. We hung it over his head, sayin' we would leave and never come back if he touched us again. It kept him calm, and then he went off to war soon after. We made it through the war and he came back so much worse." Her accent was thick which meant she was upset. Telling him was so much harder than telling Francesca, she would never judge her. She tightened her hold around her knees, her hands white. "So to get away, we started travelin' to rescue girls and even boys from terrible slave lives, and then send them to a safe home, Liberty Houses." She closed her eyes. "I was nearly seventeen when I got kidnapped by one of the men we were buying girls from. He is known as Cutty. For his formal name Cuthbert. We didn't know the girls were his when we bought them. We had been trying for years to save his girls. Cutty held me for a month. I fought back a lot, but his men took what they wanted from me. They took everythin' I had in that month." She bit her lip so hard, it nearly bled. "I have nothing to give you. They took everything." She had never felt so humiliated and ashamed. "Cutty was never caught."

After some time of silence, she looked over at his hand. It was white from squeezing the chair. He moved his hand like he wanted to take her hand, but he pulled back. She couldn't make herself look at his face.

"You're wrong," he finally said. His throat was raw and his accent thick. "You have so much to give and you have given so much to me already. You give your heart and soul. You give me your love."

She finally looked at him. He had tears running down his dark cheeks. She knew he didn't cry often. He was now crying for her. His eyes were full of love and compassion for her. She shook her head. He would tire of her when he got close, she just knew it.

He nodded. "I didn't understand your past before Fran opened her big mouth. It makes me feel like I used you. I didn't treasure you. I wasn't listening to what I felt God tell me that night. I was listenin' to my flesh. I was so wrong."

"It's all right," she said, though it wasn't.

"I feel like I failed you in so many ways. I didn't know how to love you right and I might still have issues, but I am workin' on loving you properly through Christ."

She didn't know if she could believe him. His words were melting her heart.

"I desire you so much." He looked ready to touch her face, but he did it so slowly that she knew he was waiting for her to pull away. She stayed still and let him touch her cheek ever so softly, like a feather. He let it rest there. "I desire like a man desires his pure Angel Bride. That is what you are on the inside and the outside, a pure white beautiful bride. You do not belong to me now. You are the King's Daughter. I want to show you, by my actions, that you are a treasured angel. I might mess up, but I want to know how to treat you right. I want to help the angel come out of you. I know the real you is in there. I have seen it when you are with Kat, Fran, and the young girls. I can see that you don't show me that side. And I understand why you don't. I have not been the man you needed. I will try to have that side come out because I love you. I love everything about you." He pushed a stray hair behind her ear. Again, being ever so gentle with his rough calloused hands. "When you thought to do this without touching as much and being not alone, I wasn't sold on it. But I see it's what you need. Will you let me prove to you what kind of man you need? Give me another chance to love you right?"

She closed her eyes against tears. She didn't cry often. To her, she would much rather take a ride on Phoenix than waste time crying. This time she dreamed of hearing these words. She slowly nodded and met his eyes. "Why do you call me Angel?"

He gave her a soft, sad smile. "Ma told me you were an angel. My angel, God gave me. To be careful about how I treat you." He frowned. "She is the one who knew I had struggles. She wouldn't be happy with how I treated you."

"I think she would be proud of you right now." She touched his hand.

He gave her another sad smile. "She knew me so well. She knew I was afraid to move forward in the relationship without her. She was always a part of everythin'."

She smiled back, putting her legs down, relaxing a little. That is why he didn't propose romantically. Ellen had been a part of Cole's proposal. She was all right with not having a lot of romance. He hadn't been ready for something that big. "She will be watchin' us."

He stood up, walked over to the edge of the porch, and faced her. He had a very serious look on his face. He walked in front of her and kneeled down. "When I asked you the first time, I didn't understand what love was. I didn't know how to love you, I did everything wrong." He put his hands on her lap. "I have come to love you so much more in the last few weeks. I can't imagine loving you more than I do right now. I love everythin' about you, how givin' you are, how you love without limits, how you make the best sweet tea in all the west. I love everythin' about you, here and now and in the past." He held his hand out to her. "Will you take my hand with God this time, my Angel?"

She looked down at his hand. She saw it. It was a necklace with a ring on it. The ring was white gold and shone in the sunset. It was stunning.

"No one knows this, but Ma gave me her weddin' ring before she passed. And she wanted me to give it to the woman of my dreams. She already knew it was probably you. I want you to have it. She knew you were my angel before I knew it. But I do now, you have my whole heart."

She nodded and let the tears fall. "I will give you my heart."

He stood and then pulled her up. Taking the necklace, he put it on her. "Would you wear this till I can put it on your finger on our weddin' day?"

She nodded and then faced him, holding the ring. It felt wonderful in her hand. The promise it held.

He took her chin. He ran his thumb over her lower lip. Asking silently. She had always been smart. She hadn't kissed him since he came back from the mountains. She had learned to enjoy and trust his touch again. Leaning a little closer, he got the message. His lips met hers, his lips tasting of tears. Tears he had shed for her. He had handled her past with such gentleness and care. Even now he was gentle and caring like this was their first kiss. She moved her hand to put it on his chest. It was like he was giving something to her and not taking. Breaking the kiss, he smiled and then kissed her again. Soft and quick. So loving again, giving something to her.

Moving her head to rest against his shoulder, she softly sighed. He was strong enough, yet gentle enough to handle her past.

Chapter 31

Izzy walked into the kitchen with a mission, finding the person she sought, Francesca. She helped Francesca bake a peach pie like all was normal.

Francesca eyed her like she couldn't be fooled. "So did I hurt what you have with Jesse?"

Izzy looked at her. Her heart hurt for Francesca. "No, you didn't. I know why you did what you did. I tried the same thing with my cousin and her beau. I was mad at her for moving on with her life and I felt she was leaving me behind. But that wasn't true. I found Jesse and you will find a man too."

Francesca laughed like she had to be kidding her. "Me? What man will be with a woman who has been with hundreds of men? He will grow tired of me! Just like Jesse will." She glared at the older woman. Her eyes hurt, so broken and confused. "You think Jesse won't grow tired of you. That is what men do with a woman like us. There is something wrong with us. Why do they keep moving on to more women? There is something wrong with us. Soon enough Jesse will see it."

Izzy shook her head. "No, he won't." She couldn't say any more. She had no more words. It hit too close to home for her. Maybe Francesca was right, even in her hurting words. Maybe Jesse would grow tired of her. No, that was not true. She turned to the sink, feeling tears come to her eyes. She rarely let them fall.

"See, I am right. In your heart, you know it too," Francesca told her smugly.

Izzy closed her eyes against the tears, knowing she couldn't speak right now. She didn't have the fight in her to change Francesca's reflection on life.

"You are wrong, Francesca," Jesse said as he stood in the doorway. Izzy's eyes met his, then she looked away as he spoke. "Francesca, you are wrong. When you get to know the man God has sent you, he will love you for you and not what you can do for him. He will honor and protect you as God commands him to. If he is listenin' to God's will and respecting you, he will wait till marriage to be with you."

Izzy looked up at him. He was looking at Francesca, so caring but trying to guard his look. He walked over to her and took her hand, squeezing it in comfort.

Francesca glared, her hands in fists. "That is a great thing to say, but have you ever been with a woman? Have you ever slept with a prostitute? Cause I hear there is nuttin' better!"

Izzy didn't know when she had felt so vulnerable, so exposed, like her sins were out there in the open. Francesca's words hurt more than she could say. She just wished Jesse would hold her closer cause she was about to break. Holding his hand wasn't enough. She needed to know he didn't believe these lies. She needed to know he didn't believe these lies.

Jesse put his arm around Izzy, sensing what she needed. No matter what Francesca said, in her eyes she was a child calling them to love her and not forsake her as everyone else had in her young life. Her eyes said prove me wrong. "I had been tempted to, but I never did. Some would say it was because I had a good God-fearing mother. Others would say because my ma was a prostitute and probably died in that life. But the truth is I couldn't ever do it. I had learned from a young boy that a woman's body was never something to buy. Ever. Do you want to know why I believe that?"

"You were too good for them?" Francesca crossed her arms in a way that made her almost flirting with him.

"No, I knew they were real women who had a soul. I heard my older brother cry out almost every night for a sister he would never get back. We hardly ever spoke of Clara, but I knew her well from her brother's cries. They never ended. He still cries for her in his heart. And will probably until the day he dies. It is a silent cry for someone who was taken at the young age of twelve. She never got the chance to live in freedom from men. You have that chance, Fran. You have that chance to live free of that. Andrew and Katrina are givin' you that chance."

Francesca looked shocked and maybe behind those eyes she looked hopeful, but her eyes still held distrust, like she could never have that life. "What am I trying to do to be a good daughter to them? What will it matter? I will never get a man who won't grow tired of me. You just wait and see, you will grow tired of being with Izzy!"

Izzy flinched at the words.

Jesse held her tighter, a little closer. "No! Don't you ever say that again. I know why you would believe that. You have seen it with men. Passing you by for another. For someone better." He gave Izzy one last squeeze and then walked closer to Francesca and met her hard eyes. "The reason you think men will move on with something better is because you have seen what the men's sin has done. Not your sin, but the men's sin. It is their selfish desire that hurt you. It was their lust that they moved to another woman. It was not love, and that is what God designed sex to be. God didn't make it evil or to hurt, but men have done that. Men moved on because they were sinful and lustful. It had nothing to do with you. You are beautiful inside and out." He paused. "I will never grow tired of Izzy because I love her the way a man should love a woman. And when we get married, I will love her the way a husband loves a wife. Because that is what God made sex for in a marriage. But what is more important is that I will care for Izzy's heart. Caring for her heart and soul to make sure she is happy and content and at peace. The same way I know Katrina would want to do with you."

Francesca shook her head, putting her hands on the flour-covered counter, and stayed hard, like a rock unmoved. "So what, you know how to be content?"

Jesse tried to meet her eyes, but he looked down. "I thought I learned to be content when I first believed at sixteen, but I realized this year I didn't know contentment. When I first believed, I depended on my ma way too much. When she was close, I felt like I could handle life. I was just a minute away from falling apart. You know that she passed away. When she did, my world ended. I had lost my lifeline. I didn't realize God was there for me all along. So instead of going to Him, I made Izzy my new world for contentment. It was wrong, and a while ago I realized God is a jealous God. And He wanted me to be content with him, not with Izzy or Ellen. And He is now. He is my life. He is where my contentment comes from."

Francesca's eyes showed anger, as if she didn't know a thing of what he said. She understood none of it. "You try that God thing. It will be a matter of time until you grow tired of it." She dusted off her hands and then shook them off on him. She glared at Izzy. "You'll see I am right. Why else would your pa beat you as a child?" And then she walked out, slamming the door.

Izzy didn't flinch, but Fran's words stung. So much for opening up to her, trying to help her understand. It had gotten thrown back in her face.

Jesse just shook his head, feeling heavy. He heard Izzy walk up behind him. She slid her arms around his waist. He held onto her arms, knowing how hard it was hard for her to touch him. She put her chin on his shoulder and watched Francesca walk to the corral toward Poder and whispered, "She doesn't have the ears to hear."

He turned around in her arms and looked at her. He stepped back. He had been trying to show he loved her by not always touching her, but by touching her heart. "What she said was lies."

She nodded, understanding what Francesca felt and believed.

He brushed her cheek ever so softly. "I will never grow tired of you. When you walk into a room, my eyes cannot get enough of you. When I touch you it makes my heart beat a mile a minute. It takes my breath away. Feeling you is like holding a pure white angel. I will never stop desiring you. You will forever be my beloved bride. Forever."

She could melt in those chocolate eyes. His words were like a salve to her wounded heart. It made her feel like she was a pure maiden. She winked. "Forever is a long time, cowboy."

He leaned closer, and breathed, "Forever will be like a day with you."

She turned her head into his hand. His voice was crazy to her heart. For the first time, she was feeling. She didn't want it to stop. His touch made her stomach do butterflies. She closed her eyes, not wanting this to end.

He ran his hand down her cheek and then stepped back like he knew what she was feeling. Looking into those beautiful eyes, he said, "Isabella Donovan, I also promise to do the best I can to care for and protect your heart. To care for the person who was hurt. To remember to be the man God made me to be."

What Cole said, Julia ran over and over in her mind. Could Charity be doing too much? Too much of the mother?

Suddenly the boys ran in, with Charity chasing after them.

Julia stopped them. "Now what is wrong?"

"Julia, I have it under control," Charity told her. Not disrespectful, just a statement.

Julia's eyes widened. Charity had never acted like this before. "Boys, go to your room," she told them. They both looked to Charity and then to Julia. "Now, boys."

As they ran off, Julia was gentle with Charity. "Now, why do you think you are in charge? You are a child."

Charity looked hurt. "I am more of a woman than you think. I know how the boys can be and I need to help."

Julia sat down at the table. "Come sit, dear."

Charity obeyed, playing with her napkin.

"Hon, me and Cole can parent the boys. You can just be a child. Do normal child things, play with your ponies, go swimming and when we get to Colorado, there will be school and church friends."

"I ain't been a child for years. And you can't do it alone."

"I won't be alone. Cole is here to help me."

Charity looked at her in disbelief. "Yeah, right. Do you know how many times David hit Ma in front of Owen? And he did nothin' while he got all of David's love. He would say you are their ma, you do the work. She had to do it alone. Just like you. Cole is never going to help. David loves him." She sounded too sure. "It just won't happen."

Cole walked in carrying flowers. Setting them on the table, he was silent.

"I am sorry, Cole, for sayin' that." Charity almost cowered.

Cole took a deep breath. "Darlin, never apologize for being honest with me." He sat in the chair across from her. "I am not the same as your pa. I do plan to help raise y'all. I won't say Julia and I won't make mistakes, but we will try to do what God says and try to raise you because we love you all." Charity looked surprised. "I do love you. My greatest wish right now is for you to be a child. Can you do that?"

She nodded. "I will try... Do you really love me?"

His heart melted. "I really, really love you, darlin." He picked up the flowers and smiled. "These are for you. To show much I love you and for all the work you do around here."

"Thanks." She gave him a small shy smile. Getting up, she added, "I will go show Mel."

When Charity left, Julia looked to her handsome husband. "Do you know I really, really love you?"

He took her hands as he pulled her closer to him. She sat on his lap. "I can hear it again."

"The flowers were for me," she whispered in his ear.

"You will have to realize there are other women in my life." He sighed like he didn't have a choice.

"Well, you got good taste." She kissed his cheek. Sighing, she turned serious. "I should have realized what a bad pa Owen was. I moved out around the time Ben passed."

"Well, you couldn't have known any difference. Owen and Ben were your only father figures."

"Well, Owen could never match up to Ben in a million years."

He raised an eyebrow.

"What?" she wondered out loud.

"Well, it's just Owen had a lot to live up to." He cleared his throat. "Just makes me think of the children. They don't expect a lot from me. They never had a proper pa, from what they can remember."

Her eyes went wide. "But they do expect a lot from me. Because I can never match up to Ellen." She bit her lip.

He hugged her tighter. "That is not what I meant. You aren't meant to be Ellen. You are meant to be the best ma you can be, and that is what you are doing, love. That is all a person can ask."

She nodded. "You're right."

He kissed the top of her head. "Of course, I am, Rose." He turned serious. "You know I will be here when you need me to be. I will try to parent David with you and figure out what works and what doesn't."

She felt such a peace, like she wasn't doing all on her own anymore. She had a man that she could stand by. This is what God wanted marriages to look like.

"How are my fine ladies today?" Cole asked. He had all the boys so the girls could get a break. They had taken the time to get some much needed chores and packing done before the big move. He had spent it in the barn getting it ready for sale. He couldn't wait till they were gone.

The girls were outside sipping sweet tea under the big shade tree.

Melody ran up and jumped in his arms. "Great. We got most of the fun stuff packed. Now it is just dishes, food, and canned goods."

"Oh, you forgot..." Cole teased her. "Remember to pack all the candy I just bought. That is the real good stuff."

Melody's eyes danced. "Oh, we will remember, Pa." She moved around in his arms. "I will go tell Mama now!"

Cole put her down. He didn't mean right then. He was just funning her.

Moving to where Charity sat, she stood when he walked up, her defenses high. "How are you doing, Char?"

"Fine," she told him in a monotone voice. She didn't meet his gaze.

He prayed he could reach her. He would have to be patient. Suddenly he heard something. Staying still, his eyes moved over the ground. His heart stopped as he saw a rattlesnake by the tree near Charity. Just then, Charity met his eyes and her head turned toward the snake. Gasping, she stayed still. Didn't move. Only wisdom from what she had lived through would teach her that self-control. Staying still, he prayed he was fast enough. Taking his gun, he shot it before it could bite.

What he didn't expect was when Charity started screaming, and ran into the woods. She was not seeing where she was going, she just ran. Cole wasn't sure if he should go after her. He might make it worse since he was a man, but Julia wasn't there. He walked into the woods, waiting to hear from her. If he ran after her it would make her more afraid. He could hear her moving through the fallen leaves.

Two hours later, he finally tracked her to one of the biggest hills on Silkwood. It overlooked Daphne. To the right was a beautiful view of the gulf. He would miss the water. He thought it strange, Charity normally would have run to the beach, but she ran to the mountains. Praying, he walked up to where she sat. She said nothing. She looked calm and in control. He sat next to her, acting like he didn't have a care in the world. "I am sorry I scared you. I didn't see another way of getting rid of the rattler."

Charity shrugged. "I should be sorry. It was foolish of me, running like that." She looked up at him. "Thank you for saving me."

He smiled. "I always will, darlin'."

Charity did the bravest thing she had ever done. She laid her head against his shoulder. "You remind me of Ben, Pa," she said, so softly Cole almost missed it.

Cole praised God for this miracle. She hadn't even called Julia ma yet. He stayed still and let her control what she wanted in their relationship. He looked down at her and eventually found her asleep. God was healing this little girl's heart. He knew she had a long road to

221

travel, but this was the start and he would be there for her.

Cole wrapped Julia in his arms. She seemed to be worried about something. Cole heard the laughter of the children as they landed in the water from the slide. It was hot and muggy but Cole still held her knowing she needed it. "Do you need a hug?"

Julia nodded against him. "Yes, but I also need to talk to you," she murmured in his wet shirt.

Cole stepped back to where he could meet her eyes, turning serious. "What is it?"

Julia sighed. "It is time to give you this." She pulled up the hem of her skirt and reached into her boot, taking out her knife and then a very small gun from her boot. She handed him the weapons.

"What is this?" Cole asked as he took them. He had never asked her to give them up. He put the gun in his waistband, and the knife in his side pocket.

"I don't want to live in fear any more." She bit her lip. "I trust you and the brothers to protect me and the kids."

Cole hugged her again. "Do you know how proud I am of you? You are so brave." He took her chin in his hand. "Thank you for trusting me."

"No problem." She smiled. "I love you and trust you."

Cole turned and held her hand, looking out at the mountains. "I never asked you to give them up. I know even after the men after me were killed that fear doesn't leave. Izzy still wears her guns and probably always will." He sighed sadly.

Julia squeezed his hand. "Maybe one day she will also give it up. With your love and Jesse's, healing is possible." She turned to watch the kids, knowing they could be interrupted at any time. "I just wanted to trust you. Actually Charity helped me with it. And I was afraid that David could get his hands on the gun."

Cole looked at her. "You know we can't keep guns out of the house, especially on the ranch. It is more dangerous than Alabama."

"Oh, I know that. But we still have to keep him safe, and the other children." She had to know. "Have you thought about what to do about guns when we get worse children on the ranch?"

He looked thoughtful. "Yeah, Juan Jose and Drew have been talkin' about it. We will have to be like most ranches and teach them gun safety. With all the dangers around we don't have much of a choice."

Chapter 32

Katrina walked on the sidewalk, laughing. She needed this today. They all did. It was a way to decompress — a day of shopping, eating at the diner, and girl talk.

Suddenly she walked into Izzy, who had come to a stop and stood still, staring at something ahead. Her back went straight, her jaw set. "What's wrong, Iz?"

Izzy just took a step back and looked at Mabel, then back again.

Mabel followed her gaze and her eyes went wide. So much for hiding one's emotion.

Katrina looked over at the person they were staring at. He was a richly dressed man with a dark mustache, wearing a fancy hat over his combed hair. Nothing about him said much besides he was not from Deer Trail, that was for sure.

Mabel stepped behind Katrina and whispered closely, "That is Teal Heyman. He is the operator of the Denver asylum."

Katrina gasped. "How is he allowed in Deer Trail?"

"Everything he does is legal," Izzy muttered bitterly. "Even gets paid for it."

Suddenly Mr. Heyman spotted them and started walking toward them.

Katrina wanted to run, but to do that wouldn't help. They should know why he was in town.

Mr. Heyman stopped in front of them. "Ladies." He tipped his hat. His eyes landed on Izzy. "Isabella Donovan, the talk of your beauty does not do you justice." He looked at her openly, up and down, seeing she was dressed in a fashionable but simple and modest dress.

Katrina tried to get past Izzy, but Mabel held her back. If only one of the Starry men were here. They would never let a man do that.

Izzy acted like she wasn't noticing his rudeness. "Mr. Heyman, if you don't have a reason for speaking to us, I would ask you to move."

Mr. Heyman chuckled and met her gaze. "Well, my dear, always to the point. I have business with you. Or I should say, with your brother.

He has two of my asylum children. Two girls, a little redhead terror and a tall pretty blond. I want them back."

Katrina gasped. *No, this can't be happening.* Again she tried to pass Izzy. Mabel held her tighter.

Izzy was calm and said smoothly, "The children have not been in your care in over a year. They have been at Liberty House for that time and so you can't take them back. That is a part of the agreement we came to when we took some asylum children off your hands. Dorothea Dix even signed the agreement, if you remember correctly, so I don't see any other business we have to discuss." Izzy tried to pass him.

Mr. Heyman didn't touch her, but he blocked her way. "I have read the contract, that's why I know they are my girls. They belong in the asylum for being touched in the head." He cleared his throat. "That contract works if they have lived at Liberty House for longer than a year or find parents to sign papers from me." He made a hissing sound like Izzy had been a bad girl. "I came to find out the older one only lived at Liberty House for a few weeks at a time. The terror never did. So I will be in the hotel and you can bring the girls later today, Miss Donovan."

Izzy stepped closer, her eyes blazing. Her voice was firm and sure. "You are not getting those children. Part of the contract says we wait for a judge to decide on what to do. So that is what we will do. I will see you in court, Mr. Heyman."

Mr. Heyman glared down at her. "Well, do it the hard way. In the end, I will still win." Before walking away, he winked at her. "See you in court, my dear."

Katrina almost fell back. This couldn't be happening. Izzy didn't turn, just looked off after the man as he walked away. "Izzy, what are our chances?"

Silent, Izzy stayed still. Glancing at Annie then looked off.

Mabel stayed behind her, holding her shoulders, not speaking.

Annie spoke up for the first time, her voice soft and comforting. "Izzy and Cole will get this worked out. They have been to court many times. Oh, everything will be fine, Katrina."

Izzy turned and stared at her twin, but said nothing.

Annie kept at it. "Everything will work out fine, my dear. They have done this in the past. They have got it under control."

Izzy took her anger out on her sister. "Shut up, Annie," she snapped. "We have never been to court. Ever." She groaned. "He is expectin' a fight. That is what he will get." Her eyes showed determination, but they also showed hopelessness.

Katrina cried out, "No!" She felt hopeless for her girls. Is that what court would be? She promised her girls she would always be there. Would always feed them. Who will feed her babies? Who would care for them like her? She stepped back again. *Oh, Lord God, please. My babies, don't let them take my babies.* A pain like she couldn't describe hit her. It made her knees feel weak, her head spin. She wondered if her heart stopped beating because she could hardly feel it. For the first time in her life, she felt this kind of despair. Worse than when she found out Ellen was dying. Everything was ending. She was losing everything. Falling to the ground was the last thing she remembered.

Chapter 33

As they were sitting around Andrew's kitchen table, Annie poured coffee for them all, then she went out to watch the girls.

No one wanted food. All the faces were solemn.

Katrina hadn't slept the night before, just staring off into space, wondering if her girls were being taken. They hadn't told the girls yet they were in danger of being taken away by the courts.

Maverick looked at them. "Hey, we have been through worse before. This is just another trial we will have to get through." He tried to encourage them all. "Since Cole will not be here by the time the judge gets here," he looked at Charles, "Can we depend on you to help with answers? And maybe even a doctor's report?"

"Of course, that is why I am here." He took Mabel's hand.

Andrew spoke up. "Now Charles, we don't want to put your own children at risk."

"It's no problem. They are with my older daughters in Colorado Springs, so are my grandchildren. We didn't want them around when this hit the news," Charles told him.

Andrew nodded.

Maverick spoke again. "We are putting up watches all around the ranch. Night and day. We can take rounds."

Charles spoke up. "My sons and some friends from town can help if need be, and I plan to be here to help with the court."

"Good, I appreciate it," Maverick said.

"I will warn you, the news will be all over this soon." Juan Jose looked sober but hopeful. "We will have newspapers from Denver and Colorado Springs here by the time the judge gets here. Nothing will be a secret anymore. Even what y'all did in the south will come out. They will find out things like medical reports, the issues at home, and pretty much anything to get the girls taken away."

Andrew nodded. "We have handled that before."

Sawyer agreed. "I will cover the story."

"They will go after your hearing loss, Katrina," Mabel told her.

Katrina flinched, and then shrugged. "I have dealt with that before." She paused. "If we had legally adopted them would this have been an issue?" She kept her eyes on the table.

Izzy spoke. "No, they wouldn't have cared one bit. We have an agreement with the asylum that works. Most of the time they don't mess with it but we know there is always a chance the children will go back. Adoption papers wouldn't matter because it has to do with the state."

Katrina bit her lip and nodded solemnly. "What I am worried about is how we can hide this from the girls. They will notice the men around. They probably know something is up already."

"Can you keep them inside for the next three days till the judge gets here?" Izzy asked.

Izzy looked like she had aged ten years overnight. Katrina thought the only one who looked worse was Jesse. He sat there with a stiff look on his face, like he was about to leave the moment he was free. "I can try. I can keep them occupied with cookin'," Katrina mumbled. She had almost started baking in the middle of night but she didn't want to wake the girls.

Gloria winked at her. "And more bakin'." Her voice was light. "I could move in if that would be easier."

Izzy shook her head.

Katrina agreed, shaking her head. "They would know something was up. I want life to stay the same as can be, but thank you."

"So Charles would like to meet with us at Sawyer's house in town in two days?" Maverick asked.

Charles nodded. "I will be there."

Andrew fidgeted next to Katrina. She wished he would take her hand like he always used to in the past when they had meetings like this, but his hands were around the coffee mug. He held it like it was somebody's throat. Probably Mr. Heyman's throat. "Then we got a plan." Andrew tried to be encouraging, but it didn't reach his eyes. "We will keep in touch in the next few days."

So this is what it was like to walk through the valley of despair, Katrina thought.

"Would you mind if we prayed?" Charles asked.

Maverick nodded since he seemed in charge.

"We would appreciate it, Charles," Juan Jose told him. He was such a humble man, caring and honest to a fault.

Katrina couldn't look at Mabel. The older woman was such a help, but her children were safe. She didn't worry about her children being taken. They were all at a place where they would stay safe till this blew over. They weren't in any danger. Mabel had adopted for years, and had helped others. Their children were safe. Why not hers? Izzy said it was because they were Starrys. It was time for the asylum to get them back. Izzy had said, going after Alexanders wouldn't hit the same as going after someone related to the Donovan's. For the Donovans has been a thorn in their side for too long. It was time for revenge. She felt like screaming. The look on Mabel's face made her worried. Her children were still safe. She felt selfish but didn't know how else to feel. She wanted them all safe, and that would not happen.

As they bowed their heads, Katrina was glad Charles prayed. He was not only a father, but a grandfather many times over. And he was one Godly man that understood what they faced. She put a hand on Andrew's hard one. He took her hand in his, but she felt nothing of what they used to have. She signed in his hand, *I love you.* He didn't respond. She let tears form in her eyes. She was also losing her husband along with her children. Maybe this is what a fever was like, a slow wait to lose all you have in a matter of days. She had lost it all.

Andrew stormed out of the house after Charles finished praying. He couldn't breathe. He was so angry he couldn't think straight.

Charles' prayer ran through his head. "Father God, we come here as humble servants. You know our needs and what we are facing. Be with us, give us guidance and give us wisdom. Protect your children, especially your two little girls, Sara and Carlissa. Take care of their parents you have blessed these children with. Give Andrew and Katrina peace that passes all understanding. Give wisdom to the judge that hears this trial. Teach us what you want us to learn. Father, protect your children. May your will be done. In Jesus' name, amen."

Every word reminded him of the past. Of a man he hated. He walked to the woods. He should have grabbed his jacket, it had been cold lately. He wasn't about to go back to the house for anything. He was losing everything. His precious girls. He would give anything to protect them. He kept walking and then cried out as he smashed his fist into a tree. He pulled his hand back, and it was raw, blood started to seep through the broken skin. It didn't take the pain from his heart. Oh, how was he going to face such a quiet house? How was he going to fix the pain in Katrina's eyes?

He heard Maverick behind him. He didn't want to talk to his brother. He had already heard from Maverick how he wasn't meeting Katrina's needs. He didn't want to hear it again. It hurt too much. He felt a rough hand on his shoulder. "Go away, Mav. I can handle this," he raged.

"I don't believe you, son," Charles told him.

Andrew turned to find Charles standing there, looking at him with such compassionate eyes. He was about a head shorter than Andrew, but looked like he could hold his own in a fight. "I'm sorry for yellin'." He stepped back and grunted. "But like I said, I am fine."

Charles looked down at Andrew's bloody hand. "Why don't I believe you?"

Andrew looked at the ground. He wasn't in the mood to talk to anyone, especially Charles. Thunder rumbled in the distance.

"What is your problem with me?" Charles asked. He was not angry, but wanting to know.

Andrew looked at him, muttering, "Nottin.'"

"Well, I don't believe that either. You will talk to the young men in the church and when I come up you close up." He demanded, "What is your problem with me? What?"

Andrew's eyes went wide. "Nothin'. I don't know what you're talkin' about." His eyes turned dark, wanting this conversation to end.

"What are you so angry about? What pain do you have in you, Andrew?" Charles walked closer to him.

"I am losing my children," Andrew cried.

"It is more than that. You have a bitterness that is eating you up. You can't seem to think past it. It's all you think about. It's hurting you, and your relationships." Charles put a hand on his shoulder. "Am I right, son?"

Andrew had a lot of self-control or he would have decked Charles at that moment. But he just pulled back as his face crumbled. "Never call me that. I ain't anyone's son! Not anymore," he yelled. The pain was so deep, so raw. He couldn't handle it.

Charles stood there and the light came into his eyes. "Now I see. Sawyer told me what happened to your pa. What he did. He was a terrible man for doing that to all of you children. But Andrew, you have to let go of what he did to you all."

Andrew shook his head. "You don't understand." Giving up. What did it matter? He was losing his children.

"What? What is wrong?" Charles got in his face.

Andrew couldn't do this. He closed his eyes, and that night flashed before his eyes. He glared at Charles with all the hate and rage he could, and Charles never even flinched. He just stood there waiting for Andrew to come to him with the truth. What would it hurt to tell the man? He was losing his kids so Katrina and him wouldn't have to come to him or Mabel anymore. He turned as he spoke in such anger, such pain, "I killed him. It was my hand that pulled the trigger. It was me." He caught his breath, glad Charles stayed silent. "I watched him closely, he had a gun pointed at Matt. I aimed my rifle. I had done it many times in the past. This time I felt nothin' like all the other times. It is just a job. Then I saw him fall, and I knew it had been my gun." He hung his head beside a tree, breathing like he had run a mile.

Charles stepped beside him but didn't touch him. "I am so sorry, Andrew. You didn't have a choice in the matter. He would have shot your brother. You can forgive yourself, with God's help."

Andrew shook his head. "I don't know if God can. I have never been so alone that night. I haven't felt right with God since. I didn't see God that night. And even if I saw God, I hate Owen. I hate him with all my whole being."

Charles blinked. "You haven't seen God at work in your girls? In your wife? Or even in your family in the last few months? God didn't just drop off the face of the earth when Owen died. He was there that night. You need to ask God where He was that night. Where He was in your darkest part of your life. He will answer."

"You have all the answers, Doc," he said sarcastically as the rain started to fall.

Charles looked at him with sad eyes. "If you don't let go of bitterness, Andrew, it will kill you."

Andrew looked away as the rain came down harder, like God was crying for His children. "It already has, Doc."

Chapter 34

Waking in a cold sweat, Andrew sat up in bed breathing hard. He hadn't had a dream like that in a long time. He looked over at Katrina, who lay sleeping finally after crying for hours last night. She looked peaceful, her hair over her soft face. The only note was the red rims around her eyes. He took one of her curls in his hand, loving the soft feel against his rough fingers. Maverick was right. He should make more time for her. He would after this ended. He let the curl fall and got up.

Walking past the girls' bedrooms, he was quiet as he went down the stairs. The night air was chilly as he stood on the porch, the cool wood against his feet.

He sat on the steps and looked up at all the stars. 'When I consider thy heavens, the work of thy fingers, the moon and the stars, which thou hast ordained.'

God took such care for the stars and the world. Why wouldn't He care for His children? Was He always there? Ask God where He was that night. He will answer. Was Charles right? He ran a hand through his hair thinking of the bible verse, But the very hairs of your head are all numbered. Fear ye not, therefore, ye are of more value than many sparrows.

The sparrows reminded him of his girls. He placed such value on his children. Incredible to know God had that much care for him. He closed his eyes. *God, it's been too long since I have come to you like this. I need to ask, where were you that night? Did you care? Show me how you were there.* He put his head in his hands and went back in his mind to the night that he had tried so hard to forget.

He saw it all like he was watching it play out in his mind. He could see where all his brothers were, and he could see himself holding that rifle. Then he spotted Owen aiming a gun at Matt, who didn't even see him. He saw it then. There was a light around Andrew as he pulled the trigger. He saw there was the same light around all his brothers. God or angels? Did it matter that God protected them? He saw himself drop the rifle and fall to his knees. He saw a bright light, like a man holding him right there in the woods. Then he saw tears in the man's eyes. They had shed the same tears that night after taking his father's life. Jesus wept. He had wept with Andrew that night.

Oh, God, could I be so blind? Andrew wept now. He let the tears fall, and as they did, he felt himself forgive Owen. It was like he didn't have a choice. God came to him like he could do anything. Bring his marriage back to what it was. And maybe, maybe even save his girls. With God, all things were possible. He wiped his eyes, looking up. He hadn't felt this light in such a long time. Though he had a mountain of problems yet to face, his heart was free and so he could face those problems head-on.

Andrew's heart felt light despite his inner pain of what might happen. He enjoyed watching Katrina with his little blond angel, though most would not call her that. He saw the inside; she was one and that could come out in time. But they didn't have time.

"Look, Sally is taking the last kitten!" Sara pointed at the barn cat carrying the last of her four kittens to inside the stall where she had found a new home, farther away from the curious little puppy.

Katrina smiled.

Sara looked thoughtful. "I have learned something while living here on a real ranch." She stayed silent for so long Andrew didn't think she would tell them. But then she softly said, "Mothers are supposed to love their babies. Ember, the mama pig, hates us if we get close to her piglets. The cows and horses will take out a person to protect their young. The mother hens will pick at us for even taking eggs." She added, "They don't abandon or sell their babies."

Katrina leaned closer. "No mother should do that. I love you, baby. Like the mother hen, and I will protect you like the pig." She smiled lightly. "And you know how crazy Ember can get."

Sara shrugged and curved her lip. "But mistakes happen."

Katrina put a hand over her mouth and tried to stop a sob.

Sara's eyes got wide like they did when someone cried, but this time with fear.

Francesca and Carlissa walked in just as Katrina literally ran out.

Andrew ran a hand through his hair. This was not going well.

"What is wrong with Ma?" Sara asked.

Francesca shrugged and stated, "I know the signs. She will abandon us and is feeling a little guilty."

"Francesca, your ma would never abandon you," Andrew told her. "She truly loves you."

"Then what is wrong?" Sara stared at him. "Pa, did you make a mistake?"

Andrew put a hand on her shoulder. "No, my darlin', we didn't. We have not and will never regret adopting you girls. But this world ain't perfect, and some things are happening out of our control." He prayed. His heart felt like it was in pieces. "The owner of the Denver asylum is back. We will go to court and will try our best to keep you girls with us."

Sara didn't react.

Francesca's eyes nearly popped out of her head, then her eyes went dark like a raging storm.

Carlissa just looked up at him with her beautiful blues. "It's all right, Pa. We knew this place would not last. But is Francesca coming along?"

Andrew had never felt pain so great, and once someone had burned half of his body. He would rather feel that pain again than to see the look on his children's faces. His face almost gave way. He picked up Carlissa. "I meant this to be your home and we will try our best to make sure that happens."

"How could you keep this from us?" Francesca yelled. "That is why everyone has been around so much and Katrina looks like death?"

"We wanted to have a plan, Francesca," Andrew told her truthfully.

"Why? Why are Sara and Carlissa being taken when Mrs. Alexander's brats are safe? Why the girls?" Francesca shook her fist at him. "Oh, I get it. You are getting money for them. See, I know you are selling them!"

Andrew's jaw popped and tried to remember the pain she was going through. "I would never do that, Fran. Now calm down. We are trying our best in this." He looked to Sara, who never said a word. "How are you, Sara?"

Sara looked at him, her eyes lifeless. "Like I said, everyone makes mistakes. Can I go get some cake?"

Andrew nodded, having no words to her quiet turmoil. Watching her leave, his heart broke.

Carlissa rested her head against his shoulder, her red curls touching his chin. He saw her eyes closed. He wished she could always have this kind of peace. His family was being ripped from him one by one. And it was breaking his heart. God had to have an answer for him. *Please, God, save my babies.*

Chapter 35

Maverick dismounted in front of the church, looking like he was on a mission. Andrew knew that look well. He prayed Maverick had answers before court started. He walked down the stairs to greet him.

"I might know of a lawyer in Denver that will help." Maverick got to the point. "But one of us will have to travel there."

Andrew nodded. "I will. It will only be a few days' ride."

"Take Juan Jose with you. He knows the area the best."

Andrew looked into the church. "I'd hoped your first time here would be for a picnic or church social."

Maverick put a hand on his shoulder. "We will get time to do that."

Andrew knew if he lost the girls, he could never look at the church without mourning. Entering the church, he felt like he was walking to his death sentence.

He walked to the front where Katrina and Izzy sat. Maverick sat down next to Izzy. The peaceful church had been turned into a courtroom. There were two tables up front, and a table for the judge up front. Sitting next to Katrina, Andrew saw Jesse and Sawyer seated in the front pew of the church.

They all stood as Judge Bower came up to sit behind the table. Bower had a small build. He had gray hair and dark eyes under bushy eyebrows. Glancing down at some papers, he looked up again. "Well, this will be a hearing and not a trial. The parties involved areAndrew and Katrina Starry who have been caring for Sara and Carlissa and the party of Mr. Heyman, the director of the Denver alsyum. Who would like to make your case first?"

Mr. Heyman stood up. "I would like to call Mabel Alexander to the stand."

After swearing Mabel in, she looked calm and in control. "Ma'am, you were one of the first ones to meet the girls after Mrs. Starry, is that correct?"

She nodded. "Yes."

"So you saw that Mrs. Starry was afraid to be their mother." Before

Mabel could argue he added, "How long did it take for them to adopt the girls?"

"A couple days." She bit her lip. "A week, but most parents take longer to decide."

"But Mrs. Starry was afraid to be their mother, was she not?"

"You are not a father. So you can't understand that..." Mabel gave him an amused look. "Many mamas are terrified. But we do it because it is a part of us."

Mr. Heyman looked bothered by not having shaken her. "Are you the one who fixed Sara's broken arm?"

Mabel nodded. "Yes."

"Why didn't your husband? Odd that a woman would do something like that. You are not a doctor, you could have done something wrong."

Mabel frowned. "I have been caring and helping women and children in this area for decades. Everyone knows that. I would never make a mistake like that. My husband wasn't able to help me."

"Really? I heard he wasn't busy at the time. Why was she unable to help you?"

Mabel looked to Charles.

Andrew made a fist, ready to punch someone. The whole town knew Mabel took care of many different needs for the women in town. This was so wrong. The whole town would know his children's fears. Was it worth it? They didn't have much choice.

"Answer the question, Mrs. Alexander," Mr. Heyman told her.

Mabel looked ready to kill someone. "Sara wouldn't let him help her."

"So you are saying she was putting herself in more danger by not letting a professional work on her. Because of her fear." Mr. Heyman looked too smug. "And how did she break her arm in the first place?"

"She fell off of a cliff," Mabel said simply.

It was a simple accident, nothing more. But what did the man have up his sleeve? Andrew thought.

"So no one was watching her then? She was all alone on that cliff?"

Mabel looked at him with shock. "She is a teenager. What teenager do you know is watched all the time? Teenagers I know and raise can ride off alone by themselves. It was an accident, she slipped, nothing more."

"But her parents didn't find her for a while? Her pa didn't get to her right away."

"She is alive, ain't she? He found her in enough time," Mabel answered sarcastically.

Andrew prayed all the people they put on the stand could be as good as Mabel, but he was afraid they wouldn't be. Mabel knew how to deal with professionals. Say just enough to answer, but not too much detail.

"Have you ever seen Mr. Starry or one of his male relatives being improper with the young women?"

"First, they are not young women. They are children and no, I have seen none of the Starry men be improper with any of his children," Mabel told him firmly.

"Why then would he take in a Mexican young woman who lacks values?"

"Maybe because he loves her." Mabel shook her head. "A father's love. One that will do anything for a child, even the difficult things."

"And how many children have you adopted?"

"What does that matter? I am not on trial."

"It will show that an adoptive mother's heart will say anything to see a child have a home. Even a child who is too old and too loose to belong anywhere."

Mabel put her hand on her thighs, leaning forward. "Francesca Starry is one of the bravest girls I have ever met and she is not on trial right now, Mr. Heyman."

"I have one last question. Has Katrina's deafness ever affected her parenting of the children?"

Mabel gasped. She didn't look at Katrina or Andrew, but kept her eyes straight ahead. Choosing her words carefully, she proved she knew what she was doing. "No, it has never hurt her parenting."

"That is not what I asked. Can she hear the children every time they call? Are there times she can't hear them?"

Mabel bit her lip. "Yes, but her children are older, so they work with her lack of hearing. It doesn't bother them."

"Does it bother Carlissa?"

Mabel glared at him. "I have a question for you, while you stand there and tear apart the Starrys the rest of the trial, you didn't even give Carlissa a name. She was known as the Terror. Where have you been the last year since the children went missing? Answer me that, Mr. Heyman!"

The judge looked at her. "Ma'am, Mr. Heyman is not on trial."

She looked at him respectfully. "Yes, sir, but will you make him answer the question? It is for the well being of the children, sir."

Andrew could tell it killed her to be respectful to the judge who gave this man too much power, but for his girls she remained respectful and in control.

Bower looked at Mr. Heyman. "Answer the woman's questions."

"But sir..." Mr. Heyman stuttered.

"I happen to know that the Alexanders have several of your former children, so I would answer the question."

Mr. Heyman looked at her, his face full of disgust. "I was out of town when they ran away. I didn't have the resources to find them."

"Really?" Mabel looked surprised. "The children have run away a couple times since living here, and Andrew had many of his new friends looking for them. They have the resources for what matters."

Andrew hid his smile. The friends were her relatives and his brothers and friends, but what did it matter. They cared and helped. Mabel had won the battle with him.

Mr. Heyman glared at her. "No further questions, Mrs. Alexander."

Maverick stood up in his new suit, looking like he had it under control and knew what he was doing. "Mrs. Alexander, you were there for the Starrys since adopting the girls. Have you seen the girls get healthier with the Starrys?"

"Yes, both Sara and Carly have gained weight, and their hair and skin are looking much healthier."

"Have you seen any mistreatment of the girls while living in the Starry home?"

"No, I haven't."

"And can you tell me what you have seen the Denver Asylum do? Can you explain how you came to this knowledge?"

"Well, like Mr. Heyman said, some of my children are adopted. And I support helping others adopt. So I have heard their stories of how they found their children. One ma found her baby left to die on the porch of an asylum. When the babies get sick or are too loud, they leave them in the sun so they will dehydrate faster or they will freeze in a matter of minutes in the winter." Mabel shut down her feelings to share all this. It must tear her heart. "One man found his boy nearly naked, tied up in a big bucket they left outside in January. Another family found their five-year-old twins being beaten and tortured in front of each other. One family found two children under a porch in the middle of winter. Another boy was eating in a pig pen out back. This is hard to hear, but you might wonder where all these children were found. Well, Mr. Maverick Starry, we found them in that man's hell." She pointed to Mr. Heyman. "The Denver asylum." She pushed graying hair from her face. "Those are just the places they found the children. Not the stories of what happened before this. Their little bodies suffered so much trauma. It hurts their development of their body and brain. It makes them think, act, and behave in strange and different ways. All I know is from what I learned, and sometimes that ain't much. These children need love, structure, consistency, care, and support from parents, relatives and yeah, church families. What did God call His people to do? Care for the fatherless and that doesn't always mean raising them. Just supporting and caring for ones who have been called to adopt."

"Thank you, ma'am. That will be all."

Andrew didn't know how much more he could handle. This didn't look good. Though Mabel had been right. The judge looked indifferent and he understood the law unlike most.

After a couple of other people spoke, Gabby got on the stand.

Mr. Heyman gave her his full attention, acting like a gentleman. "Well, Gabby Herman, I hear you know pretty much everything in town."

She grinned. "That is for sure." Then she looked at Katrina and frowned.

"So you got to know the Starrys pretty well since moving here. Have you noticed any problems between the couple?"

Mabel shrugged. "Well, I think all married couples have issues at one time or another. My husband and I sure did. I am a widow now."

"Did you ever see any bruises on Mrs. Starry?"

Gabby looked to Andrew, her eyes pleading with him. "Well, Kat said a box fell on her face." She looked back at Mr. Heyman. "I had a wood box fall on me at the store and give me a big ol' black eye." She grimaced. "And no one said my Luke did it. You should be more of a gentleman. And there was this one time..."

Mr. Heyman interrupted her story. "Have you ever wondered why Katrina and Andrew adopted right after moving here? Did Mabel pressure them?"

"No, she doesn't pressure people to adopt, but they come here to help adoptive families so I wasn't too surprised." Gabby looked lovingly at them.

"And why did Katrina never have her own child?"

Gabby gasped. "Now that is something a gentleman would never ask." She glared at him. "I never could have any children, so I know that pain. My Luke would never let me raise a child. When he passed, I was too old, but then Mabel let me be a granny to her youngins. Andrew and Katrina supported each other in adopting these children."

"If Katrina raised a baby, it might meet her disabilities better. Her hearing affects the girls and how she parents them, doesn't it?"

Gabby raised an eyebrow. "I thought Mabel put you in your place over that one."

"Answer the question." He didn't seem threatened by her.

Gabby looked to Katrina, her eyes pleading to be told what to say. Then she nodded. "Yes, it does, but she has a lot of help from her sisters and Andrew."

Mr. Heyman ignored her comment. "Have you ever seen odd or strange behaviors from Carlissa or Sara?"

Gabby looked panicked again. "Well, sometimes little Carly will scream and thrash around, but most of the time she is a very nice little girl."

"I am sure, but you have to agree she is touched in the head. She does not act right. And should be somewhere where she will be safe, and others will be safe."

"She is safe."

"Are others around her safe?"

Gabby shrugged. "I think so. She has wonderful parents."

"But is she a danger to others and to herself?"

Gabby looked at her hands and nodded.

"I can't hear you?"

"Yes, she is." Gabby started talking quickly. "But I am sure with the Starrys she will be just fine. She is better now. She doesn't run out of a church no more or hit people with hymn books."

Andrew tried to meet her eyes, but she kept talking about what the girls didn't do anymore. It wasn't helping, though she thought it was.

She finished with, "They now ride and work the land with their pa and Izzy. They are good little riders and are now roping."

Mr. Heyman again looked smug. "That is all, Mrs. Herman. You have been helpful."

Gabby smiled brightly at Andrew as she stepped down, not knowing what she had just done. Andrew felt bad, so he tried to give her a smile. She had pretty much said he adopted the girls to work the land. She forgot to mention how much they loved the foals and newborn calves, how they were learning to cook. How they were children at the ranch. Closing his eyes, he prayed again.

The last one for the day was Maryanne Smith. She was the one who had spread lies about Mabel. She hated Katrina just as much. Mr. Heyman looked the smuggest with this one. He seemed to know what she would say. "Now you have some thoughts about the Starrys?"

"Yes, when Katrina Starry first moved here, she was a bright, outgoing young woman. I was excited to get to know her. But I saw Mabel Alexander was fast becoming her friend and she always pressures people to adopt. So when she ended up adopting the girls, I wasn't surprised. I noticed slowly how the changes were on her. She struggled with her new children and her relationship with Andrew could use some work. I saw it with my own eyes. They would glare at each other in town. And the children were just so bad. If it wasn't all of them, it was that oldest one. Who would take in an illiterate young Mexican woman? She is not even the same color and they are about the same size, so she ain't anyone's child. Nor would she ever be again."

Andrew bit his lip, wanting to grab his gun, but Maverick had made sure none of them brought their guns in, including Izzy. Though with her line of work, she probably had one in her boot. He hated how this woman talked of his children. She was lying. All of it was lies. He took Katrina's hand and saw her go all white. How she wasn't crying was beyond him.

"Did you notice Mrs. Starry was afraid of her husband, Mr. Starry?"

She nodded. "I did. He was mad that she let one girl play with her friends. She backed up like he would hit her and you know how big he is. It wouldn't take much. It could be why she lost so much of her hearing. Hitting can do that."

Before Mr. Heyman could ask another question, Maverick stood up. "Judge, Mrs. Smith has no proof of this."

Bower looked at Mr. Heyman. "Change the line of questions."

"Have you noticed Mrs. Starry is very strict with her children?"

"Yes, it is probably she doesn't want them disobeying because of her deafness. Doesn't want to look like a bad mother. She doesn't let them play unless they eat. She always watches them as they play. She doesn't even let anyone hold the little one, even her hand. She makes them sit in the middle of the seat when they want to sit along the edge of the wagon."

"And are the children allowed in school?"

"Well, they do not allow touched children in our school. So they will never fit in this town anyhow."

"No further questions."

Maverick asked a few questions, which she tried to turn around to her own gain, then he stepped down, knowing it was just hurting their cause.

Andrew looked over to Katrina to find her eyes wet with tears. She had kept them at bay so far.

Bower stood. "Well, this is all for today. We will meet in two days. It will be a three-day trial. Thank you all who came."

Katrina walked out feeling like the blood was drained out of her.

Chapter 36

"How did Maryanne know all that? Andrew and I don't fight in public. We have never had a fight in front of the girls. Ask them! How did she come up with such lies?" Katrina asked Mabel as they took a walk the next day. "I have never felt more useless or dumb." She made a sarcastic sound. "And don't worry, the south tried their best."

Mabel nodded. "I am sure they did. Maryanne can be a very hard woman. She made up lies about me and my children when she first moved here. It hurt, but the rumors died away. And so will this." She took her arm as they walked around the pond. "And most of the people, at least the church ladies, know Maryanne can be spiteful. I just believe there is more than what she is saying. Something painful, deep inside causes her to act like this."

"But what about my pain?" Katrina cried. "I am sorry. That is selfish."

"No, you were hurt and so was I. You also have to remember that not many people will understand how we raise our children. Why do we make them eat before playing? Well, it might help them try to not kill their friends." She gave Katrina a sarcastic look. "You know what I mean? Not many of the church ladies do. When they first heard about us raising touched children, they said time and love would cure it, and when it didn't they didn't know how to react. It was like God wasn't answering our prayers. He is and He always will. But it might not be in the way we think or in the time we want. Just because something we make breaks doesn't mean we can fix it without a few issues. I pray in the future that they will understand what all our children can be."

Katrina looked at the ground, feeling the cold air in her lungs, waiting for the first winter snowfall. "But what if they are right? What if I am a bad mama because I can't hear them all the time?"

"You know that is not true. Those are just lies. They come from Satan. You have a lot of help. A husband that is working the ranch from home, you have sisters and brothers who are understanding and supportive." She grinned. "And you have me. What more could you ask for?"

"Ellen," Katrina whispered. Then she looked up. "I am sorry. I just miss her and now..."

Mabel took her hand, comforting her."You don't have to explain. I understand that mother's love. Just don't let your pain over Ellen and your hurts over Maryanne change you."

"I feel like I have changed already. I am harder, I feel like I can't control a thing in my life."

"Honey, we aren't meant to control our lives. God is always in control. But yes, times like this, all of it is in chaos."

"We should head back to the house now. Gloria is not used to the girl's behaviors yet."

"Is Julia or Annie used to them?"

Katrina shook her head. "No, Annie ain't used to much. And Julia is pretty good with everything and now she is raising the younger children. It has grown her up some."

"Marriage does that." Mabel winked. "Motherhood makes sure it happens."

Katrina chuckled. "You are never afraid of it."

Mabel shrugged. "I have been, but I try to find humor in almost everything."

Katrina heard screaming before she opened the door to see Carlissa, lying flat on her back, her legs flailing, her arms hitting everything. Gloria looked to be at a loss on what to do. Katrina didn't want to fix this problem this time. It hurt too much. Mabel came in behind her. The older woman had no emotion on her face. Mabel whispered, "You will always be a mother. You are their strong mama."

Katrina didn't even cry. She felt so frail. She didn't have it in her to get her daughter calm, but she was hurting herself. Suddenly Carlissa sat up and saw Katrina. Her anger and hate was so loud it was like she screamed it. Katrina didn't see it coming; Mabel pushed her out of the way as a glass hit the wall and shattered. Katrina walked over to her. She got down and didn't talk to her. Carlissa was too angry to think, to reason.

She had her arms around her and held her legs down so Carlissa didn't kick her. She tried rocking her. She closed her eyes but couldn't pray. She wasn't bitter at God. She just didn't know if it did any good. Was God with her while she held her child? Was He with her when she talked to her children about their past? Was He answering her prayers? Her heart cried out.

Suddenly Carlissa jerked and added curse words to her screaming. She became more forceful. Katrina wondered what she was doing here. Was she doing any good in her child's life? What had she done for them? Maybe she wasn't made to be a mother. Maybe God had made a mistake by giving her the girls. She knew she loved them and wanted what was best for them. But was that enough? Did her love not meet her children's needs?

When Sara had slapped at her, Sara's eyes had held such hate, She remembered in that moment thinking she just wanted her daughter gone. She had thought it, and now God was making it come true. Maybe it was her? Maybe she was the reason they were being sent away? She wanted to cry out; she didn't mean to think such a thing. She would take it back if she could. She just wanted her babies. Her heart was open and breaking. She couldn't do anything well, parenting or being a wife. What was God trying to teach her? *Why are You doing this?*

Just like that, Carlissa stopped. She looked up at Mabel. "Hi, Mrs. Alexander." She even smiled.

Mabel took it like she did everything, calmly. "Hello, Carlissa."

Katrina let her go. Both stood up. She looked at everyone in the room. She couldn't take the look of pity and compassion. "I need to go." She partly ran out. She didn't enjoy riding, so she just pulled up her skirt and ran.

Running across the field until her legs burned, she couldn't breathe. Falling to her knees, sobs from deep in her heart came out. She leaned against a tree near the creek, only hearing her own cries. She didn't know how much she could take. Ellen had told her she might get to a breaking point. Katrina was at her breaking point. It was here, and she didn't know if she could handle it. The tears made her feel like she couldn't breathe. It was more than just pain, but physically she couldn't take the suffering. This truly was the valley of the shadow of death. Deliver us from evil. Though her girls weren't gone yet, she ached to hold them. Oh, how she ached for them.

"Is this a new painting, Rose?" Cole asked as he packed away another one of Julia's paintings.

Julia held some smaller ones and looked over where he was packing one of the larger ones. She smiled softly as she saw it, the one with the Great Shepherd watching over His sheep. "Yeah, something I did a bit ago."

Cole looked at her like he would find out the story behind it. Julia just winked at him, knowing they enjoyed finding new things about each other. Cole eyed her like he didn't have the time to respond to that wink. He told her with his eyes they would finish it later.

Julia planned to wear David on her chest; she wrapped him like a baby and not a toddler. She only did it now when Cole was around. If he left the room, she would get David's full anger. She knew Cole couldn't always be there, but for now, he could be. She didn't know if it was helping, but it made her notice things about him she had never noticed before.

Hannah, Susan's mother, had not come to see her daughter off. Julia could tell by Susan's face, there would be tears on the train.

Julia saw a boy run away and from the look on Cole's face that something was wrong on that note. "What does it say?"

Cole shook his head. He handed her the note. Matt held a screaming baby Mary and read over her shoulder. It read that Katrina and Andrew were losing their two little girls to an asylum.

He looked at the children. "On the train, kids. Westward ho!," he tried to say excitedly. Too nervous and excited, the children missed what was going on with the adults.

Julia almost fell back. "No." She looked at Cole. "Is there anything we can do for them?"

Cole frowned. "Izzy and Juan Jose are there. There is nothing I can do from this far, but I will send a telegram saying we will pray and send another telegram in the following towns." He slammed his fist in his palm. "In all the years of running the home, our work never went to court. This ain't good." He looked at Julia. "Get everything loaded and I will reply."

Julia nodded, feeling so much dread for Katrina and Andrew. How they must be in such despair, such pain over this.

Susan took her hand. "Let's pray for them and our trip."

Matt came along with Mary, who had calmed a little. They all prayed for God to help Andrew and Katrina in their time of need, for a miracle to happen in the Starry family.

Katrina stood up after the service. Her legs shook and she hoped no one noticed. Andrew would have if he was there, but he was away with Juan Jose. After looking at Pastor Peter one more time, she knew she would never be back in this church. She wanted to weep. So many dreams gone. He had meant his sermon for them.

Holding Carlissa's hand and having Sara walk next to her, she headed to the door. Old Mrs. Landon stopped her before she got to the door. She took Katrina's hand like she was a dear old friend. "Mrs. Starry, don't you worry yourself. This is all for the best. These girls will go back to where they belong and the older girl will move on. Then you and Andrew can start with a baby. Like it's supposed to be." She said it so friendly like, it was the truth and she even meant well.

It cut Katrina like a knife. She pulled her hand away as if she had been burned. Biting her lip so she couldn't speak, she wished Andrew were there to set this woman straight. She could feel Sara harden next to her. She felt Carlissa withdraw more. She knew Francesca was ready to explode, a fire about to be lit. She couldn't speak. If she did, she knew she would cry, and she had been doing good at not crying in front of the girls.

Jerry stepped up with his arm around his wife, Gloria. "Now Mrs. Landon, I am sorry you believe that. That you accept the lie so many believe. I used to believe the same way about God. Some believe he is all about judgment and no mercy. Some believe He is all love and mercy and no judgment. I believed the first, and I believe you have too. You see God as a God who set out to hurt and judge everyone, but He is a merciful God. He was merciful to the thief on the cross. He was merciful to the woman at the well. He is merciful to the weak and the blind. He is loving and merciful. Yes, he is also a God of judgment, and I believe He will also judge His church, His people for turning away His children. It says whoever hurt my little ones will not go on without judgment. He will protect the orphans. Yes, even ones who are touched. See you might know of God, but in your heart, you don't know God."

Mrs. Landon blinked back like she hadn't thought of it that way.

"What do you say, Pastor Peter?" Jesse challenged the pastor listening to them. He held Izzy's hand.

Pastor Peter walked closer and held his head high, like he was glad they finally asked his advice. "Well, I won't comment on what Mr. Emerson just spoke of. He is a young, naive man. I believe the asylum should be used sparingly and with care. Katrina and Andrew have tried their best, but think of what the Bible says about giving Caesar what is his. Leave it up to the law to decide what is best for these children."

Katrina gasped at his words. Pastors had hurt her in the past, but nothing like this. This cut to the core. This was her children he was speaking of so cheaply as if they belonged to the government. She stood there and watched the pastor's face in disbelief. How could he turn on them like that? She let the tears fall for the first time in front of her daughters as she cried. In front of the church members. In front of a man who was supposed to lead the children of God, she cried.

Katrina watched Annie step outside as she wanted away from the conflict. Odd how one sister ran from any dispute while one sister stood in front of it, no matter what it cost her.

Sara walked up to him, her face red, her back straight. Her entire body was shaking in fear as she stood in front of Pastor Peter. "I will see you in Hell, Pastor!" She leaned up and spit in his face, then ran out like he would chase her.

Izzy went after her, silently walking past the pastor. Katrina could tell she had turned her feelings off. She was just going through the motions, Mabel called it.

Katrina still couldn't seem to move or speak. She held onto Carlissa tightly. The child looked confused from all the conflict. Katrina just held her and cried. For a child who had to learn too early that life was hard. She cried because her own mama was not there to fight for her. To fight with her. She cried because no matter what, Ellen was right. It wasn't about what state, what part of the country, even what year it was. It mattered if they knew the value of human life and really treated everyone equally. Colorado territory did not differ from Alabama. It was the same people. It was just how they viewed God's children.

Katrina might not be able to speak, but her oldest daughter's fuse broke loose. Francesca walked up to the pastor, her arms crossed, her jaw set. Her face was as hard as a rock, like anything the pastor would say to her wouldn't make a dent in her heart. Katrina saw through her facade - if the pastor said anything, Fran could be crushed again as she had by so many others.

"Do you know why she wants to meet you in hell? Because before she goes back to the asylum, that is where she will go. Pa can't protect her, neither can Ma, not Preacher Juan Jose, and even Maverick can't help her. It will be up to the government. You preacher man, as you call it." She swore. "You know what, Katrina was right. You might be a learned man, but you don't understand the value of life. You don't understand how hard life in an asylum is. I wish you could walk a day in Sara's life at the asylum. You can't imagine what life is like for her. But you can't, you're a man." Francesca looked at Katrina.

The look in Francesca's eyes made Katrina cry all the harder for her. She was so broken. So lost in believing the doubts this pastor believed. Katrina didn't know what to say. Her whole world was coming down. "I loved you, Mama." Francesca shrugged like she couldn't help it. "I can't do it anymore. They have won."

Katrina shook her head and stepped forward and took her hand. "I love you and will always love you no matter what."

Francesca's face didn't soften, she just looked at her with angry eyes, almost black. Katrina kept her gaze. Francesca's eyes were asking her to make this hurt go away.

Katrina kept her gaze and kept it lovingly. Kept it light no matter how hard she wanted to fall to the ground and just sob.

She almost shook her head. She couldn't fix this. Only a miracle could. Francesca was right, she knew the outcome. The state had won. She wept as her daughter glared at her to fix her life. Knowing she couldn't was one of the hardest things she had ever had to face.

Chapter 37

Katrina had almost everyone looking for Francesca again. With the hearing underway, it made everything more dangerous. They had three more days until the last hearing. She walked out to the creek to see if she was there. If not, Andrew said he would check the brothels again. She closed her eyes and prayed her daughter wasn't back in one of those places. Walking to the edge of the woods, she spotted Phoenix. Izzy was furious when Francesca took Phoenix without asking. Well, she had to get in line. She walked closer and saw Francesca sitting against a tree looking over at the river. She looked tired, but almost at peace. Her face and body were relaxed. The girl was hardly ever relaxed.

Katrina was about to walk over when she heard someone call Francesca's name. Looking around like Francesca did, she saw Timmy ride up. He dismounted and looked concerned, but not angry. "What are you doing here, Francesca?"

Francesca didn't move and shrugged like she didn't care. "Nothin'," she muttered.

Katrina could read her lips very well from where she stood behind an enormous tree. She could also read Timmy's lips. She waited and watched what would happen.

Timmy tied his horse, walked over to the tree across from her, and sat down. "What are you doing here?" he asked again.

"I was sick of being watched and needed a break. When I couldn't get past anyone, Sawyer was in the barn watching. I started to cry and I told him I needed to talk to Katrina. Like I ever would do that. I made a break for it," Francesca told him, as a matter of fact.

The words hurt Katrina. She wanted to be needed.

Timmy smiled. "And you took off with Miss Izzy's horse. She is madder than a wet hen."

Francesca chuckled. "I am sure she is. Phoenix knows the land. He is fast enough to pass all the men."

Timmy grinned. "The men are good at protecting others."

251

"I reckon." Francesca nodded. "They should get work with the US. Marshalls."

"And work the hearing. They do that pretty well." He looked concerned. "Are you all right, Fran?"

Francesca shrugged again. "I am just so tired of it all."

He frowned. "I am sorry for what Pastor Peter told you. He was so wrong."

"How have you gone to that church for so long?" Francesca asked. "Y'all are so different from Peter."

Timmy nodded. "He is a hard preacher man. We went through some pretty hard stuff with him when we adopted my brothers, but a lot of that is in the past now."

"Did your parents pay for your brothers?" Francesca's mouth was hard. "For you?"

Katrina would have laughed at Francesca. She was trying so hard to offend Timmy and he just shrugged like it was nothing. He was tough as nails, for sure.

"Nope. I was a freebie," he stated with lightness. "If you expect to offend me, I have heard it all before. Strangers will tell you everything. I was a free baby because of the birthmark on my face. My parents paid for my brothers. And the other boys we got from the streets of Denver."

"Do you know anything about your real parents?" Francesca asked, softer.

Timmy nodded. "My real parents, I live with every day." He grinned and gave her a knowing look. "Yes, my ma looked for my tummy mamma. She died a couple months after I was born. Because of my good looks, I am probably Mexican or Italian. There was nothing of a pa. I was blessed, and I got great parents who love me."

Francesca frowned. "You never doubted them. Never wondered if they loved you."

Timmy shook his head. "I have doubts. Many times I explode in anger and I have so many fears that the anger will set me back."

Francesca glared at him. "But you remember nothing."

Timmy nodded. "I don't remember anything but I feel different sometimes. I still scream in the night and I don't know why. I yell, wondering why I am doing this." He shrugged. "My ma said I am like a cannon ready to light. I hide what I feel. My brothers are like a lit fuse all the time." His face lightened.

Francesca's lip came up in a smile. "Us girls would be a lit fuse."

Timmy shrugged. "It will pass in time and then you will feel like you have better control of your emotions."

"Did that come from your mama?" Francesca asked sarcastically.

Timmy shook his head. "Nope, I have felt it and seen it."

"Why did you stay here? And not go with your siblings?" Francesca's lips pouted a bit. Katrina could tell Francesca was acting, she wanted to be kissed. She was teasing him with her body.

"I wanted to be here for you. And I worry about mama getting enough rest when she is in a fight like this."

Francesca's eyebrow rose. "You worry about your mama?"

"Yeah, I do." Timmy chuckled at her shock. "Mothers are pretty sweet, you just have to get used to the rules with love. What is the best thing Katrina taught you?"

Francesca pouted her lips more, thinking about it. Katrina was afraid of what she would say. "She taught me how to cook. I like cooking. Andrew says if a woman can bake a peach pie, then she is ready for marriage." She chuckled. "I made my first pie a couple days ago and I think it turned out pretty well."

Timmy blushed to his roots.

Francesca laughed. "I can get Katrina to blush at the drop of a hat." She winked at him. "Though I can't get Andrew to blush one bit. But I keep trying."

Timmy shook his head, chuckling. "Your lot in life should not be how much can you get people to blush."

Francesca put her hand on the ground and leaned over to him, her lips close to his. "Maybe I just want you, Timmy," she whispered. If either moved, they would be kissing.

Katrina watched it play out before her. The struggle on Timmy's face was evident. Katrina prayed he would fight it.

Timmy put his hand up and Katrina thought it was to pull her close, but he put a hand on her shoulder and pushed her back, shaking his head. His face struggled. "You do not belong to me. To take even a kiss would be wrong."

"And who do I belong to?" Francesca asked angrily. She didn't enjoy being rejected, but if Katrina didn't see it, there was a light in her eyes that he wasn't just a man that took another kiss from her. It still confused her. According to Francesca, her body was the only reason a man wanted her.

"You belong to the King of kings, and you are Andrew's beloved daughter," Timmy told her.

Francesca rolled her eyes. "Sure," she muttered. "Sometimes I wonder why Katrina and Andrew do this. Their life could be so much easier." She looked confused. "They have lost Isaiah over us."

Timmy looked thoughtfully at her. "Nah, he just doesn't understand what Andrew is trying to do."

Francesca sighed. "Your ma still kept you when she had a baby."

Timmy looked confused. "Yeah. What makes you say that, Francesca?"

Francesca leaned against the tree. "I had a friend, Anna. Her real mama had left her. When she was still young and pretty, she went home to this rich couple. Anna never forgot about me. She brought me food. I didn't go hungry anymore. I tried to be a good child, to stop cursing and stealing. It was not easy. We would play and I would dream that they needed two daughters. Maybe they would forget I was Mexican. Then something happened, and I knew it was too late for a family." She stopped talking.

Katrina let tears fall. She wiped her eyes and watched Timmy's hand cover Francesca's hand, just in comfort, not grabbing.

Francesca allowed it and continued. "In her barn, we would sit on her pony. It was always safe there with lots of food. Three winters went by. We stayed just as close, then her mama was with child." Francesca's voice hardened. "We loved the baby and talked of holdin' the little sister and protectin' it." Francesca's mouth curved. "The baby came and Anna forgot about me. I would sit in the barn and wait for her to bring food and she forgot." Francesca's face went hard. "I went hungry and started stealing again. Then one night, Anna got dropped off by her adoptive mama. Her mama said she was a child from bad blood." She shook her head and ran a hand through her hair. "The madam of the house cussed and slapped Anna. We called the madam the witch of the village, because of how dark she was inside and out. Anna said her mama didn't want a daughter with scars."

Katrina wanted so much to hug her, but she watched as Timmy stayed silent and just held her hand in both of his.

"Anna taught me to read and write. When she was adopted, she would write me notes and I could never read them. She taught me to read and write from those notes. We couldn't afford books. Katrina also writes me notes." Her face crumbled.

"What happened to Anna?" Timmy was so gentle.

Francesca's face was full of guilt and grief. "I got sick and Anna took care of me. I got better and then she got it, but she wasn't getting better. I kept trying. I stayed up two nights caring for her. I fell asleep, and when I woke up, I was on a train. I tried to go back. But the train was too fast and it was heading west." Her hands curled into fists. Her face was furious. "I found out later she passed away. Our papers probably got burned. I have nothing of her."

"You have what she taught you," Timmy told her.

Francesca pulled away and stood. "Now I am losing my sisters and my parents."

Timmy stood, facing her. "You are not losing Katrina or Andrew. They will always love you. You are their daughter, Princess."

The wrath on Francesca's face was so full of hate and distrust. She yelled, "I will never be their baby. I will be no one's baby. I was born filthy and dirty. When I came out, my own mother hated me. I was nothing. If you knew what men had done to me, what I did with them, you would run and never say that. It's only a matter of time till Kat or Andrew sees what I am." Francesca let loose a string of swear words.

Katrina had never heard those filthy words come out of her mouth.

Timmy walked up close to her, his face full of compassion and care. He held out a hand and put it to her lips. "No, Francesca, you listen to me. You are the daughter of Katrina. You are a Princess." His voice was firm and angry. "Francesca, you are none of those things. Men made you think you were those things. You were made to be a perfect child. You were made to be loved. You, only you, are the one God chose. He chose you to be His and His alone. He chose you to be his daughter. When your father and my mother forsake you, then the LORD will take you up. The Lord has chosen you to be His treasured possession. That is what the Lord thinks of you, Francesca. He gave you to Andrew and Katrina as a gift. He chose you just for them. Who can say different? You lived in their house before they got there. You were meant to be Andrew and Katrina's daughter. You were meant to be Sara and Carlissa's big sister, even if for a short time. God decided it. You are God's beloved daughter." His face was close to hers while his eyes begged her to realize the truth.

"You didn't stutter," Francesca told him.

Timmy stared at her. "What? Have you heard anything I said?"

Francesca nodded. "Yes, but I just can't believe it. Trusting them would be like trusting a God who is taking my sisters from a safe home. No one can stop them from going, not even Andrew and Maverick. No one. Not even God can stop them." She shrugged. Her eyes were full of pain. "So what is the point?"

Timmy shook his head. "Oh, my dear. You have ears to hear and eyes to see." He took her head in his hands. "But you still are so hard of believing." He let her head lean against his chest. He let his other hand drop and with the other hand, he ran it over her head from the top to her shoulders, like he would a child. Her head rested against him, but her body wasn't touching him. His touch was pure. "You are Andrew's baby forever and always. You are Katrina's little girl," he whispered over and over.

Katrina backed away. What Timmy had just done was more than any man, except Andrew, had ever done. If this boy could make a difference in her little girl, then what could a nation do for children like hers? What if every town treated children like Jesus did? If only all of God's people would do what this one boy did. Her little girl was in God's hand.

Chapter 38

"We need more days like this." Izzy smiled.

Jesse agreed as they walked from the diner to the general store. It had been such a light day. "Even if I had to make you take a day off."

Izzy almost sighed the second trial was in two days. She forced herself to wink at him. "I was going to go anyway."

"What am I going to do with you?" He poked her side and then settled down as they walked in. Many people said they were praying and supporting the Starrys. For most of them, this was the first time seeing and hearing firsthand the evils of the asylum. Izzy nodded and tried to keep it light. She was getting married soon and would be happy with her man.

When someone touched her shoulder, she turned to find Mabel standing there.

"Hi, dear," Mabel said. She gave Izzy a hug and then nodded to Jesse.

Izzy kept her face light. She just wanted to cry in the woman's arms. That wasn't like her. What was wrong with her lately? She didn't let her emotions control her. "We just came from the diner and thought we would get a few items for our home."

Mabel kept her mood and met it, keeping it light. "I have an idea for some supplies."

"That would be great." She walked over to the general store together, taking tips from the older woman. After a bit Mabel asked, "So when should your ma come?"

"A couple of days. I hope when she gets here maybe things could get better between us." Izzy shrugged, afraid she admitted too much. "Or maybe I am wishin' for too much."

"Anything can happen." Mabel touched her arm gently. "If she sees the trial, maybe she will see how she can change. It has changed many."

Izzy made a long face. "My ma doesn't change." Finding the can of cherries a few minutes later, she turned to see Mabel talking to Annie and another woman Izzy couldn't see behind a shelf. She walked up beside Mabel and to her shock, her mother stood there. Jesse came up right next to her.

"So you just got in today, Rosa?" Mabel asked.

Annie answered, "No, she got here two days ago. We have had such fun."

Mabel's face showed shock.

Izzy's mouth dropped open. She felt Jesse's hand claim hers. "You have been here for two days and didn't think of coming to the ranch?"

Rosa looked surprised to see her, and guilty. "Well, we didn't want to bother your work."

"Sawyer didn't tell me." Izzy shook her head.

Annie looked at her twin like she was making far too big a deal of this.

Jesse spoke up, a bite to his words. "Sawyer has been at the ranch before she came because we were talking about our mother-in-law coming."

"You have been talking about us," Annie snapped.

Izzy cocked her head, raising an eyebrow. "Sawyer would never do that. He was just askin' why were you so mad about him helping." Letting go of Jesse's hand, she walked out.

Mabel was right by her side and stopped her before the alley way. "Are you all right, dear?"

Izzy shook her head, sorrow on her face. "I wish I had a ma that loved me."

"You do, she is coming next week. You have a wonderful aunt," Mabel told her. "But it doesn't change the hurt."

Izzy couldn't agree more.

Rosa walked up to them, her hands on her hips. "What is wrong, Izzy? You always have to make a scene."

Izzy laughed hard. "You just don't get it."

Jesse took Izzy's hand, and added softly, "Miss Rosa, I can't imagine my ma ever comin' without seeing all of her children. You haven't seen your children in months. Sawyer and I were just talkin' about what great parents we had and how sad our girls didn't get that chance. Even if Annie gets your love now, you didn't love her when she was a child. You lacked a mother's love. Why? There had to be a reason. What is the pain you have?"

Izzy was proud of Jesse. He was being compassionate and truthful. She knew he had issues with her mother, but Jesse was right. Annie would wake up to their pa beating Ma, Cole, or Izzy. Yeah, Annie had it bad, even if she never got hurt physically.

Rosa went pale while looking down. Maybe in shame?

Annie was red, her hands in fists. "You have no right to say that to my ma. I know Sawyer doesn't agree. I am glad I got the better man than you."

Izzy flinched at her words, crossing her arms. Annie might not say it, but she meant she was worthy enough for a good man. Would she ever be as good as Annie? Annie was pure as a bride. Izzy would never be pure. That would never change, even if Jesse could accept it. She still worried Jesse would see the truth in her or even grow tired of her. She bit her lip, trying to fight off those thoughts and feelings. Having her family here made her feel all the old feelings she had hoped were gone. If Cole were here, he would have helped. She always felt safe with him.

Jesse rubbed her arms like he was trying to warm her after her family's cold wrath. His voice had a bite to it. "You are right, Sawyer is a great man." He moved like he was ready to walk away. "I got the better half of the twins."

After hiding all the knives, guns, rifles, and any other weapons in the house, Andrew worried about the girls. What if the girls did something to themselves? Or others? All he could do was keep them safe. Walking into his room, he looked over to see the girls playing outside. He looked to his nightstand to find his picture was gone. He spotted it on the bed. His heart broke, picking up the picture. He wanted to weep. Literally. He hadn't cried in all this mess. But this picture was his priceless childhood memory. One of the first ones he had of the family.

He looked at it now. A fire had burned the edges of the frame and now the glass had been broken. He wasn't sure how but someone had taken out the picture and crumbled it. The sides were slightly ripped, but the faces of the children looked like they could save it.

Katrina walked in, looking at him like he did something wrong. "I called you, Drew." She saw the picture in his hands and rushed over.

"Oh, no." She took it out of his hands. Her face crumbled, angry. "I am so sorry, Andrew."

"It doesn't matter." He walked into the kitchen. He knew if he asked the girls, they would just lie. He closed his eyes. This picture had gotten him through so much doubt, grief, and so much pain he didn't think he would have made it without it. The picture reminded him he belonged in the Starry family.

Katrina put a hand on his back. "It matters, Andrew."

Putting the picture on the table, his hands went into fists. "Julia saved this picture from the fire when our cabin burned. It's not fair. Why? It's one of the few pictures we have of when Ben was alive! Why?" He shouted through ground teeth.

"Because they are in pain. When a person is in pain, they create more pain," Mabel said as she walked into the kitchen.

Andrew turned to face her and saw Charles behind her. They had pretty much lived at the ranch. He could never repay all they had done. He had to let them into his personal life but now he didn't want to face them. He didn't want them to see him at his worst. It made him feel like a heel coming in on him, yelling at his wife. He still held out his hand to her. They were connecting this time, not separating. "I don't see your point," he told them honestly.

Charles spoke up. "This picture looks like it has been through a lot and now it has been cracked through the anger of your children. It can be fixed with a little care." He picked up the picture frame, taking the back off. The glass was in sizable pieces and fell out. Taking the frame off, he left the picture. He picked up a large piece of glass and held it up. "God designed us to have protection around us. He made us have parents, grandparents, and providers in life. Sin took that away. Our children didn't get that. At first, it was like a glass got cracked, then broke. A little more each time. The community, the church, the state, and the government did nothing for their pain. The glass just kept chipping away because the protection wasn't there. Finally, their lives shattered, and they had to do everything on their own. They had to be ma and pa to themselves and siblings. They had to find shelter, food, and safety." He met Andrew's gaze. "They couldn't protect themselves from the evils of men. Our children know the evil no person should know." Charles was a man of few words unless they needed it.

Andrew's heart hurt over the image Charles made, but he still loved that picture. It held so much memories for him. Did he always forgive and let go?

Mabel spoke up. "When a person is hurting, they hurt. When a person is in pain, they cause pain." She shook her head, her face in pain. "They want to hurt their parents the most. They seem to know how it will hurt us most. It doesn't excuse what they do, but they are in so much pain they can't see straight. As much as they hurt us, someone has hurt them the same way or worse. Repeatedly. It's all they know, so they continue the pain. The pain and rejection have been great. They build walls around their heart to protect themselves. Getting through those walls they put up will be hard. It will be heartbreaking, but I believe through God you can do it. And it's up to the girls to decide how they will live. It's between God and each child. He will get her attention."

Andrew let the tears fall. "I don't know if I can be the pa they need." He sighed. "I don't know if I am made to be their pa."

"You know it's not up to you. I am always glad that it's left up to God," Charles said. "It's up to God, and He gave you those children."

Andrew looked down at the picture. Picking it up, he looked at his father's face like he always did. How did Ben feel when they spread lies about him? How would he have handled the case? Charles was right. God had chosen him to be their father. He touched Ben's face, wishing he could speak with the man once again. It was like God was touching his face and blessing him with Katrina, great siblings, and blessing him with God's children. God had given them to Andrew to love and care for. Despite what they did to him.

Chapter 39

"I need to send a telegram to the manager at Liberty House," Izzy said with emptiness in her voice. The last day in court had really done her in. It hadn't gone well. Mr. Heyman had so much power over the trial. The only positive thing she saw so many of the townspeople were seeing the asylum life for the first time. And it made them angry and to know Mr. Heyman got paid for every person in the asylum.

"Sure," the telegrapher said and did as she asked.

As Izzy walked out, Johnny told her he was praying for her and the Starrys. She smiled at him. As she walked out, she went to get Phoenix and suddenly felt nauseated. She threw up right in front of the alley, but at least her stomach was empty. Closing her eyes, she held her stomach. She had thrown up every day for the last two weeks, so this was normal for her lately. But it felt different. Her stomach was cramping like the monthly.

Suddenly she felt someone at her side. Hoping it was Jesse, she opened her eyes to see Maverick looking at her, concerned. He didn't touch her. "What is wrong, Izzy?"

Izzy shook her head and then threw up again. Embarrassed, she couldn't believe Maverick was seeing her like this.

"You're sick. We need to get you to Doc Charles," Maverick ordered in his authoritative voice.

She shook her head. "I am fine. I just haven't been feelin' well lately."

Maverick's eyes went wide. "You mean this has been happening for a while? Izzy, why have you been hiding this? Ellen hid she was sick and she died. Please go to Charles."

She shook her head. "I can't." She threw up again. Wiping her mouth, she knew she had to see Mabel. "Take me to the Alexander ranch. I will see Mabel."

Walking into Mabel's parlor, Izzy sat on the couch. She was so relieved to just sit, though she was still feeling cramps. Maybe she was starting her monthly back again. Mabel put a cold cloth on her head.

Mabel handed her a drink, Izzy drank some, glad it stayed down.

Mabel cleaned her face. "Now I need you to lay back."

Izzy obeyed, feeling dizzy.

Mabel felt her stomach and then moved down gently. "I will have to check you, Izzy."

Izzy nodded. "That is fine. I told Maverick I am just fine."

"Well, you aren't," Mabel told her gently. "You have lost weight. I should have seen it. When was the last time you ate?"

Izzy frowned as she tried to think. "I think yesterday. I haven't been hungry lately."

"Izzy, you know how bad that is. You have been working too hard on the trial."

Izzy nodded. "I have done it before. Don't go on treatin' me like I am a child."

Mabel nodded. "You are right, but I am also your friend and you have been doing too much, am I right?"

Izzy knew she had.

"When was your last monthly?"

Izzy didn't want to answer. It was embarrassing. She didn't have them normally, probably why she was barren. "Six months ago." When she heard Mabel gasp, she explained, "My monthly has not been normal since I was sixteen."

"I am sorry," Mabel said compassionately.

Izzy met her gaze. Mabel knew the truth. Izzy knew that Mabel knew some of it, but with that look of compassion and understanding, Mabel knew all of it. With Mabel, she didn't feel the old shame rise.

"So how has it been going with your ma?" Mabel asked.

Izzy gave her a long face. She had been trying to make up for not caring and it was smothering. "I don't handle being treated like a daughter by her. I do appreciate it from Aunt Mary because she knows me inside and out. Ma doesn't."

Mabel listened to her talk and then helped her sit up. Sitting next to her, her face was very serious. "Izzy dear, we are both women here. I think we should be honest with each other."

Izzy nodded. Was she dying like Ellen? She was there when Ellen told her children. Would she have to do the same?

"You are with child," Mabel told her gently.

Stunned, Izzy's eyes went wide. "Are...you...sure?"

Mabel nodded. "The child is Jesse's?"

Izzy nodded. She closed her eyes. How could she be carrying a child? She had been told she could never bear children. Well, God had different plans. She was caring for a baby! She had never felt such shock or joy. She knew she shouldn't be pregnant with a child, but she had dreamed of a child as long as she could remember. That dream had ended when she was sixteen. Secretly she had wished for a child to look like her that she could care for, keep safe, and be a loving mother to.

Suddenly she thought of what they might call her child. She looked at Mabel, feeling an ache in her stomach. What if her child had a childhood like hers? What if the child never felt like she belonged? "Mabel. Mabel, I didn't have a good childhood." She put a hand over her stomach, like holding the little one safe from the world. "What if my child is known as a bastard?"

Mabel put a hand on her shoulder. "Your child will have a father and a loving mother. Your child will know the love and the security of a God-fearing family."

Mabel was right, but what if Cole found out? It would devastate him. She could handle this. It wasn't the first mistake she had made. She would love this child. She would start now and go eat something. She would be a splendid mother.

Mabel looked at her seriously. "You need to face this. You need to tell Jesse."

Though the wedding was a little over a week away, she had to tell him. "I know." She felt ashamed. "It was just one time. I wanted to feel loved. I thought I would understand what love meant." Her eyes filled.

Mabel put an arm around her. "You looked for it in the wrong ways, dear."

She put her head in her hands. More than emotional, it exhausted her. Crying, she said, "I want my child to know love and to belong. Not always being used and abused by someone."

Mabel took the younger woman in her arms as she cried her pain away. She just wanted to be a little girl again, crying in her aunt's arms.

When she stopped crying, she had to face life, because her baby was given life and would never be known as a problem. Izzy had made her own mistakes and had to face the problems she had made, but her child wasn't one. She would face life as a mother.

Izzy thought leaving the Alexander ranch would make her feel better, but it didn't. She had eaten an apple and taken another one for the ride home. Walking next to Maverick instead of riding, she felt uneasy. He was being way too comforting which made her feel so much guilt. She didn't deserve his care.

Suddenly she felt another wave of nausea. She held her stomach and threw up. Leaning against a tree, Maverick stood by her. "I need to know, Izzy. What is wrong? You are sick."

"I will be fine," she muttered. If she could get to the ranch, hopefully he would leave her alone. She threw up again. Was this a normal part of pregnancy? Was she going to puke her guts out?

"No, you are not fine. I need to know. I can help you tell the others." His voice was high pitched and rushed, so unlike him. "We will find you help to solve this illness."

"I am not sick," she told him. Her stomach settling, her head still ached. She took a sip of his water. His face was full of worry and concern. "I'll be fine."

"This is not normal. What is wrong?" Maverick demanded. He was getting more aggressive, but also gentle.

She didn't feel threatened by his actions, which she should. Maybe she felt safe with him because he knew of her past. She genuinely didn't care. She just didn't want to answer. She wanted to go to bed. She was so exhausted. Maybe the baby had been taking her energy. Or the court had. Way too many people were depending on her. And now a child was. She leaned her head against Phoenix, feeling better.

"No." He stopped her. "What is the matter? Mabel told you something. I could tell when you walked out." His face softened. "Please."

She couldn't think anymore. He knew how to push. She glared at him. She knew how to fight back.

"Keepin' it to yourself will not help," he told her. "What is wrong?"

"I will be fine." Another wave of nausea went through her and she closed her eyes. She couldn't hear Maverick's voice. How was she going to tell Jesse? He was not doing well because of the trial. She feared he would even go back to alcohol during the worst. But he hadn't. Tomorrow was the sentence, and she would have to wait till after that. She knew the outcome of that day. It made her sick. Finally, Maverick's voice came through again. "Tell me."

She couldn't handle his nagging. Glaring at him, she said, "I am with child." What had overcome her? She didn't let anyone make her do what she didn't want to do.

His eyes went wide, and he gasped. "What?"

Embarrassment and shame came over her. "It wasn't supposed to happen."

"How could Jesse do that?" Maverick asked angrily. "He didn't love you."

"Mav, shut up." She glared at him. "We made a mistake. We will make do, but this baby is not a mistake." She sighed, thinking about what she had to ask him. She wanted to ask Andrew, but with his knowledge and being there for Katrina, it was too much and everyone was watching him. "Now I need your help with the girls. We both know what will happen tomorrow."

"Why are you worried about Andrew and Katrina's children when you are with child?" Maverick asked, shocked.

"Yes, my child is safe inside me and these girls are going to hell. I have a plan, but I need your help."

Maverick frowned. "Why don't you ask your man?" he asked sarcastically.

"I would, but you know how this is hitting him. And I think you know why it is. So I can't ask Jesse." She put her hands on her hips.

Maverick looked away, like he was trying to hide what he knew.

Izzy had wondered if Maverick had gotten Jesse out of the asylum. Now she knew. "You are one of a kind. You make your sister feel safe enough to talk. You help a brother hide a secret for years. And you got my fiancée out of hell. Is there anything you can't do?"

His face crumbled. Then in a split second he had no emotions. "This."

"I wish I could shut off my emotions like you do."

"You have in the past," he told her.

"Yeah, and I almost didn't feel again. Women are made a little different."

A soft smile came to his lips. "You got that right." His eyes turned dark. "You deserve better, Iz."

"Well, I am getting married in a week and I need you to make sure I am not in jail for my wedding." She folded her arms.

His eyes went wide. She could get reactions from him and it was fun. "I don't think I want to hear your plan, girl."

For the first time in as long as she could remember, she smiled. Then chuckled. Cole would call it her evil laugh when she had done something crazy. That was the same thing Cole would tell her when she came up with a grand idea. She missed this about working on the rescues. She missed the high rush of the job. "Will you do it?"

He narrowed his eyes and nodded like he was going to his death sentence. "But we stay out of jail."

She couldn't resist, she gave him a grin. "Aww, now, why would I do that?"

Maverick just shook his head.

Chuckling, Izzy told him her plan.

Chapter 40

Katrina put the last dish on the table. She didn't even know why she tried. Sara hardly ate and Carlissa ate so much she would throw up. Francesca would throw her food like a toddler. Lunch and supper time was turning into a war. Jesse and Izzy were pretty good at handling it, but they were at the Alexander ranch trying to find an answer to the court. She just wanted life to get back to normal. But what was normal? They didn't have time to make a routine longer than a couple of weeks.

The girls all sat and Andrew dished out the food for Carlissa. Katrina poured them sweet tea. Francesca drank it like she couldn't get enough. She loved the sweetness along with the ice.

When Katrina sat, Andrew bowed his head and began to pray.

Katrina bowed her head but felt like a hypocrite. She had a hard time praying since the first day of court. All she could do was cry and weep for all she lost.

In the middle of the prayer, Francesca stopped him. "Why are you even prayin', Pa?"

Andrew looked at her with sadness in his eyes. "Because I believe in God and believe He will work everythin' out to His plans."

"What? What are His plans for Sara and Carlissa? To go back to that asylum? Cause it sure looks like it," Francesca yelled. "What is God's plan, Pa? What?"

Sara shuddered in her chair, sinking down like she was trying to hide from Francesca's rage. Her face was white with fear. Her hands started to sweat.

Carlissa looked indifferent as if none of this bothered her.

Andrew stood his ground. "I wish I knew God's plan, but I don't. I know He will never leave or forsake us." He cleared his throat. "The evilness in this world was brought on by sin. What we are fighting in court is due to the sin of man."

Katrina felt like such a hypocrite because she knew what he was saying was true but she wanted to argue as her daughter did. She pulled Carlissa closer to her side.

"I don't know why you pray!" Francesca stood up, her anger in full force now. "I have never seen what your God has done for me. I have slept with many church family men. I have slept with preachers, judges, and lawyers. And you tell me these men serve God. Pastor Peter says the girls need to go back to the asylum. What ya think of that?"

Katrina saw Carlissa start to panic and maybe even go into a terror, so she pulled Carlissa into her arms. Carlissa held onto her tight and curled up like she could hide in Katrina's arms forever. Katrina had no words. She couldn't speak, for all she wanted to do was shout at Andrew the same way. Why was God taking her babies? Why?

"Honey, I know many men and even women have hurt you." He paused. "You need to calm down. I wish I could give back what has been stolen from you. I wish I could answer your questions on why some people call themselves God's people and are anything but that. God does say He will look at the men who do so much in the name of God, and He will say He never knew them. He will judge every person who has hurt His children. All I know is the men like Peter believe the world's lie."

Sara stood up and walked outside. She couldn't handle it anymore. Katrina knew one of the brothers was out there so she wouldn't go far.

Francesca stood and shook her head. "Tell me what your God has done for me. For Sara and Carlissa. I hate you and your God." She picked up her glass and threw the sweet tea at him. She set it down and ran upstairs. Normally she ran outside to the barn, but with the boys all around the land, she was staying inside more often. Katrina thought it might help to have the brothers all around. It kept her children in a better mood and in the house.

The ice tea hit Andrew's face and ran down his chest. His face was full of shock and distress.

Katrina could not believe Francesca had just done that. She knew if Carlissa didn't eat soon she would go into a rage. She took a piece of bread and handed it to Carlissa who was still curled up in her lap. She took it and started nibbling on it.

"Well, at least it wasn't full," Andrew said dryly, taking his napkin and wiping it up. "And it tastes good." He licked his lips.

Katrina chuckled and then full out laughed along with Andrew.

Carlissa chuckled. "You are awful funny, Pa."

His eyes danced with humor. "I am so glad I can amuse you, darlin'." He stood and picked her up carefully so as not to get her sticky, giving her kisses on the cheek till she giggled. Then he sat her in the chair. "Eat up, Punkin. I need to talk to your mama."

Katrina kissed her head. "Want me to warm the plate?" It had gone lukewarm.

She took a bite. "Nah, I should get used to eating cold food. Soon I won't be able to eat any food at all." She took another bite. "Sara says I should get used to being hungry. She says she won't be there. But she is always there."

Katrina closed her eyes and was glad her little girl couldn't see the pain on her face. She knew where Sara would be and didn't want to think about it. She didn't know how her children could just talk of their past like it was nothing. No emotion whatsoever. How they could talk of going back like it was nothing. Carlissa seemed to do so much better. Was it because she knew Katrina would be out of her life soon enough so she wasn't a threat anymore?

Katrina stood up and walked over to the sink with him. Taking the warm water already on the stove and putting soap into it, she took a wash rag and wiped his chest.

He took her hands that rested on his chest, his eyes on her and not the work. "Katrina," he whispered.

She kept her eyes on their hands. She knew something was on his mind. She was pretty sure it had to do with his talk with Francesca. She suddenly felt like a child going to get set straight. She didn't really want to. She just hated feeling this hopelessness.

"Katrina, talk to me," he whispered so lightly.

She tried to pull away. He knew how to hold her. She knew she needed to be this close to him. They had talked about not letting things or the children divide them. Andrew had been meeting her needs and now he was trying his best to do it again. She closed her eyes and nodded. When she pulled away, he let her go. With Carlissa eating behind them, she didn't want anyone to know her doubts. Her face in grief, she signed, *I can't tell you what I think! I am too ashamed because I wanted to yell at you with my daughter. I don't see what God is trying to do. I just don't.*

Andrew shook his head, in such sadness. He signed, *I should have known you were struggling. I am sorry. What we need to do is get back to God.* He took her hands again. "Let's just ask Him what He is trying to do. Let's take this to prayer. To the Lord. He will answer, baby."

Katrina put her head on their hands and again let the tears flow but this time it was in prayer. She cried in her heart. Repenting for not trusting Him. She had been a rebellious daughter. Her sobs came harder as she prayed. God, I give you my babies. Do with them what You will. They are all yours. Feeling a peace in her heart, she knew she had been right to do this. should have done it a long time ago. But her heart still hurt for her babies.

Jesse had never known nightmares like this before. He was afraid of sleep. He was staying in his dreams. It made him feel sick and he thought he would throw up. He hadn't slept in days. waking up nightmares and being there for Izzy as she thought of ways to win in court. After the second court hearing, he didn't know if he could take it anymore. Living in the memories, he was about to break.

Walking to the barn, he found the bottle in the hayloft. He figured Francesca had been drinking again. He took the bottle, looking at the amber liquid. If he took a couple sips the memories would fade. He looked around; anyone could walk in. He didn't have any time alone. So he mounted and rode to the south of the ranch.

Not really paying attention, he ended up at the place where Izzy and he had talked honestly for the first time. Dismounting, he leaned against the large rock, feeling like he was going to throw up. So many bad memories clouded in. One took him away. He let his mind run and thought about it. It was a couple weeks after he got to the asylum. They had kept him in a small cell, all brick. His backside and sides had sores all over from the cement floor. He had never been so alone. Even on the streets, he had been with Pedro. It was a loneliness that went deep into his soul. Then an older boy in the asylum came into his cell, feeding him and telling him to keep quiet. Who would he tell? No one cared. Molestation started and he hated it, but it made the loneliness bearable. He felt so guilty over it. So filthy and helpless. He was one of the smallest boys there, especially for his age. Ellen said his weight might be because of his starvation on the streets. One memory was so bad, he had forgotten it. He couldn't go there. Last night he had remembered it in the few hours before he went to sleep. Holding the neck of the bottle, he almost took off the lid. The memory came back to him now. He closed his eyes and threw up, feeling utterly destroyed and hopeless. *God, why did you allow it to happen? I can't deal with this anymore.*

Feeling so hopeless he took the top of the bottle off and smelled the amber drink. He knew it would sting going down, but it would make him forget the pain.

He held it to his lips and then heard a voice. "That ain't gonna help what ails ya!"

In a daze he wondered if he heard God, then he looked to see Juan Jose walking up. He held the bottle, fighting the anger. "What, are you checkin' up on me?"

"No, I wanted to make sure you were all right." He leaned against a tree. "You drink that and you will never get Izzy's trust back again."

"What do you know?" Jesse yelled.

"I know you are fighting nightmares. I know you are having a hard time sleeping or functioning during the day. I know the hearing is making you remember things you haven't remembered in years. Am I right?" Juan Jose looked relaxed, like he could take what Jesse gave out. Well, he had already proved he could.

Jesse shook his head.

"You want to tell me what haunts you?" Juan Jose asked gently.

Jesse shook his head, his rage taking over.

"Since there ain't a brother here you can speak to, I might be your only choice for a while," Juan Jose tried again.

Jesse felt like his heart would explode. He threw the bottle against the tree, watching it shatter like his heart. His soul had been so damaged. The one he would go to get advice was Andrew or Matt. However, Andrew was a mess. Matt wasn't here. Juan Jose cared. He could tell by his actions. He was a kindred heart, Ellen would say. "You're right. I can't deal with the nightmares. They are all there. I kept it out of my mind for years, but now it came all back and I can't deal with it. It makes me sick." He looked away, feeling like a coward, feeling so low and vulnerable.

Juan Jose spoke softly. "Ask God where He was in the painful place. Ask Him to show you. Ask Him to heal you from it."

Jesse looked into his eyes. "The most painful place?" He didn't know if he could.

Juan Jose nodded. "You need not tell me anything. Just ask God how He cared."

Jesse fell to his knees on the dry ground. Juan Jose kneeled next to him and put a hand on his shoulder as Jesse sobbed. This was a new healing cry to the only One who could touch the hard places. *God, where were You when all those boys attacked me? Where were You when I was taken? I felt so alone!* He prayed, then listened. He didn't know what he was waiting for, but he just waited silently.

Then he saw it. The older boys attacked him and held him down. It was like he was watching it happen from outside his body. He had felt so helpless to stop it. He screamed, but no one came to his aid. This time though, he knew God was inside him. Feeling his pain, feeling his bruises and his brokenness. God had felt every pain he felt, every feeling he had felt that night and so long after.

He cried like he had never cried before. This was the first time he cried and he could feel his heart heal and coming back together in one piece.

Then he saw a broken boy who was wearing rags, skin and bones with sunken eyes. Lice and fleas covered him. He was walking towards the plantation, towards his first and only home. Ellen was running out to him like in the prodigal son. He could still remember her warm, caring arms come around him. He would never forget that. He had wished for it for so long. She just held him covered in dirt, feces, and vermin, not caring. She just held and rocked him. He could still remember her tears in his hair. He often wondered if she was crying for him or for losing Pedro. He knew now Ellen cried for him and all the pain. In everything, his mama loved him. God had been there for him even in the worst moments and then given him a mama and a godly caring pa in Ben. God had blessed him with a family.

Chapter 41

Walking arm in arm, Izzy gazed at the setting sun. Another day had ended and the hearing was still not over. She feared for it to be done, because when it was, the girls would be gone. Unless a miracle happened. And they could use a big miracle. One that would stop this town short and open their eyes. Izzy and Jesse talked lightly of the case, their wedding, and everyday things.

Jesse tried to keep things light as they walked around the pond. As he noticed her look like she had a ton of weight on her shoulders, he said, "Hey, we will get through this."

Izzy nodded and looked at him. "That is because we don't have a choice. Starry's always do what they have to."

Jesse stopped and took her in his arms. "You got that right," he muttered in her hair. The sun was dropping below the mountains and it was getting chilly. He took her chin in his hand. Gazing into her beautiful face, he couldn't believe how he was blessed to have her want him. He was so unworthy. The orange from the sun shone on her face. Her brown eyes were like bright stars. Her hair had a glow around it that made him want to run his fingers through it.

Glancing at Jesse, she noticed a peace in him, something she hadn't seen in him before. What was it? He resisted and held her close, where she couldn't go help the girls or answer to someone's need. She could just be safe in his arms. He was slow as he pecked her lips. It was a quiet, sweet kiss.

Izzy leaned into it and wanted more when he pulled away.

He just smiled softly at her. "We should head in, Angel." If they didn't, he was going to do something he would regret. He had already made so many mistakes with her. He was doing things right this time around. God's way.

Izzy followed him. As exhausted as she was, she felt safe in his arms.

By the time they got to the door, the stars were coming out. Jesse leaned against the door, looking very content.

"Why don't you come in for some coffee?" Izzy invited him. "Katrina is probably still up. The poor girl never sleeps anymore."

"Aww, not tonight." He pushed a curl behind her hair and let his hand rest on her shoulder. "I am doing what I told Francesca I would do. Not in just words, but actions."

Izzy looked confused. "What is that?"

He leaned close and whispered in her ear. "I am honoring you. Protecting you."

Izzy looked down. "You don't trust me."

Jesse gave a soft laugh. "No, I trust you," he muttered. "I don't trust myself. I am weak in the flesh. I love you and want the best for you. Iz, I am doing it God's way."

Izzy's eyes softened as she met his gaze.

For Jesse, gazing into those eyes was like getting lost in a wonderful place. He could tell she was trusting him. He had to go, he kept telling himself. But he stood there, just gazing into her eyes.

"Juan Jose got to you, didn't he?" Izzy winked.

Jesse's eyes widened. "How did you know?"

Izzy softly laughed. "I know my cousin in the making. He has brought the life to your eyes I always knew was there. Ellen told me you would open up one day, and it probably wouldn't be me making that happen."

He looked away, then back at her. "Juan Jose helped me let go of some demons."

"He is good at that." She placed a hand on his chest. "It's cold tonight. I will get you an extra blanket." Then she rushed back inside and came back a couple moments later.

Jesse thanked her and then told her, "You need to get some sleep tonight. Don't let Kat drain you anymore."

Izzy shrugged. "I don't run out of energy."

Jesse's eyes narrowed. He didn't believe that for a second. "Tell me you will go to bed or I will make sure Kat makes you do it. You know I can."

Izzy shook her head. "Fine, but I probably won't sleep." She folded her hands. "I am dreading tomorrow."

Jesse took her icy hands and bowed his head. "Lord, protect Izzy tonight. Comfort her and let her sleep peacefully. Hold her in Your protection. Give the whole family peace. Lord God, protect Your children. Protect the girls. Keep them safe. We trust You to do your will. Your will be done in this situation. Amen."

Izzy felt peace come over her. Too emotional to speak, she blew him a kiss and walked away. Entering the kitchen, she saw her mother, Annie, and Katrina sitting at the table enjoying coffee. Suddenly she was feeling the cold seep into her and it had nothing to do with the night. It smelled like Katrina had brought out Gloria's peach pie.

"What are you doing here at this late hour? I didn't see your wagon," Izzy asked.

Annie got up and smiled brightly, "Oh, Sawyer is just getting it for us." She smiled brighter. "Guess what?" She almost giggled. "Mama is with child!"

Izzy's eyes went to her mother who still sat at the table. "Wow, this is a surprise. What does Marshall think?"

Rosa didn't meet her gaze, almost fearful. "I haven't telegraphed him yet. I am just so surprised."

Izzy's hand under her coat went to her flat stomach where the baby was safe. Safe from her mother's indifference. "You can say that again."

Katrina gave her a sympathetic look. Almost like pity.

Annie frowned. "Well, you don't seem too excited, Iz."

Izzy eyes narrowed. "I am just so happy. Can't you tell?" Every word dripped with rough sarcasm. She wanted out. Where was Cole or Jesse when she needed them? What would Cole say? This child shouldn't grow up with an indifferent mother. Would Marshal love and cherish this baby? Or be as emotionless as their mother. "Well, I wonder if Marshal will protect this child."

"Whatever do you mean?" Annie asked.

"What do you think? He watched us get beat for years and then he married Ma, after doing nothin."

Annie crossed her arms. "Marshal loves us," She muttered. "You never liked him. You didn't even come to the wedding. Cole came."

Izzy rolled her eyes. Cole only went to the wedding because he was already on his way home from Alabama. Right after the wedding, he went to Colorado instead of staying like he normally did. Actually she loved Marshal and that was why when he saw her bruises and did nothing, it hurt more than words could say. She wasn't ready for all this. Tears came to her eyes. She turned to leave and met her mother's eyes for just a second before Rosa looked away. "I will love this baby, you know that. That means I won't stand by if she or he gets hurt." She felt nauseous. "I just hope this baby has a better life than we did, because this child is wanted by his siblings." And just like she thought, her mother's eyes didn't change. No emotion crossed her face. Izzy covered her mouth from a sob and ran to her room.

Throwing herself on the bed, she sobbed. Her mother didn't want or deserve another child. Pulling her knees up, she put her arms around her belly protecting her beloved child. *God, help me. Help my beloved baby and mamma's baby. Take this cold away, Lord. Heal my heart.* She fell asleep and for the first time since the trial started, she slept peacefully.

Katrina played with a piece of wire in her hands. Izzy had given it to her, saying it would help with the nervousness. Katrina wanted to tell her it was more like heart-wrenching pain. The wire wouldn't mold in her hands.

Glancing behind her eyes met Julia who had just walked in. Katraina gave a wink smile then glanced back up front.

The judge sat, looking over the crowd. He didn't show any emotions. "Well, for the final time the Denver asylum will present their case on why the girls should be with them."

Mr. Heyman stood. "Thank you, Judge." He walked to the front. "You might think I am not a moral man. I do run a place that is a little hard to live in, but I ask, would you want these dangerous children to live in your town, your homes, and to be your neighbors? These girls are young, but they need so much more care and help. More help than the Starrys can give. I made the asylum for children like this. You know as well as I do, that touched children are created by the devil. They are not meant to have normal families. There is a reason I have them, their own parents didn't want them or couldn't handle them. You don't want strangers coming to your town seeing touched children in your stores, blacksmiths, or church. Of course, you don't. It would bring shame to everyone. People like Sara and Carlissa are not made to be seen by the public unless they want to look through my asylum. They are not meant to live in a family. It is not how America does things. We don't want this to change. All I ask is that you ask yourself if you want two touched children to live dangerously in your town or safely in an asylum." He sat down.

Maverick stood up, looking in full control, his emotions shut off. "You had some well-meaning points, if that is what you meant. Some children need more care and structure than a family gives, and so they go to Liberty House, where they live on structure. The touched children do very well in their care. If Mr. Heyman's asylum was like a home or provided any care, then I would support him if the girls needed to go to a place like that, but they do not. And his place is nothing good." He looked down at the paper in his hands. "I would like all the children to leave and some sensitive women. Everything I have to say is true, and it is not for the weak of heart." He waited for the children and some of the people to leave, while others leaned forward. The room held an early silence as Maverick began to speak. "I want y'all to close your eyes." His speech was slow and smooth with no hint of an accent. "Imagine a child born the way God made them. In His image, no matter how they came out. Imagine a perfect child that just wants love. Really only wants food and care, a kind touch. But this baby is left for days without food or being left in a mess. It leaves them to stop trusting anyone because no one met their needs. It changes their young body and brain to go without. As the child becomes older he wants love. He needs a kind touch. He doesn't have toys to play with. So being a child who doesn't know better, he plays with the body of a baby who passed away too early." He heard women sob and men gasp, but he continued. No one could say anyone in this town didn't know the truth of an asylum life. "He doesn't know what it is or can't see the life that was taken too early. As he grows up he becomes…"

Katrina closed her eyes. She wanted to cover her ears and shut it out, but she didn't. She listened to every word Maverick spoke.

It made her slowly weep for she had heard nothing worse. It made her dizzy, listening to the pain her girls and so many others had suffered. Her heart felt like she was going to break. It was worse than the pain of the fire. It filled her whole being. It made her whole body ache.

Maverick finished with, "Now I want you to picture in your mind this is your son or your daughter."

Juan Jose was next to stand up and take the stand. He was confident and sure. He had an air about him that was powerful but also humble. "I can say a lot up here on what I have done in life to help the touched. I can say what I feel about the touched, but I would rather tell you what God feels about the touched. And that means all of them, and not the ones you pick. Children are born to shine, love, and live. They want to learn to love and not hate. When their whole world is hate and anger, are you surprised that they are filled with it? God adopted them into His Family. He chooses each person for a purpose, we just have to listen to it. Here is what God tells us about His children: 'For ye are all the children of God by faith in Christ Jesus. For ye have not received the spirit of bondage again to fear; but YE HAVE RECEIVED THE SPIRIT OF ADOPTION, whereby we cry, Abba, Father. The Spirit itself beareth witness with our spirit, that we are the children of God: And if children, then heirs; heirs of God, and joint-heirs with Christ; if so be that we suffer with him, that we may be also glorified together . . . And not only they but ourselves also, which have the first fruits of the Spirit, even we ourselves groan within ourselves, WAITING FOR THE ADOPTION, to wit, the redemption of our body. Children were fearfully and wonderfully made. Being the image of God is the title of both honor and humility. Now, therefore, ye are no more strangers and foreigners, but fellow citizens with the saints, and of the household of God. The Lord takes pleasure in His people.'" He paused. "Pleasure means acceptance. He delights in us and wants us to serve Him. He did not create us to be alone or forsaken. He wants us to love one another as we love Him. He called for us to care for the fatherless. As you well know, many touched are fatherless due to illness and abandonment." He was about to step down when he finished with, "I will end with what God feels about His children. May we all see children through God's eyes. 'THE LORD KNOWETH THEM THAT ARE HIS. And, Let everyone that nameth the name of Christ depart from iniquity.'"

Katrina looked behind her and saw women wiping their tears. Even some older men wiped their eyes with hankies. The men looked angry and ready to take on a fight for these children. Ben would call it righteous anger. Glancing at Andrew, her husband, who faced so much in his life and who continued to rescue others, she saw he also shed tears. His face was full of pain and anger.

The judge sat back in his chair, looking like a king in his castle. "Will all rise?"

Katrina stood up, holding Andrew to give her strength. 'God, please keep my babies safe.' She could do this.

"After hearing both sides. Andrew and Katrina Starry have done a

279

very good job of raising the two wards of the state for a short time. The facts are that the children, Sara and Carlissa, are wards of the state." He paused. "Given the facts, the children are wards of the state. Tomorrow the children will return to the asylum in Denver."

The words he spoke were knives slashing and slicing at any hope Katrina had. By the time he had finished, she stood motionless and silent, unable to speak, unable to bear the crushing weight of guilt that she hadn't stopped this. Those girls were bound for hell and she had to stand by and allow that devil to take them.

It was like her head was fuzzy. She walked out of the church. The air was still cold as it rained. Like Izzy said, God was weeping with them. She still couldn't breathe. She walked to the back of the church, leaning against the building. She leaned over and threw up, wiping her mouth on a handkerchief. She hadn't eaten since that morning. She had felt nauseous for days. She had never known this kind of pain.

Katrina walked away from what looked like chaos, but she couldn't seem to think straight. She just sank. She shut it all down. Just as she looked up she saw Julia walking to her. It was the last straw. If one person knew her pain, it was Julia. She was a mother. Tears fell as Julia's arms came around her. She held onto her sister, feeling utterly broken. They had crushed her spirit. Her arms would be empty soon.

Izzy walked to the back of the church, knowing what the judge would say. Jesse had stayed in front. Walking out, her ears were still ringing from the judge's verdict. She took off at a run to Annie's house. She nodded to Maverick, who looked ready to shoot someone.

He went inside and a few minutes later he walked back out with the girls. As Izzy put Carlissa on a gentle, fast little mare, she hoped Carlissa could make the ride. As fast as they were going, they couldn't ride double. She told Carlissa to hold on to the horn and just let the horse follow them.

Maverick put Sara on her horse as the people came out of the church. Since few people were in the street, they made a scene.

Izzy mounted with a hand on her gun. If need be, she would shoot to protect these children. She felt cold. It scared her to feel this cold.

She looked over at Sara. "Sara, ride like you stole it."

Sara smirked. "I am good at stealin'."

Izzy dug her heels into Phoenix's sides. The horse took off at a ground-eating run. The other two horses followed as she'd hoped. She didn't even hear the people screaming after them. She knew they couldn't follow. Timmy had let all the horses go. Only wagons lined the streets, and where Izzy was going no one would find her. She knew how to cover her tracks. She prayed it was enough to keep the children safe. Just until her friend could come and save the day.

Chapter 42

The air had cleared and the sun was out, much to Katrina's misery. Going to find Andrew, she had a plan.

Finding Andrew behind the barn chopping wood, it looked like he had chopped enough for three full Colorado winters. "Andrew, we need to talk." She crossed her arms.

Andrew swung the ax again. "What?" he muttered.

She looked around, feeling like maybe someone from the court was spying on them. No, they were probably still searching for the girls they wouldn't find. Izzy knew these mountains and she knew how to protect. Especially the ones she loved. "We need to find the girls, take Francesca, and run away. We can go as far as the Oregon territory, up into Washington or Dakotas."

He stood up but he didn't face her. "We can't."

Feeling rage go through her, she walked up in front of him and hit his chest. "Why? You have never denied me anything. These are my babies. The first ones I ever had and they are headed to hell, Andy!" She grabbed his vest with her fists, her eyes shooting bullets at him.

Andrew grimaced. "Kat, we would always be on the run. It would be wrong. We would never make it through the northern winters with no help. It wouldn't happen."

She dug her face in his sweaty shirt, too exhausted to cry. "Then what are we going to do?"

"I don't know." His arms came around her. "I am praying for a miracle."

She agreed a miracle is what they needed. Trust in God with all your might, actions, and power. He would lead her paths. Closing her eyes she prayed, when Alice ran up. "Mrs. and Mr. Starry, my grandma wants you up at the chapel." She nearly danced. "It's a miracle. You have to meet her. She is here. She came!"

Alice was talking so fast it was hard for Katrina to keep up. It didn't matter because Andrew took her hand and nearly ran to the chapel. Like it had been for a while, there were horses, wagons, and buggies all around Liberty Ranch from people helping and visiting.

Nearly running into the chapel, Katrina's eyes had to get used to the dim light. Then she spotted Cole, Juan Jose, Mabel, Jesse, Mr. Heyman, and another woman she didn't know sitting around a table. There were papers lying on the table.

All eyes turned towards them as they walked down the aisle. Mabel greeted Katrina with a hug. "I would like to introduce you to Dorothea Dix. Miss Dix, this is Andrew and Katrina Starry."

Katrina's mouth fell open. She couldn't believe this woman, who couldn't stand more than 5'6", was the woman who changed the north and south for the asylum people. Mabel put a hand under Katrina's chin and shut her mouth. She nearly gasped in embarrassment. "I am sorry. I am just so surprised to meet you."

Miss Dix smiled. Her brown hair was pulled back in a loose, becoming bun, her brown eyes showed compassion and discernment. "I am honored to meet you. Anyone that has the courage to have a ranch for touched people is very open minded. I have promoted this for many years now." She shook Andrew's hand like a man would. She was serious and business-like. "Please have a seat." She sat down. "Now I was just talking with Mr. Heyman here about giving the girls to you. And any other children who are too sick or need more than he can give." She spoke softly but also firmly like she had done this many times.

Katrina didn't know why she was being so kind to the man. He was so evil. She just nodded.

"Now I have wired Judge Boyer and he has agreed to this as long as everyone is in agreement. What do you say, Mr. Starry?"

Andrew blinked. For a man that didn't get surprised by much, he was in shock. "Yes, I will do my best to raise Sara and Carlissa."

"Very well." Miss Dix nodded. "Mr. Heyman, you are in agreement."

He grunted. "If I have to…" He started to make excuses.

Andrew's hand went into a fist. Katrina covered his hand when she spotted a dark look from Miss Dix.

She spoke up. "You know you are overrun with people at the asylum already, and if you agree to let the children be raised by the Starrys, you can all work together, and never go to court again." Miss Dix allowed an edge to her voice but said the words with such sweetness it was hard to miss. She pushed the papers to him.

Mr. Heyman nodded and sighed as he signed his name to the paper.

He shoved them at Andrew. "Here, now the brats are yours to keep, but stay out of my way."

Katrina took his arm with both of her hands.

Miss Dix nodded to him. "Now you can sign it and no one will take your children from you again."

Andrew looked over the paperwork and signed. As he did, tears came to his eyes. "I don't know what to say, Miss Dix. I can't thank you enough."

She smiled. "Thank me by continuing your work with the touched. Now I have to go and see how Mr. Heyman runs the asylum." She gave Cole a big motherly hug. "Now give your sister a big hug for me. I will see her again one day."

Cole nodded. "She will be sorry to miss you. Thank you so much for coming."

Miss Dix just nodded like this was her life's work. As she started down the aisle, Andrew called out to her.

She turned and raised an eyebrow.

"Why were you nice to Mr. Heyman?"

Miss Dix had that same compassionate look. "You can get better results with honey than vinegar." Before leaving she added, "God bless your work."

Katrina cried tears of joy.

Someone touched Izzy's shoulder. It took her a second to wake from slumber and point her rifle at the abuser. "Izz, it's me," Andrew spoke softly.

She nodded and stood. As she felt unsteady, he held her arms. Getting her balance, she smiled. "So she came?"

Andrew gave her a fool grin. "Yes, she came to save the day. They signed the papers already. The girls can stay forever."

She nodded, feeling so exhausted after this ordeal.

Jesse rode up. Nearly jumping off, he stalked over to her and took her in a hug, holding her out so he could see her. "I was so worried, Angel."

She hugged him back, then glanced at Andrew.

Andrew took Carlissa in his big arms. "A lady from the east made sure you stay with us forever."

Carlissa's eyes got big. "Forever!" She smiled brightly.

Andrew laughed. "Forever and always."

Izzy was so overcome with joy that she hugged Sara. "You get to stay, sweetie."

"Let's head back to the ranch," Sara muttered and mounted Whisper.

After packing up, Andrew took the lead down the mountain. "Don't wait too long comin'."

Jesse took him in her arms.

Izzy stepped closer. Feeling small and safe as his arms wrapped around her, she closed her eyes, enjoying his touch, his comfort. "The girls are safe, Jess."

She felt him nod. "They are very safe because of you. You are so brave and reckless."

She stepped back, knowing the shock she was about to tell him. "Jesse, I need to tell you somethin'." She knew it would be better to get it over with. They had hours to get home. She didn't want this between them. She turned her back to him.

"Izzy, what is it?" Jesse asked, concern in his voice. "Nothin' could be worse than these last few weeks, Angel."

Her legs feeling weak, she sat on a rock. She was not facing him when she whispered, "I am with child." She heard Jesse gasp.

She turned to face him, his face showing shock and then horror. "How?"

Her eyes got wide. Crossing her arms, she gave him a look like he was a fool.

"All right, I know." He ran a hand through his hair. "I can't believe this. I never even thought you could be in that way."

She put her arms around her waist, feeling sick. Feeling cheap. So ashamed.

Jesse was not seeing what she was going through. "What are we goin' to do?"

Standing, she glared. "What do you think?"

He paced back and forth. "I don't know. This is a mess."

She placed her hands on her hips. "This is a mess we caused, Jesse." If looks could kill, he would be dead. "My baby is not a mistake and if you don't want the child, then I can raise him on my own. I don't want to trap you in somethin' you don't want."

"No, that is not what I meant," he drawled. He looked at her

285

stomach, as if he were finally realizing what this meant. He stepped closer. "I just didn't think of this happenin'. It makes me think of what my family would say or yours." He ran a hand threw his hair. "What would Ellen think?"

Izzy wasn't ready to touch him, to comfort him. "She would say mistakes are mistakes. Now we move on and make do with what we have been given."

Jesse's eyes misted over. "She would have loved our baby."

Izzy felt too cold. And it had nothing to do with the cold of the mountains.

He walked closer, taking her hands. "All I know is I want you and I want this baby. We will be married in less than a week and be startin' a whole new life together."

Izzy couldn't take it anymore. Maybe it was the baby? Maybe it was being exhausted? Maybe it was wearing thin for weeks? All she knew was she let the tears fall. She put her hands on her face and sobbed.

Jesse put his arms around her. "Oh, Angel, don't cry."

It made Izzy cry all the harder. The cold she felt was softening, but she knew it had to leave. She just didn't know how. She cried till she felt sick and knew she wouldn't be able to make it down the mountain if they didn't get going. She wasn't staying up here alone with him. Even for one night. She pulled away, wiping her eyes.

Jesse handed her a cloth, handing her a canteen. "Drink this," he told her, and then he started picking up the camp.

Izzy was feeling better by the time Jesse had everything ready, though her headache stayed on. She said nothing as Jesse helped her up. Knowing she didn't need help, she was thankful for his kindness. She took the lead.

After a while, her head started bobbing, feeling her body relax, her eyes closing.

At a meadow, Jesse stopped Phoenix. He took her hand. "Izzy, come here." Before she could say anything he picked her up and put her on his lap, her legs to one side. "I will not have you fall off this mountain, Angel." He tied Phoenix's reins around his horn.

Izzy tried to argue, but it felt wonderful, relaxing and taking the weight off. She felt fat and ugly. She would never be a little maiden on her wedding night. Looking up at him she put a hand on his chest as she whispered, "Jesse, can you kiss me?"

His eyes melted. He took her cheek in his hand. His calloused hand was ever so gentle. Right above her lips he teasingly whispered,

"Angel."

Izzy felt a tingle in her. When his lips met hers, she felt her heart fly, feeling safe. He tasted of salt from the tears she had shed. His lips were as light as a feather. He was giving to her as he deepened the kiss. He pulled back with a content sigh. "My lovely angel. You are my treasure," he whispered breathlessly.

Izzy leaned against his chest. "You are my man."

Jesse put his hand on her flat stomach. "Ellen always said, 'The parents might make a mistake, but babies are never a mistake'."

Izzy looked up at him. "She would have loved this little one." She touched his face when his eyes grew sad. "I thought if the baby was a girl, we could name her Ellie May."

His eyes misted as he smiled. "I think she would have liked that." He let tears run down his face this time. "Do you know you are perfect for me?"

Izzy nodded contently. "I know, love." She settled back down in his arms, feeling content like she belonged there. Heading down the mountain, they could face their choices, their actions, and the future together.

Chapter 43

Mabel took Katrina in her arms as she met her on the walkway the next day. Andrew and Charles stood back watching. Katrina had needed to get out of the house so they went to town for lunch. They were still rejoicing over the good news.

Andrew greeted Charles. "We have hope we never had before."

"You got that right," Charles said. "Dorothea Dix is a remarkable lady."

Katrina was rejoicing all that had happened. "She is a very gracious lady."

Mabel was recalling what Miss Dorothea Dix had done until she glanced over and saw Peter walking up to them. She quickly took Andrew's hand as fear overcame her.

Andrew's stance was full of control. His look was not inviting.

When Peter reached them, he smiled lightly. "Hello."

When no one knew what to say, Peter cleared his throat. "Well, I made you all speechless. I deserve what you have to say or think."

Katrina agreed with that. She could see he had thought the way of most of the world on touched people.

He looked at Andrew and Katrina. "I want to ask you to forgive me. What I have done to you was wrong. I didn't support you and I believed lies about your children." He took off his hat and ran a hand through his hair. "When the hearing started, I still believed the lies, but something changed. You have such faith like your God can do anything. It might be funny coming from a pastor, but I haven't believed in God like you do. You know what your children can do and you believe in them. You believe God will help you through this trial, even when it didn't look good. I have been so wrong on so many things. Will you forgive me?"

Katrina stared at him. Hearing him say these things was like she was in a daze. Was he honest or just using them?

Andrew spoke first. "Yes, I do forgive you. Thank you."

Katrina nodded. He seemed to be honest. "I forgive you."

"Thank you so much." He turned to Mabel and Charles. "I am glad you both are here. I would also like to apologize to you both as well. I know none of my words can take what I have done to your good name." He looked at Mabel. "I have hurt you and blamed you for many things, Mabel. I took it out on you and not Charles. I knew I would have to work with Charles occasionally. He was quieter, even though I knew he thought the same way as you did. You were so outspoken and I knew you were right. Deep down I knew you were right, even past the lies and judgment. It made me feel guilty. So, I acted out in anger. I hurt you in ways I can't go back on. I went after you by using your children and that was so wrong. Can I ask your forgiveness, Mabel?"

Mabel showed little emotion during this. Now she just held out her hand. "I have forgiven you a long time ago. Most of my children have as well." She shook his hand. "Friends."

Peter nodded. "Friends." He shook Charles's hand. "I have decided to give up being a pastor for a while. I need to look at what God wants me to do in life. I plan to have Juan Jose take it over."

Katrina smiled. She couldn't be more surprised or happier; she loved Juan Jose and his kind ways.

Charles nodded. "He is a good man. He will do good to the church."

"I know. Well, I have to get something for the missus." With that, he walked away.

Mabel took Katrina's arm as they started to the ranch. "You don't know how I have prayed for this. To finally have my children and myself accepted in the church. I didn't think it would ever happen."

"I am so glad, Mabel," Katrina told her honestly.

"I am just sorry it took a court trial for him to see the truth."

"It has been a long road to get to this day." Charles looked content.

"And it will be a long road for us to prove to the world that our children have value," Andrew added.

"Why don't we just teach the church?" Charles told him with a grin. "It can be hard. It took Peter over twenty years to see it."

Andrew smiled. "I am up for the challenge. I am young."

Charles slapped him on the back, laughing. "You might be gray by the time they learn."

Izzy turned as she was about to walk into Cole's house, to find Jesse behind her. The wind was blowing and clouds building up like a storm was about to start. He held the door open for her. "How are you feelin'?" he asked.

She shrugged. "Fine." She walked in and found it warm and dim. Walking in the parlor, she found Cole and Julia having coffee near the fire.

Cole looked up, surprised, and drawled, "Hey, Izzy'-Bab." Standing, he hugged her. "Come join us."

Izzy hugged him back, "It's so good to see you." She stood back for a moment. She didn't know if they should tell him.

Jesse kept his gaze on the floor.

Cole looked between them. "What is wrong?"

They needed to tell him. She didn't think she wanted to tell him with Julia there. She felt like Julia was so much more worthy than her.

Suddenly she felt sick, and this time it had nothing to do with the baby. Holding her stomach, she moved to sit on the sofa.

Cole came alert. "What is wrong, Izzy? Are you ill?"

Jesse came to her side and sat down next to her. His eyes clearly signaled they needed to tell them.

Julia came back with a glass of water. Izzy shook her head. "I am fine, but I need to tell you somethin'."

Sitting next to her, Cole's eyes got wide. He was always so calm and in control, but he lost it when it came to Izzy. She knew it had to do with the past and having no control over his life being ruined, not once, but twice. She glanced at Julia, who looked worried. Cole couldn't take it anymore. "You're dying, ain't you?"

Izzy sighed. "No, can you sit down?"

Julia was the only one standing. She sat in a chair.

Izzy thought she could be sick again. She never expected this to be so hard. Looking at her hands, she said, "Jesse and I made a mistake." She didn't want to see Cole's face when she told him. "I am with child."

Julia gasped.

Cole stood up and glared at them. "What? How could you?"

Jesse took a deep breath and stood, taking it like a man. "It was me.

I wasn't being a Godly man."

Cole walked closer to him and grabbed him about his shirt collar. "You bet you are the one who did it! How could you do that?" he yelled, punching him in the face. "You used her." Jesse held his jaw, lying on the ground. "You took what didn't belong to you! You took a priceless gift."

Julia's eyes were wide. "What would Ellen say, Jesse?"

Jesse flinched at her words. They caused more pain than Cole's fist.

Izzy stood up, taking a hold of Cole's arm. "Stop! It wasn't only him. I was also in the wrong. We shouldn't have put ourselves in that position," she tried explaining. His face was hot, hands in a fist. "Stop! My child won't know anger. Please!" Her eyes misted.

Cole looked at her, her words hurting him. His eyes were wide with rage and pain. "I failed you. I let you get hurt, Izzy-bab."

"No, it was our choice. Our mistake," Izzy reassured him.

Jesse stood up. "No words or pounding can cause me more pain than knowing how I hurt Izzy." He rubbed his jaw. "No amount of apologizin' will make up for what I did."

Cole still glared at him, not letting his anger go that easily. "I trusted you, Jesse."

Izzy sat back on the sofa. This was too much.

Julia stood, shocked, also glaring at Jesse. "You were so wrong, Jesse. What would Ellen think? What would Ben say?"

Jesse covered his face with guilt. "I don't want to think of what they would say." His voice was full of anger. "But I would think in the end, Ellen and Ben would love this baby!" His voice was tight. "I am so sorry, Julia!"

Tears stung her eyes. She couldn't speak.

Cole kneeled in front of Izzy. He took her hands. "I failed you, Izzy-baby." Tears came to his eyes. "I let you get hurt. I wasn't being a real brother." Tears poured down his face. "I want so much for you. I want the best for you and this baby."

Izzy choked on a sob. "I am so sorry to hurt you." She had never expected to cause anyone else pain. She had never thought her decision would affect others. She prayed for Cole and her family.

Only He could work another miracle in the Starry and Donovan family.

Katrina sat at her kitchen table with Mabel. She ran a hand through her red curly hair, feeling more relaxed than she had in a long time. Her blue eyes landed on Mabel, one of the truest and bravest women she knew. "Does the fear ever go away? I keep waking up and checking on them to see if they will get taken."

"That is very normal. Just pray about it and let go each time," Mabel told her.

"I don't know how you do it. I am having such a hard time with the church right now." Katrina turned her head. "All right, maybe not the whole church. Just Maryanne and some other older ladies. They are hard."

"They are set in their ways and you are young and trying to change things. It doesn't sit well with them." Mabel sighed. "And you know Maryanne is just a hard woman with so much damage. I think she says too much. Like there is a reason she hates us so much."

Katrina nodded, not really caring about the lady. She had done so much damage to Katrina and hadn't cared about any of it. "I reckon so…"

Just then she heard a knock on the door. Getting up, she opened the door to find the very woman they spoke of. She slammed the door right on Maryanne. Turning, her eyes were blazing when she met Mabel's questioning gaze.

"Katrina, why did you just do that?" Mabel asked.

"The woman we were talking about is here," Katrina said bitterly.

"Oh." Mabel stood up and opened the door, not looking any happier to see her than Katrina was. "What are you doing here, Maryanne? You have hurt Katrina more than you can ever know. I won't let you do it again. Especially on her land."

Maryanne looked at the floor. "I know. I would just like to say some things." She looked up. "May I come in?"

Mabel sighed and stepped out of the way.

Katrina couldn't believe this woman was here. "What are you doing here, Maryanne?" She crossed her arms and glared. "Are you here to tell me what a terrible mother I am? Or why I was not put in an asylum when I should have been? Are you here to learn something about my children and why I do the things you accused me of? Why don't I let my children eat because I value how they treat their friends? And being hungry sends them into a rage, though they don't know that. And I do the other things because if they make their own decisions, it could be a mess. And just so you know, I never fight Andrew in public. I don't even fight in front of my family." She turned around. "What are you doin' here?"

Maryanne had gone very pale. She looked to Mabel and then to Katrina. "I am here to say I am very sorry for the lies I told. I also came to tell you why I did it."

Katrina turned and glared at her. "Do you think I care? No reason you give will matter. I almost lost my babies because of you."

"I am so sorry. I just lost it when I saw you adopting."

Katrina couldn't believe it. "Why? You don't make any sense! Why do you hate me and my kids? Why?"

"Because I gave my babies to an asylum!" Maryanne said, then walked to the door.

Mabel grabbed her hand. "No, stay."

Maryanne stared at her with pain-filled eyes. "I can't."

"I think you are finally ready to be honest," Mabel murmured. "Come sit."

Maryanne sat, or more like collapsed, into the chair. She sat across from Mabel while Katrina stood on the side, holding a chair like it was holding her up.

Maryanne stared at her hands. "When I moved here, I hated you Mabel, and you did nothing to me and never even fought back when I said anything against you, even when I made rumors about your family I knew weren't true. I knew I was wrong for doing it." Her eyes came up. "Then you came, Katrina, and you had everything. I liked you, knew you were a pioneer coming here, and then you took in those girls. I couldn't stand it. You were becoming crazy like Mabel."

Had Katrina not been so mad, she would have smiled. She had been called that before, and Maryanne made it sound humorous.

She put some sugar in her coffee and then more. "Back east I was born into wealth and I married wealth, I had friends in all the right places." She looked ready to be sick. "I had my first child, a baby boy. He was a fine baby, though he looked a little different in the face. At around a year, he had issues, no talking, no walking, and not doing anything normal babies did. I took him to the doctor, and he said he could do nothing for our son. No one ever did for an insane child or a touched child. I wouldn't believe him. My second son was that way. By the time, I had my third son and he came out looking the same way. At six months my friends started saying that my boys were different. They wouldn't let their children play with mine. I started distancing myself from them emotionally, and then Paul noticed the difference. The only one who could relate to them was my sister. She loved them."

"We took our precious little boys to the New York state asylum and left them there. I walked out and never looked back. Our friends said we would have more children that were normal or that maybe we could adopt. It took us two years, and I was with child. I prayed this one would be normal because that mattered for having a perfect family. My first daughter was born, and I knew right away she had the same thing the boys had. I went back to the doctor. He said the same thing, that it was something my husband and I were making like this. My husband blamed me." She started shaking. "By the time I had my second girl, we went back to the asylum and dropped off my last two children. I fell on the ground when they took my screaming baby from my arms. I couldn't believe it, I was doing it again."

"Why didn't you end the pregnancy? You expected them to come out touched, why not kill them in the womb? They would be with the Lord and not a man like Mr. Heyman or worse!" Mabel asked bitterly.

Katrina gasped.

Maryanne flinched. "I tried with my third boy, but it almost killed me. I am not proud of what I did." She continued, "We went home to a big rich empty house. After my last child, my doctor made sure I wouldn't give birth to another child again. I gave up the hope to have a normal child."

"I fell into depression badly, then Paul came home with a baby boy. He was perfect and from a normal family who just couldn't afford him. I expected my life to get back to normal, everything perfect again, but it didn't. I couldn't bond with my little boy. All I could see were my boys I gave away. Then Paul came home with my little girl and we became a happy family. Everything was perfect. But then we lost everything - our house, our friends, and then we moved to the poor part of town. I just got hard... I couldn't fake it anymore. My children noticed, and then Paul did. We came here, leaving my babies behind. I continued to live hard and ugly here. Then I met Lucy, and I kept thinking that is what my babies should look like, but I never would admit it." She groaned. "I put up a face, a big one. I hated my life and even my children. Paul and I don't even talk like we have these five children." She paused. "I saw how both of you chose your children and they aren't normal. After finding out what happens in the asylums, due to the court trial, I have had nightmares since and thrown up every day. I just can't take it anymore, so here it is." She wiped her eyes of tears which couldn't come. "I knew asylums were terrible places, I knew it was wrong in my heart, but everyone says that is where they belong, not with you. I knew in my heart it was wrong, but I believed the world's lie."

Both ladies looked at her. Katrina got up and checked the coffee, her back to them so she couldn't hear them as well. She wanted to weep.

Mabel touched her hand. "I am sorry you went through this."

Maryanne looked surprised.

Katrina walked back over, set the pot down too hard and looked at her, eyes stinging. "Did no one love your children?"

Maryanne flinched. "Yes, my sister Amy did. She loved my boys so much. She cried and even yelled at me and Paul for doing this. She tried to get the boys, but she was a single woman and couldn't. She wouldn't talk to us until we had the girls. She didn't expect me to send them away like the boys. She came with us, wept and wept. She told us, 'God will judge you for the things you have done to the gift He gave you'." Her face turned hard. "She never spoke to me again, but she sends letters to my children. I won't let them read them. She was never the same again after that day, she changed."

Mabel looked at her, trying to understand Amy. If she had been in that place, she might have taken the girls before they went to the asylum, but she also had a husband who shared her love for the touched and Amy had been single with no help to support two touched children. Paul could have also gone after her with the law. That is where the church should have stood up for the helpless who had no voice. "Could you get your children back?"

Katrina finally sat and decided not to bother with more coffee since no one had drank it.

Maryanne shook her head. "No, Amy never stopped visiting them when she could and they had all passed away in a fever that went through two years ago. That is the only time she wrote to me, said I should know they didn't get a funeral. Just graves with no names like they didn't live. She had wept over every one of them, mourned over their short lives."

Mabel had never heard from a mom who had given her children up like that. She often wondered if she could have met her children's parents, knowing it would never happen. But she often wondered about them, and she never considered them to be someone like Maryanne, but more like a saloon girl or an unwed young mother. She felt sick for Maryanne's children and the life they had lived in the asylum before they met their Creator who wanted them. She thought of where they were today, singing and running with their Creator.

Katrina couldn't help she glared at Maryanne, "You make me sick. After all these years, you are still thinking of only yourself. About how you wanted a normal child. God didn't want you to have a normal child, and maybe He would have or not. But how would your life had been like if you still had them? The reason you are still hard and depressed is that you are selfish. Only thinkin' of you, never another person."

"What could you know?" she spat back.

"What do I know?" She stood up and put her hands on the back of her chair to keep herself from hitting the other woman. "What do I know? I see it every time one of my little girls won't let me hold them. I hear in it their hurt little voices when they are crying out for help. I hear it by seeing the man in court who hurt my babies, wanting to kill him with my hands." She let the tears fall. "My children have to live with what you did to yours so long ago. Every day they have to live in abuse more than you have ever felt. You might have lived hard, but nothing like your children because you chose that for yourself." She was shaking now. "Their mother did this to them. A mother just like you!"

Maryanne sat back like someone had slapped her. "I know this. I just don't know how to live with this."

Katrina turned around. She cried more on the inside. This woman could have been one of the mothers to her daughters. She knew her girls needed to forgive the parents who gave them away, but this was so hard. She never thought it would be so hard. It hit too close to home.

Mabel took her hand, and she turned around, letting the tears fall. "My feelings are close to Katrina's. You understand the way you have hurt your children. That is good because God can forgive you for what you did. He can heal your heart and make you soft again. God will be there when you confess what you did and He can save you. Paul might as well see the change in you and come to see what he did to his little ones. Let God heal that heart of yours. He wants to; He wants to make you whole again."

Maryanne shook her head. "But I have wasted my life and my children's lives. Nothing can make up for that. Nothing I can do will be enough."

"You're right, but it doesn't matter to God what you have done. He can make you beautiful."

Maryanne shook her head. "I've done too much."

Mabel looked at Katrina and told her to sit with her eyes.

Katrina sat hard in the chair, sighed, wiping her eyes with a hankie. "Mabel's right. I would love to know my girls' mothers. They would see them again one day, whether in heaven or here on earth. I would have loved to know I would see my parents one day again, but I don't know if I will. Believe and you will see your babies. Because they are in heaven where Jesus is holding them tightly in His arms," she told her gently, though she didn't feel it.

Maryanne let the first tear come. She wiped it away.

Mabel took her hands in hers. "Let them come, hon. Let them come, it's time to mourn."

Maryanne looked at them. "I threw my precious babies away for what the world said was right. I believed the lie and lost my children." She sobbed like she couldn't handle it any longer.

Katrina touched her head. "My mama gave me away to get more out of life. Your children are in a better place."

Maryann looked up like she couldn't believe her ears. "Thank you, dear girl."

Chapter 44

As Izzy sat on the sofa in Cole's parlor, she had never felt so relaxed with her mom in the room. Her mom sat in the chair looking indifferent while Cole and Julia softly talked on the sofa. Annie and Sawyer sat in chairs as they glared at each other. They had something big between them. At last Jaun Jose walked in and stood by the door.

"So why are we here?" Jesse asked, looking content, acting so much more confident than he felt.

"To talk about the rumors," Annie snapped.

Izzy shrugged. "I wouldn't worry about it. Even Pastor Pete is on our side now. The rumors will end." She cocked her head. "One day."

"That might work for you, but do you know what she is saying about the brothers?" Annie glared at her.

"What is Francesca doing now?" Cole asked, bored. He leaned his head against the back of his hands.

Izzy shrugged again, like it was no big deal. "Oh, you know neighbors, they love to talk. They ask Fran questions." She winked at her brother. "You know she lets them believe some of the lies."

Cole grinned. "I reckon that is so." None of it was a laughing matter, but after what they had been through, it was so great to laugh. They had so much to be thankful for. Even if healing from this would take years, they could heal and that was what counted.

"This ain't funny. She is telling people that the only reason she is at the ranch is so the brothers can..." Annie couldn't finish the sentence. They all knew the rumors.

"Let it go, Annie. It will go away," Izzy told her.

"Well, you don't have to live here. You are going to the mountains," Annie said bitterly.

Cole opened his mouth, but Sawyer stepped in. "Leave your sister alone. I agree the rumors will end. Unless you believe them?"

Annie bit her lip in anger. "You know I don't, but what if it happens?"

Sawyer's eyes widened. "I am married to you and will always be. I will never look at another woman. Let alone one that is my brother's child."

Annie looked away. "She ain't no child."

Sawyer took her chin in her hand and looked at her. "Maybe in body she is a woman." He tapped her gently on the head. "But inside she is a child."

Annie didn't look convinced.

Izzy leaned back and looked at Jesse.

He leaned back and enjoyed just looking at her. He was serious. "I reckon this is how Ellen felt when we lied about her."

Izzy knew Jesse and Matt had made up most of the lies, while Andrew's lies had stuck longer. No one really cared what no-accounts kids thought, but Andrew had a name. His rumors stuck. "She lived through it and so will we."

"The rumors don't bother you?" Jesse asked, concerned for her.

Izzy winked at him. She was thankful for his concern, but mostly rumors were her entire life. "You are asking the girl that was told she was buying other women with her abuser. I was also told I deserved what I got for not being a normal girl and staying at home. I was too wild at heart."

Jesse flinched at her words, but he smiled lightly and touched her cheek. "I fell in love with that wild free spirit."

Izzy giggled softly.

Jesse's eyes turned so soft. "Do you know what Ben always said?"

Izzy loved hearing what his parents had taught him. It was like getting to know him better. "Mmmm?"

"He always said you knew you had a woman's heart by hearing her giggle." Jesse winked at her. His eyes were peaceful. "Missy always had that giggle."

Izzy's heart melted. To know Missy had been through some rough times and still had a giggle was wonderful. "You know my aunt taught me I will know my man by the look in his eyes. I saw that look when you were protecting me."

Jesse sighed. "I am so glad."

Annie yelled something at Sawyer. It surprised Izzy that Cole or Juan Jose was not trying to stop their arguing.

Jesse must have seen her look, and he breathed, "They should try to do things our way. We are a perfect couple." He sighed. "We did everything right."

Izzy burst out laughing, for that was the farthest thing from the truth.

Annie looked over at her. "Is there something funny?"

Izzy just shook her head and laughed harder. Jesse joined her. It was so good to laugh. She hadn't known if she would get her laugh back.

After everyone turned serious, Juan Jose found a seat. "I thought we should all talk."

Suddenly Izzy tensed. She didn't like family talks, they didn't end well. She crossed her arms, feeling the cold come into her.

"Well, I thought we could talk of past issues and maybe bring things out into the open." Juan Jose looked at Rosa. She was pale. "We are all family here and it is time we act like it. I think as couples y'all are having issues."

When they all argued, Cole spoke up. "What Juan Jose means is we need to talk better without a partner. We need to know why they might be strugglin'. It might help to bring stuff out into the open."

Jesse looked at Izzy. Izzy looked at him questioningly and then shook her head. She did not want her mama knowing about her child.

Rosa looked to Izzy. "What is this about? Has something happened, Izzy?"

"Izzy always does something," Annie snapped.

"Annie, stop it." Sawyer told her. "She has been more supportive this time than anyone. I think we need to bring to light what has been eatin' you."

Annie pulled her hand away, glaring at him. "I just didn't want you being at the ranch all the time. I told you not to go."

"I told you, when a Starry needs help there are no questions asked. We just do what they need," Sawyer tried again.

Izzy looked to Juan Jose, which was not helping. Rosa kept looking at her oddly. She couldn't handle it. All she knew was she would love this child, unlike her mother did for her. She looked down, closing her eyes against the threatening tears. Her child would have it all. She knew there would be struggles, fights, and hard times, but the child would have a mother's love that she had lacked. She put a hand over her flat stomach.

With Annie and Sawyer still bickering, Rosa gasped. "No, no it can't be!"

The entire room went silent. Izzy met her mother's eyes, so much like hers. Her mother's eyes were wide with shock and pain. She closed her eyes and held her head in her hands. "No, no, child."

Her response shocked Izzy. "What do you care? Are you

300

embarrassed I am carryin' your grandchild?" She made a hard laugh. "Well, I wasn't expectin' you to be much of a grandma. So I don't care what you think of me or my child."

Rosa just shook her head over and over.

"How could you do that, Izzy?" Annie looked disgusted. "You have brought shame to the family."

Sawyer took her hand again to quiet her. Donovan women didn't get quiet often.

Izzy just shook her head. "Brought shame like the time they took me." Her voice was hard. "When I came back, everyone was afraid I would be with child because of what those men did to me. Well, I have a child now. And I want this child. I want this child more than I want my own life."

Annie was about to come back, but Juan Jose spoke. "Stop it, Annie. We will not cause more pain." He tried to get her to see. "We have a child to think of in this room. He or she will never be told they are unwanted. Even unborn."

Izzy looked at Juan Jose. "How did you know?"

Juan Jose looked to Jesse and then back. "I didn't know for sure, but I wondered. I think we need to work as a family before Jesse and Izzy leave to start their new life."

Jesse spoke up. He took Izzy's hand. "I was the one in the wrong. I wasn't leading Izzy properly. Don't blame Iz." He looked to Juan Jose and then back to them all. "We are takin' responsibility. I want to lead my bride and child God's way from now on."

Izzy glanced at him.

Rosa finally looked up at Izzy. She seemed so aged, so hurt. "I am so sorry, child. I am just so sorry."

Izzy pulled her legs up to her chest. She tried to pull her hand away from Jesse, but he didn't let her go. She was feeling cold, and tried looking anywhere but at her mother.

"Sorry for what?" Cole asked.

Rosa shook her head. "I messed up so much of my life. I let my man hurt my children. I caused so much pain to you all."

"You tried your best, Mama," Annie said.

Rosa shook her head. "No, I was wrong. I was a terrible mother. I need to ask you to forgive me." She looked right at Izzy.

Izzy couldn't believe what was happening. All she knew was she couldn't do it. Everything in her hated her mother. She just shook her head and held her legs tighter.

Rosa looked so broken. "I understand, I have caused so much pain, but I need to tell y'all somethin'." She looked around. "I hadn't ever told anyone this. I was young when I met your father, he was many years older. I was naïve and in love with him, though I knew he was not a believer. I knew it was wrong, but I was angry at my parents. I wanted them to pay for hurting me. So, I got pregnant."

Cole stared at her in shock like the others. "You conceived me before you were married?"

Rosa nodded. "I wanted you. I always did. When I told your pa, he hit the roof. It was the first time he hit me. I felt shocked but knew I didn't have much of a choice but to marry him. So, I did."

Cole looked so broken. "That is why he hated me. He blamed me for having to get married."

Rosa nodded. "He wanted Amy. And then he said no more children. Then the twins came. I felt so alone but I wanted you both. Izzy, you have to believe that."

All of this was a shock to Izzy, to realize her mama had done the same thing she had done. She just shook her head in disbelief. "You're so wrong! I don't believe you. I don't think you wanted me." She stood up, feeling like she couldn't take much more. "You never wanted me. I was your shamed, abused, Mexican daughter." She walked to the doorway to the kitchen but stopped when Cole softly told her to stop.

Rosa stood up and walked closer to her. "I love you. I loved you so much I couldn't show it. You were such a strong child. And then you got hurt. I didn't know how to help. I was..."

Izzy stared at her. She had too many questions to stop now.

"My uncle raped me," Rosa cried out.

Izzy just stared at her mother, feeling crushed. Leaning heavily on the wall, she just couldn't believe it.

Rosa's whole body shook. "I was in grief over what happened when I met your father. No one knew what had happened. I never told anyone."

Izzy stared at her, feeling so cold, so much hate. She thought she could never see her mother again and she would be just fine. "You were raped?" she whispered. "You must have really hated me!" she yelled. "Do you know how much I wanted you then? Do you know how much I wanted a person to understand my pain?" She walked into the kitchen, and then turned her back to her. Her whole body was shaking. "How much did you hate me? I felt so rejected by you when I came back. It had ruined me. I felt worthless in your eyes. I hated you.

I hate you." She slipped down to the door, sobs overtaking her body.

Rosa sat next to her on the floor, not touching her. "Please forgive me. I love you." She said it so softly.

Izzy looked at her through teary eyes. The cold was deep in her bones, more than ever before. "When Jesse and I slept together, I felt cheap and used again," she admitted softly through sobs.

Rosa nodded. "I felt the same way. I knew I was wrong, but I kept doing it. I wanted to be loved. I wanted to feel love. I wanted to escape the feelin' my abuser put on me."

Izzy shook her head. "Why did you tell me now? I wanted you so much then," she yelled. "I felt so alone. I went to Colorado to heal. It was like you had abandoned me all over again."

"I am so sorry." Rosa met her eyes, tears pouring down her face. "I wanted to talk to you. I knew you were so broken. But I couldn't, my mind and body had tried so hard to forget that I couldn't bring it up. I just wanted you to heal. I know I didn't heal. So I thought sending you away from the memories of the abuse would help. I thought of you every day." She stopped talking and took her hand. "That first night those men took you, a part of my soul died." Rosa let the tears flow, for the first time Izzy had ever seen. "I knew what was happening to my baby and I couldn't stop it. I knew your pain and I know your pain now, baby."

Izzy shook as sobs overtook her body. For the first time, she could remember her mama holding her. She felt like she was on fire, feeling so much hate for this woman. Also, much love under layers and layers of bitterness. It was there, like a candle that had been burned out. But could always be re-lit.

Beloved daughter, give me your pain. I can heal the brokenhearted and mend their wounds.

It was like she was being held by her Father. It was like Father God was holding her in His big arms. She still felt cold. Deep eating cold. She knew she had to let it go. It was so hard.

My beloved daughter, I have given you the power of love. The power of forgiveness. Give Me your pain.

She felt like her heart was dividing. Never had she felt such pain. Not even after coming back home. She felt like she could finally be free from the cold. "Mama, I love you." She wrapped her arms around her. "I forgive you, mama."

Rosa cried all the harder. "Oh, thank you, Father God. Thank you, baby."

Izzy felt emotionally drained but so free. The coldness was gone. It had been there since she had been kidnapped. For the first time, she felt warmth.

Chapter 45

The room smelled of flowers and sweet perfume as Izzy's hair was done up in curls. She was still in her undergarments when she heard a knock on the door. She put a robe on, and then opened the door. Katrina walked in carrying a large box, and Annie and Mabel followed.

Katrina put the box on the bed. She took Izzy's hand. "You don't know how much your knowledge and your support has helped me these last months. I could never repay you for what your friendship has meant to me. I love you as a sister. "She smiled. "And now you will be."

Izzy hugged her, feeling so light.

Mabel stood next to Katrina. "You have come to mean so much to me. We wanted you to have something special, so this is a little token of our love for you."

Izzy hugged her and then turned to the box. She opened the lid, moving the tissue to find a white dress. She picked it up, holding it to her chest, feeling for the first time like she could wear white proudly. Pulling the dress out, she saw the length was perfect. "Thank you so much. I love it." She pushed her curls away from her eyes.

Hugging them both again, Mabel whispered, "You are a white pure treasure."

Izzy's eyes watered, looking at this older woman who meant so much to her in such a short time. Izzy heard another knock; Katrina opened the door to find Rosa.

For the first time Izzy could remember, the coldness was gone and love was there.

Rosa hugged her like she meant it. "Jesse is such a blessed man."

Izzy blushed. "Want to help me get into this thing?"

"It would be an honor."

The others filed out to get ready. Katrina said something about Sara having a meltdown over the color she had to wear.

After helping her into the dress, Izzy noticed that Rosa also looked stunning. Her skirt was a bright blue, ruffled full and wide to, cover her growing belly. The blouse was of the same color with beads. Her hair hung down in curls, looking so elegant. "I have somethin' for you." She held out her hand and placed a bracelet on Izzy's wrist. "I wore this when I married Marshall. He was my soulmate, though I didn't know it on that day. And now we are having our first child together."

Tears ran down her face. She hugged her tightly. "Mama, I am excited."

Rosa squealed like a young bride and mother. "Me too. Now let's finish this." She took the necklace and placed it on her wrist. It had little hearts all around it, and one little red jewel in the center. She looked in the mirror as her mama hugged her side. The dress was pure white satin, so soft. It had a round neckline, with lace around it along with little white flowers. The bodice and the skirt on one line had a little white flower down to the floor. The train was long and had flowers covering it. She wore Jesse's necklace, holding her ring on it. The dress made her look like an angel. She knew she had a bump, but the dress hid it. She knew she couldn't hide it much longer, which is why she needed to get to the mountains, though she would never hide her child from anyone.

Rosa put a hand over Izzy's flat stomach and smiled in delight. "I will always love this child. I will try to be a good grandma." She placed a hand over her own belly. "Who thought I would get a chance at being a proper mother."

Izzy felt so much love for her and the little one. "It will be like they are twins far away."

"Well." Rosa smiled like she had a secret. "I was telegraphing with Marshall, he is coming for a visit." She laughed, looking years younger. "I plan to talk to him about staying for a while."

Izzy hugged her. "Oh, Mama, I would love that." Hearing a knock, they turned as Cole walked in.

"Almost ready?" He rolled his eyes and drawled, "I should know having two daughters, girls are never ready."

Rosa gave him a playful pat. "Be nice to your sister." She winked at Izzy. "I love you, girl."

Izzy sighed constantly. "I love you too, Mama."

Cole walked up to her, his eyes melting at the sight of her. "Izzy-baby." Using her childhood nickname. "You look so beautiful. You will make Jesse a beautiful, priceless, elegant, fun, wild bride." He stepped closer and placed a gentle hand to her stomach. "You are a wonderful, fun-loving, carin', mama bear, and wild mama. I can't wait to meet this little one."

Izzy put her hand over his, feeling his love, his protection. "You have been like a father I never had. You have been my support, my strength when I was weak."

Cole kissed her head like a child. "I will think of you near Christmas. I will pray for you every day."

"I will do the same for you all here," Izzy whispered.

Cole held out his arm. "Ready to become Isabella Donovan Starry?"

Izzy smiled. "More than ready."

Cole led her towards the chapel. Buggies, wagons, carriages, and horses lined the whole yard. It must be a packed chapel. This is where they wanted to get married. They first felt loved here. Cole whispered, "I wanted to visit your place on the mountain before winter, but it doesn't look like I can get away."

"Don't worry. Andrew and the others have been up there. It is a fine cabin." Izzy knew he was worried about her living in a place like their first cabin.

"I know you can handle pretty much everythin'. I appreciate what you have done with Liberty Ranch. It is running much better because of you. You showed the Starrys the ropes out here."

Izzy smiled softly. "It was nothin'. You know how much I love it here."

They came to the steps of the chapel. Izzy beamed, the music beginning when they entered the chapel. Izzy almost gasped. The girls had done a wonderful job at making the chapel look so elegant. Satin bows and flowers were everywhere, and wildflowers all over the building.

As they came to the back of the benches, Juan Jose came to her side. She took his arm. "Thank you, Juan Jose."

Juan Jose looked at her in that way that made her feel priceless. "No, it is an honor to give you to Jesse."

Everyone rose as Izzy walked down the aisle. The room was decked out in flowers Sara and Alice had picked. The front of the church was covered in a white canopy. Everything was bright and cheery. Perfect for a wedding. She was nervous, but then she spotted Jesse. When their eyes met, her nerves went away. The love she saw in those eyes was unforgettable. After taking Jesse's hand, she kissed both Cole and Juan Jose's cheeks.

Juan Jose stood as their pastor, marrying them. Matt stood by

Jesse's side, and Francesca stood by Izzy.

Izzy said softly, "I love you more than I ever thought I could love anyone. I have come to trust you in ways I have never trusted anyone. I promise to honor and love you for the rest of our life. I can't wait to grow old with you."

As Jesse took the necklace off of her, his hands shook. She winked at him. He almost laughed out loud. His eyes danced with her.

He took her hand and placed the ring on her finger. "I have come to love you as a friend and then I loved you as a woman. I love you as my soulmate. I give you my heart today as I care for yours." He whispered for her ears only, "If God did nothing but give me you, I will live a content life."

When Juan Jose told him to kiss her, she got nervous like a schoolgirl getting her first kiss. One hand came around her waist, his other hand touched her cheek as he drew her in. His lips were soft and hungry at the same time. She felt like a treasure in his arms. His lips firm, achingly soft, as if showing her he would always desire her. This kiss was a promise of what was to come, their second chance at love. God's way of love. She touched his cheek, deepening it. She felt like a priceless pure bride for the first time, like he was giving her so much more.

Their bedroom had a light glow to it. There were wildflowers all around that made it smell heavenly. All this added to the room was bliss to Izzy as she looked into Jesse's eyes. Oh, how she loved him. Willingly, she went into his arms. Sitting on the bed, Jesse leaned against the back of it and held her. She laid her head against his chest, loving to hear his heartbeat. She was content, at peace. She spoke softly, "The wedding was wonderful. I never thought I could be so happy."

"It was," Jesse murmured, just as relaxed. "You know I promised Ma I would give you the wedding you wanted?"

She sat up, looking at him. "No, I didn't."

His eyes misted. "I think she knew I would probably elope like Sawyer and Annie. She knew you wouldn't want that. And I see it too, now. So I promised to do what you want."

She touched his cheek. "Thank you, Jess. For doing this for me. I know today was hard. I thought of her often."

He nodded, his face crumbling. "This is the first wedding without her... and seein' the children after months. It was just all so much harder than I thought it would be."

She wiped his tears like he had done for her so often. "I know it was." She snuggled back with him.

"I hear your mama might stay here longer?" he asked, knowing while he had a strong God-fearing loving mother, she had a mother who wasn't any of those things.

"Yeah, I think it might be the baby."

"I think it is because she wants a second chance with all her children."

"You know, I never thought I would have so much in common with my ma. It makes sense why she married such a horrible, Godless man. I wish she would have told me she was pregnant before marriage."

He flinched. "Would you have done our courtship differently?" He couldn't help but put his hand over her stomach that had a little bump, though no one could tell by the clothes she wore. This was the first time they had gotten to talk alone since they found out all the family secrets hidden by one mother.

"I am not sure, but I would have liked to understand why my pa hated Cole and me so much. It was like he blamed us, especially Cole, for marrying his wife."

"If they hadn't married, you wouldn't be here or your sisters," he stated. "And I wouldn't trade a day without you. I know your life was hard growing up with him, but your pa gave you life and our life had crossed because of our families. It was meant to be, though it was hard."

She sighed. "I can't say I wouldn't trade my life, but I can learn from it. To teach our child somethin' better than the choices we made. We won't hide what we did from him."

"But our child will also know that she is loved and wanted, though her parents didn't plan and weren't obeying God's way. We want this child. She will never doubt that. She is a gift from God, no matter if we didn't plan to be parents this early. We will be wonderful parents to our girl."

She shook her head, chuckling. "Or our son."

He kissed her head and whispered, "Or both."

She tried to sit up, but he just laughed and took the clips out of her hair. She giggled. "One child this time, I am sure." Though twins would be twice the work and joy.

She growled, "So we will plan on two next time."

He got her hair undone and ran his fingers through it. She must have liked it, for she made a purring sound. He kept at it, and then placed a few kisses on her neck, sending chills through her. She turned and kissed him. Deepening the kiss, she dug her fingers through his curly hair.

He broke the kiss, laid on the bed and gazed at her, not touching. "Izzy, I have grown to love you in ways that I never dreamed possible. I have learned to trust you and put my heart safely in your hands, knowin' you will care for it. Like the Godly, loving woman I know you are." He placed his callused hand on her cheek, being so gentle. "I love you to more than words can say. I hope I can be the man you can trust and depend on when things get hard. I pray with God's help he will keep showing me how to love you. He sent you to me. You are my Angel. My gift. My treasure."

She let tears fall, happy tears. His words were so reassuring, so comforting, with all they had been through the last couple weeks. "I never thought I would love someone like I love you. For me, love was always hard. I kept my heart from it for so long. I never thought I would feel again. When I came into your life, I learned to love in new ways I never thought possible. I have learned..." She reached out and touched his jaw. "You have taught love can be fun, be trusting, and can be treated like a genuine treasure, and you have taught me that it's all right to touch. To open your heart is nothing to fear. I pray with God's help I will be the wife you need me to be, a caring, loving, and trusting helpmeet. I love you more than I thought possible."

She kissed him, feeling his passion but also his care, his tenderness. She never thought she could enjoy the feeling of being truly loved by her man. A man God sent to her. When his hands dug into her hair deepening the kiss, she felt the passion, the love from her heart. Then he pulled away and gazed at her lovingly.

She sat up and felt a bout of nausea. She held her stomach.

He was at her side in a minute. "Is it the baby?" he asked.

She shrugged and took a deep breath.

He poured her a glass of water and handed it to her.

She drank, then handed it back, feeling better. But she had to tell him she wasn't ready. She turned away, whispering, "You saw with the trial I stopped feelin'. I went through the motions and just didn't feel. I knew if I had walked in that courtroom the last day they sentenced the girls, I knew I would stop feeling ever again. But you stopped me. You kept me feeling." Jesse took her hand. "When we fell that night I didn't feel, it was like my body was there, but I was not."

He gasped. "I am so sorry, Iz. I didn't know... I..."

She touched his lips with her hand. "Don't. God forgave us, and our family did. We are getting a second chance at true love." Her shoulders sagged. Not feeling shame or guilt. Feeling vulnerable, so open, so raw and exposed. "When the men would hurt me, I would try to stop feeling." She had to stop. She had never told anyone this personally before. He took her in his arms and held her so tight. It made her feel safe. "It was a way to survive. When they got near me, I would leave my body or pass out. I don't want to do that when we touch."

He was shaking a little. He kept his eyes gentle, kind. "Oh, my brave, brave girl. I love you."

She looked up at him. "I am ready to touch and not leave like before. I am ready to trust you. To love you."

He sighed like he didn't know how to handle all this. He wanted to be strong for her. He wanted to do right by her. "Are you sure, Angel? I can wait."

She nodded, moving his hair back from his forehead. "I love you, Jesse."

"Oh, I love you, Angel." He kissed her, passionately and lovingly, yet so gentle he made her feel treasured.

For the first time, she realized that love and intimacy in the bed was nothing to fear or feel ashamed of. God had designed it to be this way, had made it to be with the man she loved. That God made her for this man. Isabella felt true love. She left all her feelings of unworthiness behind her.

Chapter 46

"When I heard they would take the girls, my first thought was who would feed them." Katrina told Gloria, who sat on the swing with her. "I promised my girls I would always feed them, but I just kept thinking no one will feed them. Odd, right?"

Izzy walked out, swinging the door shut behind her. "Nah, you kinda feed everyone." She sat on the railing. "You made a promise and you know how to keep it. It's normal." She sighed. "When I first heard my initial thought was I can't kill these men legally." She shook her head in disbelief. "These men get paid for being as bad as saloon owners, and I can't kill them legally."

Katrina and Gloria's eyes went wide when they realized she was being honest.

Izzy felt uncomfortable. She had told too much. What had overcome her?

Julia walked out. "Cole told me he had the same thoughts." She took Izzy's hand. "I appreciate all the times you protected my man. He wouldn't be here if it weren't for you. In more ways than one."

Izzy shrugged. "It goes both ways." She sighed. "Maybe one day these men will be put where they belong."

Katrina nodded. "We can only hope and try to change it. One day they will see life as it is." She looked at Julia. "How is David doing? Are things getting better?"

Julia shrugged. "Cole and I have been talking about it. While things are still hard they may get better in time. For we have never had friends or a church family. That might heal him. Be what he needs." She sighed. "And he might not get better with me but I am not going to give up. There is always hope."

Before anyone could respond they turned to see the first wagon pull in. A new part of life.

Dressed in her full blue skirt and a white blouse, Francesca walked away from Liberty Ranch. Carrying a bag with food and clothes, she didn't look back.

By the time she had hitched on a ride to Denver, her feet hurt, her back ached, and she was cold. She stopped by the train station. She knew how to get a ticket, and had done it all before. But for the first time, she was afraid of the work. She was so tired of running. Tired of that line of work. She knew with her education, she couldn't do much. She had no plans for the future. That was before Katrina tried to push her to make plans for her future.

Sitting on the bench, she thought it over. She wasn't that good at cooking. She could ride, but not well enough, but with Andrew's teaching, she would have gotten good. She hated to clean. That was out of the question. Sighing, she didn't know what she wanted. The only thing she was good at, she didn't want to do. If she went home, Timmy would grin saying, "It's about time you came back to where you belong, Princess."

Her mama had always said, "Only thing you will ever be good at is pleasing a man. A whore is all you will be."

Katrina said she could be whatever she wanted. She could make it happen with hard work. She wanted to believe that, but it was so hard. Doubts came in and fear took over, making her want to flee when they pressured her. Katrina made her feel things she never felt. She got out of the bitter cold and walked into the station. A man walked out, and nearly knocked her over. He caught her arm gently. "Sorry, miss, twas my fault," he said mannerly.

She looked at the older man and nodded. She couldn't get used to men being a gentleman, but she knew if he found out what she was, he wouldn't treat her with any kindness. "You are a pretty little lady. Best get home in this weather. You are someone's special little girl."

Francesca took a step back in shock. Those were Andrew's words. He always told her, "You are my special little girl." Her legs shook. Sitting back on the bench, she glared at the ground. What was she doing? She was running from people that loved and cared for her. Why? She may not believe what they did, she might not believe in their

313

God, but they showed they would love her. They didn't make Maverick believe, and they still loved him. They still loved Jesse, and he could be a pain. All the Starrys had come together and fought to keep the girls safe, though they hardly knew them. They bickered and fought, but always loved each other. How?

Looking up, the man was gone. Where had he gone? Andrew would call him an angel who God put there just to help a body out. Shaking her head, God had never shown her His care. That didn't mean she couldn't go back to the Starrys. She could try to be a family.

Now determined, ready to walk all the way back home, about an hour down the road, doubts came in. They won't want you. How many times have you run away? How many chances can you give them? Second chances run out. They won't love you forever. No one has before. Remember what your mama said, and she knew better than Katrina did. Francesca stopped in the middle of the road. What if they didn't want her?

Frozen in fear, she saw a wagon full of children drive up and stop in front of her. The driver asked, "You need a ride, Missy? We are on our way to Deer Trail." He looked up at the clouds gathering. "It looks like rain."

Francesca glanced at the children and the wife. The man wouldn't try anything with his family there. Nodding, she climbed in the back.

The wife smiled at her as they moved on. "Hello, honey. Where are you headin'?"

Maybe the movement of the wagon, the horse's hooves, or staying up all night made her eyes close. Leaning against some feed, she said, "Mmm, Liberty Ranch." Then she dozed off.

She woke up as they entered Liberty Ranch land. She looked around with fresh eyes. This was home and would be forever. Pulling up to the house, she jumped out. It looked empty. She knew Izzy and Jesse were already in the mountains. But where were the others? Maybe they hadn't gone looking for her? What if they were partying? Or doing chores like she never left? Fear built again. She should just leave and save herself from the hurt.

Walking into the kitchen, she saw it empty. The fire was still warm. She took off her coat and set it on the table. She found a piece of paper on the table. Her name was on it. She picked it up and read. She caught about every other word. She wished she could read better to get it all.

Mama, I feel so lost. Francesca has run away again. Andrew and the boys are out looking again. I wondered if she would run away after almost losing the girls. Mama, I wish you could meet her. She is so wonderful. She is smart, sarcastic, and funny. She works so hard at what she does. She has such a bright future. I love her so much, Mama. I want my baby Francesca back and safe in my arms.

Francesca put the letter down. She was worried about her mama. Her mama cared. How could she be so blind? Stepping back, she walked back outside. The wagon and family were still there.

Then, in the yard, she saw Katrina walking out of the woods from the chapel. Her head down, then she looked up.

Francesca had never run to a mama. Never had a time where she ran to meet her mama as a child does. Her tummy mama hadn't been safe. She ran to her mama now. Her first real mama. Feeling her mama's arms around her, she felt safe for the first time.

Katrina held Francesca tightly, not believing it was her coming home. She really came home. She whispered over and over, "I love you, baby." Francesca cried for the first time Katrina had ever seen. Her daughter didn't cry when men took her body, when her sisters had been taken, or when she screamed for hours because of nightmares. But now her daughter sobbed. Katrina knew these tears were a breaking point. Her daughter was softening. Mama had said, 'when a heart is soft enough to cry out in tears, healing can start.'

The wind was picking up; Katrina didn't stop what Francesca needed to do. She needed this moment. But she wasn't wearing a coat. Moving her arms to still hold her as she picked her up and carried her to the short distance to the house like she would a toddler. She often wondered why God made her so tall and big-boned. As a child, she wanted to be like Julia. Now she knew so she could carry her older children like a baby they never got to be. As she walked into the house, she prayed her daughter had finally come home for good.

Epilogue

Christmas day, 1873

Colorado territory had its beauty of mountains and snow, but on Christmas Eve it seemed so much more special. Katrina looked out the kitchen window at the children building a snowman in the fresh snow that had fallen the night before. Never had she remembered it snowing on a Christmas eve before. Being Colorado, she was sure it would probably snow every Christmas. That was fine with her. She was learning to love the snow, even the bitter cold that came with it.

The entire family was going to Cole's house for Christmas eve supper. They got together often. First, they would put up the Christmas tree and decorate it. The girls had such fun making the decorations.

Julia walked in, taking off her coat and boots. "Wow, it's an iceberg out there."

Katrina smiled and poured hot coffee for Julia, who had not gotten used to the weather. She was always complaining about it. "Here, sit and thaw. I don't know how the children handle the cold so well."

Julia sat, taking a sip of the hot drink. "I know. The southern kids have gotten used to it." She winked at her. "I am the one who gave their snowman the hat."

Katrina chuckled, glancing out the window. The hat was a summer straw one. The snowman looked like a southern redneck. "The southern kids knew how to do it their way. Who would have thought this is the first Christmas in Colorado? So much has changed."

Julia agreed. "So much good and struggles have come from this year."

"So much has improved, even Fran and Sara are happier." Katrina was so glad for that. Oh, there were days when the moods were so hard, but they were getting through those struggles. Healing was coming slowly. Katrina sat across from her, took another sip of coffee.

Just then the front door opened and the children piled in, along with Andrew pulling in a tree they had cut together earlier.

Katrina helped Carlissa take off her many layers of clothing. Then she picked her up and put her on her hip as Andrew put the tree in the parlor. After Andrew moved it back and forth until it was perfect, the children got out the decorations, and with no order, put them on.

The Donovan children started talking of past Christmases as they worked. Then Melody asked Sara and Carlissa, "What was your favorite Christmas memory?"

Katrina almost flinched. The girls likely didn't have a good memory of any Christmas.

Carlissa just shrugged as she put the glass angel on the tree.

Sara mumbled, "This is my first Christmas."

Melody's mouth dropped open.

Francesca shrugged. "This is my favorite." She added bitterly, "Past Christmases were drunken men and parties."

Katrina looked at her lovingly. "I am glad you are here this Christmas and hopefully every Christmas with us."

Francesca looked uncomfortable but smiled lightly, putting the wooden bear she had carved, with Andrew's help, on a branch.

At supper, Katrina looked around, seeing the joy, the laughter on their faces. She was so blessed. It again showed her how this came about. They were all here because two mixed-race couples took in seven no-account orphans and raised them into these wonderfully reasonable adults. Because of that, they now had spouses and many grandchildren. She knew Ellen, Missy, and Ben were looking down at them —Joyful over what they saw.

Izzy had never felt pain like this before. It was Christmas morning and her body was about to explode. So this is how it would end. She was going to die on Christmas. She was as big as a cow, and now her stomach felt like it would break in half. She was sure this wasn't what labor felt like. "Jesse!" Taking the bedsheets in her hands, she screamed.

You are my beloved daughter.

Jesse came right to her side. "I have the water ready, Angel. You are doing wonderful. You are so strong, love."

I have raised you to do great things.

Izzy didn't know how much more she could take. All she knew was she couldn't do this again. It was just too painful. Something had to be wrong. She would die, she knew it. Jesse kept at his praises. It was driving her crazy. "Shut up!" she said through grinding teeth.

You are my chosen child.

Jesse nodded. "Of course, love, whatever you need." He panicked. "What can I get you? Food? Coffee? Water?"

I am your Lord. King of Kings.

Closing her eyes, she leaned back. Maybe a towel so she could put it in his mouth. He was the one who did this to her, anyway. "Nothing'." Suddenly she needed to push. Her body was breaking. She would surely die.

You are a child of the King. You can do everything with the Lord's strength.

Pushing, she grunted. She would not scream. She was not a child. She was a woman who could handle this like a cowgirl. It's not like having a child was a new thing. Women had been having babies since the beginning of time.

Jesus' Beloved daughter, adopted into the family of God.

Another push. "Jesse, I need you to get that clean towel. You are going to have to catch the baby," she told him. Then another push came. Stronger this time.

You are my beloved daughter.

Jesse's eyes went wide. "Me? You want me to catch the baby."

Every life is a gift from God.

Izzy moaned. She had told him this before. The labor must have wiped his mind clear. "Yes!" Another push came. The baby was getting closer or she was going to burst.

He healeth the broken in heart, and bindeth up their wounds.

She could do this. Jesse moved to get the towel. Then he got near her legs. He looked like he was scared out of his wits. She almost laughed at the look on his face, but another pain came and she pushed.

God is the strength of my heart.

"I see the head! I see the baby's head!" Jesse nearly shouted.

The gift of God.

Izzy gritted her teeth. This was it. This was time. She had to do this.

Pushing, she couldn't breathe. She was sure this child would never come. The pain was like she had never felt, but her heart filled. This was her child she was fighting for. This was the child God had given her, even though she didn't deserve it. Love filled her like she never felt before. It was all-consuming love, as if God was showing this was how much He loved her. God loved her as much as she loved this child. God was giving her this child as a gift. Showing her how worthy she was. How precious she was in His eyes. How He treasured her for just being her. She didn't have to change to be His daughter. She could just be herself. She gave one last push. This is what it felt like to be truly consumed, loved, and it felt wonderful despite the pain she was in.

The LORD is merciful. We love him because He first loved us.

Jesse had never had so much fear and joy. Izzy was in such pain he wanted to take it from her. He wanted to help her. He saw the baby's dark hair, feeling so much love for this child. Feeling a bit of fear. What if he wasn't a good father? Owen hadn't been.

When your mother and father forsake you, I will be there. I am your Father.

God was trying to get his attention. He had been trying for some time. Jesse hadn't been listening very well. God wanted him to give up all his bitterness. Give all your pain to God. Give Him all your fears and anger. Replace fear with faith.

You are my beloved son.

Then he saw the baby's face, and it was pink and wrinkly. Oh, how he already loved this child. God had given him such a wonderful gift. A beloved, beautiful bride and now a child. How much God must have loved him.

Children are a heritage of the LORD: and the fruit of the womb is his reward.

Tears ran down his cheeks as the baby came. Tears of joy and of release. It is like God came into his heart and took out all the bitterness. Cleaned his heart for only love to come in. Then the baby fell into his hands.

Every life is precious.

"Izzy! Angel! It's a girl," Jesse said over the blinding tears that came. "We have a baby girl." The baby let out a soft cry, upset for being woken up. Jesse gently wrapped her.

Izzy held out her arms, waiting for the child to come to her. "Give me my baby."

Jesse gently handed Izzy the baby girl who now cried louder, like she wanted to go back to sleep.

Izzy held her baby girl. Her arms shook, but she lay her crying, wet, wiggling baby on her chest. Oh, she felt so good to hold.

Jesse leaned close to look the baby over, who now lay quietly against her mother's chest. "Look how beautiful she is." His gaze met Izzy's. "Thank you for giving me such a wonderful daughter. I am so proud of you."

Izzy melted. "Ellen is so proud of you. She would love her namesake."

Jesse nodded. "Ellie May, did you hear that, you have a wonderful Grandma, who watches over you."

Izzy kissed her head. "Yes, Ellie May, you will now have love from your family and God." Jesse kissed her. Like his touch did every time, it brought such joy and peace. God had truly loved her to give her so much.

The END

Acknowledgments

So many people have helped me along this journey I can't mention all of them. But you know who you are and you are greatly appreciated.

First to my heavenly Father for putting this story in my heart. I would never be able to push forward if it hadn't felt like I had to. To get this story out in the world. God, you have given me a passion for children and women in need. I pray I did this story justice.

To Angie for helping me perfect the scenes. One of my favorite parts in the story where Izzy and Francesca talk, you helped me get that scene perfect with your input. Thanks for always being there. And I hope we get to meet one day in person on this side of heaven.

To my family that always supports me in this journey. Y'all are the best.

Rose Hale for all of your support. You are an awesome, encouraging reader.

A big thanks to Samantha Fury, who formatted this book last minute. You did a great job. I just love the pictures.

Many people have asked why I have written this book, especially about this touchy subject. I wrote it so people could see their Value in God. To see everything comes down to the value of human life. We haven't changed as a country, we have just gotten better at hiding it. We have more slaves today than at any other time in history. Yes, in 2021. Many people might say the abuser comes in a black van and takes the girls. That is not true. 95% of the abusers know their victims. They trap the victim's mind to their way of thinking, just like Francesca struggled with. Much of the techniques haven't changed over the years. A lot of the research I gathered was from the Operation underground railroad. They are a wonderful nonprofit mission. God Bless their work.

What made me do a story? Well, it started when I started to research adoptions and foster care placements that didn't end well. I wanted to know why and it started me to find out Rad, (Radiative

Attachment disorder). And that changed my life. So I started to research. I knew Rad couldn't just be a modern-day thing. Actually writing this book, I did many years of research. Many more years than actually writing the book. Haha.

I wanted it perfect and very to the times of the 1800s. I read books from orphanages, prostitutes, and asylums. I wanted to dig deeper to find the facts no one knows about. And guess what I found Rad in many people from Ann Sullivan to children on the frontier, in orphanages, and yes, many in asylums. You might wonder why I mention Ann Sullivan. She was raised in an asylum and then school with no attachments. Her first attachment was Helen Keller and she never let anyone close to her. While we often remember the survivor, we forget about the people that got them there.

When Andrew asks Dorthea Dix, how can she be kind to the master of the asylum? Her answer was word for word. She was always kind to the guards, owners, matrons, and anyone in the asylum. She knew many were evil and unkind to the touched people but she knew she couldn't change them or fire them. So she would go about it with the law. She was one of the first women to go before the House and Senate. She was truly a woman who made such a difference in her time.

So I took what I learned and wrote this story. What I hope you come out of is knowing your value in God. Whether you are like Katrina, Izzy, Francesca, Jesse, Andrew, or even like Maryanne. There is always healing in Christ. He always forgives. Always look for the value of human life. It is all around us. You are valued, never forget that. Until next time, always believe.

One Star at a Time.

Until next you can find me on FB, Instagram, and other platforms. I love to talk, especially to my readers.

Liberty Mountain
Is coming out in the Summer of 2022.

Made in the USA
Middletown, DE
01 October 2021